PRAISE FOR CHUCK WENDIG

"Think *Six Feet Under* co-written by Stephen King and Chuck Pahniuk... Wendig's surefooted prose means that this ride is ll worth sticking your thumb out for."
SFX Magazine

Fast, ferocious, sharp as a switchblade and fucking ntastic."
Lauren Beukes, author of Zoo City *and* The Shining Girls

eral and often brutal, this tale vibrates with emotional ess that helps to paint a bleak, unrelenting picture of life ie edge."
ublishers Weekly

uck Wendig is one of the stars of 21st century genre on, and *The Blue Blazes* is exactly my kind of supernatural crime novel: dark and visceral, with an everyman hero oot for and Lovecraftian god-horror to keep you awake ght. Like Mookie Pearl's beloved charcuterie, this is the l stuff, right here."
dam Christopher, author of Empire State *and* The Age omic

lls-to-the-wall, take-no-prisoners storytelling at its best."
Bill Cameron, author of County Line

lackbirds is] a gleefully dark, twisted road trip for everyone o thought *Fight Club* was too warm and fuzzy. If you enjoy ook, you're probably deeply wrong in the head. I loved ...nd will be seeking professional help as soon as Chuck lets me out of his basement."
James Moran, Severance *and* Doctor Who *screenwriter*

ALSO BY CHUCK WENDIG

CHUCK WENDIG

THE BLUE BLAZES

ANGRY
ROBOT

ANGRY ROBOT
A member of the Osprey Group

Lace Market House,
54-56 High Pavement,
Nottingham NG1 1HW
UK

www.angryrobotbooks.com
Mookie take it off again

An Angry Robot paperback original 2013
1

A catalogue record for this book is available
from the British Library.

ISBN 978 0 85766 334 4
Ebook ISBN 978 0 85766 336 8

Set in Meridien and Dirty Headline by EpubServices

Printed and bound by CPI Group (UK) Ltd, Croydon, CR0 4YY

PART ONE

SALT & SMOKE

PROLOGUE

They have a name for it, in myth. Katabasis. The descent. To descend. Mythically speaking, into the Underworld – the so-called "Harrowing of Hell." Inanna passes through the seven gates to see her sister. Izanagi's wife Izanami is burned to death while giving birth to the fire god, and so he travels into the land of Yomi to defy death. Eurydice is envenomed by a nest of vipers after fleeing a satyr's attack, and upon her demise her lover Orpheus descends into Hades to rescue her from that subterranean place. The Katabasis has its opposite, the Anabasis, or the ascent. But one's ascent is not guaranteed. Izanami turns to a monster and refuses to go home, so Izanagi is forced to close the world of the living from the land of the dead to keep her from dragging him back to be with her. Orpheus betrays the one rule he is given and looks back at his bride as they flee, thus sealing off the worlds and losing his love. Inanna finds that despite the costs she has paid, another secret price will be extracted: she must choose someone to enter the Great Below and take her place. And so it is with the Underworld: you may enter its depths and walk into the dark, but something is always taken from you. And it remains ever-uncertain whether your entrance will be mirrored again by your escape.

– from the Journals of John Atticus Oakes
Cartographer of the Great Below

1

They want what we have. The denizens of the Great Below care little for the humans of the Infinite Above except as providers, as resources, as dogs or toys or tools. They rape and kill and feed. They drink our pain, supping at it like we're each an endless goblet of wine and blood. But we are not endless. We can be used up. And they don't care, for they are predators and parasites to the last. This is why the intersection of our world and theirs is found most cleanly in the places where the mythic and monstrous Underworld clashes with the more criminal one. For the criminals – organized crime and violent gangs and the whole miscellaneous lot of murderers and human monsters – feed on us the same way. Another set of parasites and predators. And so it falls to these criminals, the most selfish among us, to act against the terrors that lurk and writhe in the darkest chambers of the Earth's own ugly heart.

– from the Journals of John Atticus Oakes
Cartographer of the Great Below

This, then, is Mookie Pearl.

He's a high wall of flesh stuffed into a white wife-beater stained with brown (once red), a man whose big bones are wreathed in fat and gristle and muscle and sealed tight in a final layer of scar-tissue skin. At the top of his ox-yoke shoulders sits a head like a wrecking ball with black eyes and shorn scalp and a mouth full of teeth that look like white pebbles fished from a dark river. He's got hands that could break a horse's neck. He's got Frankenstein feet and a Godzilla hunch.

He's built like a brick shithouse made of a hundred smaller brick shithouses.

Mookie the Mook. Mookie the Meat-Man. Mookie the Monster.

Butcher. Bruiser. Breaker of legs. Some legs human. Most not.

Some call him "Mook." Most don't call him anything.

Tonight and every night he's scarred up like the walls of his bar. The walls are carved with names, and Mookie's carved with the scratches and teeth-marks of subterranean monsters, monsters who wanted to take what he earned: a shipment of the Blue stuff.

They tried. They died.

He rounds the bar, pops the door on a micro-fridge beneath it. Pulls out a paper plate covered in plastic wrap. The oaken bartop's got the texture of an old cowboy's face: creases and canyons in the dark wood. He sets the plate down.

This is Mookie's bar. He is its sole employee. He is its only customer.

It's also the place he calls home.

Mookie feels old. Every one of his forty-some years on this Earth have come back to haunt him, each bringing another friend – the age is settling into his bones like a cold damp, the years chewing at his joints like rats eating wires.

He reaches up, grabs a bottle of cheap vodka. Most of the liquor behind the bar is firewater. Bad Polish vodkas and off-off-brand tequilas. But there are a few bottles of good stuff, too. Basil Hayden's bourbon. Bluecoat gin. Macallen 18, a Balvenie Madeira cask, a Laphroaig 18-year. Somewhere in the back, a bottle of Pappy van Winkle. None of that tonight. He won the day, but it feels hollow. No celebration here.

Mookie sits. Spins the cap off the bottle. Pries the plastic wrap off the plate with a delicateness one would not suspect of his thick, callus-upon-callus fingers. But it's surgical the way he pulls it off, folds it once over, then twice, before revealing the whole of the plate.

Before him, a variety of meats. A soft square of rabbit galantine. An oily circle of salumi. A couple cold blood sausages, each as black as the Devil in the night. Far end of the plate is his favorite: lardo. Chilled, cured fatback.

There exists a moment when he stares down at the array of charcuterie – meats he prepared himself in an act that brings him peace and satisfaction in this violent life – when the pain almost overwhelms him. It's not the physical pain, though that's most certainly there, what with the scabbed knuckles and the fat lip and all the other bumps and cuts and pummeled flesh.

This pain runs deeper. His heart a puddle of slushy water that hides an endless well of regret. His heart hurts. It hurts into his stomach and his lungs, makes it hard to breathe, makes it hard to eat. He breathes deep through his nose, then pops the lardo in his mouth–

The hurt fades. The fat melts on his tongue. Salty and sweet. Faintly herby. A true cold comfort, melting over teeth and gums. Eyes closed. Boulder head rolling back on mountain shoulders. He moans. He can't help it. One of the few things he truly enjoys: the preparation and the consumption. He's lost to it. He can feel it in his *toes*.

Until–

His phone rings.

And like that, the moment is ruined. A kite that comes crashing down to earth. Caught in briar. Dashed on rocks.

Mookie palms the phone in his pocket, brings the tiny digital brick to his ear. "Yeah?"

It's Werth. The old goat.

"How'd it go?" Werth asks, stepping across all the pleasantries, which is what Mookie prefers anyway. "It get done?"

"It always gets done." Mookie looks down at the knuckles on his left hand. As he flexes, scabs split. Red runs fresh. He rolls those knuckles on a bar napkin. "I ran into problems."

"There's always problems. What kind?"

"The gobbos. They're all riled up. Like wasps that know winter's coming."

Werth is silent for a moment. "Was bound to happen."

"Yeah. But this is different. They're agitated."

"But the shipment's good?"

"Shipment's good."

"Good. Good. Real fuckin' good. Hey. The Boss wants to see everybody."

The Boss. The big man at the top. Konrad Zoladski. He's been out-of-sight for the better part of a year, now.

A spike of worry lances through Mook's chest. "Why?"

"Not sure."

"Unh. When?"

"Tomorrow morning. You want me to pick you up? I'll bring the car."

"No. I'll take the train."

"Call me when you're in the city. I'll text you the address when you get here. I need you to dress like a…"

Werth keeps talking, but Mookie stops listening.

Because he smells something.

He smells flowers.

The bundled flesh at the back of his neck prickles and turns to chicken-skin. That scent crawls into his nose. All-too-familiar.

"Did you hear me?" Werth says on the other end. "I said, don't dress like a thug tomorrow. I need you to dress like a professional. Put on a fuckin' shirt. Something with buttons. Definitely nothing with bloodstains on it. Hey. Mook?"

"I gotta go."

"Hey, goddamnit, I'm talking to you–"

"I'm tired," is all Mookie says.

Then Mookie ends the call with a punch of his thumb.

He slides off the barstool. Big boots make the floorboards whine.

That smell again. Like snippets of a melody in the air, a song you know but thought you'd forgotten, a song whose sound conjures memories of long ago.

"Nora," he says. Voice a croak. "I know you're here."

From the back booth, a shuffle of a heel scuffing the floor.

But nobody's there.

Until she is. One minute: nothing. The next, Nora stands there like she was never *not* there. That smile, curled up at one corner like it's tugged by a fish-hook. Those eyes, mean and bright like match-tips at the moment of striking. Chestnut hair down over her shoulders, longer than Mookie remembers it.

She appears, plucking something out from under her tongue. He doesn't see what.

She still looks like a schoolgirl. Tartan skirt. Blue cardigan. It's her look these days.

"Nora." He feels like a tree hollowed out by termites. Ready to fall in a stiff wind.

"Mookie."

"Don't. Don't do that to me. Please."

Her eyes flash: sympathy? Pity? Something more sinister. "Fine. *Daddy.*"

He lets out the breath he didn't realize he'd been holding. Another whiff of perfume–

A little girl, brown hair a mess, squealing as Daddy bounces her on his knee, each squeal interrupted by each bounce – "Eee! Eee! EEE!" The same little girl, a little older now, crying and hiding under her bed as Mommy and Daddy scream at one another and throw lamps and then Mommy stabs Daddy with a fork and Daddy punches an old microwave into a lump of glass and metal and sparking circuitry. The little girl, not little at all now, watching out her window as Daddy goes

*back to the city, both of them knowing it'll be months before they see one
another again, and truth be told, even that's being optimistic. Finally,
the little girl mostly-grown-up, with a revolver in her hand, a smudge
of blue at her temples, a wicked boomerang smile on her once sweet face.*

Behind him, his cell phone on the bar top vibrates across
the wood. *Vbbbbt. Vbbbbt.* Werth again. Mookie grabs it, turns
it off. Wings it back onto the bar. Never once taking his eyes
off Nora.

He says, "Maybe I should call you – what is it they call you?"

"Persephone." A flicker of amusement in her face.

"Yeah." That's the name she's been going by on the streets.
"Why that name, exactly?"

"It's pretty."

"Uh-huh. At least you didn't bring a gun this time."

She shrugs. "Decided I didn't need it. I know where
we stand."

"Where's that?"

"You know." A wink. She goes to the bar, curls the tip of
a red Converse Hi-Top around a stool-leg and pulls it to her.
She sits on it, slumps forward: the posture of a surly teen. And
that, Mookie has to remind himself, is what she is: a surly,
pouty, pissy, mean-ass, don't-give-a-shit-about-nobody-
but-herself teen.

Or is that underestimating her? A year ago she shows up,
tricks Mookie into clearing out a major nest of goblins and
leaving their stash of Blue untended so she can steal it, then
shows up at the bar and shoots Werth in the gut? Then she sets
up shop in the city, paying off players and buying up resources
with money that couldn't have come from the Blue she'd
just stolen. Suddenly: Mookie's own daughter, a new player
in town. One who doesn't play by the Organization rules. A
constant thorn in everybody's paw. Depending on who you
ask, she's either a cryptic mastermind or a talented – and lucky
– amateur. Mookie's not sure which it is.

Nobody in the Organization knows who she is to him. Nobody but Werth.

"How'd you hide from me?" he asks, standing there in the middle of the floor, feeling like a broken thumb.

She shrugs. Coy. Playful.

He takes a guess. "Snakeface trick. Gotta be."

Nora grins a Cheshire Cat grin – as a girl he rarely saw her smile and even this one doesn't seem all that happy. She always was a good actress.

"Got it in one, Daddy-o."

Daddy-o. So she *has* been hanging out with the Get-Em-Girls. "Why are you here, Nora? Ain't safe." He starts to feel weird. Dizzy in her presence.

"I'm always safe with you around." She twirls her hair. "I want to put my offer on the table one last time."

"Not workin' for you, Nora. I got people. I got loyalties."

"Your 'people' don't know what's coming."

"And you do?"

"Maybe I do. And maybe I'm giving you a chance to be on the winning side of things. Because it's all gonna fall apart and if you don't move from where you're standing? You'll be underneath it when it does."

He snorts. "You gotta lotta nerve, little girl. Last I checked your apple had lost its shine." That isn't just him being cocky. Her stock has dropped in the city. She made her move and for a while it worked, but the gobbos came back, the gangs got her measure, the Boss made his own play to block her at every turn. He bought back her allies. Killed a few of her customers. Her circle of influence is growing ever tighter. Nora – *Persephone* – doesn't have much left. "Go home. Go back to your mother. Quit playing like you're a gangster. You don't have it. We both know you just did it to piss me off."

The smile falls away like the last leaf off an autumn tree.

"Why I do what I do isn't your concern. I'm here offering you a chance."

"I'm good where I'm at."

"Something you ought to know about Zoladski."

The Boss. You didn't say his name out loud. Not if you worked for him. Not if you didn't want to end up in the river.

"I know all I need to know," he says.

"Then you know he's dying."

That hits Mookie like an ice-ball to the face. He flinches. "What?"

"Cancer. The real bad kind. His expiration date is coming up fast."

"How do you know this?"

Mischievous twinkle. "What can I say? I'm *good*."

"You're bad."

"That too." She shrugs. "But you're not exactly a boy scout, Daddy."

"I do what I have to do."

She taps her temple then. A sign. A gesture from one Blazehead to another. That kills him. That little acknowledgement – a recognition of a shared sin – cuts all the way through the fat and meat and gristle.

"Damnit, Nora."

"Hey, we are who we are, Daddy. We all have our roles to play. I just thought you'd like one last chance to get onboard. Boat's leaving. Once it's out of port, you'll be shit out of luck, old man. Stuck on shore as the world burns."

"I told you, Eleanor. Go home. I know your mother misses you."

Nora bristles. Goes quiet for a few moments and her gaze is a pair of hot pins through his eyes. Again he feels dizzy – sick, too. Nora unmoors him but this is different. Something's wrong.

"You don't know anything about Mom," Nora hisses. "You never did." Those words, dripping with poison, like a sponge soaked in snake venom. "You don't look so hot. How was the lardo?" At first he thinks she cares, but then he sees her lips tug into another smile.

"You…" He can barely find his words. *Snake venom.*

"Poisoned you?" She laughs. "Just a little."

He tries to step forward. His leg doesn't comply. It feels mushy. Like a rubber band dangling.

"Something big is coming, Mookie. I'm going to change the game." Nora waggles her fingers. She mouths, "Buh-bye."

Then Mookie drops like a hammer-struck bull.

2

The saying goes that there is more below the streets of New York City than there is above them. An exaggeration by those who say it, perhaps, but they don't know just how accurate that statement truly is. Hell's heart, as it turns out, has many chambers.

> – from the Journals of John Atticus Oakes,
> Cartographer of the Great Below

Daddy… Daaaaaaddyyyy…

I need your help, Daddy.

I'm hooked on Blue. These awful things sold it to me.

Goblins. They hurt me. They hurt my boyfriend.

If only someone would kill them for me…

Daaaaddyyy…

He awakens in the morning. Still alive. The poison ran its course, scraped him out like a knife. Every movement feels slow. Like he's walking underwater. Glances up. Sees the time. He's running late. For the Boss' meeting. Shit. *Shit.*

He grabs a stool and shatters it against the bar top, then staggers out the door.

Mookie takes the train out of Edison.

Train's late. And it's not the express. Time escapes. His body's starting to rebound from whatever Snakeface venom his daughter must've used to poison his meat – and now everything feels toothy and raw. Like coming down off the Blue.

His feet tap. He keeps cracking his knuckles.

Finally, the train moves. North on Jersey Transit toward the city. Through trees and tracks, past Rahway, Elizabeth, into the bleak industrial waste that is Newark, and finally down through darkness toward the city proper.

When the train hits the tunnel, Mookie stiffens. His whole body, tensing up like he just stepped on the third rail. Out there in the shadows of the underground, anything could be hiding. Monsters of known quantity: a band of war-whooping gobbos, a handful of all-mad half-and-halfs, a cult of Blazeheads looking to score. Or creatures of unknown measure: they exist, too. Things that have no name. That have never been seen before and will never be seen again once they crawl back down into the deep. They could rush the train, break the windows, drag passengers out through the holes screaming into the black.

It won't happen. Probably. Hasn't yet. Most know better. And the trains move fast.

But Mookie knows what could happen. He's seen worse.

So when the train plunges through the tunnel before Penn Station, when his cell signal goes dead and out there in the darkness he sees the sparking blue of powerlines snapping, he feels his teeth grit, his eyes water, his balls cinch up toward his belly. He thinks he sees something, or someone, standing out there on an abandoned platform, lit by the sparking blue, but then the train moves and the shape is gone.

Then it's light and the muffled voice coming over the speakers.

Penn Station, New York City.

Mookie gets off the train.

Everyone avoids him as he exits. It's not just because he's a big sonofabitch. It's because he looks like he could knock the heads off their shoulders with but a flick of his wrist. It's because he looks like he might eat them if he gets hungry enough. It's because he looks like something out of a bad dream.

Maybe he is.

Dreams of hands pulling her down through water. Then into the muddy bottom. Bubbles in black muck. Down, through the mud, wriggling like a reverse worm, into the catacombs. The maze like a bundle of snakes, loops and whorls against loops and whorls, her running through tight tunnels that empty out into epic chambers, past glowing rock like tropical coral, past fungal shelves that smell of rotting meat, past an overturned shopping cart with a human skeleton draped upon it – skull-teeth *clack-clack-clack*ing.

Something chasing her. Away and into the dark.

A black shape. Flinty, silver eyes – like hematite catching light. It's faster than she is.

Suddenly she's above. City streets. Flickering lights. People are screaming. The earth shudders. Something dark coils around the Chrysler Building.

Then: another sound. Feet stomping on rock. Like hooves on cobblestone.

A hand falls on her shoulder–

Big hand. Hard hand with scabs on the knuckles. A hard shove and she's down on the ground. Palms stinging against asphalt. She rolls over. She sees. It's him.

"Daddy?" she says, voice damp and smothered – something in her throat –

Nora awakens. Mouth gaping as if emerging back up through the water in her dreams, gasping and then gagging and then coughing. Mouth thick with the treacly mouth-breather spit-crust. She makes an *ugh* sound, fumbles on the coffee table – she fell asleep on the couch last night – for a bottle of iced tea. Not much in it and it tastes foul, but wet is wet and she doesn't feel like getting up, not yet.

There, next to the bottle, on the far side of a cat-chewed remote control, lies a small Altoids tin. She grabs for it, gently opens it, the little metal hinges squeaking.

In the corner of the tin sits a small residue of blue powder.

Just looking at it makes her heart flutter. Makes her brow hot.

So little left. Less than a thimble's worth. One use, maybe two.

Part of her itches to use it. Grab it. Smudge it. Give into it.

But she doesn't. There's no point. She has to be practical with this stuff. Reserve it for when she'll need it most – and that time may be coming soon.

As though on cue, her phone vibrates on the table. Screen lights up with a text.

From her boy-toy:

Will I see you tonight? <3 C.

Another swig of rancid tea to wash down the bad taste and the worse dreams.

"You bet your ass you will," Nora says, texting him with a more moderate:

l8r, yes.

She holds the phone to her chest and smiles. The whole thing will flip soon enough. Thanks to her. And then she'll have all the Cerulean she could ever want.

And Daddy will have to ask *her* for permission to get a taste.

Mookie gets a text from Werth. It's the address. Then a follow-up text, all caps:

WHERE THE HELL ARE YOU YOURE LATE

Mookie doesn't know what to say so he texts back nothing.

He knows the address, at least. East Village. Little Poland. Tiny hole-in-the-wall restaurant called Wila's. Good golabki. Killer kielbasa.

He thinks to take a cab, but most the time they don't stop for a big scary bastard like him. And fitting into the back of a cab sucks. It always feels like one of his elbows is going to bust out a window, or his head is going to pop up through the roof. He's been in tighter places – the Great Below isn't always roomy, what with its tight labyrinthine hallways and suffocating chambers – but somehow the back of a cab always makes him feel claustrophobic. And out of control.

And Mookie doesn't like to feel out of control.

But today, no choice. Cab'll move quicker than he can on foot. And he's already late.

To stop a cab he steps out in front of one. Brakes screech.

He gives the chipmunk-cheeked Sikh behind the wheel the address. The Sikh gives him a look of bewilderment and maybe even fear. But Mookie just growls and the man flips the meter and drives.

At this hour, the streets are crowded. People going to work. Or looking for work. Or tourists coming into the city. A hippy woman on her cell bumps into a reedy little black dude struggling past with a Great Dane that looks more horse than dog. A Korean pushes a bike with a bent wheel. Homeless guys push shopping carts filled with cats and blankets, booze and busted-ass dreams. Men with loud ties pass women with short skirts. Children run to school, mothers trailing after.

None of these people get it.

It's not their fault. He knows that. They're ignorant. *Blind.* Eyes stapled shut. It's like how nobody in this city looks at anybody else. They don't look because they don't want to see. Someone gets mugged, another yells "rape," and nobody comes calling. People get beaten to death in stairwells, cries rising up through the building so that half the apartments can hear it, and by the time someone calls the cops, the body is cold, the blood is thick, and the killer is on the L train ten blocks away.

They don't know what lies beneath. What walks around them.

Maybe it's because they know. Secretly. They feel it vibrating in the deep of their bones, twisting in their stomach like an unspoken and misunderstood fear. Some part of the primal animal mind tells them, *hey, right now, something awful – not someone, but some*thing *– might be walking right next to you. Sizing you up for a snack. Thinking to drag you down into the dark and stuff you full of its fingers and tongues and lay eggs in all your holes. The monsters are here. You know it, I know it – so why even look?*

Mookie's not blazing. Not right now. So he's just as blind as the rest of them.

But that doesn't change what he knows.

He knows that the monsters are real.

And they're here. Hidden in plain sight.

Skint is an ashy, dry-skinned albino. Sells flowers all around TriBeCa to make a buck. At least, that's what he wants people to think. Nora knows him for something else: he's a guy who brings people together. He knows everybody. Sets up meetings. He's not an info broker like that Snakeface in Chinatown, but he can plant a whisper in every ear that matters.

He's also not human. Not all the way, anyway.

He's a half-and-half. Were she Blazing, she'd see a long-limbed freak with skin like cracked vellum and eyes like unpopped blood blisters.

Thankfully, right now she's Blind.

She shoves a cuppa coffee in his free hand. In the other hand, he holds a bundle of roses. Other flowers sit in makeshift containers around his feet.

"Little Miss Thing," Skint says. "Whadda you want?"

"Bought you Starbucks," she says, smiling.

"I don't drink Starbucks. Their coffee tastes like burned pubes."

"I think you'll like it."

"I said I don't drink this nasty-ass–" Suddenly he stops. Weighs the cup, finds it lacking. Skint's dusty eyebrows lift in a curious arch and he pops the top. He sees the money curled inside. "Yeah, OK. What?"

"Don't act so surprised I'm coming to you."

"I just figured you were done in this town. Hadn't heard much from you in the last few months. One minute you were selling Blue, next minute, poof."

A jogger in a blue knit cap almost knocks her off her feet. She gives him the finger and barks some profanity about the jogger's mother, then turns back to the albino. "Yeah, well. Things cooled down. But I'm back. I need you to get word out."

"To who?"

"To everybody. All the gang heads."

He looks at the cup. Then back at her. "This for that?"

"It's enough. Besides, when I'm done, there'll be more. A lot more."

He's dubious. That's fine. Let him think she's blowing hot air. He says, "I think you're a bad investment, so let's just call this charity, eh? What's the message?"

"I want you to tell them that the Boss is a dead man. That it's time to take back the city. You tell them I have a guy on the inside and a plan to bring it all crashing down."

He laughs. "Big talk. And sounds like bullshit."

"Just tell them, already. Unless you like all this?" She sweeps her arms as if to encompass the grandeur of standing on a shitty city corner. "The Organization doesn't think a split-skinned freak like you is fit to kiss Zoladski's dirty shoes. You're a nobody out here. A piece of monster trash. But that can change. You can make *them* kiss *your* feet. Then kick them in the teeth as they pucker up."

He pauses. Shifts from foot to foot, all anxious-like.

"Yeah. Yeah, fine. I'll tell them."

"Tell them all. And let them know I'll be in touch."

Skint lifts the coffee cup as if to toast. "To the future, then."

••••

Wila's.

Counter on the left. Register. Seats at the counter and a bunch of rickety tables and ratty booths. Everything cast in a color like old lemon meringue pie.

No hostess here. Just a tired-looking waitress with hound-dog eyes and hair dyed so red it's almost purple. She shows off a set of nicotine teeth, tells Mookie he can sit anywhere. He shakes his head. Points upstairs.

"Oh," she says. Then she gives him a sad smile. "You look like a growing boy. You want something to take up? Pierogie?"

He does. He wants a pierogie. Or a link of kielbasa. But no time. He feels his mouth water like a dog staring at a steak.

The waitress leads the way upstairs.

The smells of the kitchen are strong here. Paprika and vinegar. Sharp bite of fennel. Garlic, too. Mookie wants to pause here on the steps, take it all in.

But–

The Boss awaits.

At the top of the steps is a door with peeling blue paint. Mookie walks through.

Nora stands across the street. Under the awning of a little café, pigeons dancing around her feet.

She watches her father go into the Polish joint. Dumb monkey. The old man looks rougher than usual. Her poison did a number on him, but here he is, anyway. She knew it wouldn't kill him; that was never a question. The Snakeface that sold it to her made sure it wasn't the deadly stuff – just the "go the fuck to sleep" stuff. (She's not sure how they know to milk different venoms from their nasty little... fang glands or whatever, they just do. And she's content with that answer.)

It's in this moment that she realizes she has a lot of power.

Right now, she's privy to a secret meeting of lieutenants and higher-ups in the Organization. All gathered under a single, ill-defended roof.

I could call the gangs.

I could leak it to Smiley.

I could stir up a pack of pissed-off gobbos looking for a chance to get back at the group of humans who have helped keep them bottled up and kept below.

I could call up some hobo with a shotgun to kick down the door and blast all those a-holes into bloody bits.

But she just stands there. Eating a Luna bar.

She could do a lot of things. Instead, she does nothing. Just stands there. Eating a Luna bar.

It's all going to shake out the right way no matter what. Patience will win the day. She has her way in. The old man is going bye-bye. The house of cards will fall and she will be the one to help rebuild it.

She tells herself it has nothing to do with the fact her father's inside. Instead of sleeping off the Snakeface venom on the floor of his Podunk bar. That's definitely not it. Because she hates him. That's what she tells herself.

The door bangs as it shuts. A big banquet room full of the Organization's lieutenants turn and stare at him as Mookie comes through. Jimmy Luscas in his sharkskin suit. Maria O'Malley in a heavy wool turtleneck. Not far away, Saul Bloom gives him an irritated look over his dark-rimmed glasses like, *The fuck is wrong with you?* But fear flashes in Bloom's eyes, too – fear of who Mookie is and what he does.

These aren't Mookie's people. Not really. They know him. Or know of him. They operate business in the city: gambling, protection, prostitution, imports, exports, all of it. They don't handle what goes on beneath the streets. That's what Werth does. And beneath Werth is Mookie. On paper, Werth's a lieutenant and Mookie's a soldier, but that ain't quite right, either. They're a two-man operation, a broken branch of the Organization's family tree. Werth's got Mookie, and Mookie has his own people. Mole Men. Blue-sifters. Informants. Addicts.

Werth appears, catches Mookie's elbow. Werth, the old goat. Wiry chin hairs. One half-lidded eye. One gray tooth. And now, thanks to Mookie's own daughter, a cane. Werth isn't a classy guy – given half a chance he'll hang around in a dirty polo shirt drinking bad beer – but he's got a top-shelf cane. Black like volcanic glass. Topped with a silver goat head. He gives Mookie the same look Bloom gave him, and whispers: "You're late, you big asshole."

"I know." He doesn't say why.

"You look like hot hell. I told you to dress nice."

"Didn't have time."

"Didn't have–? You had *all night*. You know what, never mind. I swear to fuck, Mook, sometimes..." He shakes his head. "Haversham talked for a little while. The company man ran the numbers, I 'bout fell asleep standing up. No Boss yet."

"Yeah." The lieutenants start to mill and mumble. Impatient types. Mookie says, "Sorry I'm late."

Werth sizes him up. Keeps his voice low. "You didn't call me back last night."

"Like I said, I was–"

"Tired, I heard you. Was it her?"

"Her who?" But Mookie knows what he's asking and who he's asking about.

"Don't fuck with me, Mook. You get a chance to take her out, you need to take her out." He lowers his voice to a scratchy, rheumy whisper: "The Boss doesn't know. Who she is to you. But the longer she's out there the bigger the chance he's going to figure it out. And that's bad news. You hear?"

He's about to tell him, *yeah, yeah, I hear*, but then the crowd hushes.

Up on the dais – a dais still ringed with crêpe ribbon and cut-out paper wedding bells from some event nights before – steps the Boss.

The dread realization strikes him: *Nora was right*.

The Boss has always been a small man: sharp and etched like a peach-pit, mean and jagged like a little kidney stone. But here he looks smaller. And weaker. Skin like paper. Hair like wisps of white silk.

Haversham trails behind, wheeling an oxygen tank. In an Italian family he'd be considered a *consigliere*, but this isn't an Italian family – and Haversham's about the furthest thing from Italian you'll get: pinched accountant face, white blond hair as thin and airy as a cottonball.

The wheels on the oxygen tank squeak.

The Boss steps up. Takes a hit off of the tank's mask, then hands it to Haversham.

The old man speaks.

"I've got–"

Voice like dry leaves in a closing fist. He coughs into his armpit. Something wet rumbles in his lungs and he pulls his arm away and tries again.

"I've got six months to live. Lung cancer."

3

The criminal organization found in other cities is barely that — "organization" is a joke, a lie, an easy bit of short-code spoken by people who don't understand. It's gang against gang. No quarter. No peace. No treaty. No cleanly-drawn territorial lines. A constant push-and-pull of drug corners and gun-runs and stables of foreign girls made into sex slaves. The battle lines redrawn in new blood day after day. That's not New York. Here the Great Below altered the landscape both literally and figuratively. The monsters that came crawling up out of the broken mantle forced the game to change. Here the gangs found a tense, but effective, peace. They operate under a central authority: the Organization.

> – from the Journals of John Atticus Oakes,
> Cartographer of the Great Below

The Boss stares out over a room with eyes so brown they're almost black. Coals in cotton. The Lieutenants shift uncomfortably. Mookie feels gut-shot. The Boss being off the radar for so long — that was a mystery on its own but they figured, well, they figured a lot of things. Maybe he was running things on the down-low; he was old, approaching eighty, and the Organization was a creaky-but-effective machine. Maybe he was off somewhere talking to other criminal organizations – Philly, Boston,

29

DC. Maybe he was taking an extended vacation. But this? Cancer?

Behind the Boss, Haversham steeples his fingers – each hand a spider on a mirror. He looks ever the accountant, the company man.

"I'm dying," the Boss says again. He's a small man, but the lights behind him lend him a long shadow. "The cancer's all up in me. It's, ahh–" Here he looks to Haversham. "What's the word?" Haversham whispers and the Boss returns his gaze to the crowd. "Metastasized. Like bedbugs in city hotels. By the time they saw it, well." He gives a shrug, takes another hit off the oxygen, throws the mask down like it's a dirty rag. "I hate that thing. The oxygen tastes funny. Like minerals. Or pool chemicals."

Everybody's quiet. After a few moments, Zoladski resumes speaking:

"I built this thing we do from the ground-up fifty fucking years ago. I came up out of Philly, me and just a couple other guys. Alfie Luscas – Little Jimmy's pop. Cyril Bartosiewicz. Max Dombrowski and his little brother, Joshy. I stole business from the Italians–" He pronounces it *Eye-talians*. "–and then me and my boys pushed back the Irish all the way to the Bowery and then we took the Bowery a few years later. Little gangs popped up, the Puerto Ricans, the Jamaicans, the Lantern Jacks, the Black Sleeves, the Railroad Boys..." He takes a moment, starts to cough. Haversham hands him the mask, but he swipes it away. "And instead of beating them back we brought them in. Made them a part of it. A real coalition. A fucking *Organization*, all official-like. You're either in it and alive or outside it and dead. And the time came that we learned what lurked underneath our feet, we stood tall and kept what was ours."

Thirty years ago. When the Sandhogs opened up the Great Below and hell came spilling out. The monsters wanted a slice. Between the Sandhogs and Zoladski's crime coalition, the nightmares got pushed back into the dark.

"Hell with it. Nobody came to listen to an old man talk about bullshit everybody already knows. Business is good. And business is gonna stay good. This thing that we do runs itself and me being six feet under ain't gonna change that – not like I was getting any younger. Every day is a day gone, a day you don't get back, and that shouldn't come as a surprise to any one of us. Still, somebody needs to step up. Take the reins."

Mookie looks around the room. The lieuts look anxious. And suddenly excited. Like one of them is going to be called up here and now and handed the keys to the city. Zoladski had a son, but the son died in a deal gone bad with one of the gangs, the Crimson Kings. The Kings paid for that transgression – heads cut off and sent to the other gangs as a message: *This is what you get when you fuck with a Zoladski.*

But it's then that Haversham gives a nod to the far corner of the room and out from behind a stack of trays and chairs walks this young, reedy kid in an ill-fitting black suit with a narrow black tie. The kid hurries up to the front like a couple mop handles falling out of a hallway closet. Got two gold rings on his bulbous knuckles. Thin gold chain around his neck. It's then Mookie sees the resemblance – square-shaped head, hair styled the same way (even though the kid's is penny-red and the old man's is like fresh snow). Same nose, too. Nose like an owl's beak.

Mookie's seen him before. But last time he saw him he was, what, knee-high to a chipmunk? Just a little boy then.

"My grandson," the Boss says, the words a rheumy rattle. "Casimir Zoladski. Some of you have met him. He's a good kid. He'll succeed me in this. When I'm gone, he's the new Boss, so give him the respect he deserves or he'll cut your balls off. And I'll come back from the dead to eat 'em."

A moment hangs in the air before the applause, a handful of seconds bundled in the string of uncertainty where the lieuts shift nervously and wonder if this is some kind of fucking joke, that the Boss is going to hand over the entire Organization to a twenty-year-old wet-behind-the-ears *whelp* like this.

"So there it is," the Boss says. Like he just pissed on the floor and is daring anybody to say something about it. "Let's eat."

Servers from downstairs put out chairs and tables and bring out food. A lot of it. Trays over burners. It's a whole Polish spread: pierogies, three different types of kielbasa, golabki, pyzy dumplings, tomato soup, poppy seed rolls. Mookie wants to eat it all. He's starving. He's always starving but now's worse than ever because the venom has him feeling gutted, like his blood sugar has fallen through the floor – and then this news? Cancer? Casimir? Mookie's always been the type to eat his emotions and right now his emotions want him to shovel pierogies and sausage into his mouth until he passes out.

Then there's that nagging thought: *Nora knew about this. She told me he was sick.*

How the hell did she know?

Mookie moves to get in line. He jostles Shawndell Washington, who turns to say something but then sees who he's dealing with and then shuts up. Sometimes Mookie likes scaring people. Other times it makes him sad. Right now he just wants to eat.

Which is why it sucks that Werth comes up, grabs him out of line.

"Hey goddamnit," Mookie protests with a grindstone growl.

"Shut up, you'll get to eat. You're like one of those goddamn Hungry Hungry Hippos." He waves Mookie on. "Let's go see the Boss."

"He doesn't want to see us."

"He doesn't want to see *you*. But we gotta pay our respects."

"All right, all right. But then we eat?"

As they head over to the corner table where the Boss has parked himself, his tank, and Haversham, Werth slaps Mookie's gut through his stained shirt. "I remember when you were cut like a slab of mountain rock. You got fat."

"I got old."

"I'm older than you," Werth says. "And I'm thinner than ever."

"You got a tapeworm. And you're part goat."

They stand in line behind a couple of other lieuts looking to kiss the ring, metaphorically-speaking. Werth keeps egging Mookie on: "I'm just saying, Mookie, you used to be a mean cut of meat. Now you're like a... flabby chuck roast."

"I can still hit things." He snorts. "And chuck makes a damn good pot roast."

"Oh, here we go. You and your little... froofy foodie obsession."

"It's charcuterie."

"*Shark cootery.* Sounds French."

"It is."

"You're too dumb to speak froofy French."

Mookie shrugs. "Only French word I know. And it ain't froofy. It's meat. I kill pigs. I take their meat. I put it in sausages. I cure the fat. I eat it."

"Whatever. You know what I like? That two cheeseburger meal at McDonald's. Same every time. Couple bucks. Greasy and sweet. The pickle? The ketchup and mustard? Right on the money. And those fucking French fries, Jesus

Christ on a cupcake those are like, the perfect– Oh, here we go."

Ahead of them, Marla Koladky-Pinsky steps out of their way, gives them a pissy look like they're the last pair of dingleberries hanging, and then–

There he is. The Boss. Looking small and crumpled. Like an origami tiger on the seat that somebody sat on without realizing.

The Boss stands. Steps around his oxygen tank, thrusts out a hand. That's his thing. He shakes your hand no matter who you are.

Mookie takes the hand.

"Don't break my arm," the Boss says with a wink. He stifles a hard cough.

"I won't."

"You got a good grip. Confident. But not too confident." The Boss doesn't let go. He casts a squinty look down at the two hands – his own hand dwarfed by the human oven mitt that is Mookie's. "I can tell everything with a handshake. Everything. It all comes together in that moment. I can tell if I like a guy. Or if I want to stick him in the gills with a switchblade. I can tell if he's gonna betray me or if he'll stand by me as Hell pisses on my head." He licks his teeth. "You're rock fucking solid, you are. Not just physically. You're loyal. A good soldier. And you–"

He turns to Werth. Werth says, "Boss, I'm sorry as hell to hear about this."

Zoladski waves a hand.

"God comes for all of us in the end. You know how he got me? Asbestos. This is a fuckin' *asbestos cancer*."

Haversham, in a clipped tone, adds: "Mesothiolioma."

"Right. Asbestos cancer. Some time in my life, way back when, a little shitty *speck* of asbestos embedded in my lung-meat and now here we are. Death sentence." He sniffs. "We had that shit in our house down in Kensington. In the roof shingles. In the siding. Wrapped around the pipes. Inevitable, I guess."

"They got surgery they can do," Werth says. "Right? Lung transplants. And then there's chemo and radiation and, and—what?"

"Hell with all that," the Boss says, flecks of saliva dotting his lip and gathering at the corners of his mouth like sea foam. "I go that way they maybe give me another three, four months, and my quality of life goes down the crapper. I'll look like a baby bird what lost his feathers. No. We have to project strength. Continuance. We got a good thing going here in the Organization, but soon as those fuckin' gangland piranhas smell blood in the water, it's over. They'll churn the river good trying to get to me. What we got here, boys, is a real *fragile situation*. Like an egg balanced on the tip of the finger, could get messy. Could all go *tits up* in a blink." His voice goes low and his eyes lose focus. "All because of a little piece of asbestos."

The Boss's gaze returns to Mookie.

"You used to work with asbestos."

"Uh. Yeah." How'd he know that?

"You were a Sandhog."

Mookie grunts in assent.

"Family thing?"

"My Pop. My Grampop, too."

"But not for you, not anymore. Why you'd quit?"

Mookie shrugs. "This is my thing."

"This thing we do," the Boss says, the words almost musical, like a Sinatra croon lurks somewhere behind the words, a sing-song ghost. "Christ, I'm hungry. But the cancer's a jealous mistress. It eats me; I don't get to eat anything else. Food here's good, though. Kielbasa's solid." He pronounces it *kill-baasy*. "They know a good kilbo. Still ain't like in my

Philly days, though. They, *they* knew kilbos. Before we came here they called us the Kielbasa Gang. You know that? Maybe you did. I repeat myself in my old age – forgive me that sin, yeah? Where you come from, Mookie?"

"Jersey originally."

"Good. Well. You go eat." Then the Boss waves them off. Sits back down. And that's that. *You're dismissed.*

On the way back to the food line, Werth says, "Fuckin' cancer, am I right?"

"Fuckin' cancer," Mookie says.

The plate is heavy. Pierogies – fat dough pockets filled with cheese, slathered with butter and onions. Kielbasa red like a Russian rocket. Beet salad. He's tempted to toss the plastic fork away and just use his hands, but people would stare.

Fuck it. They stare anyway. He starts using his hands.

Mookie sits by himself in the corner. Rips apart a pierogie. Cheesy filling spills; steam rises. Just as he's about to cram it in his salivating mouth, a hand falls on his forearm.

It's the kid. The grandson. Casimir.

"You're Mookie Pearl," he says.

Mookie looks left, looks right. Like this is some kind of joke.

"That's me." He almost adds, *Whaddya want, kid?* but then remembers that this "kid" is going to be the Big Boss with the Red Hot Sauce before too long.

"Can I sit?"

"You can do anything you want."

And yet the kid doesn't sit. He stands there. Hands in his pockets.

Casimir lowers his voice. "I'm not ready for this."

"To sit down?"

"To take over."

"Oh." Mookie looks down at the drippy blob of butter-ooze dough at the end of the pierogie and sighs. *Be rude to eat in front of the next Boss.* He sets the food down, an act that is almost painful to perform. "You got some time yet."

Now, Casimir sits. "Not much. Not enough."

"You'll be OK."

"Up until now, he kept me out of it. The business. Now it's like–" He knocks two fists together. "Boom. Crash course. And I'm not ready."

"I don't know what you want me to say."

"I need you to do something."

Can he do that? Does the kid have the power yet? He's more important than Mookie by a hundred miles. A thousand. So, yeah, probably. "OK, sure."

"I need you to cure my *dziadzia*."

"Your who?"

"My Pop-Pop. The Boss."

"Cure. Like, the cancer."

"That's right. I need you to cure his cancer."

Mookie almost laughs. This kid isn't too bright. "I know I don't look like a doctor."

"But you know things. You've been..." The kid points toward the floor. "Downstairs." He means the Great Below. The Underworld. *Hell itself.* Mookie's surprised the kid knows about that, but if they've been giving him a real crash course and he's going to take the wheel...

"Hell's not a hospital. It's the... opposite of one. No help there for your grandfather."

"I've been reading."

"Good for you. I hear it's fundamental."

"No, I mean– I have these pages. From this journal? This guy named Oakes..."

Shit. *This.* "John Atticus, yeah. He went down fifteen, twenty years ago. Went nuts. Never came back. End of story."

"He says that the..." And here Casimir lowers his voice even further as if he's summoning the Devil. "Blue stuff isn't the only pigment. That there are *five* in addition to the Blue and that one of them can cure anything, can end death itself–"

All anybody has of Oakes' journal are a dozen or so pages that have been found scattered around the Underworld over the years. Mookie knew him. Well, met him, anyway. Was a reformed thief-turned-explorer. A self-proclaimed "cartographer". Like the dead of Daisypusher, he wanted to chart the whole Underworld. Thousands of miles of subterranean labyrinth. He got a lot of things right but some stuff...

"You're talking about Death's Head. *Caput Mortuum*. It's not real. Nobody's ever seen the stuff. Nobody's seen anything but the Blue."

"They say that they found the Red–"

"Fuck the Red." The kid flinches. It's only then Mookie hears the anger in his own voice. He's tired. Hungry. Seeing Nora didn't do him any favors. "I just mean, until I see it, I don't buy it."

"But if Death's Head were real, it could cure him."

Mookie shrugs. "If it does what Oakes said it could do, yeah."

"So you'll find it."

"Kid–"

"You'd be helping me. And him. And the whole Organization. Can you imagine it? Curing his cancer?" Casimir runs his hands through his copper hair. "I'm not ready. I need more time."

"Why me? Why not go to Werth?"

"James Werth is a half-and-half. A hybrid."

So, he knows what that is. Mookie wonders if the kid's ever Blazed, torn the scales off of his eyes to see what's really out there. "So? You some kind of racist?"

"No. I mean – I don't know. You're human. And you come highly recommended."

"From who?"

The kid blanches. "From, I dunno. People."

"Jesus. Fine. I'll look."

Casimir offers a hand to shake. "Thank you, Mookie."

Mookie takes the hand. Shakes it. Tries not to roll the kid's knuckles. If the measure of a handshake really matters, then Mookie wonders what it means that it feels like he's shaking a dead carp instead of the kid's hand. Maybe the kid really isn't ready.

Which is bad news for everybody.

Mookie heads for the door. He ate. His stomach feels fit to burst. In a good way. He likes that feeling beyond satiety – the fullness of the flesh, the sense of being somehow completed by a good meal.

Werth hobbles over to him. "You leaving?"

"I figure." He doesn't say anything about what Casimir wanted. Werth would call it crazy. It *is* crazy. "I got things to check on while I'm in the city."

"You should move back. Get an apartment in the village. Or Brooklyn at least."

"I got my bar."

"It's not a bar. It's a house with a bar in it."

He shrugs. "Got a freezer for meat. Got shelves for liquor." But he notices that Werth has mentally checked out. His tongue is fidgeting with his loose gray tooth and he's staring off toward the door.

"Who's that?" Werth asks, lifting his whiskery chin.

The man that enters the small banquet room isn't one Mookie recognizes. Definitely not a thug. Nobody from a gang. He's too well-dressed. Like he's in a Cuban café – tan fedora, red embroidered guayabera shirt, a gold watch, and shoes so shiny other shoes might use them as mirrors.

Mookie doesn't know what makes one guy good looking and another guy ugly, but he knows that if he's at the ass-end of the spectrum, this guy's at the other. He looks like someone out of a movie. Dark-drawn lines around the eyes, a glimmer in his gaze.

Following behind is a thin slip of a man, skin so pale it might as well be gray, sliding along with all the posture of a broken coat-rack. A black V-neck T-shirt hangs loose over his sickly frame – his match-stick arms are inked with symbols and sigils, ones Mookie's seen but can't place, ones that tell him right away what he's looking at even without blazing.

"Ten to one that guy in the black shirt is a Snakeface," Mookie says.

"Shit, yeah. Look at the arms."

The man in the suit and his wormy attaché head toward the Boss's table in the back of the room, the pair gliding through the crowd, earning stares. They don't belong.

Mookie feels himself tense up. This could be it. This could be a hit. Maybe one of the gangs is sending someone. Or maybe this is from another city: the Sicilians, the Irish, or any number of Mexican, Aryan, or Dominican gangs. Or maybe it's someone from the Deep Downstairs – some pissed off half-and-half wants to take over.

Mookie reaches into his pocket and starts to move toward the new guests. His big hand fumbles for his little tin of Cerulean – he's ready to powder up, rip open his third eye and become *aware*. But then he sees Haversham stand and cross the room. Haversham and the man in the suit shake hands.

"Mr Candlefly?" Haversham says.

Mookie lets the tin drop back into his pocket.

Haversham greets the man in the suit. This man, Candlefly, speaks with a European accent. A Spanish roll to it. The voice warm, dark, like a fresh cup of black coffee. "Good day, Mr

Haversham. Nice to finally meet in person." Candlefly gestures toward the Snakeface: "This is my associate, Mr Sorago."

The Snakeface – Sorago – bows his already bent head.

And with that, Haversham ushers them toward the Boss.

Werth pops up again by Mookie's side. He's eating a roll. "Why would a Snakeface be hanging out with the Boss?"

Mookie grunts: a wordless answer of, *not sure.*

Around a mouthful of bread, Werth says, "Strange. The Boss doesn't usually deal with... that type."

"Times are changing."

"Hope they don't change out from under us."

Mookie shrugs. "I gotta go."

4

Cerulean. The bright blue mineral vein shot through the prehistoric schist of the Great Below. Equal parts pigment and drug. It goes by many names: Peacock Powder, Truth Talc, the Straight Dope, Blue Jay (or just, "Jay"), Bluebird or Blue Butterfly (or simply "BB"), Blue Mascara, Cobalt, Azure. But many just call it – and the effects it engenders – the Blue Blazes. Users smudge some of the blue powder on the temples to bring on effects that include: preternatural strength, preternatural toughness, as well as a wiping away of the illusions that keep mortal men from seeing the truth of the denizens of the Underworld. In first-time users the Blue Blazes create an adrenalin rush and an eerie, powerful focus – a high that peaks with the initial use and is never again matched. Blazeheads are said in this way to "chase the blue" or "hunt the peacock". Many never know that the visions they sometimes see are true – they believe them to be by-products of the drug, hallucinations that accompany the feelings of invulnerability and clarity. As a drug it's quite rare and fetches a high price among those who know of its existence. The Organization controls Cerulean. Or, at least, they think they do.

> – from the Journals of John Atticus Oakes,
> Cartographer of the Great Below

A passing subway train shakes the walls. Fluorescent lights swing.

As they do, the shadows of the room move – shadows of crooked card tables, of antique scales, of the little towers of tins that tilt and teeter as the train passes.

Once the noise has calmed down, the half-man, Octavio, says, "C'mon, man. Death's Head isn't real, Mookie. You know that."

Mookie's not Blazing right now: if he were, he'd see a man with hair like braided vines, with skin like tree bark and fingernails like rose-thorns. Octavio's a half-and-half, like Werth: but, while Blind, all Mookie sees is a broad-shouldered black man with long, puffy dreads going halfway down his back. Behind him, a couple other workers – ex-Mole People – pull out a few softball-sized hunks of Cerulean, the blue of the pigment an unearthly hue, here in the bright lights of the secret room not far from the Brooklyn Bridge Station.

Mookie shrugs. "I know. But I was told to ask."

The ex-Moles use the bottom of plastic buckets to crush the Cerulean. They pulverize it to a powder. They measure it out into neat little piles. The piles go onto scales and then into little unmatched tins. Each equaling one ounce of Blue. Rumor has it it's starting to catch on with rich kids and celebrities: folks who've finally caught wind that there's some secret hush-hush drug out there, some trip-balls hallucinogen that makes you "see things" and "feel like you could take over the world."

If Blue really catches on after all these years, it may be time to upgrade from little operations like this one. Mookie has a hard time envisioning rows and rows of trailers in some abandoned Jersey lot like they're cooking meth or unbundling bales of weed. Besides, it's not like Blue is in endless supply down here: you can always grow more marijuana or make more meth. Cerulean is like gold: you find the vein, you tap it, then it's gone. It doesn't come back. And one day they're gonna get tapped out.

Speaking of that, Octavio says:

"Heard you found a new vein, bruh."

Mookie nods. Reflexively he reaches for the leather satchel he carries over his shoulder and pulls it tight. He trusts Octavio, but the other Moles – they pulverize the Blue just hoping to get a taste. Addicts, all of them. "Under the Garment District, yeah. The Hell's Kitchen crew knows their shit pretty well. They're the ones that found it."

You use Blue to find Blue – when you Blaze, you can sense more Blue through the walls. Like a heartbeat dully thudding behind the rock. A vein in every sense.

"No more problems with the gobs?" Mookie asks.

Octavio shakes his head; his dreads stay still as his head moves. "Nah, bruh. Thanks for saving our bacon."

Mookie looks down at his scabbed over knuckles. "It's fine."

"They're gettin' worse, though. The gobbos. All riled up and shit."

"I know." Before Octavio can continue down this topic, Mookie asks again: "You sure you haven't heard nothing about the Purple? No Death's Head anywhere?"

"Nah. But I know I guy who knows a guy who got a hold of some of the Red."

"Bullshit." Always a *friend of a friend* story.

"For real! Said that shit's like bath salts had a baby with steroids or something, man. Makes you go crazy. He went nuts. Tore up his mother's house. Ate her dog."

"Ate her dog."

"Scout's fuckin' honor, yo."

"You were a Scout?"

"Do I look like a damn Boy Scout to you?"

"I dunno, Octavio. Go back to work. You hear anything about Death's Head–"

"Yeah, yeah, I'll call you."

It's all a myth. The Five Occulted Pigments. Sacred blah blah blah. Way Mookie sees it isn't much different than talking about Jesus or Buddha or any of that other stuff: yeah, maybe there's a grain of truth in that bag of rice, but for the most part, it's all stuff people make up to feel better about all the other stuff they don't understand. The stories folks tell about the Great Below – ancient gods in at the heart of the Labyrinth, mystical mineral pigments nobody's ever seen but everybody's got a story about, monsters that folks have only ever seen once – they're all just that. Stories.

And Mookie doesn't have time for stories. But Casimir Zoladski, he's got his brain wrapped around one such story the way a car wraps around a telephone pole – it's *inextricable*. He's gonna be the Boss one day. So Mookie's doing the deed. He won't find anything, but hopefully Casimir will one day say, "Good job", and maybe give him another couple crews, or maybe make him a proper lieutenant instead of a soldier, or best of all, just let him retire with one last suitcase full of money.

Mookie asks everybody he can ask. He knows a couple rock-flesh Trogbodies that hang out at a boxing gym in Brooklyn: Morg has a clumpy basalt body and he's strong, but slow. His mate, Gannog, is taller, a little leaner, a body of all iron-blue limestone. Gannog's quick on his feet, Morg is slow. Better at wrestling than boxing. Mookie shows up and the two of them are training – all the humans of the gym know them as Morgan and Gary, don't know that they're monsters, don't know that they go down into the dark when night falls and sleep together by merging with the rock.

When he asks about Death's Head, Morg says it's all a lie. Gannog's on the other end of the spectrum: he's a believer. He says he sometimes hears the whispers of the Hungry Ones echoing up through the tunnels of the Tangle like someone talking through a cardboard paper towel tube. Says that the old gods make *Caput Mortuum* – sometimes they call it the Violet Void. Says that some folks claim it's not even a proper

Pigment in the rock. Then the two of them go on to talk about the other colors, too: Red's real bad news, they heard tell of a quartzite Trogbody who got hold of some Golden Gate, but it didn't do anything when he ate it, whatever, all crap, none of it useful.

After that, as afternoon settles in, Mookie grabs a couple tacos from a taco truck and heads to see a couple kooks from the Skein, one of the lesser and more harmless cults of zealots who venerate the Great Below. The Skein contains a bunch of rich-folk academic-types who think that the power of the Underworld is to show humans the way to enlightenment – something about men and women "walking the Labyrinth in their own hearts" and "confronting Satan in his own house", which is all well and good except Mookie's never met Satan or Lucifer or anybody in the Deep Downstairs who would claim the title.

They invite him into their loft space in Chelsea and he asks them about Death's Head and of course they sit him down and give him some tea that tastes like they filtered water from a potted plant through a jockstrap stuffed with old gym-socks, a tea that has "live and active cultures... oh, and *love*." Then they want to give him all the academic foo-faw, all the *wisdom* of the ages that *Caput Mortuum* is Latin for "worthless remains" and that in the world of painting and also in alchemy the pigment is iron oxide on hematite, though did Mookie *also* know that *Caput Mortuum* sometimes refers to a *brown* pigment which was made from ground-up mummies and–

None of this matters, so Mookie gives them their gym-sock tea back and moves on.

By the time night falls, he's talked to a couple amateur spelunkers, a few Blue addicts, a Snakeface named Sirko (they always have *S*-names, those slithery sneaky pricks), and a homeless squid-faced half-and-half who calls himself "The Bishop of New York City." He hits the few mystical bazaars and visits a few bars. Asks a lot of questions.

Everybody says the same thing. Death's Head is a myth.

Eventually, evening settles on the city. Night closes like an iron door.

Mookie has a few more options. None of them he much likes.

He could go see Smiley. Chinatown Snakeface, sells information. Under Organization protection because, well, he pays for it. And he's good to have around. But that doesn't mean he's trustworthy. No Naga is. Some Snakefaces are assassins in that they'll kill your body, but Smiley, he's a *character assassin* – he'd sell your social security number and your mother's anal virginity for a half-a-secret.

So, for now: no Smiley.

Which means it's time to go under. Into the Great Below. The Deep Downstairs.

It's time to descend.

Mookie runs crews of Mole Men. Or, to be politically correct, Mole *People*, since a good half of them are women.

Now, in the city of New York, you have Mole People, and then you have *Mookie's* Mole People. The city has a whole contingent of homeless lunatics who live under the city – a lot of them live in a ramshackle shantytown under the Freedom Tunnel. They put up little plywood houses and burn barrels and live with the rats and the dogs. Some of them know about the Underworld – what goes on deeper beneath their rag-swaddled feet – but a lot of them don't. Mookie's Mole People know. It's their *job* to know.

The work of the Mole Men is straightforward: they live down in the dark, away from the light. They track gobbo movements. They keep their ears to the walls. And most importantly, they find and dig veins of Blue. In payment: they get a little money and a free supply of the Peacock Powder. (Which in turn helps them find more Blue.)

They're all addicts.

Some are insane.

Mookie doesn't like dealing with them, but it's his job. A soldier doesn't usually run a crew, but Werth sure as hell doesn't want this part of the life. He doesn't come down here. And it's not like he and Werth are a part of the usual hierarchy, anyway.

So, Werth delegates. To Mookie.

Once Below, Mookie canvasses the Moles. Many as he can find. He finds the Hell's Kitchen crew first: they're a good bunch. Solid. Stable. Dependable. Four-Top leads that crew: big black shambling dude, was once one a waiter at several of the hottest, trendiest restaurants in the city. Then he got hit by a cab. Knocked his brain funny. Funny enough where he can't wait tables but not so funny he can't run a gang of Moles.

Sometimes, Mookie brings him charcuterie – a little salami, a little lardo.

He finds Four-Top and his crew working on the Hell's Kitchen vein, chipping hunks of Cerulean out of black stone under the swimmy light of a couple camping lanterns. He sees Mookie, he comes up, gives a fist-bump–

"Hey, hey, whatchoo got, Mookie the Meat Man?"

Mookie knows what he wants. Mookie shrugs, shakes his head. "I don't got any meat for you, Four-Top. Next time. I promise."

Four-Top makes a pained face, holds his fists to his rag-swaddled chest and drops to his knees. "You're killing me, Mook! You're *killing* me."

Mookie tells him that he knows. Then tells him what he's looking for.

"Death's Head's just a dream," Four-Top says. "People get lost down here lookin' for that shit. It don't exist."

Behind him, the Moles continue working at the vein, pulling chunks out of the wall and dropping it into a rusty

Red Ryder wagon, *ka-gung*. A couple of them stare at Mookie from under ratty bangs or dark scarves. He knows two of them: Benny Scafidi's got a winky eye and a poochy belly like he's eight months pregnant. Next to him is the Mole who calls herself "Jenny Greenteeth". Curiously, her teeth aren't green but rather, the color and consistency of melted nubs of black licorice. They want to see if he's going to treat them with a little taste of the Blazes. Mookie just gives them a *get back to work* look and they quick pretend like they never saw him in the first place.

"Tell you what I did see," Four-Top says, eye twitching. He leans in, so the others don't hear: "I saw this thing, yo. It came with a pack of goblins, right? Looked like the cloak off the Grim Reaper, just a black blank space, like a... I dunno what. Shiny eyes and long fingers. Floated there. I hid and then, boom, they was gone."

"Hrm," Mookie says. Normally he wouldn't trust a story like that. But while Four-Top might be twitchy, he's trustworthy. And, surprisingly, not hooked on the Blue. Some guys control it. Some don't, or can't. Four-Top handles it. Mookie does, too – though even now he feels the need for Blue crawling through him like ants through a tunnel. He's just lucky enough he doesn't have to give into it. Some folks, they get a taste for it and need more and more and more. Some'll even kill for a tin.

Which is why it's important to have loyal crews like this one. Once in a while, the Moles try to steal what's in the walls. That's where guys like Four-Top come in. They tell Mookie and Mookie steps in. Might break some fingers. Pop off some kneecaps, use them as candy dishes. They get paid in Blue if they play nice. They get paid in pain if they take more than they're owed.

"Never seen one," Mookie says. "But I'll keep my eyes out."

"I could feel it, yo. Thing was like a... hole in space

with a pair of eyes. Like it wanted to suck me up, vacuum-style. I hid behind some busted-ass boulders. Thing that got me was, the gobbos followed behind like it was leading them somewhere."

"Gobbos don't like to be led."

"Damn straight."

It's strange. Still, could've been a trick of the eyes. Easy to lose your way down here, think you're seeing something you're not. Especially the deeper you go. You leave the Shallows and wander around the Tangle for a few days, every shadow jumps out at you, every glint of light on wet stone is a pair of eyes, every underground river has shapes swimming beneath the milky waters. Once Mookie was down here and he swore he saw his wife – er, ex-wife – Jess. That's how this place is: it makes you see crazy shit.

Mookie tells Four-Top to keep an ear to the ground for anything. Another "reaper-cloak" sighting, any hints of Death's Head, whatever.

Then, tired, Mookie ascends back up out of the Underworld. He's got boltholes and doorways everywhere, some everybody knows about, others only for him. This one takes him up through a shattered piece of old sewer where the bricks are the color of old blood. It dumps him out into the basement of an Irish bar – McGlinchey's – on the Lower East Side.

It's night. The city's lighting up with night time traffic. Streaks of brake lights. Bleary headlights. Honking. A whiff of perfume. Club kids shuttling past.

Mookie's tired. And hungry again.

Tomorrow, it continues. For tonight, home.

Mookie sits at the bar. Sipping a Yuengling, eating some blood sausage. The TV's on: some bullshit sports game. Mookie doesn't give a shit about any kind of sports and usually he'd change the channel, watch an old WWII movie on AMC or maybe pop on the Food Network and see what they're cooking up. But now he's zoning out.

The day bugs him like a hangnail. He can't quit tugging on it. The Boss with his cancer. The man, Candlefly and what was surely a Snakeface associate. Casimir's request. Four-Top spotting that black shadowy thing.

And over all of it, his daughter. Nora. Looking down like he's trapped in the belly of a big iron cauldron and she's the witch stirring the soup. Standing here just last night. She'd known the Boss was sick. Said something big was coming. Then she poisoned him.

For months he thought she'd quieted down. Gone dark. Maybe even gone home. Not that he'd bothered to check. Now she's back. Messing with him again. Messing with his life, his work. With the Organization.

On the bar top, his phone. He knows he should pick it up. Call his ex-wife, Jess. Tell her about Nora. They could talk. He could check in. Maybe she doesn't hate him anymore. Or maybe the hate has quieted, like a campfire gone to gray ash.

He pulls out an old picture from behind the bar. Pops out the thumbtack that kept it hanging there. The photo's faded. Fraying on the edges. A Polaroid. Little blurry. Twenty years ago, wasn't it? Coney Island. Bleary carnival lights in the background. Mookie smiling. (When was the last time he smiled?) Looking thinner, too. His arms had shape – biceps under white T-sleeves like a mountain range under a blanket of snow. Now they're just big hams. He's still strong but... well.

And Jess – goddamn, so beautiful. She always reminded him of autumn. Lips painted like the leaves fallen off a red maple. Hair the color of apple cider. Freckles like the flecks of cinnamon floating in the mug. He grunts. Reaches over, tacks the picture back.

Looks at the phone.

Call her.

He reaches over it, grabs the remote control to change the channel.

5

The Sandhogs. Local 147. The unsung architects of New York City's past, present, and future. The men of that union are the ones that go hundreds of feet below the city and they dig. They dug all the water tunnels. They dug all the subway tunnels. They sank the caissons for the Brooklyn Bridge. For a long time they owned the underground. That is, of course, until they opened a hole to hell in 1976. That happened at the start of the biggest Sandhog project yet: Water Tunnel #3, a tunnel 800 feet below the surface of Manhattan that would run 60 miles upstate to pull water from a new reservoir. They'd never gone deeper. They had no idea what waited for them there, but they would soon find out what horrors lurked beneath the schist.

– from the Journals of John Atticus Oakes,
Cartographer of the Great Below

He's got one option left before he heads off to see Smiley: the Sandhogs.

Come morning it's back into the city. He slings his satchel over a beefy shoulder. Throws some loose provisions in there: some jerky, couple bottles of water, bandages, some other odds and ends. Then it's off to the dig site.

See, in the middle of Lower Manhattan sits a big fucking hole.

It's as wide as the base of the Chrysler Building. Not nearly as deep – not this one, anyway. This one's maybe four stories down, with a series of branching tunnels leading off it. It's a hub. A hub to bring the diggers to various jobsites – the new water tunnel (#3), the new tunnel opening the 7 line of the subway, and other smaller projects.

All around the hole is a massive worksite. Forklifts rumbling. Shipping containers clanging. Wire bails and fuel tanks and thousands of bags of concrete.

He never worked this site, but he worked others just like it. Smells of churned dirt and blown stone, of grease and exhaust and oil. And sweat. Above it all, the vinegar stink of sweat. Sometimes it's hot down in the dark, sometimes it's cold, but with all the gear the Sandhogs have to wear – the galoshes, the slickers, the overalls, the hardhats, the masks – you can't help but sweat.

I don't belong here. That's the thought that keeps going through Mookie's head, tumbling over and over again like a rock bouncing down a mountain.

He used to belong here. Thirty years ago. When he was a young buck, just out of high school (more like just *failed* out of high school). Working his father's crew. His grampop up in the work trailer, pushing a broom, shoving a mop, missing his left leg at the knee and hobbling around on a leg the guys made for him, a heavy-ass limb made out of a wooden salad bowl, some leather straps from an old hospital gurney, and a length of rebar.

Grampop was tough as they came. Like the beef jerky in Mookie's bag. No fat, no gristle, just dehydrated muscle and hard leather.

Not to say his father wasn't tough, too. Pop was built like an oil drum. Lower teeth missing from when a rock popped up, dislodged by a hammering jack-leg, smacked Pop right in the mouth. Tongue swollen for weeks. It earned him a new nickname: Rocky.

Pop was a fire-plug of a man, but even he was afraid of Grampop.

Grampop would hear about something you did on a job and he'd thump you with a mop-handle and dress you down in front of all the guys – and he was a quick wit, his tongue a loose and lashing cable. Mookie remembered him calling Pop a "thick-necked buffalo with a brain like a shit-bucket". One time Mookie wasn't paying attention in the tunnels and put a ladder down on loose scree – the ladder came falling on top of him, cracked him in the head, gave him a concussion. Grampop said, "You're dumber than a truck full of broken toilets, slower than cold molasses, lazier than a car-struck cat, and uglier than the inside of a donkey's asshole." All the men brayed with laughter as Mookie stood there, his face a mask of dried blood from where the ladder had hit him, and that made Mookie mad – he suddenly took a swing at his father's father. The old man ducked the fist like a bum sidestepping a slow-moving train.

Then he fired a knee up into Mookie's balls.

He followed it up with, "You got a hard head, Mikey. Hard as diamond, but nowhere near as pretty." Then he shoved Mookie back into the lockers.

More laughs. Haw, haw, haw. Assholes.

And it's those laughs Mookie hears when he steps into the work office – really, a trailer, but a trailer that probably hasn't moved in ten years. Up on cinderblocks. The side of the trailer facing the hole is caked with dust, the rime of blasted rock.

Inside are the Sandhogs – some about to go on shift, some about to go off, others who are new to Local 147 and hoping to get some work for the day. Mookie walks on the dirt-smeared linoleum, past rows of lockers marked with masking-tape labels showing nicknames like "Weasel" and "Little Blue" and "Mudcrab".

He steps into the main area – guys sitting on benches, guys playing cards around a little side table – and eyes turn to him. They're all hard-asses. You can't be a Sandhog – one of the best-paid and most dangerous union jobs in the whole goddamn country – and not be a hard-ass, because candy-asses either get pounded to silt (and quit) or turn hard as stone (and stay on the job). So, these hard-asses know another hard-ass when they see one.

They don't recognize his face, though. And he doesn't recognize them, either. These are younger guys, mostly. He sees a couple veterans in the back: some old ratty strip of rope with his hard hat still on standing next to a doughy three-chinned dumpling of a man with a Santa's beard and a pair of industrial-grade eyeglasses too big for his already big head.

Mookie maybe recognizes Santa, though doesn't remember his name.

It's the two old vets who stand and wave him toward the back. As it should be. The young guys are faster, tougher, but they're not the alpha dogs in an operation like this. The old hats, they're the ones who know what's up; you piss them off, they'll leave you down there, floundering in the dark with your dick in your hand.

The shriveled length of rope whistles through busted teeth. "You need something, big fella?" The Santa Claus motherfucker just eyes him up.

Mookie nods. "Looking for Davey Morgan."

"Davey Morgan?" Skinny Rope lifts a furry eyebrow. "He's on site."

"Then I need to go on site."

"He's in the tunnels. Way down."

"Then I need to go way down."

"He's not available. Sorry, big fella. Now scram the fuck out of here."

Mookie feels agitated. And suddenly angry. Half-afraid that Grampop's ghost is going to come up out of nowhere and whack him on the back of the head with a loaded dustpan, tell him he's "more useless than pair of tits on a lawnmower".

It's then that Santa speaks up. "You're the Pearl boy."

A turn of the worm inside Mookie's heart.

Mookie gives him a look like, *Yeah, so?*

"I remember you. Hard not to. Geez. You're built like a stack of boulders. I knew your dad a bit. Good Hog. Knew his way around a concrete mix."

Skinny Rope lifts the other eyebrow. "Pearl. You mean Brosie Pearl?"

"Nah," Santa says, waving a hand that Mookie can see has the crinkly flesh of a burn scar all up the back of it. "Ambrose was the old man. I'm talking about Henry. The son. Rocky, we called him. And that makes you…" He snaps his crusty fingers. "Little Mikey."

"Mookie. I go by Mookie these days."

"Right. Right. You worked with Davey Morgan down there."

"Uh-huh."

Santa leans in. "I remember it right, you bailed on us. Left the union."

"I had other things to do."

"I bet you did. I bet you did." The way Santa is sizing him up, he knows. "You were with Davey, that means you were with the 147½. That right?"

"That's right." The 147-and-a-half: the union inside the union, a cabal of Sandhogs who know what's down there and who serve as the first line of defense between the city above and Hell below. They don't usually run afoul of the Organization, but it happens – the Organization wants the resources the Deep Downstairs has to offer, but the Sandhogs think all of it should stay corked up and kept from the light. "What of it?"

Mookie doesn't bother answering.

"So then you know Davey's busy. And you know that there's no way I'm letting a quitter like you down in the dark on our territory. Davey's not your business. OK? His business is not your business. So, go home, Little Mikey. Go back to your *other* friends."

He knows. He knows who Mookie works for. Santa Claus knows that he's been naughty, not nice. Skinny Rope doesn't know elf-piss from egg-nog: he's following the conversation the way one does when the other speakers are talking a different language. But not Santa. Santa sees all.

Mookie growls. He's not fond of being told "no".

"Ease off the stick, Cochise," Santa says. "You're a big ape used to throwing your weight around, and I don't doubt you could punch my fat old head into next week. But you got a whole trailer of mean sonofabitches behind you, and worse, this site is watched by Homeland Security. We got big projects going on. Important projects. Not to mention an unholy hell's load of dynamite down there. You go knocking guys around here and they'll throw your ass in an unlabeled hole for the rest of your years. That what you want?"

Homeland Security? Jesus. Things have really changed since 9/11.

Mookie just shakes his head.

"Then let's just cut this short and say goodbye. Goodbye, Mikey Pearl."

"Mookie."

"Whatever, kid. Get outta here."

Kid. The old lump of bearded fat called him "kid". Mookie's a couple years shy of his fiftieth birthday, and even still, some senior citizen Sandhog calling him "kid" gets under his skin, lays eggs there, eggs that hatch and whose larvae burrow deep.

The ghost of Grampop is somewhere here, laughing at him.

He can still get down there. Into the tunnel. Mookie's always got a bolthole and long ago he made sure to carve himself a couple doors into the length of the tunnel – doors that'll one day need to be sealed up before the gates open and the water comes rushing in, but that's three years off, easy.

It's just a long fucking walk. He was hoping to circumvent the trip. He's tired.

But, what else is he gonna do?

Once more, descent awaits.

It's eight or nine hours of crawling around through too-tight tunnels and ducking his stubbly dome underneath jagged rock that Mookie finally comes to one of his bolthole doors. It's hidden. It has to be – elsewise any goblin or cult freak or amateur explorer could find it. This one behind a crumpled old refrigerator (the Shallows of the Underworld end up as home to lots of junk and trash, the debris of a humanity that doesn't care where its waste goes long as it's out of sight). Mookie has to hunker down, shimmy the fridge out, then squeeze through.

Then, twenty feet down, a big rectangle of schist. Which he cut through using a gas-powered cut-off saw about four years ago.

Mookie steps into the tunnel. He turns off his flashlight – the space is well-lit and his eyes take a moment to adjust.

The tunnel's big enough to drive a tractor trailer through. It's cool in here. Up above, strings of sodium lights hang. Everything in a yellow glow, like morning light through a windshield smeared with tree pollen.

Here, the distant sound of the city. The *gung-gung-gung* of subway trains. The rumble-and-hiss of steam somewhere behind and above the rock. The white noise of a million machines and devices: cars, trucks, boats, cranes, drills, all forming a meaningless mumbling hum. Mookie finds it all oddly comforting.

This isn't the Water Tunnel proper. That's further down – he's got boltholes that'll take him right into the tunnel, but getting there would take him another half-a-day's walk and right now there's just no need.

It isn't long before he gets to another hole, this one ringed by lights. Bundles of cables and pipes disappear down over the craggy lip and into the pit. The pit sits ringed by a metal handrail. Mookie steps up. Looks down.

Down, down, way the fuck down.

The skyscrapers in the city above do as their name suggests: they are physical objects that scrape the sky.

This is the opposite. This is negative space, a carved out channel of rock and stone that's over four hundred million years old – it doesn't scrape the sky, but like a needle plunged too deep, it perforates the membrane between this world and the next. Or, it did, when they first dug it out. Now it's walled off, fortified in ways not easily seen or understood.

But Mookie remembers this shaft.

This isn't how a lot of the Sandhogs get to the Tunnel #3 dig now – no, there's a much bigger hole down in Battery Park, a straight shot eight hundred feet into the earth where they can drop trucks and where just a few years ago they lowered a mammoth tunnel boring machine, "The Mole". That beast, a 450-ton driller, meant to do a lot of the dirty work of making the tunnels, work that once necessitated tons of dynamite and guys who knew how to make the right blasting plans so as not to bring half the city down on their heads. Dangerous work – one of the Sandhog mottos is "a man a mile". Because for every mile of tunnel they dig, another man dies.

This way's easier for Mook.

The way down the shaft: a blue cage. Meant to hold five men, but Sandhogs cram ten or twelve guys in there, easy. Still. Mookie steps in and it's cramped. A feeling of claustrophobia tightens around him like a fist: part of it's the cage, but part of it's the fact that a whole city is above his head. Like he's Atlas holding up the Earth on those big-ass shoulders. Once upon a time that feeling comforted him the same way that feeling a belly full of good food comforted him. But time hasn't been kind to his nerves.

Mookie punches the button. The motor grinds. The cable thrums.

The cage drops.

A pair of wavy yellow cables snake along the wall. A big fan blows air. A pipe for concrete is bracketed against the wall – it's a "slick line", used to pump the wet mix over a thousand feet from the worksite above. Glimpses of civilization. Of human work and effort. The Sandhogs have claimed this part of the Underworld for mankind. The trappings of man are all here: a pickaxe in the stone with a hardhat on the handle's end, a discarded and dented lunchbox, a crumpled-pack of cigarettes, a lone boot crusted and made heavy with dry cement.

So much cleaner than many of the low places he finds himself in. Rooms laden with glowing polyps. Black stalactites like swords dripping blood. Hell, a month ago he found an old subway train car down at in the Tangle when he was looking for a couple wayward Mole Men. The train sat on a soft sand island out in the middle of a steaming subterranean lake – it was the moans that drew him to it, the *very human* moans. Inside: bodies. Vagrants, by the look of them. Mostly dead but kept alive by the gobbo eggs in their mouths, under their armpits, between their legs. The moist places of the human form.

Mookie burned the whole car. Not much else to do. The eggs, bulbous and red, were ready to hatch. The guys were dead anyway, they just didn't know it yet.

He wonders what normal people would think of the way the eggs popped and squealed, like bacon fat in an iron skillet. What face they'd make when they saw the bodies thrashing around, the little gobbo hatchlings born premature, splashing up against the sooty train windows before finally expiring in a red squeak down the hot glass.

People just don't know.

Finally, Mookie gets to the start of the tunnel proper. A massive concrete tube. Lit up like it's practically daylight down here. Floodlights eliminate darkness. Big fans blow cool, musty air. In the middle of the tunnel runs a set of tracks – the Sandhogs don't use old-school mine carts anymore. They use powered ones. "Pigs." That's what they call them. As in, "Hop on, the pig's about to leave."

There's a small three-man pig nearby, sitting away on an ancillary track. Mookie feels relieved. The powered mine carts don't move fast, but they move a lot faster than walking. And it'll save him a ten-mile walk to wherever Davey and his crew are working.

He hops in. Starts it up with a growl.

Doesn't take long to ease it on the track–

Soon Mookie's chugging along. Bright lights passing overhead.

Chug chug chug.

This tunnel, Mookie thinks, is the Sandhogs' legacy.

They've been working on this for years. Hell, this tunnel's where Mookie got his start, and really, that's what he's thinking about: how *this* could've been his legacy instead of what it is now. Ex-wife. Daughter who hates him. Breaking the heads of goblins and the knees of addicts.

He never gave much of a shit about the tunnel. To him it was just work. To the city of New York, it was them building a parachute while falling down to earth. Both of the original water tunnels are on their way out and the water in the city is undrinkable. Repair either of the original tunnels, you turn the water off for weeks, maybe months – and if the valves break, then longer. The city loses water, the city loses everything. But for Mookie, it was always just work. Because that's what he does. And that's who he is.

Though now it occurs to Mookie: that's why Homeland Security is invested. They don't want terrorists messing with the city's water supply.

Up ahead, he hears it:

The sound of *work*.

Hammering. Drilling. The murmur of men yelling.

But that's when he hears something else, too:

The scrape of claws on concrete. The whisper of flesh on stone.

Goddamnit, Mookie thinks. I'm being hunted.

6

The monsters of the Abyss. Offspring of the Void. The children of the Hungry Ones, of the Deep Shadows, of Those Who Eat. Birthed from the Maw-Womb, given life down in the dark – wriggling, screaming, baying for blood and singing lamentations to the lack of light. The gobbos, or goblins, those most common denizens of the Great Below – half-mindless, willing to eat their own young grubs, a tribe or hive of peons and pawns, Hell's own foot-soldiers. The Trogbodies or troglodytes, blind golems of stone and clay and silt. The Snakefaces – or Nagas and Naginis – those hidden seducers, those worms in the rock. They, the named races, the sentient entities. Some are lesser beings with minimal minds: the roach-rats, the milk spiders, the gelled waste, the rimstone cankerpedes. Others are smart but have no names: I have seen a dripstone that unmoored from the rock and spoke riddles before scurrying away. I have seen a flying thing, with gray vented wings and eyes on telescoping stalks. And I have seen a tenebrous shape stalking the depths, darker than the dark, like a black sheet on a clothesline rippling in a hard wind.

– from the Journals of John Atticus Oakes,
Cartographer of the Great Below

Something is following him. Some*things* by the sound of it.

He prays it's nothing dangerous. Which is a lie in its own way – nothing down here could be categorized as "safe". Even a starving brood of roach-rats (and they are *always* starving) offers up a thousand mean teeth and a hundred long claws and the light-only-knows how many strange diseases and parasites. But those he can handle.

The thought nags at him: what if it's something else?

As the pig grumbles forward, Mookie fumbles with the tin in his pocket, a tin sized well for normal hands, but in his hand it looks the size of a button popped off a shirt. With a thumb he lifts the rust-rimmed top (it's an old lip balm tin, same tin he's been using for coming up on ten years now) and reveals the peacock-blue powder inside. Just the sight of it makes his temples tingle, his knees go weak, his brow flush with sweat.

He looks down at his cakey blue thumb, a "Smurf thumb" in Blazehead parlance, a classic tell for those looking for Cerulean addicts – and then he thinks, here it is, here's where I rip open my third eye and see what's following me.

Mookie pops a callused thumb into the powder–

He presses one thumb to one temple–

Then the other–

The Blue Blazes washes over him.

It's like being in a ship that's just starting to capsize. Listing on an unforgiving ocean. Then: a wind of wet heat on his forehead – a hot breath – and at the edges of his vision the ripple of blue flame like a puddle of vodka lit with a Zippo, a ripple that fades fast, taking with it the scales that cover the eyes, that protect the mind, that hide the happy dumb people from the truth of what lies beneath.

It's then that he sees.

Not roach-rats. Or cankerpedes.

It's gobbos. Gray snot-slick heads. Yellow fangs. Some loping like dogs, others hurrying along on bent and rubbery legs. A dozen of them. Many with weapons.

Fifty feet in and closing. Forty. *Thirty*.

A few of the gobbos are naked – bulbous genitals like tumors slapping against hairless thighs – while others are robed in tattered rags, rags once the clothing of humans but stolen and torn to ribbons and knotted together in motley patchwork clothing.

Twenty feet.

The pig won't go faster. Mookie's going to have to fight. Last thing he wants to do is bring some mob of the Underworld's finest to the Sandhogs' door. They'll never help him if he does something like that.

Ten feet.

It's then he sees something else–

Behind the Gobbos, something else. Shiny eyes. Long, flashing fingers. A black shape, blacker than night, black like a hole in the Devil's heart.

Like a Grim Reaper's cloak.

Through the walls, the *lub-dub oonch-oonch* of pounding bass.

Nora steps on the gobbo's arm. Bones crackle like bubble wrap popping. Anybody poking their head past the door of this strip club back room would see Nora standing on a skinny, greasy man – a divot-cheeked, sallow-faced weasel with thinning black hair matted to his bulbous scalp – with a .38 snubnose pointed at his face.

But she's Blazing. One of her last doses.

And it shows her that this is a goblin. Little fucker's been hiding out here at Double Delilah's, hired as the janitor – which translates to "jizz-mopper" – of this back alley strip joint. While on the side, he's been slinging bits of Blue to top-shelf customers and well-paid dancers. And, worse, once in a while he kidnaps one of the girls and takes her down into the dark where…

Nora doesn't want to think about that.

The gobbo bleats and babbles at her in a guttural tongue.

"Oh, no, no, nuh-uh," she says, pressing down harder on its arm and cocking the hammer of the gun. "Don't play with me, gob. You're up here wearing your ugly-ass mask which means you speak English well enough to get by. So speak English."

"You eat dick!" the gob cries out. "You eat it hard."

She presses down again. The goblin keens through his wet mouth, eyes shut.

"Why?" the gob asks. "Why do this?"

"First, because you got Blue, and ta-da, I need it. Second, because you're going to send a message to all your gross little fuck-buddies downstairs." This, a different message than the one she paid Skint to pass along. "I want you to tell them I'm going to wipe them out. Every last one of you nasty mutants."

"You?" The gob laughs. "You just a *girl*."

She puts all her weight on it. The arm-bone beneath gray rubbery flesh cracks. The gobbo howls. "And oh, what a bad girl I am. Daughter of Mookie Pearl, if that name means anything to you." She sees by the widening bulge of his bulbous eyes that he does. "Now cough up the Blue, freak."

The gobbos hit him hard, a truck slamming into a guardrail–

The first two are fucked from the get-go. Mookie's chokes one snot-slick monster with the shoulder strap of his satchel. The other gets stuffed up under his armpit. Then the rest are on him, clambering up his shoulders, wrapping themselves around his legs. Yellow teeth tear at his shirt, his jeans. He sees a flash of green above. Sees one atop the others, holding a weapon made of an old wrench – the end spackled with a Q-tip wad of black gunk, which is in turn riddled with shards of green glass from a beer bottle–

The thing brings the green-glass mace down, but Mookie uses the naked gobbo in his grip as a shield. He holds the thrashing creature up just as the mace crashes down on its head, sticking in the thing's skull and spraying up a mist of oily goblin blood.

They shriek in his ears. Whooping and cackling.

Fucking gobbos.

They must have formed a hunting pack a while back. Been waiting in the dark. Invisible – down here, that's an option for them. Can't play that trick up above. Up top they've got to look like somebody, so to the Blind they look like miscreants, vagrants, thugs. Some go the effort to get gussied up in other outfits and play different roles – maître d', cop, pimp. But most just stay at the fringes, acting like one of the many freaks New York City has to offer. Such simple camouflage.

The question here is: how the hell did they breach this tunnel? The easy answer: *They found one of my boltholes.* Probably not the one he just used, but he's got dozens of the hidden doorways around here. Hell, so does Davey. Maybe one of those doorways isn't so hidden anymore.

No time to worry about that now.

Mookie tosses the ruined creature in his hand – it splats limp against the curve of the concrete pipe-wall. The one under his arm is starting to bite at his side; he feels teeth sink into the meat encasing his ribs, and he snarls, pressing down with his bicep and squeezing arm to body hard enough that he hears the thing's spine *snap* like a piece of celery.

Pop. Drop. *Splurch.*

A pair of gobbos tries to dart past him. But Mookie pivots – a slow turn, as his body is weighed down by shrieking gobbos clinging to him like wolves trying to bring down a charging moose – and reaches out, grabs one by the heel. He drops, using the momentum of his fall to fling the one into the other. They bowl into one another, a tangle of limbs, a clatter of bludgeoning weapons.

Now Mookie is on his back. A gobbo grabs his ear. Tries to rip it off. Another takes a shiv made out of a sharpened toothbrush, starts stitching it in and out of his forearm – *punch punch punch*, blood welling up red and hot. Hands in his mouth. A lashing tubule tongue trying to force its way past his lips. One is pulling at his boot.

But the Blazes run through him full-bore now: a bullet spinning down a rifled barrel, a sweep of fire across a gas-soaked floor. And with the Blazes comes more than just sight. It brings with it high-test clarity and a double-dose of extra strength.

Even off the stuff Mookie's no weak-kneed Girl Scout – he's all grizzly, no Care Bear. But on the Blue Blazes, he's like if an M1 Abrams tank made mad monkey-love with an eight hundred pound silverback gorilla and had a baby, all black fur and olive iron, all guns and treads and swinging fists.

He grabs the stabber gobbo, cranks its shiv-arm upward, smashes its head down on its own weapon – the end of the toothbrush popping up through a rotten eggshell head. The ear-grabber gibbers and wails, and Mookie slams his head sideways into the monster, bowling the goblin backward. Oily gob fingers are still in his mouth; he bites down. The blood is bitter, cloying, tastes like infection – it's not the first time he's tasted their blood. Won't be the last. And as the gobbo opens its mouth to scream in pain, Mookie spits the fingers into the former owner's wailing mouth. *Ptoo.*

He kicks out with a hard boot. Bones crack, yellow teeth clatter.

He grabs the tongue – a female's tongue, probably hoping to plant eggs somewhere moist and warm, because once those eggs attach they release toxins into your bloodstream that'll make you slow and stupid – and winds it around the gobbo's neck like a weedwacker string. Then he pulls taught.

Gray face goes blue. Cheeks bulging. Black capillaries bursting in ugly goldfish eyes.

Then, for a moment–

All goes dark.

A rippling shape, black as tar, flutters over his head–

Blocking out the light. Whispering as it passes.

What the hell–?

Mookie roars. Stands up, unsure what he just saw. Whatever the hell it is, it's moving further down the tunnel, toward the distant Sandhogs – and fast. But as he stands, he sees: the two goblins he tossed into the wall aren't dead or even knocked out. They're up and at 'em, coming right for him. One's barehanded, swiping at the air with dirty claws.

But the other's got a weapon.

A gobbo pop-gun. Not a gun at all, but a short length of iron pipe with a pull tab at the back of it like one of those party-poppers where you yank the string and loose confetti into the air–

This doesn't release confetti. It barks a big bang and makes a hard flash – and Mookie suddenly catches a scattershot spray of shrapnel in his side. No idea what it is, but probably nails, glass, stones, gobbo teeth, shattered crystal. And when it starts to burn, sending screaming tentacles of pain up through the wounds in his side, Mookie knows that the stuff was first dipped in goblin poison – rock-snot, or dung-thistle, maybe.

Ahead, the tunnel is swallowed by a haze of smoke–

Mookie staggers left, tries to barrel ahead, but the pain is an immense thing, a thing with shape and presence all its own, pushing on his side and slowing him down–

The gobbos leap for him.

And somewhere ahead, he hears his old friend Davey Morgan scream.

Davey Morgan's got explosives on his mind.

Dynamite, in particular.

Dynamite's how the tunnel grows. Sure, for a lot of it they can use that big bitch machine, but for sensitive areas of the rock, it's dynamite all the way.

You drill holes. Drop dynamite into the cavities. Head back upstairs, hit the button and – the ground shakes, the earth booms, and the tunnel's dug another thirty, forty feet. Then the men clear the rubble, put up more wire cage to keep rocks from dropping on their heads, and the process begins anew.

That's the job. That's *been* the job for twenty years.

Davey's good. They say he's the best, but he doesn't care for that kind of talk. He knows he's good, and that's enough.

But things are changing soon.

In less than a week's time he and his men – loyal men, good men, *capable* men – will be underneath the juncture between all three water tunnels. Dynamite's not a scalpel. It's not even a fire axe. It's precise like a hand grenade. You don't control an explosion so much as politely suggest what you want it to do and then pray. Maybe God gives you what you need. Or maybe God decides to blow your ass sky-high to Saint Pete's doorstep. You accept the judgment of the blast and move on.

A man a mile.

But soon, they'll be detonating rock with two other water tunnels fifty feet and a hundred feet above their heads, respectively.

Which means this has to be done right. They're going to be using dynamite to thread a needle. Davey can no longer be good. He *has* to be great.

Has to get this right or they're all, as he is wont to say, "fuckered".

And it doesn't help that they work down here. On the edge of oblivion. With any number of horrible things coming up out of the dark, smelling the sweat, hankering for blood. They're the union-within-a-union. The 147½. The last line between the light and the dark. Only makes the job, oh, a thousand times harder.

Someone taps him on his helmet. It's Boise – young kid from Jersey who when he was first asked where he was from said *Boise* instead of *Joisey* because he's a nervous kid who stammers when he talks, but he's also a hard worker and that's all that matters to Davey. Boise says, "I hear a pig comin' down the tunnel, Davey."

Davey tilts his head. Gets away from the boys chipping and hauling blown rock.

Sure enough, he hears it–

The *chug chug chug* of a powered mine cart.

Now who the hell would that be? All his boys are here.

Some fucko from the EPA? Or Home-Sec? Bah.

He gives the tunnel a good look. Feels the Blue crackling at the edges of his vision – he's looking for anything that belongs to this place, that shines of the Great Below. At least half his crew are Blazing at any given time. They take shifts. Half on, half off to cool down, ease off the powder. Some of them end up addicts. When they go that way, Davey puts them through his own personal treatment program. Which isn't a fun program to go through, but he can't have shaky hands playing with dynamite.

He doesn't see squat down the tunnel.

Davey turns back to the crew. Whoops and twirls his hand like he's got a fake lasso to get their attention. Men in hardhats with grime-streaked cheeks and goggles stand against the backdrop of a forbidding stone wall that will need to be blasted – others off to the side pouring concrete that will eventually get made into the walls of the tunnel proper.

Davey yells to them in his muddy one-generation-removed Irish accent:

"Any of you boys know who might be comin' down the tunnel? Dutch–" He points to an old stoop-backed Hog with a scar across the bridge of his bent nose. Dutch is the radio-man. "Any news from above?"

Dutch starts to shake his head, but then his eyes go wide.

The other men start to yell and point–

One reaches alongside a mine cart and Davey sees a shotgun coming up–

Another grabs for a pick-ax.

Davey turns. Almost falls.

Sees something he's never seen before and it's coming at him fast–

It appears out of nothing – like a car riding through a heat haze on a long desert highway that seems to drive out of the vapor. All black. A shifting shape – like a kite, a bird, a flying *puddle of dark oil*. Big, too, big as a tarp.

He catches sight of shiny eyes, eyes like polished buttons.

And fingers, too. And teeth. Both like knives. Long knives. Hunting knives.

It casts fear in Davey's heart. Turns to run, to find a weapon – but these boots aren't meant for running. The toe of one boot catches the bulging heel of the other and Davey Morgan pitches forward.

The ripple of fabric is right on him. So is the clatter of knife-teeth and blade-claws. He hits the ground. Shoulder taking the brunt. Pain. Like a baseball through a window: *ksshhh*. The monster is upon him. Covering him. All light is extinguished. A horrible thought crosses Davey's mind: I'm too old for this now. I'm too old and too slow and I've let fear creep in like black mold and now it's all over.

He hears a shotgun boom. Men yelling, though they sound so distant…

He can't breathe. The creature sounds like fabric but feels like liquid. Davey tries to swing a fist, but it's like thrashing around underwater – a slow-motion freakout.

He sees those eyes. Just the eyes. Gleaming buttons. Coins in black water.

Then knives plunge out of the liquid and into his chest.

Then into his head.

But the pain is strange – hardly a pain at all, not in the physical sense. It's like a spear punching a hole through his thoughts, through his mind. What he feels instead is something far deeper and ultimately worse than physical pain:

Grief and guilt holding hands, la la la. In his mind, memories burst bright like fireworks: *pop pop pop*. His first day as a shaper on the bench at the Sandhog office, feeling the pinprick stick of shame as he secretly hopes some poor Hog breaks his foot so that Davey has a shot down below; him losing his virginity with a Bronx whore on a dirty afghan on a mattress that smells like beer and cigarettes; the day his daughter Cassie was born and he was down here working; the day his wife died from an aneurysm and once more he was down here in the dark while she flopped around on the kitchen floor like a fish trying to find water. Image after image, memory after memory, too-bright and too-loud fireworks launching into the sky of his mind before fading anew. All of it feels bad, sour, like a kind of *mind poison* – every memory robed in rotten ribbon, a mummy's gauze, dusty and cursed.

Then one image stays fixed in his mind: blueprints and blasting plans for Water Tunnel #3, a yellow notebook with scribbles sitting under his left hand, a cold Coors Light in his right, the can sweating–

Cassie walks into the room. He says, "Hey, lollipop–"

He hears a sound. A familiar voice. A familiar *roar*.

And then it's all over.

The goblins hang on him like boat anchors. He doesn't have time to care. Mookie runs. The Blue gives him speed. Puts power in his legs. The Pig churns ahead of him around the bend of the tunnel. Gobbos bite. Claw. He feels blood wet his shirt.

He leaps for the Pig. Grabs hold. Barely. Legs dragging behind him. Gobbo hanging off the legs.

The pig rounds the curve. There. Ahead Davey. Lying underneath the black thing, the reaper's cloak, men leaping on top of the monster – the monster flinging them off like they're straw-stuffed poppets.

They're not Mookie.

The pig lurches forward–

Mookie clambers up over it, toward the front of the cart–

It crashes into the deadstop. Mookie uses the momentum to leap.

He tackles the shadow-thing. Goblins screeching behind him. One gob catches a shotgun blast to the dome – buckshot peels back its scalp like the skin of an orange. A Sandhog's six-shooter punches a hole in the other.

Mookie wrestles with the reaper-cloak. He pulls it off Davey Morgan – but it has weight and energy like Mookie can't believe and before he knows it the thing has him pinned. Bullets cut through the shadow and disappear inside it – the shadow-thing continues its assault unfazed. Knife fingers stick through Mookie's breastbone like the flesh isn't even there – he feels them cutting apart not his heart but rather, his soul –

Nora. Jess. Grampop. Pop. Worthless. Dumb. Bad Dad.

Ugly thoughts like tentacles reach up, coil around him, threaten to drag him down.

No. No time for this.

He roars. Lifts his head. Opens his mouth.

And bites for one of the only exposed features he can find.

He bites off one of its shiny eyes. Spits it out.

Light shines through the hole – a bloom of illumination like a sunbeam through morning mist. And then the thing keens, a high-pitched tone before diving off Mookie and through the floor. Like a wraith without substance, its flesh unreal.

And then it's over.

7

A union within a union. A guild within a guild. Local 147-and-a-half. The men of the Sandhogs know about it, though they've little idea what it actually is. They think it's some manner of "inner circle" composed of veterans of the Sandhog life who help shape policy and who know all the tricks. They know tricks, yes. They know a great deal. They're the ones who know what's really down there. The night the Sandhog demolition crew blew a hole in prehistoric rock and opened up a cave into a forgotten gobbo temple, the men there on that crew were the first. The ones that lived formed the pact. They wrote the charter. In union speak, everyone there bought the buck. Any Sandhog who sees something he's not supposed to see, they rope him in. Though some find themselves invited, too. Tested by the others. Strong, smart, tough, and a little deranged: these are the traits that those men need. These are the traits necessary to stand between the safety and sanctity of the world above and the named and unnamed monsters of the Great Below.

> – from the Journals of John Atticus Oakes,
> Cartographer of the Great Below

The reaper-cloak gone, the gobbos dead, gun barrels swing toward Mookie.

Davey stands. Shaking. Flinty eyes casting about, trying to find a slippery grip on the world. The man – older now than Mookie is – looks rattled. He brushes it off, finally levels his stare at Mookie. "Mookie Pearl, as I live and breathe."

"Davey Morgan."

"Been a long fucking while, Pearl." *Loooong fookin' wall*.

"It has."

Morgan shows his palms, lowers them – and as he does, the rest of the Sandhogs, a dozen or so men, lower their guns, axes, hammers.

"You bring these monsters to my doorstep?"

"Maybe. I dunno."

Davey steps up to Mookie. His bushy caterpillar eyebrows arch. He clucks his tongue, then seems to make some internal decision.

Mookie knows it's coming long before it hits – the old man telegraphs the punch so far in advance he might as well have sent message by way of an old limping donkey. Just the same, Mookie takes the hit. It's owed to him.

But just to be sure, he growls:

"You get that one. But you won't get a second."

Davey cocks his fist back again.

The hand trembles.

Mookie gently shakes his head. *Don't*.

Davey's fist uncurls and he waves Mookie off. "Ain't worth breaking my hand on your ugly underbitten jaw, Pearl." He takes a bit of snuff from a Skor can, stuffs it between gum and lip. The other Sandhogs start to back away – they can sense the body language of their crew chief. They slowly move back to work, always keeping one eye on Mookie – a stranger in this place. "Fuck are you doin' down here anyway?"

"On a job."

"Listen to you. *Job*. This is a job, Pearl. The Sandhogs know the work." Davey spits and the tobacco juice splashes against the gray back of a dead gobbo. "So, spill it. Whaddya looking for this time?"

"Looking for Death's Head."

Davey ill-stifles a bark of a laugh. "Right. You're smarter than that. Or I thought you were – maybe I've been overestimating you all this time."

"I know it's a dead-end, but they told me to look so I'm looking."

Suddenly, Davey switches tracks. "How's the wife, the kid?"

Mookie knows what he's doing. Davey's sizing him up. Why, Mookie's not sure. Maybe he really knows something.

"Been apart from the wife. Years now."

"I think I remember hearing that. Your kid?"

"She's fine."

Davey smiles. "You're lying. You got a bad tell, Pearl." He taps his jaw. "You get tight right here. Muscles bunch up. Like the lie doesn't want to come out and you have to *force* out of your mouth."

"Fine. My daughter hates my guts."

Another laugh from Davey. "Mine hates me, too. Cassie."

"I remember her." Their girls went to junior high together.

"Cassie's a good kid. Wants to be a Hog."

"They let women in now?"

"They do, at that. Oh, I scoffed at first too but some of these broads swing a hammer or hang wire-net better than a lot of the fat bastards that work on other crews. That fella over there–" Davey points to a Hog's broad back in a reflective vest and slicker. "That's no fella. That's Honolulu. Samoan girl. Tireless worker. Doesn't sleep." Davey shrugs. "Just the same, Cassie can't be a Sandhog. I won't let her. It's too crazy down here."

As if for proof, he nudges a goblin corpse with a boot.

"You know what that thing was?" Mookie asked.

"The shadowy fucker? No. Never seen one. Came right for me, though."

"It did." Mookie sniffs. "Why'd it do that, you figure?"

"Fuck if I know." Davey shifts from foot to foot, shoves his tongue in his cheek pocket. "What are you saying, Pearlie-boy?"

"I'm saying it went right over my head. Like it was coming for you."

"You're the one that brought this thing to my boys. Don't go pointing fingers at me, 'less you want another jab to the chops–"

"What'd it come for, Davey?"

Davey's hands curl into fists. "Fuck off, you asking me questions like that. Like I answer to you."

"If they came once they'll come again."

"Let 'em come. I'll be more ready next time."

One of the Hogs behind Davey comes up. Mookie knows him from way back. Dutch, the radio guy. Not as old as Davey, but older than he was. Someone who's been around. He sets a long-fingered hand on Davey's shoulder and peers over a nose broken long ago by an errant pick-ax. Mookie hears the man mutter: "Just give it to him. Not doing us any good, is it?"

"Give me what?"

"I'm not giving it to this big bastard–" Davey, suddenly cagey, narrows his eyes and looks Mookie up and down. "Fine. You know what? Fuck it. *Fook it.*

Davey fishes in his overalls underneath his slicker, withdraws something that looks like a little jeweled tea ball. Fake jewels. Just a trinket. Hangs on a small chain. He tosses it to Mookie. "I found a vein of it way down. About two years back one of my guys, Goosey, got taken down past the Shallows, into the Tangle. I went after him, found this in the wall of a dead-end passage, next to a thread of rose quartz. I didn't think it was anything but…"

Mookie flips the cheap little latch.

Inside, powder the color of blood. Bright and fresh. Like something spilled out of a throat-slit calf and dried to a flaky dust.

Holy crow. "This is Vermilion?"

"Uh-huh. I can't vouch for the other colors, but now we know that Red and Blue are the real deal. Oakes maybe got something right."

If Red is real...

Then maybe Death's Head is, too.

"How do you know? You try it?"

"Once," Davey says. "And never again."

"Bad?"

"Never been out of control like that before. Way beyond what the Blue does for you. They call it the Red Rage for a reason." Davey shudders. "Felt like it... took something from me, too. Can't say what. Years of my life, maybe. So, fine. Take it. You can carry that burden. I don't want it anymore."

Mookie looks down at the little ball of red powder before snapping it closed again. No idea what he'll ever do with this or what good it will be. Barter, maybe. Not that he wants some Mole Man jacked up on the Red Rage, but if it gets him closer to the Death's Head, so be it.

Davey says suddenly, "You could come back, you know. To the guild. To the 147½. Once a Hog, always a Hog. Turn yourself around. Get away from that crowd you work with. Do some good down here. I got a place on my crew. Young fella, West Indian, name of Jamie that we called Cheeto, he caught a mean burn on his legs from the lye in the concrete and he's out for a good long while – and you know, a man a mile and all."

Mookie shuts him down. "No. I'm good where I'm at."

"Course you are." Davey scowls. "Whatever. Fine. Go on out of here, then. We've got work to do."

"Can I take the pig?"

"You could use the walk."

Mookie growls. "Later, Morgan."

"Fuck you, *Mikey*."

••••

Nora's on her way to meet a Trogbody called Kortz – she doesn't know him, but what she does know is that soon the shit is really going to hit the fan and that means she's going to need someone to protect her. The Trogs are good at that. Loyal to a fault. Thick body, thick skull. Dumb as the rocks they're made of, most times.

Reminds her of her father.

But then, as she's crossing the street to hit the subway, the text comes in.

Nobody's gonna b home come ovr <3

She smiles. Texts back: **No guards?**

The reply: **No guards all clear**

She texts back:

OMW

And then she is truly on her way.

It's almost midnight when Mookie emerges, born out of the dark. Night in New York is never dark, not really; the sun may set, but the lights are always on. Traffic lights, streetlights, headlights, lights from many windows and many doors. All of it painting the sky in a rusty glow, an orange-brown smear that sometimes stands punctuated with pockets of other color – a blue wash from the tip of a skyscraper, a purple spotlight from some new club opening up. Muddy watercolors.

Even if all those lights went out, it'd still be brighter than the spaces beneath.

And so when Mookie once again rises into the world, he's once more forced to narrow his eyes. Soon his brow hurts from squinting.

Sometimes he thinks: maybe I belong down there.

He knows he's gotta call Casimir. Tell the kid something.

Should've never taken this job, Mookie thinks. Should've never told that kid I'd have a look. Because even if the Red is real, the Purple probably ain't. And if it *is*, Mookie's no closer to finding it – which means the old man is going to die and this coltish kid is going to end up as Boss. Worse, he's going to blame Mookie for failing him.

Damned in all directions.

All that sits in his gut like a ten-pound barbell. The Red, the Blue, the search for Death's Hand, the changing of the guard. It's all too much for Mookie. He looks at his phone – again that thought: you better call Casimir, get it over with – and then swiftly pockets it. He'll call the kid later. For now, he cleaves to comfort: his stomach growls like a starving bear.

He'll put off the call. Just for tonight. Time to murder some food. Not literally. Not this time. To do that – to go select a hog (a real hog, not a Sandhog), he's gotta take a trip out of the city to one of the farms. Maybe Butter Moon, where Charlie Predwick raises beautiful Berkshire hogs, or maybe Red Bridge Farm, where Maeby and Mark Cunningham have a pen of wild Mangalitsa – close enough to boar that the pork is wild, gamy, musky. For now, that's not an option. He's in the city and he's got work to do, so he figures it's off to see Karyn.

Karyn McClaskey – little hipster chick inked from wrists to neck to ankles. Butcher. The girl loves all parts of the pork, especially the strange parts. Ears and face-meats, guts and gonads. She'll even cook the tail. Braise it in beer. Then bread it. Then fry it.

His stomach does happy somersaults just thinking about it.

Last time Mookie checked, she's dating one of the Get-Em-Girls, too. Not his place to judge. (Though Karyn's always picked the crazy girls.)

A trip to Karyn's will be good. He needs something to distract him. He's still riding the tail-end of the Blazes. Makes him feel buzzy and bee-stung. An antenna drawing in too much noise, not enough signal. When that dark shadow-thing attacked him, it poked holes inside him, holes he can't seem to plug up, holes through which gush visions of Nora and Jess, images of cancer and shadow.

Mookie comes up out of a metal cellar door in a West side alley, and his phone suddenly goes full tilt like a juggled pinball machine. It buzzes and lights up once, twice, again and again.

He's got ten new messages.

They're all from Werth. The old goat has the patience of a coked-up mosquito.

Mookie sighs, then thumbs redial without listening to the messages.

"Fuck, Mook, where you been?" That's how Werth answers.

"Downstairs. I got something. We thought it wasn't real, but I got–"

"No time for that. Later. Something bad has happened."

"What?"

"Someone murdered Casimir Zoladski."

PART TWO
BLOOD & BRINE

8

The Underworld in myth has long been associated with the dead – it is in the low places that the souls and spirits of the departed go in many of the old stories, sometimes to be castigated for their earthly ways, sometimes because that's where the dead must go. It has long been believed that this Underworld, our own Great Below, was not like that: it was a physical place, not a spiritual one. Its walls were granite and quartz, basalt and schist – they were neither slick with spectral ectoplasm nor formed of the non-corporeal dreams of the freshly demised. The monsters of the deep were real, it seemed, and ghosts – if they were real at all – were not part of that place. We were, of course, wrong.

– from the Journals of John Atticus Oakes,
Cartographer of the Great Below

Mookie doesn't belong in this neighborhood. Upper East Side, Museum Mile, Central Park – it smells of money. It's all trees and top-shelf condos and mansions crammed next to mansions. It's restaurants that wouldn't let him through the front door (much as he might secretly like the chance), people with dogs from breeds he's never heard of and probably couldn't pronounce, views of the city and the park that some buyers would literally *kill* for.

The air, fresh, crisp. Like the bite of an apple.

No gangs here. Nobody owns this territory – not the Get-Em-Girls, not the Three-Eyed Jacks or the Switchblade Charlies.

The gobbos try once in a while, but neighborhoods like this are well-lit, clean, lots of cops. The gobs and other Underworld beasties can masquerade, but the mask is imperfect. And it's only skin deep. Besides, the Organization has a strong presence here. The Boss. Couple lieutenants living in the neighborhood. Most they get is some gobbos slinging Blue where they shouldn't.

Mookie comes up on the Boss's place – middle of the block off of 5th on 82nd Street. In some ways the mansion looks like a long, lean face with many eyes and a mean, hungry mouth.

Through the front door.

He thinks for a moment he has the wrong house. His heavy boots fall on black marble, kicking up little clouds of powder and leaving behind a small trail of sand, and all of it echoes, and nobody's here, and for a second, Mookie's about to back out slowly–

He smells something. A whiff of a scent…

Then: Mookie hears a ding, and crossing the foyer comes Werth, hobbling along on his cane.

Werth, the old goat. Literally so. He with a pair of cracked hooves clomping on the floor and a set of ram's horns jutting out over his furry, crooked ears. Chin whiskers now more than that – from his jaw sprouts a wispy salt-and-pepper goat's beard. His face is still human. Hands, too. The rest of him: not so much. All this, revealed by the Blue.

Mookie asks, "What happened?"

"C'mon. Upstairs."

"Where is everybody?"

"We're the ones they called."

"Are we at war?"

Werth pauses. "Not yet. Like I said: upstairs, let's go, let's go."

Mookie feels suddenly raw, like skin peeling off a popped blister. When Cerulean leaves you, it'll do that. Make you feel restless, listless, tired and wound up all at the same time as if you just pounded a double-espresso right before sucking down half-a-bottle of codeine cough syrup.

The Blazes gutter and go out. Werth goes from *goatman* to *just a man* in the blink of an eye. The Blue is gone. Blindness to that world returns.

Werth asks, "You OK?"

Mookie doesn't say shit. He just keeps walking.

Upstairs, then.

Werth steps into the elevator. Mookie pulls the wrought iron door across. Inside are old elevator buttons like something off an antique typewriter.

As they go up, Werth looks at Mookie's side. The shirt soaked through from where the gobbos got him. Arm, too. "You tussle with someone?"

"Gobbos."

Elevator, top floor. *Ding.*

The smell of blood and human waste hits him even before the doors open.

The body. Not ten feet away.

The hallway is all creams. Walls like cream-in-coffee. Floors like cream before the coffee. A few punctuations of darkness here and there – a black lampshade, a couple dark lines in the wainscoting, the wrought-iron of the elevator.

And blood.

Dark blood. A lot of it.

Casimir Zoladski is face down on the marble. Sticky dark stuff spreading beneath a face smashed too far into the floor, so far that his face must be crushed and crumpled like an empty egg carton.

The grandson's black jacket lies another ten feet to the left. His white shirt has been cut open. Not ripped, but cut. Delicately. Surgically, Mookie thinks. Like a pig's belly opened by a careful hand with a sharp knife. *Or a claw.*

Symbols lie carved in the pale stretch of his dead back. Symbols Mookie doesn't recognize – the rifts in the flesh form an inverted triangle (one point ending at each shoulder blade), and inside that triangle are lines that suggest a maze. And at the center of that maze is something that Mookie can only describe as a mouth. A circle with crude pointed teeth and forked tongue cut in the flesh.

Werth tilts his head toward the body. "Check the hands."

Mookie stoops down. Knees popping. He grabs the wrist. Already stiffening. Turns it, sees a flash of orange: withered marigold. In this hand, and in the other.

"Two broken links of iron chain in the pockets," Werth says.

Mookie grunts.

Sees something else, too. The fingertips. Smudgy with – at first he thinks, *blood, his own blood*, but no, it's something else. Mookie bends down almost like he's praying. He has to get close to smell it.

He knows the smell. Because he knows food.

"Chocolate," he says. "Dark chocolate."

Then, something else. A whiff of the familiar.

He crawls around to the front of the body.

Lifts the head. Hates to do it but has to. There's the sound of peeling skin, like he's scraping a car-smashed raccoon off the road–

In the middle of the stink of blood and human waste, he can smell something else.

A smoky, briny stink. Like the wind off the ocean. Like a peaty swamp.

And an acrid tang with it, too. Fruity and sour.

Booze. Like a peaty Islay Scotch. No. Wait. Like the roasted whiff of mezcal, tequila's stranger, smokier cousin. That's what it is. He's about to say as much when two figures enter from a side door.

Haversham and the Boss. Oxygen tank squeaking behind.

The Boss looks a thousand miles away. Like he's barely there inside his own skin, like what's here and walking around is just a saggy scarecrow, his mind's somewhere else, somewhere distant. He barely even notices Mookie and Werth.

Haversham in alarm: "What are you *doing*?"

Mookie swiftly stands, moving his prodigious bulk fast as he can, stammering out, "I was just – I thought I smelled something–"

The Boss, staring off at nothing, whispers, "Fucking tragedy." The old man's body trembles, as if cold.

"Fucking tragedy," Werth echoes.

The kill, Mookie thinks, is ritual. Some of it he understands – if only loosely. *Ofrendas*. Offerings. Marigolds, chocolate, liquor. Day of the Dead-style gifts to those who have passed on: not something you usually find on a fresh corpse. The links of broken chain, though, and that symbol – those are different.

"You want us to get who did this?" Mookie asks.

"We know who did it," the Boss says. Voice a rattling wind stirring dry leaves. He takes a hit off the oxygen and closes his eyes.

"Who?" Werth finally says after a few seconds of silence. "Point us at 'em."

"Walk with me," the Boss says.

He and Haversham walk forward. The old man creeps slow, rasping and wheezing, sometimes coughing and taking a hit from the oxygen. Mookie and Werth share a bewildered, uncomfortable look and follow after like dutiful children. As Mookie walks, his nose catches that same scent from downstairs, a scent suddenly and dreadfully familiar: a perfume of flowers.

Nora sits on a park bench just inside Central Park off Fifth Avenue. Her hands shake. People hurry past, laughing, talking, texting.

Every moment feels hyper-real. Part of it's the Blue. But only a small part.

She turns her palms up on her knees. Sees the blood on her hands.

Oh god, oh god, oh god.

A taxi honks.

A siren somewhere in the distance.

Her mouth is dry. The taste of Snakeface magic lingers under her tongue.

She's afraid to blink because of what she'll see behind her lidded eyes. So she keeps them open. Tries to regulate her breath. Tries to still her trembling limbs.

Keep it together. This can work.

No time to feel anything, you dumb girl.

Stop! Stop thinking about it!

Everything is an opportunity.

You're going to text Skelly.

You're going to tell her it's beginning.

Then you're going to stand up, and you're going to move.

But first, you're going to stop crying.

She blinks back tears. Wipes her eyes.

Then she texts Skelly.

Back downstairs. A small room past the door to the wine cellar, near the kitchen. Inside: a bank of eight monitors next to a shelf full of fireproof file boxes. Surveillance for cameras watching the Boss' house. The room isn't big, and it feels like everybody's having to crowd around and cram in next to Mookie. Which only serves to make Mookie feel awkward, a man in a dress shop, a vegetarian at a slaughterhouse. And all that time, the smell of his daughter's perfume lingering in his nose.

He suddenly worries about what he's going to see in this room, on these monitors.

Haversham reaches past Mookie, flips one switch of eight on the wall–

The top left monitor comes to life.

The black-and-white feed shows the front door of the building. Catches people walking up and down the street, but only in periphery: one arm, feet, part of a face, a head. Incomplete shapes, nothing more.

Haversham reaches for a second panel – this one with a set of dials. He turns one of them left – and instantly the live feed starts to rewind behind a curtain of static.

The time on the screen – which Mookie hadn't even noticed – zooms backward.

"Here," Haversham says. The feed stops. Then starts playing.

8:30pm.

Ten seconds, fifteen. Nothing.

Then the door opens.

Then closes.

Haversham stops it.

"There," he says. Like, voila, *I just did a magic trick*, except nobody sees that anything changed. No dove out of the hat, no card from the sleeve.

The Boss looks at them, taps his head: "You need to powder up for this."

The denizens of the Underworld don't show up on video, film, even audio – at least, not to those without Blue wrenching open the third-eye. Every once in a while some philosopher gets it in his head to talk about whether or not the powers of the Underworld are mystical or natural – something evolved out of nature or born from occult powers, but Mookie doesn't know and doesn't care. All he knows is, you want to see the monsters, you need to play with the peacock. And that's what the Boss is telling him.

Except, no peacock smear around the Boss' temples – nor Haversham's. So how's he know?

Doesn't matter. The Boss knows. That's good enough for Mookie.

Werth pulls a palm-sized tin. It's an old hair pomade container: "Doan Brothers' Hair Pomade Dressing Pat Pending". Rust flakes rain as he screws it open.

Mookie pulls out his own tin. Hands shaking. The Blue is the key to a door he no longer wants to open. *Nora...*

Werth gives him a look.

"You don't need to jump in on this," Werth says.

"I want to see." He doesn't. But he has to.

"You're just coming off a high. Your pupils are like pencil points."

"Doesn't matter."

Werth lowers his voice. "You're gonna run yourself ragged."

"I said I'm *in*," Mookie growls. And that ends it.

Big thumbs in the blue, back to the temples, smudge one, smudge two. The stuff rolls in rougher this time: like a horse kick to the psychic center. Werth dips a pinkie in, does the same – the true denizens of the Great Below don't need Cerulean to see their own kind, but a half-and-half like Werth needs to. His eyelids flutter like fly-wings against window blinds and then he's blazing, too.

Haversham replays the video.

Fifteen seconds in: a shape.

It emerges from the side, as if crossing the road.

The closet suddenly feels to Mookie like an elevator. The floor dropping out. His heart and all his substantial viscera left in the air as everything else falls.

Werth sees it, too. Sees *her*. "That little fucking bitch."

Nora.

Something big is coming, Mookie.

I'm going to change the game.

Jesus.

On the video feed, Nora walks right up to the front door. Pulls out a key. Unlocks. Opens. And then she's gone.

Mookie swallows a hard knot that feels like a baseball in his throat. He shoves Haversham out of the way, grabs the dial, fast-forwards in fifteen-minute increments. The door never opens again. Nora never comes back out.

"Persephone," the Boss says. He doesn't know her as Nora. Nobody here but Werth knows that she's Mookie's daughter. If they were to ever find out...

But Werth, he *does* know, and he stares icicles right through Mookie.

"I thought the girl was pushed out," Werth says, his voice barely containing the fact he's talking more to Mookie than to Haversham or Zoladski. "I thought she was done in this city. And yet, *here she is.*"

"This must be her last play," the Boss says. "Last-ditch effort. And it's a fucking doozy. I'm dying. And my only heir is..." His voice cracks. He looks away. "I need some air." Haversham tries to hand him the oxygen mask but the Boss waves it away, says, "Leave the tank. I need some *real* air. You two. Come on. Let's go outside."

Outside, the Boss lights a cigarette. Takes a deep inhale. Coughs like he swallowed fiberglass insulation. But then the coughs abate.

"Haven't smoked in fifteen fucking years," the Boss says. "And tonight I had a nic-fit like you wouldn't believe." He looks up, scowls at Mookie and Werth. "What? Not like it's going to give me *more* cancer, Christ."

People pass by. A few stares reserved for this motley crew – giant dude, cancer man, crippled old goat. The Boss spits a nit of nicotine out of his mouth.

"You two are gonna handle this," he says.

"We need *everybody* on this–" Werth starts to say, but Mookie interrupts:

"We can handle it."

"This is about our *Southern* business," the Boss says. That's what he calls their dealings with the Deep Downstairs. *Southern business*. "She's been coming at us from that end all year. And the shit that she did to Casimir's body…" He coughs into a handkerchief which comes away flecked with red. "That's ritual. You wanna just kill a guy, you shoot him in the head. This means something. Find her. Figure it out."

"You got it," Werth says.

"Done," Mookie says, his blood gone to slush.

The Boss says nothing more. Just a dismissive nod, then he's hobbling back inside.

9

The Five Occulted Pigments: Cerulean, as discussed. Then: Vermilion, or the Red Rage; Viridian, the Green Grave; Ochre, the Golden Gate; and Caput Mortuum, the Violet Void – or simply, "The Dead Head". Most claim that these are a myth, but I do not believe it so. I have heard the gobbos in their gutter-tongue – yes, I've learned some of their words and sounds and crass gesticulations – speak of the other Pigments in reverent tones. We will not find the other four here in the Shallows, I suspect. But rather, they must exist in the Fathomless Tangle – or below that, in the Ravenous Expanse.

> – from the Journals of John Atticus Oakes,
> Cartographer of the Great Below

Outside the front door, Mookie starts to speak. But Werth pulls him away from the door and strides away. It's a half-a-block up before Werth finally stops, steps into an alcove between two brownstones, and wheels on Mookie.

The old goat is seething. Caprine nostrils flaring.

"Werth–"

"Don't you fuckin' start, Mook. *Don't.*"

"I didn't know–"

"That was her, wasn't it? At your place the other night. When I called, she was there." Mookie gnaws a thumbnail, but Werth grabs the hand and yanks it out of Mookie's mouth. "Look at me and don't lie. Why'd she come see you?"

97

"She knew the Boss was sick."

"What?"

"I dunno how. And then she said…" *Don't tell him, he doesn't need to know.* But Mookie hears the words coming out of his mouth: "Something was coming. Something… big. A game-changer." He neglects to say *she* was the one who promised to change the game. He reserves that much loyalty for her.

Werth snarls. "Mookie. This whole thing, *this whole fucking thing*, is on you. I told you to deal with her. I gave you a good length of leash on this one, didn't I? I didn't tell Haversham or the Boss how you were connected to her. I didn't go after her myself *even after the little cunt–*"

Mookie's hand closes around Werth's throat.

"*–shot me–*" Werth gurgles.

Mookie starts to squeeze.

The blood rushes to Werth's head, stays there like he's tying off a water balloon. Mookie feels something jabbing him in the ribs–

A .38 snubnose. Nickel-plated.

Mookie doesn't care. Keeps squeezing.

Hammer back on the gun. *Click.*

"Say you're sorry," Mookie growls.

"Ggggfffuck you." Then: "KkkaaaaI'll shhhhhooooot."

"*Apologize.*"

The gun barrel digs harder between Mookie's ribs. People are passing by, now – a Botoxed cougar with her boy-toy and her Yorkie, an old man with a newspaper under his arm. They see what's going on and hurry past.

The gun presses harder. The sights biting into his side.

Finally, Werth says, "*Zzzhhhhsssoooorry.*"

Mookie lets go. The old goat takes in a big gulp of breath, quickly pockets the gun.

"You…" *Gasp, wheeze, cough.* "You fuckin' asshole. Jesus, Mook."

"You're talking about my daughter."

"Your daughter *shot* me. And now she's gone and killed the Boss's grandson."

"No." Mookie shakes his head like a man in denial. "She... she didn't. That kid was mashed into the floor like a stepped-on banana. She's just a little girl."

"Maybe she had help."

"From who?"

"Maybe from *you*."

Mookie feels like he's been shot in the heart. "You... you know I'd never–"

With a roll of his eyes Werth says, "Yeah, yeah, you're loyal, I know. You're like a dumb dog. I know you didn't do this. But it sure matches your... style of doing business."

"He seemed like an all right kid."

"Well, now he's dead thanks to *your* kid. Don't gimme that look. Let's say she *didn't* do it. Doesn't matter. We're on the hook for this. Because if we don't find her? They're gonna send someone else. Maybe they already have. Like those two thugs, Spall and Lutkevich."

Those assholes. Two of the Organization's killers. But they're not precision men. They're messy. Spray-and-pray types. They don't do sniper rifles – they do a hand grenade chucked into an open room, even if that open room is a church or a pre-school.

"I'll find her," Mookie says.

"*We'll* find her. Split up."

"Don't kill her."

"That's what's gotta be done, Mook. It's time."

"Just... bring her in. To me. Let me deal with her." A voice asks: *can you do it? Can you kill your own daughter*? He knows he can't. He's had the chance. But something has to be done. Another voice: *She didn't do this. Bad as she is, she didn't do this...* "You owe me that much. I've done the work. I'm good."

"Owe you. Yeah. Fine. I'll call you if I find her. And if you find her? I wanna know about it. You hear me?" Mookie nods. "Don't fuck this up, Pearl. Even those big motherfucking shoulders of yours may not be able to hold the weight of all this."

Mookie heads toward the subway, hands shaking. Trying to picture Nora doing what she did – envisioning her smashing Casimir Zoladski's head into the floor, cutting open his shirt, slicing into his back. Then the rite with the marigolds, the chocolate, the liquor.

Doesn't add up. Can't be her. She's not that strong. She's a little thing. A fraction of his size – if he's the whiskey bottle, she's the shot glass. The strength it would take to pulp the kid's face against that marble, it'd have to be – well, either him or a Trogbody, because those rock-bodied sonofabitches are strong. Even someone burning the Blue Blazes candle at both ends would have a hard time making that kind of a mess. So Mookie decides. No. His daughter is not a murderer.

But Werth's right. Everyone else is going to think it's her.

And if they find out she's his daughter, they're going to think he helped.

As he walks, Mookie's thinking about where to go, how to find Nora. *Persephone*. He hates that name. *Daddy-o*. That's what she called him, wasn't it? Back there at the bar. That means she really has been hanging out with the Get-Em-Girls.

So that's the first place he needs to look.

Which means–

It's then that Mookie sees something as he heads back past the Boss' place.

A Lexus. The color of liquid pearl. It sits, parked across the street.

It's dark out but there's a streetlight above–

And in that car, Mookie sees a familiar face. The man from this morning. Candlefly, that's what Haversham called him. The one traveling with the Snakeface.

Correction: the Snakeface *killer*.

Killer. Assassin. Like so many Snakefaces. Seducers of mind, body, soul.

Life-eaters, all of them.

Casimir was at that meeting.

Mookie feels his fists ball up and he steps into the street – a coming taxi honks its horn at him and slams on the brakes, but Mookie doesn't give a shit. As he passes, he punches out one of the cab's headlights and keeps walking, bits of clear plastic falling off his knuckles.

Suddenly the Lexus lurches forward, headlights flicking on – it zips out of the parking space into the street. It takes off, and Mookie gives stomping chase. Behind him, the cab driver is out of the car – a fat white guy with flabby jowls. He's flailing his hands and yelling and pointing at the front of the car, but Mookie doesn't care. He just skids to a halt, watching the red demon eyes of the Lexus taillights turn the corner at Park and disappear.

"You better run," he says. *And if I find out that you had anything to do with Casimir's murder, I'm going to punch you into a greasy pudding.*

Karyn's isn't called Karyn's, though that's how Mookie thinks of it. She calls her place "Mackie Messer's" – but despite the name and how she looks it's not particularly hip or upscale. It's a butcher shop. Everything white. White counter, white floor. Glass case showing the cuts of the day. Couple meat scales. Grinders and other equipment in the back. Freezer, too. Basic stuff, but from that comes what Mookie considers to be the *real* magic: cuts of meat from heritage breeds of pig and cow, duck and chicken, some of which Karyn turns into charcuterie:

sausage, salumi, lardo, pate, all crafted with an expert hand and an eerie patience. Karyn is cool like that.

She's so cool, in fact, that when Mookie calls her at 2:30 in the morning, she's still awake. "Making a brine," she says. And the good news is, she's in the Chelsea shop, not in the bigger Park Slope venue.

He asks her if he can stop by. She says yeah.

He hates that he needs her for this, but he does.

Subway, then. To Chelsea. To Mackie Messer's.

Karyn lets Mookie in. She's a sight for sore eyes. White apron flecked with red hanging over a black bra. Pale skin inked with the sigils of a cook's life: a skull with a knife in its teeth on the back of her neck, a garlic bulb on the left shoulder, a giant pig's head with an apple in its mouth (and a worm poking out of the apple) covering the right shoulder all the way down to the bicep. Black punky hair in a red handkerchief.

Lipstick the color of wet cherries.

She's beautiful to him. Not in *that* way. She's gay as the day is blue – or as she puts it, "Queer as a three-dollar bill" – and he knows she'd never go for him. But she's got power. Strength. Knowledge. A confidence mitigated by an uninterrupted calm. *An even keel.*

"You're my fuckin' hero," he says.

"Hey, Mook."

They hug. He about crushes her. She gives as good as she gets.

Into the back. She pulls up a metal stool. The smell here is killing him in the best way possible. The iron tang of blood. The sweet odor of raw pork. Spices, too: garlic and cumin, rosemary and sage. He can feel the hunger in his *teeth*.

Bang. She drops a wooden cutting board in front of him.

On it? Meat.

She taps each as she tells him what it is: "Culatello with melon. Iberian chorizo from acorn-fed pigs. Cocoa nib and cayenne salami. And that last one that looks like an apostrophe, that's smoked jowl roll. Fried up in a cast iron pan."

"You have a gift."

"No such thing. I love what I do and I do what I love."

He has no answer for that because he's already plucking the chorizo from the plate and laying it on his tongue like a communion wafer. Even before his teeth cut the meat he tastes the oil coming off the sausage, oil that brings heat and spice.

"Fuck," he says, breathing out of his nose as he chews. Eyes closed.

"Good, right?"

"Good doesn't *begin* to scratch the paint."

She blushes. "Anyway. How's tricks, Mook?"

"Shitty." Here, then, the vibe of the confessional. She doesn't know what he does. Not exactly. She doesn't know what goes on beneath the streets of the city – and, sadly, often upon those streets. She's one of the Blind – the scales of ignorance blissfully closing over her eyes. And good for her. Mookie wouldn't wish the truth on someone like Karyn. Just the same, she lets him talk. He keeps it vague. She probably knows something's up with him – thinks, correctly so, that he's a made man in some way. The depths, however, remain hidden. "I got problems."

She pulls up a stool. Elbows down on the table, chin in a cradle of knuckles. "Talk while you eat."

"Work and family. Those two things…" He punches his two fists together. Sounds like two steaks slapping. "They're crashing. Into one another."

"Your daughter?"

"Getting ornery."

"Again?"

"Again."

"You still in touch with her mother?"

"Eh." Translation: *nope*. "Been awhile. A long while. She doesn't want nothin' to do with me."

"Can't she help get the girl under control?"

"I dunno. Maybe."

"Worth a shot."

He thinks but does not say: it's gone too far for that.

But still – maybe Karyn's onto something. Maybe Jess knows something about where Nora is. Or isn't. Call her, you big dummy.

"You're a smart kid," he says.

"My father's a clinical psychologist. My mother, a copyright lawyer. Two smarts don't make a dumb."

"I'm a thug and my ex-wife used to be a night nurse at a drug clinic. What's that tell you?"

"Tells me you got trouble on your hands." Karyn winks, nudges the cutting board closer. "Eat, you big bastard."

Eat. Yes. More heat. Cocoa nib and cayenne salumi. The round edges of unsweet chocolate. The fire from the pepper. The unctuous *slightly-off* taste of the meat.

He makes a sound in the back of his throat. Kind of an *nnnnggguuuuhhh*.

It's time. He doesn't want it to be, but it has to be.

An attempt at a clumsy diversion: "You still dating, uhh, what's her name?"

"Lulu?"

"Yeah. Lulu."

"Yeah. Louisa's good, she's good. Better than all the previous girls added up."

"The last one was a little crazy."

"The last *five* were a *lot* crazy. And Lulu's crazy, too, but... hey, so am I. My crazy and her crazy play well together. Run with scissors down the hall." She smiles. "She's learning the trade. She might work here soon."

"That mean she's giving up the... roller derby thing?"

"She loves that too much. The Girls are her family."

The Girls. "Her gang."

Karyn's face falls. "I know." Now it's her turn to change the subject. "You need to get yourself a girl, Mook."

"I'm too old for a girl. I need a woman." He frees his palate with the culatello and melon. Soft mild fruit with what for many is the king of charcuterie – meat from the best part of the leg preserved in the pig's emptied bladder and hung in a dark cool place for upwards of a whole year. Real-deal culatello hangs in musty old caves. Karyn hangs it in the basement of her Brooklyn joint, which is itself dark, dank, cavernous. The idea once struck Mookie that the Great Below would be a helluva place to hang meat – it wasn't. The air has something wrong with it. The meat came out bulging with fungal pods like tumors. Smelled like sour, sun-warmed death.

"Oh, hey, I got something you might wanna see," Karyn says.

She goes toward the back, grabs something from a metal table.

She lays it down in front of Mookie.

It's a cleaver. Inside a brown leather sheath.

He grabs it. Holds it. Likes its weight. The carving blade fits inside the sheath snug as anything – it slides in like a hand inside a pocket. A dark wooden handle with two inlaid brass stars encompassing the heavy pins affixing it to the blade. The handle is long. "It fits me," he says. The wood, polished to a gleam. Mookie draws it from the sheath.

The blade is bigger than a hardback book and almost as thick at the back – perfect for smashing garlic or, in Mookie's world, cracking heads. The blade itself is serrated, not on purpose but through what must be years of use – the edge a crass line of crooked razor teeth. But when Mookie slides his thumb across it, he sees how sharp it is just the same. The flesh parts like soft whitefish and a bead of dark blood draws to the surface.

He wipes it on his shirt.

"Classy," she tells him.

He gestures to her apron with his chin. "Hey, we're used to blood."

"You're maybe used to a different kind of blood."

A cold moment between them. Her eyes flick away from him. Is that fear there? She knows who he is. Maybe some of what he does.

But she pulls away from it, says, "That cleaver does me right. Not just for tenderloin or chicken bones. That'll get me through the skull of a bison if I want it to."

"Yeah, nice, nice." It fits like it belongs to him already. "What do you want for it?"

"Cost me fifty, so I'll take fifty."

"I'll pay more."

"Nah. Just next time you come into the city, bring me some of what you been making lately. Hook a lady up."

"Man, I've been busy." He folds a trio of twenties, hopes she doesn't notice as he slides the folded bills toward her. "Made some lardo I'm pretty proud of. Nowhere near like what you're bringing to the table. But it's… OK."

"Like I said. Bring some in next time you come."

"That's like a four-year-old bringing in his fingerpainting to, uhh, ahhh–" He tries to think of some kind of masterpiece painter, but nothing's coming to mind. "One of those old artist guys. But yeah. I will. Just so you can tell me what I'm doin' wrong." He stands. It's time. *Get it over with*. "I got a favor to ask."

"Favor. OK. Anything."

"I need to talk to Lulu."

Karyn bristles. She takes a step back.

"What? Why?"

"I…" He doesn't want to say too much. Karyn can't know. Can't get drawn in. "I just got some questions to ask her."

"That sounds bad."

"It ain't. It's fine. Please."

"I'm not..." She takes a deep breath. "I can't. Your world. Her world..."

"I'm not gonna hurt her."

"I don't know that."

"You know me."

"Do I?" She laughs. "You come in here, I offer you food and cut you a deal on that cleaver – I think it's a Richter Brothers cleaver if you care – and, and, and most of the time we just shoot the shit like two friends catching up on the day's... the day's whatever. But I know who you work for. I'm not stupid. And now you're asking me about my girl? My girl who belongs to a gang? I won't. OK? I won't."

"Karyn, c'mon, this is important–"

"You need to go."

He thinks for a half-a-second: I could make her talk.

That's what he does. Makes people hurt. Sometimes so they spill.

He's good at it.

It's a horrible thought. And he can't do that. Not to her.

"I'm sorry. I'll go."

"Good."

"Thanks for..." He doesn't even have to say.

"Get out."

He gets out, not sure if the bridge behind him is shaking – or burning.

10

Man will never colonize the Great Below. It is too wild. Too unreal. The chthonian labyrinth is a place of madness and I have seen it warp the mind of man the way a long damp warps a wooden beam. I myself have become twisted by the space but never enough to fool myself into thinking that we can or should stake a claim here. Yes, the Great Below has its villages and outposts – the marketplace of Yonder, the rat's nest of addicts and madmen in the Freedom Tunnel, the temple of the People of the Turning Worm, the living graveyard of Daisypusher. And, of course, they have colonized us: the denizens of the Great Below have carved out territory in the Infinite Above – warehouses and nightclubs, restaurants and abandoned houses. The Chinatown block between Mott and Elizabeth is a known haven for starry-eyed monstrosities who care little for the Great Below and who hope to give it a go in the world above. Were you to ask me, I'd again reiterate that man will never properly colonize the Great Below. But give the monsters half a chance and they will most certainly colonize us.

– from the Journals of John Atticus Oakes,
Cartographer of the Great Below

They're gonna kill her.

That thought keeps running laps through his head. They're gonna find her. They're gonna kill her. Because of what she did. Or what they *say* she did.

Mookie needs to find her, but he's going nowhere fast. Karyn wouldn't give up her girl. He shoulda known. Shouldn't have even *asked* her to do that, and now here he is, heading to deal with the Devil to see if he can't get a lead on his babygirl.

Shit. *Shit.*

He comes up out of the subway on Canal Street. Heads into Chinatown. Three-thirty in the morning. The Blazes are no longer a warm fire but a cigarette burn at the edges of everything, sizzling and searing him with a nicotine char.

Which means he's gotta get *in* quick, get *out* quick. Doesn't want to go in blind. And he knows that dipping into the Cerulean again so fast before he's had a chance to sleep could be trouble. (But here a little hungry monkey in the back of his brain screeches and hoots and rattles the bars of its cage, desperate to feed, feed, feed.)

Mookie hoofs it. Heads toward Mott and Elizabeth, where Elizabeth ends at Bayard – that last block, deep in the heart of Chinatown, that's where some of the monsters are. Monsters who play nice – or, nic*er*, at least – with the people above ground. You got Lei-Lei, the half-and-half mer-girl who runs a killer dim sum joint from her tank of ocean water in the back room. Across the street on the Elizabeth side is an antiquities shop run by another halfsie – actually a pair of them: conjoined twins, Jim and Judy, both white and blonde as the sand on a Florida beach. You look at them with a Blind eye, you don't see them conjoined – you just see a brother and sister who always stand shoulder-to-shoulder. You go in Blazing and you see the way the flesh reaches out like gooey bread-dough, her ropy flesh intertwining with his, both of them looking like each is melting into the other.

They sell *tschotschkes* to the tourists – lucky kitty clocks and Buddha statues and the like – but to those in the know, they sell artifacts found down in the deep. Strange rocks. Gobbo weapons. Above-world items dragged into the depths and infused with the magic of the Underworld, sucking it up like a kid with a straw.

It's not them that Mookie wants to talk to. Not tonight.

He wants to talk to Mr Smiley.

Smiley's a Snakeface. Runs a "teahouse and cocktail bar" at the corner. Also runs a whole stable of prostitutes. And buckets of drugs. And guns.

And, most important of all, *information*.

On the way, Mookie grabs his cell. Thinks to dial Jess, his ex. Nora's mother. It's too late – er, early? – to call. Right? He's suddenly not sure. Nora's in danger. He knows that much. And if Jess knows anything…

Then again, Mookie's the last person Jess wants to be talking to. Particularly at asshole-o'clock in the morning. That's all it is. It's late. Right?

He quickly pockets the phone.

Mookie spies the alley between the Xinhua fish market and the Golden Sun dry cleaners, ducks into the shadow between the two buildings. Back here, it smells like old fish and cleaning solution – soap and seafood in troubling combination. Mookie pushes past it, past a couple rust-eaten dumpsters, feet splashing in old puddles–

A figure steps out in front of him. Twenty feet away. Rises up from behind a small mound of black trash bags. Rats scatter.

It takes a second for Mookie's eyes to adjust – but he sees the skinny, lanky frame and what at first looks like a square head. But the head isn't square: it's just the brown paper bag *over* the head. A bag painted with a Jack-o-Lantern mask, the orange pumpkin with the triangle eyes cut out, the jagged mouth, too.

Jack-o-Lantern mask.

That means it's one of the Lantern Jacks.

They're one of the city's old-school gangs. New York isn't like other cities. The big gangs – M13, Crips, Bloods, Latin Kings, Triads – aren't here. The Organization rose up in the

1970s, made friends with the gangs that existed at that time: the Black Aces, the Black Sleeves, the Battery Park Bruisers, the Railroaders, the Majestic Immortals, the Sinner Kids, and of course the Get-Em-Girls and the Lantern Jacks. The bigger gangs never got to make a foothold because the smaller ones made a deal with the Organization – a deal that let them survive here long as they kept to the truce. Each has territory. Each does their thing.

In theory.

Chinatown belongs to the Lantern Jacks. Used to be Majestic Immortal territory but those dumb fuckers imploded about ten years back – of all things, it was family that set them on a course for self-destruction. Head of the gang, Big Chang, was married to this ball-buster, Lirong. Chang got around: had a thing for some dominatrix named Orchid on the Upper East Side. Lirong got tired of it, fucked Big Chang's brother, Little Chang. Big found out. The Chang brothers got into a very public pissing match, broke the gang in two, huge fight in the street – and Lirong was the one who ended it all. Walked into the fray, shot both of them, then walked back out. Never seen again. Gang fell apart. Lantern Jacks – white boys, not Chinese – strolled in with their pumpkin masks and their scarecrow rags, took the place over.

And now one of them stands before Mookie.

He hears footsteps behind him.

More creeping in. He glances over his shoulder, sees three of 'em back there. One of them has a thick chain ill-concealed behind his leg, the end of it draped on the ground like the head of a dead python.

"Outta my way," Mookie says.

"You Blazing?" the Jack in front of him says, then cackles. These assholes, always with the theatrics. "You carrying the Blue? Huh?"

Behind him are snickers and hisses. The chain rattles.

"You know who I am?"

From behind him, one whispers, "Mookie Pearl."

"Good. So you know to get the fuck outta my way."

"Give us what you got, Pearl."

The skinny Jack in front of him flicks his wrist – a straight razor gleams.

"We got a truce," Mookie says.

"Do we?"

More cackles.

"Last I checked. You want to throw it away?"

The razor flashes in the air. Slicing a figure eight. The skinny Jack's bag makes a crinkle-noise as he thrusts his tongue out of the mouth slit, waggling it.

Footsteps behind him. The Jacks are moving in.

Ballsy. Real ballsy. And stupid. And with the next thing the skinny Jack says, it makes sense–

"Sure glad I don't have cancer." Way he says that last word, it's a droning weasel-whine: *caaaaanceeeeeeer*. Another happy cackle. "We heard the word. Persephone's telling everybody."

Shit. *Nora*. "So that's what this is. Boss is fine. Healthy as a champion horse."

Hesitation. The skinny one lets the razor hang. Takes a half-step back with one foot.

"You're lying."

"And you're about to be lying, too. Lying *dead*." Not his best line, but Mookie's not real good at the banter. For extra spice he adds, "You little shit."

Skinny Jack screeches like an owl.

It's on. He rushes at Mookie, razor out at the side like a Samurai making a charge against a mounted soldier–

Mookie hears the three behind him close in and close in fast, feet on cracked pavement–

The chain loops around his neck.

The razor comes for his face.

His big hand catches Skinny Jack's wrist before the blade can cut him.

He wrenches the hand sideways. The arm breaks at the elbow. Sickening crunch. Bone out of skin. White bone. Red blood. Skinny Jack howls as the chain pulls tighter around his neck. The razor clatters.

One down, three to go.

Mookie tilts his body at the waist, lurching forward and down. The Jack with the chain goes launching up over him and down on top of his compound-fracture buddy – he scrambles to get up, trying to find the chain, the razor, something–

But it's too late. Mookie drop-kicks his head. Hears the jaw give way.

Mookie spins.

Gun in his face. Big fucking gun, too. Some kind of Dirty Harry revolver. Makes it all the easier to grab, which is what Mookie does – he snatches it with a twist, bashes the paper bag pumpkin mask hard enough to tear it down the center. Brown bag stained with red.

The fourth Jack – a dumpy, pudgy dipshit in baggy pants – just runs.

Mookie throws the gun.

It's heavy. It clocks the fat shit in the back of the head. He drops, face forward, into a scum-slurry puddle. Mookie stomps over. Bends down and growls in the kid's ear:

"I got my own message to send out. The Boss is alive. The Organization is strong. And Persephone better watch her back."

Then he kicks the kid in the ass as he scrambles forward on all fours.

Mookie picks up the gun, chucks it in a dumpster.

He hopes they heed his warning.

But this is a warning for Mookie, too. They know. *They fucking know* about the Boss and his cancer. If these piss-ant pumpkin-heads know, that means the other gangs know, too. And it won't be long before those big gangs outside the city like the Latin Kings and the Triads find out. The Boss is right: they're gonna smell the blood in the water like so much frothy chum. Blood begets blood. A little now. A lot later.

Shit. He can feel the edges of his world start to give in a little – it's suddenly claustrophobic here in the alley, like the walls are going to topple and crush. Mookie's world is the Organization. If that falls, what does he have?

The thought makes him feel small and weak like a starving dog. A starving *old* dog.

Then he realizes: part of it is the Cerulean. The Blazes suddenly gutter and spark and go dark – it feels like something's taken from him. Breath from his lungs. Bones from his legs. He steadies himself. Shudders like it's suddenly cold.

He hoped to have eyes on when he went to see Mr Smiley.

So – now what? Go in Blind? Or dose up and keep push-push-pushing?

Inside, the chattering voice: *Go blue! Go deep! Blaze, motherfucker, blaze! Can't hurt. Feels good! Makes you strong like ox. You're already stupid, why be stupider? Open your eyes!*

A reiterative chant: *Blue! Blue! Blue! Blaze! Blaze! Blaze!*

Without even realizing it, he's got the tin of powder already in his palm and open.

Damned if he does.

Damned if he doesn't.

Mookie dips a thumb into the powder and smudges his temples.

The ravening fire takes him, hot and cold all at the same time.

The "teahouse" has a bouncer. Mookie knows him. Trogbody named Gorth, goes by the human name of Gary. Shorter than Mookie, but not by much. Bulky stone body shoved into a black T-shirt and cargo pants. Eyes are glittering quartz deposits tucked into a pair of craggy hollows. Mouth full of stalactite and stalagmite teeth.

"Mookie Pearl," Gorth says by way of greeting. Whenever he speaks – really, when any Troggo speaks – you hear something in the back of his throat that sounds like a couple loose rocks bouncing down a mountain slope.

"Gorth," Mookie says. The Cerulean's starting to wear him down. He feels his neck tendons pulling tight like piano wire. He's gotta chill out. Focus up. His daughter's life is at stake here. Mookie takes a deep breath. "I need to see Smiley."

"We're shuttin' down for the night."

"Hell you are."

"Almost four in the morning. Sun'll be up. Smiley doesn't like the sun."

"Sun ain't up yet."

"I know, but–"

"I'm tired. I'm burning too long and too hard–" Here Mookie taps his temple. "I just need some info. Ten minutes. Tops."

"I dunno–"

Mookie's nostrils flare. "Got two ways to do this. First, you move aside, open that door. Second, I gotta find my own way in. And I'm not that smart. So that means I go through you. We'll fight. It'll be ugly. But I'm tired. And cranky. And Blazing hard. So I'll send you home with a couple cracked fingers. An arm broken off at the wrist. Head split like a geode. And I'll be beaten into mashed potatoes, too. That sound like a good way to end your night? I don't think it sounds too goddamn good."

The golem's quartz eyes flicker and flash. "That sounds bad."

"Yeah."

"OK. Go ahead in."

Gorth steps aside, his rock joints clattering.

●●●●

The teahouse. The first floor is all dark wood, so dark it might as well be black. Trim the color of matcha powder. Rice paper screens the color of red poppies.

The joint is empty. Except for Mr Smiley, sitting in the middle of the room at a two-top table. Tiny teacup to his left, with a small purple clay teapot just behind it.

This, then, is Mr Smiley:

Were Mookie here Blind, he'd see an Asian man of indiscriminate national origin – long face, big smile, hair black and oily like it's been shellacked to his scalp, like it's slick plastic snapped to the head of a LEGO figure.

What he sees instead – what the Blue Blazes *show* him – is a man whose face is a nearly perfect mix of *serpent* and *human*. The head is human-shaped but balanced on a too-long neck, the nose is just a pair of fleshy slits, the eyes are wide coppery diamonds whose irises shift and warp like you're staring through a child's kaleidoscope. The mouth – still smiling, for he is always oh-so-very *happy* – ill-conceals not just a pair of curved fangs, but rather a whole maw of them. A wet pink tongue – not forked, but thin and prehensile – slides over them like a slug over piano keys.

Mr Smiley's arms are not arms, but snake-like protrusions, tentacular and ever-undulating. The fingers are smaller versions of the arms, like little baby garter snakes attached to the tail of each substantial python.

"And here I thought we were closed," Smiley says, grinning.

"Gorth let me make a late appointment."

A twinkling fang-laden smile. "Then sit."

Mookie pulls a chair, reverses it, sits with his battleship chest against the back.

"What can I do for you, Mr Pearl?"

"I need information."

The smile doesn't leave, but Smiley's eyes flash irritation. "Yes. Obviously."

"I need to know where my–" He's about to say *daughter*, but he catches himself. The Blazes make him restless. Foolish. Like he's tap-dancing on the edge of the abyss. These people don't know Nora is his daughter. Nobody does. Nobody but Werth. "Where my *friend* Persephone is."

"Persephone. Persephone." He doesn't blink. He just stares at Mookie as he says the name again and again. "No. I don't think I know that one."

Mookie pulls his wallet. He knows how this game goes.

But Smiley stays his hand. An almost imperceptible shake of his head. "No."

"No?"

"Not this time."

"Well. What, then?"

"I want information."

"Like I got anything you don't already know?"

"Your Boss is weak."

Mookie feels heat rising off the back of his neck. "He's got it all together."

"Your Boss is *sick*."

Figures. Of course he knows.

"Don't know what you mean. That's a nasty rumor going around."

"It's not. And you know it's not. Metastatic lung cancer." The snake fingers flick and undulate. An expression of excitement? Happiness? "I want to know more about that. I want to know where he's vulnerable. I want to know where the chinks in his armor lie." Smiley laughs. "I always wondered: is that racist? Chinks in armor?"

Mookie wipes away sweat. Sneers. "I can't answer any of that."

"Can't? Or won't?"

"Ask me something else. Anything else."

"No." So petulant. And giddy at the same time.

Mookie stands. Knocks the chair over with a clatter.

"We're done here," he says.

Smiley baits him. "Don't you want to know how I know? About the cancer?"

Mookie's answer is a hard stare. His eyes like two nails trying to pin Smiley to the wall.

"Besides it being my job to know things," Mr Smiley says. "Not just my job, actually. But my pleasure, my absolute and unswerving pleasure. I like to categorize the little chips and shards of information – the sweet, sweet secrets – that come in here and, quite honestly, most are worthless. Some have a very narrow edge: a prison shiv meant only for another person, a secret useless to most but powerful to a select few. Other secrets are very powerful, indeed. A hand swept across a table, knocking everything upon it to the floor below. Your Boss's cancer is just such a secret. It's a storm that can change a coastline. An earthquake that alters the topography, a bomb that–"

"Just get to it."

"Ah. Impatient. I see that you're running ragged – look at those pupils! Fat like black flies. Blazing hard tonight, are we? Yes. That secret about your Boss? It was Persephone who told it to me."

Mookie's gut twists.

"Funny thing is, Mr Pearl, that secret truly is a big one, but it comes part and parcel with one of those very personal secrets. A piece of information that has a fingerprint pressed into its clay. It's a secret meant for you."

The world feels hot and cold. Mookie's hands form into fists so hard it's like having a pair of cinderblocks at the end of his arms.

He knows where this is going.

"Persephone is your daughter. Eleanor Pearl. And very few people know that."

"I don't know what you're talking ab–"

"Deny it all you'd like. But here comes the time where we play a lovely little game, a game called *Test Your Loyalty*. Because now you can either tell me the information I seek – and together we can explore how to undo the empire your Boss has built for the last thirty years – or I can share with that very Boss that it was *your daughter* who killed *his grandson*. How does that–"

Smiley doesn't get the chance to finish.

Mookie moves fast. Flips the table up into the Naga's face. Smiley catches the table with his writhing snake arms, flings it aside–

It's all Mookie needs. That moment of disorientation. Soon as the table clears, he drives a fist into the Snakeface's elongated neck, collapsing the throat. Suddenly Smiley is gasping a gassy squeak, trying to catch air.

Mookie grabs the neck.

Then runs at full speed to the back of the teahouse.

Wham. He slams Mr Smiley into the back wall. Snakefaces have no bones, they're just a series of tendons and muscles and cartilaginous gel that push and pull off one another. But the Naga keens in pain and hisses just the same.

Snake arms and legs wrap around Mookie. It's like trying to wrestle an angry squid. Serpentine tentacles wind around his wrists. His midsection. His throat.

Hate glows in Smiley's eyes. His smile now burned to ash. The Snakefaces flashes his fangs – the curved teeth growing out of blistery poison sacs lining the creature's grub-white gums, dripping poison the color of dying violets.

Mookie's on a fast-moving car speeding toward a broken bridge. A little voice in the back of his mind knows this is a bad move – you don't muscle someone like Smiley. He knows too much. And to kill him? That has consequences. Not the least of which is he's under the paid protection of the Boss – and Smiley pays in *big*.

And yet here Mookie is, ready to crush his windpipe. The fire of the Blazes eating up his insides like they're just twigs and newspaper.

"Tell me where she is," Mookie growls through gritted teeth. *"Where is Nora?"*

"Daddy is mad-dy," Smiley gurgles.

A baring of those fangs. Jaw snapping, teeth clacking.

It's then Mookie sees–

The fangs oozing dark fluid. Each clack milks more from the glands–

Mookie tilts his head to the right just as the Naga spits a jet of venom.

It misses. Hits a table behind them. *Squit.*

Mookie punches him in the mouth. Fangs break. A stupid move. If those fangs cut his hands, if the venom got into his bloodstream...

He finds he doesn't care. A dangerous place to be, but fuck it. All he does is ask the question again:

"Where is Nora?"

The tentacles tighten around him. Now it's not about trying to hurt Mookie – he's too jacked up for them to get much purchase, and despite Smiley's subterranean lineage, this Naga is not a trained assassin. Just a broker for information, not a fighter. Now it's about trying to get away – he's trying to wrench himself free, trying to fling himself to the far corners of the room where he'll slither out through some hidey-hole (being boneless can really have its advantages).

But Mookie isn't giving quarter. He just slams Smiley back into the wall.

"Where."

Slam.

"Is."

Slam!

"Nora?"

SLAM.

Smiley spills. "She's–" *Hiss.* "Holed up with the Get-Em-Girls."

"I know that part." *Slam.*

"Not up top! They have an enclave. Down below. Connected to a warehouse in Hell's Kitchen–"

The floor shakes. The whole teahouse shudders.

The fist comes down on the back of Mookie's head like a boulder toppling off a mountain peak. Appropriate, since the fist is made of rock.

A garden of pain blooms behind his eyes.

Mookie lets go of Smiley. The Snakeface thuds against the floor, wheezing–

And, sure enough, the Naga flings himself into the rafters of the room, swinging from beam to beam, clinging to each like an octopus in a tree–

Mookie turns, narrowly dodges another fist coming in from Gorth, the golem.

That granite fist craters a hole in the teahouse wall.

A kick follows fast after. Mookie ducks it, gets under the foot, grabs the craggy heel. Then he gives it the old heave-ho. Gorth cries out as the massive rock-body turns a teahouse table into long splinters.

Mookie knows that punching Gorth isn't going to do him any good. Hit a Trogbody and all you get for your trouble is a hand that's no longer a fist and is now a floppy skin-sack holding shattered bone-nuggets. As the golem struggles to stand, Mookie reaches into his satchel, and catches the sheathed cleaver as it tumbles out.

He utters a silent "thank you" to Karyn, then frees the blade from its sheath.

Gorth lurches to his feet. Quartz eyes gleaming red – a lava furnace of anger behind those crystal pockets.

Mookie spins the cleaver so it's the flat back of the blade facing forward.

The golem lunges.

Mookie brings the back of the cleaver down hard on Gorth's skull.

Sounds like a gunshot. The head cracks – a fissure split from forehead to skull peak, a mini canyon formed along the ridge of his uneven stone skull. From within the rift, a faint magma glow. Gorth makes a moan like a distant foghorn; then he hits the ground, utterly and eerily still.

The floorboards lie cracked and buckled beneath him.

The golem's head sizzles. Steam rises.

Mookie kneels down, pats Gorth on the shoulder. The golem will heal up eventually – the poor lunkhead will need to spend some time back down in the dark, patching himself up. But for now, he's out of commission. And Mookie, chest heaving, body throbbing, nerves jumping like sparking wires, doesn't see the Snakeface anywhere. The slippery sonofabitch must have gone up into a duct or something.

No more time to waste here.

He needs to find the Get-Em-Girls. He needs to find Nora.

11

The horror of the half-and-half is unparalleled. Consider it: you are a child with only one human parent. Your other parent is no parent at all, merely a contributor of darkly squirming seed, a mote of ill magic spawned in the cracks and crevices of the Great Below. It happens however it happens: a man stumbles into a storm drain or rocky grotto, is seduced by gobbos who to him look like lovely lasses with their bosoms bared. Or shadows creep up from the fraught fissures and take a woman in her bed – either by the lie of a human façade or by malevolent force. The result is always the same: a pregnancy. If it is the monster that is full with child, then that child will most likely be born down in the dark, and its humanity will forever be a liability. At its best, gobbos sometimes use such hybrid children as mules. At the worst, they are sacrifices to the deepest gods or test subjects for some strange new weapon. If it is a human mother whose belly has grown round with the dread energies of the Underworld, then she will most surely perish during birth; I've not yet heard of one who survived. The child is ever part human, yes – in all the weakest ways. And also part monster, in all the strangest ways. The design of the monstrous half cannot be predicted as it follows no discernible pattern nor does it seem related to the inhuman parentage. I've seen and heard tell of half-and-halfs who look like minotaurs or mermaids, or who have the flesh of reptiles or the insect limbs of pale cave crickets. One thing can be sure: they are embraced by neither world but possess the power and frailty of each. Our world sees them as human, but a human that doesn't quite seem right. The world

below sees them as human, too – a human that will never belong. It is a
horror, to be sure, but in my most sleepless nights I wonder if I would've
been better born among them. I feel as a man between worlds.

– from the Journals of John Atticus Oakes,
Cartographer of the Great Below

Werth's phone rings. He fishes for it in his pocket, tilts it up–

It's Mookie.

"Mook," Werth says, answering.

"Where you at?" Mookie asks.

"Out." He clears his throat. "And about."

"I got a line on Nora."

"Good. Whatcha got?"

"She's with the Get-Em-Girls."

Werth sniffs. "You don't say."

"Yeah. They got a little place carved out of the Great Below. It's a warehouse in Hell's Kitchen. I think I know the place. Couple blocks from Port Authority. I think the place is a gateway to the Deep Downstairs." Upstairs, downstairs. This world, that world. Earth, and Hell. Werth doesn't like that place. He likes it up here.

"And you think Nora's with them," Werth says.

"I talked to Smiley. He'd know."

"Good. I'll meet you there."

"How close are you?" Mookie asks.

"I'm uhh, a ways away yet."

"I'm in Chinatown. Meet there?"

"See you inside of an hour – 46th and 10th."

Werth punches the end call button.

Then he looks up at the warehouse where the Girls are hiding Nora Pearl. He reaches in the trunk of his 1988 Cadillac Seville, pulls a Winchester Super X 12 gauge from inside. Thumbs five shells into the gun's undercarriage, saving the sixth for the chamber.

He slides the action forward, thumbs the safety off, and heads toward the warehouse door. It's a vertical warehouse – tall, narrow, brick the color of dried blood. Looks like an old fire station.

Door's got a cage over it. Locked with a chain-and-padlock.

If Mookie were here, Werth might be able to ask the big lug to just punch it into smelt. Or bite through it like a circus performer. But this isn't a job Mookie needs to be around for. It's 4am, nobody's really up yet, and it's the same city it always was where something bad happens and nobody calls the cops...

Werth stands back. Levels the gun.

Choom.

The lock blasts open.

The cage grate squeaks open.

Werth tries the door behind it. Unlocked. Good.

Into darkness, then. He can make out shapes. A desk to his right. Ahead, narrow shelves with narrower aisles. They look empty, but it's hard to tell. He thinks to pull out the little flashlight he's got in his pocket, but all a flashlight does in a situation like this is give someone something to shoot at.

Instead, he creeps. Let's his eyes adjust. Creeping doesn't come naturally for him. He's got a limp and, to those who can see them, a pair of cracked goat hooves that would easily fit a set of Clydesdale horseshoes. Even if someone were looking at him blind, they'd still *hear* the way he clomps around like a clumsy donkey.

So, creeping takes extra effort. It's almost comical, he figures – raise one leg up, bent at the knee, gentle fall. Like Elmer Fudd sneaking up on that asshole rabbit.

He manages.

And his eyes adjust.

He keeps his finger on the shotgun trigger. Just in case.

He does a serpentine. Down one aisle. Up another. Sees now that the stacks are metal frames with splintery plywood shelves. And, like he figured, nothing on them but cobwebs and little herds of tumbling dustballs.

Finally, he makes the whole circuit.

Nothing. And no one.

Certainly no floor blown out. No way to the deep downstairs.

They're gone. Those squirrelly bitches up and left. They knew they were on the radar, and so they set up a dummy location for just such a time like this. Confirms doubly that Nora isn't operating alone; they're with her on this. With her lock, stock, and barrel.

And suddenly it makes sense. The front door is padlocked. On the outside. Nobody goes out that way. Comes in, maybe. But never goes out. This is just a ruse. A front.

Shitfuck.

He's not going to get to kill Nora Pearl today. And that, make no mistake, is what he's here to do: kill that little bitch. She tweaked Mookie's head last year, led him around by his nose until he cleaned out that big nest of goblins, then took over a little slice of the Blue trade. She's been moving and shaking ever since, and now to hear that she killed Casimir which means she's probably gunning for the Boss, well...

Oh, and then there's that other thing – *she shot Werth in the fucking hip*. He owes her for the limp. He owes her ten times what he got in pain.

So to lose the chance to pop her today...

Whoa, hold up. What's this?

Werth sees something. Just a shape of an image on the back brick wall.

Flashlight time. He pops the flashlight, turns it on, screws it between his lips like a fat cigar, and walks forward.

Well, looky-looky.

It's their mark. Their sigil. Painted on the wall like graffiti.

A girl's hand. Thorn tat on the wrist.

The hand holds an upside-down roller skate like it's a gun. The skate is Pepto pink. The wheels are robin's egg blue. Their gang colors.

Inked on the side of the skate: GEG.

Get-Em-Girls.

They use this sign to mark their territory. Which encompasses parts of Hell's Kitchen – oh, pardon, *Mid-Clinton-West-Town-Bullshitland* or whatever they're calling it now – and the northernmost blocks of Chelsea. That means this is their place. Or was, at least.

Werth runs his hands over the mark.

The floor judders beneath him. Just a faint tremor.

He starts to wonder what that means, but doesn't need to wonder long.

Because the floor drops out from under him, and he plummets into darkness.

The flashlight spins in the air. Drunken strobe.

Werth sees he's falling down a cylindrical shaft.

Sees more red brick.

And a ladder, too – a metal ladder bolted in. He reaches for it – the gun falling from his hands – and he starts to catch a cold rung, but he's falling too hard, too fast. His wrist twists. He yelps in pain. His body bounces off the shaft wall. His head hits the ladder – *gunggggg* – and stars explode behind his eyes.

Then the ladder is gone.

So too is the brick.

His hooves hit rocky ground. Pain shoots up into his hip.

That old wound reawakens like a sleeping dragon with a forge-hot sword shoved up its nethers. It's lightning and salt, fire and spear. Werth drops, rolls onto his side.

He whimpers.

He *hates* that he whimpers.

His eyes adjust. It doesn't take long.

It's lit down here. With torches bolted to rocky walls. And a shitload of candles.

Mattresses on the floor. Couple wooden barrels and oil drums – some holding candles, others turned into tables. Posters on the wall: old movie advertisements. *Scarface. Taxi Driver. Zardoz*, of all things. On the black, wet walls are pink and blue spray paint. GEG. Graffiti images of skates. Some held like guns, as in their mark. Others upright, with blue flame belching out of the top.

Not far away is the shotgun.

Werth reaches for it.

An oxblood Doc Marten stomps down on it. And pulls it away.

Shadows encircle and close in.

Here comes the girl gang.

Faux 1950s punk abounds. Hairnets and garter belts. Polka dots and cherry lips. A whiff of Rosie the Riveter meets the girls from *Grease*, with a heavy vibe of neo-future dystopian Bettie Page.

A dozen of them close in. Like wolves descending upon a fallen goat.

One steps out past the gang line. Ravensblack hair with a shock of electric blue bangs. Black button down shirt and jeans so tight they may be spray-painted on. Hanging at one side, off the girl's neon blue belt, is a pair of nuclear pink skates. Hanging at the other side is what looks to be a Bowie knife held fast in its sheath.

She's a kid to him – he's got twenty years on her at least – but older than most of the girls here.

Werth knows her. Or, knows of her.

She's the head of the Get-Em-Girls. Has been for damn near a decade. Kelly McClure is her name.

But she goes by "Skelly".

As evidenced by the white skeleton stitched into the thighs of her jeans.

And the ink-black skulls stitched into the sides of her hot pink skates.

And the silver skull – mouth open in horror – that tops the Bowie knife's hilt.

She rests her hand on that silver skull just now. Blue nails clicking against it.

"What's buzzin', cousin?" Her voice is a long slow pull of whiskey. Not the gargling glass cheap shit, but smooth stuff. An expensive pour that goes down like warm butter. "You're Werth. I got that right?"

"Yeah, that's–" He winces. Even talking sends jags of pain into his hip. "Yeah."

Skelly looks to another girl: a real dieselpunk sweetie, cherub cheeks and thick hips and a tat of a big-ass fire-wreathed wrench on her one bicep. "Lulu, gimme the gun."

The other girl tosses Skelly a gun. *His* gun. The shotgun.

Skelly looks the gun up and down. Then she racks the pump – the shell currently in the chamber flips out onto the hard rocky ground.

She does it five more times. Shells bouncing on stone. Until none are left.

Then she hands the gun back to Lulu.

"We don't like guns," she says.

"I know."

"You brought a gun into our home."

"And what a nice home."

"It does us all right."

"I gotta ask, though. You ladies piss in a communal bucket? What do you do with your tampons? Just fling them into the corner? If you're all on the same cycle–"

She steps forward, puts her boot on his hip. And presses down. Misery. Sheer misery that refuses to stay contained to that one space. It's like touching a downed power wire. White. Hot. Cold. He cries out. She steps off.

He has to blink back tears. Suck back a snot bubble.

"You know," she says, "being a woman isn't easy. It's tricky sometimes. But I'll tell you if there's one advantage we have, it's that everybody always seems to underestimate what we can and will do. Men, mostly – but even other women do it. Isn't that sad? It lets us get away with a lot, daddy-o. Lets us pull little surprises. Lets us get *tricky*."

"Fuck you."

"You want me to stand on that broken coat-rack you call a body again? Maybe we'll all have a go. Use you like a trampoline. Sound fun, sugarplum?"

He winces past the pain and offers a placating smile. "My... *apologies*. Ma'am."

"That's better. I like a puppy knows when it's licked. Keep showing your belly and maybe you'll get out of here alive."

"Wasn't sure that was an option."

Now a new voice: "We need a messenger."

He knows that voice.

He heard it *one time*. And it told him *sorry* just before a bullet tore into him.

Nora Pearl. *Persephone.*

She steps up. And he can see that she's not with these girls. Not really. Nora looks like she did a year ago, if a bit more made-up. But it's still the same costume: navy cardigan, a tartan skirt. Like she's jailbait, still in high school.

Werth can't even think of something snappy to say. He just waits there. Seething.

"You look a little pale," Nora says to him. "You feeling OK?"

"I should kill you."

"That's what you came to do. Isn't it?" With the toe of her shoe, she kicks a few 12-gauge shells around. "Oops."

"You're in deep water, little girl."

"To carry the metaphor, I'm actually sailing *on top* of the water in my pretty pink sailboat. You're the one sinking beneath the water, dude. You just fell two stories. Possibly broke your leg or, at the least, aggravated an old wound–"

"An old wound *you gave me*."

"And to make it worse, your Boss is dying. And everyone knows it. You know how everyone knows? Because I told them. They're going to come for you guys. And they're going to tear your little Organization apart, limb by limb."

"The Organization is all you piss-ant gangs have protecting you from the–"

"From the Underworld?" She snorts. "Please. I think you're keeping us *from* it. Keeping us from *all the awesome*. We want to get rich and you won't let us." She fakes a pout. "You've gotten fat and comfortable in your beds and didn't see the rats in the walls, Werth, but the rats see you." She mimes a rat gnawing and nibbling. Then laughs.

"From sailboats to rats. Now you're mixing your metaphors."

"I'll assume you can keep up."

"You're father doesn't know I'm here. Just so you know." He clears his throat. "This is all me, little girl."

"My father can go fuck a duck."

"Interesting image. He loves you very much, you know. He shouldn't. But he does."

Another laugh, this one loud and echoing and hollow. "Right. Love. Like he loved my mother? The only thing Mookie loves is you and your Boss. He loves the work so much it's not even work. *I* was always the chore. The hard work wasn't going down into the dark. The hard work was just… sitting with me. Playing dollies. Listening to my stupid stories. Pretending we were cooking food for princesses and presidents." She sighs. "After he left us, I asked him to stay… I don't know how many times. He never did. Not once. So don't sell me on his love. It's a lie, a scam, a joke."

"If you say so."

"I do."

"You said you needed a messenger."

"Yup. I want you to send a message to your Boss and all his people. Actually, I want you to tell everyone."

"Tell everyone what?"

"That I killed Casimir Zoladski. And I'm just getting warmed up."

As if the fall wasn't enough, they worked him over pretty good. The one called Lulu picked him up. Got a belt around his neck. Held him as the others brought the gauntlet to him – Skelly clubbed him with her skates. Another chick in a slashed-up mint-green poodle skirt whacked him in the face with an old-timey sap – he didn't even know they *made those* anymore. The rest just got him with fists and elbows and feet.

Then they dragged him up the ladder by a pulley. A pulley system on an old track high up in the warehouse ceiling – way they moved things around before forklifts.

Skelly patted him on his head, and then stole his tin of Blue. That crafty twat. He could've used that to feel better – a temporary fix, but a fix just the same.

After that, she tossed him out onto the sidewalk. Wound a chain around the broken lock and then popped a fresh padlock on it. Then: she was gone.

Now: everything hurts.

His head pulses like a balloon someone's flicking with an annoying finger. *Thwump thwump thwump.* He tastes his own blood. Spits it out – with it comes a tooth that clatters into the street just as an off-duty street sweeper truck passes by. He hopes that it's his dead tooth, but it's probably not. His luck it's probably one of the still-good ones.

He can barely stand. His leg is shaky, the pain almost liquid now. Sloshing up and down from heel to hip. He's not sure anything's broken. But something's torn.

Into the car. Glove compartment. Got a bottle of Vicodin. Pop the cap. Dry-crunch a couple like they're Tic-Tacs.

His phone rings.

Haversham.

Werth answers, starts to say, "You wouldn't believe–"

"Things have changed," Haversham says.

Werth listens, and it feels like the floor is dropping out from under him again – falling, falling, his guts, his heart, his head.

"OK," Werth says. Voice raw.

"We need you back. Come to the house."

"The house. Yeah."

Haversham ends the call.

Werth sits for a few minutes. Staring at the center of his steering wheel. Like it's an eye staring back, or a mouth trying to draw him close in order to eat him.

Finally he breaks the spell, starts the car, and gets the fuck out of there.

12

Some say that the Underworld is the Hell of all the myths: that it is a prison. Some say that God built it, though then others ask, why would God build such a thing? How mad must God be? The easy reply is, of course: quite mad, indeed. God's actions throughout history, if you believe in him and the purity of the Good Book, have been the actions of a psychopath. Just the same, it's difficult to reconcile the images of Hell and the ways of a Christian God with the existence and function of the Great Below – the Great Below has very few dead, after all. Some shufflers, some ghosts. But most of what lurks in the dark are not creatures of spirit; these are no spectral entities. They are flesh and blood. Gray flesh and black blood in the case of the goblins. Stone and sap in the troglodytes, slick scale and toxic slurry in the Nagas. I have heard one theory that works toward bridging the gap, suggesting that the gobbos – and perhaps the other denizens of the deep – are reincarnated sinners. Die as a sinner, be reborn as a grub in the subterrestrial prison below our feet. If that's true, if the Underworld really is a kind of jail, then it further explains why so many of the creatures just want to be free of it – at any cost.

– from the Journals of John Atticus Oakes,
Cartographer of the Great Below

Werth sits. At a kitchen table at the Boss's house – one of two kitchens, it turns out. This one has lots of white tile and dark wood, big stainless steel appliances. Two ovens. Pots hanging from a pot rack, occasionally drifting into one another – *clunk, clank, clink*. Doesn't look like anybody ever uses this kitchen – though the central butcher block has square-shaped stains on it. Maybe that's where they put the takeout containers.

He wants to lie down. Take a long nap. A long nap in a deep grave, with roots and worms and cold earth to keep him comfortable for the rest of eternity.

It's not just the pain – which by now has fought past the Vicodin like a distemper-sick dog chewing through a door.

But that's not what's really bothering him.

Haversham said, "The Boss is sick."

Master of the Obvious over here. But then Haversham said, "*Very* sick," and gave a gray-faced look, the look of the tomb, a look of fear. Werth asked how long the Boss had left. All Haversham would say was, "He's upstairs."

And then: "Things have changed."

Now Werth sits. And waits. Not sure what the hell comes next. Did they call Mookie? Is this whole Nora Pearl thing going to fall by the wayside? On the one hand, that'd be a good thing. But Werth wants to put that brat six feet deep.

A tired-looking Haversham rounds the corner. Hands held in front of him like he's an old woman pinching a coin purse to her belly.

Werth's about to speak up, but then–

Two more follow him in.

The fedora-and-beige-suit motherfucker. Candlefly. And his "associate" – the slimy one. The *Snakeface*.

Werth tries to stand. His left leg wobbles, the knee about to hyperextend. Haversham urges him to sit.

"I'll sit when I'm good and–" He winces. "Ready."

"Fine," Haversham says. His fingers working against other fingers. A nervous tic?

"Who the fuck are you?" Werth asks the two men.

"I'm Ernesto Candlefly. This is my associate. Mr Sorago."

"A Snakeface."

Candlefly corrects: "A Naga, yes. He prefers that term."

"I give a shit what he prefers."

Sorago hisses. Candlefly steadies the Snakeface with the flat of his hand.

The man in the suit continues. "I've been brought along to handle some of the business concerns as the Boss concentrates on improving his health."

Improving his health. It's terminal lung cancer.

"You. A guy the Boss just met yesterday."

"We've known each other for a while. We've been associates at a distance."

"Associates at a distance."

"Yes. My family imports Cerulean–"

"You're an addict."

"No. Oh, no. I never touch the stuff. But I do think it has value in the… broader market. It's becoming quite trendy."

Now Werth's nervous, too. He's not a fan of change. He likes things a certain way, and it's been that certain way for as long as he can remember. He feels like the ground is moving beneath his feet. Like the earth is going to swallow up him and crush him with teeth of stone and tongue of dirt.

Worse, he either has to sit down or fall down. The pain forces him to choose, and so he chooses to sit. The moment he does it, he's afraid it makes him look weak. But what's done is done: you can't put the snakes back in the can.

"Now," Candlefly says. "We have come across some… information. A troubling secret that was, I'm sure, kept from *all* of us. Did you know that Mookie Pearl has a daughter? Did you, Mr Werth?"

Shit shit shit. He musters an incredulous frown. "I know he had a family. Has. Whatever."

"Do you know who this daughter is?"

"Mmnope," Werth says. He's a good liar. But Candlefly looks like the type who can smell a lie the way a wolf smells prey from miles away. Still, Werth continues the blustery charade: "No idea who she is. CEO of Who-Gives-A-Shit, Inc.? President and dictator of I-Give-A-Fuckistan?"

"His daughter is the girl seen on the security cameras. The one we thought killed Zoladski's grandson. The one who calls herself Persephone."

Werth's no actor, but he feigns a look of shock and disappointment.

"You don't think it's Mookie that killed the grandson."

"That *is* what we think. The damage done to the body is in line with the man's... strength, is it not?" Candlefly laughs again. "He's positively giant. I don't know that I've seen any human so big." The laugh dies on the vine. "He's a murderer and the Boss would like his revenge."

"I don't buy it. Mookie's loyal."

"Are you sure? He's not loyal enough to tell us that the criminal and murderer known as Persephone is actually his daughter, Eleanor."

Now it's Werth's turn to laugh. "Not loyal enough to tell *us*? There's no *us*. There's the Organization, and then there's *you*. You come up in here like you're the new Boss and–"

The assassin moves. He steps past Candlefly, a gun materializing out of nowhere – a Snakeface trick for those who have learned it, for those Nagas in the killer's caste. The gun is small, a little four-barrel derringer, and by the look of the size of those barrels (big enough for a pinky finger each), it's a .357 or higher.

Werth winces, shields his face–

But Candlefly steps in. Eases the gun aside. With a gentle head nod, the assassin retreats and goes back to leaning on one of the stoves. Werth looks; the gun is already gone. As if it never existed.

What's left behind, however, is a bad thought hanging in the air like a rotten stink:

Candlefly is the new Boss.

Which means the old Boss is dead.

The goat-man knew, of course. That Eleanor Pearl was – *is* – Mookie's daughter. That's fine. It irritates Candlefly a little that the man would lie, but the lie is expected. He'd do the same. The irritation is irrational, and Candlefly doesn't appreciate irrationality, especially within himself.

The half-and-half goat-man, the satyr Werth, is about to speak up – but Candlefly holds up a silencing finger. The old goat is wise enough to heed the gesture, though Ernesto can see his ratty goat-ears flatten in anger.

"Where is he?" he asks James Werth.

"Where's Mookie? I'm not telling you that."

"I understand your loyalty to your soldier, but that time is done. Your loyalty goes up the chain, not down it. Does it not?"

"It does."

"Are you Mookie's boss? Or is he yours?"

Werth doesn't say anything. Just stands there, smoldering.

"Pearl has left you vulnerable. Swinging in the wind, as the saying goes. By not telling you, he makes you seem complicit in all this. You're not, are you?"

"I want to go," Werth says.

"Can I show you something, first?"

Hesitation. "Mookie didn't kill the grandson."

"You seem sure."

"I am sure. He's not like that."

"I want to know where he is."

"So you can kill him."

Now, Candlefly's turn to not say anything.

Werth says, "Sorry. No can do."

"Like I said: let me show you something. Then we'll talk."

"You gonna kill me?"

"It is not part of my plan."

He sees that flash of uncertainty. The half-and-half doesn't believe him. That's OK. Candlefly smiles. Offers up both hands in surrender. "Please. This'll only take a moment. I want to show you how I learned about Mookie's daughter. Will you permit a stranger a moment of unearned trust?"

There comes a moment when Werth thinks, maybe I'll just kill this motherfucker. Candlefly's gotta go. I'm not a killer, but I've killed. I'm older now. Slower. And I hurt like I just got thrown onto the highway and hit by every truck, bus, and car driving down it – but I can do it.

Part of it is the way Candlefly moves. Something about him radiates gentility – a refinement that suggests he doesn't have the stones for a real scrap. Sure, he can point his finger and make people do stuff. Anybody with money has that power. But the way he moves is like water following the path of least resistance. Soft-wristed gestures of the hand. The way his head rolls loose on his neck like he doesn't have a care in the world.

All this in contrast to the Boss, who for an old fucker is still a pit bull. Last year Werth saw Zoladski stick a knife in the arm of Jamarcus Kensie, a thug up out of the Black Sleeves gang. They were sitting across from each other, and Jamarcus was starting to get ballsy, dropping verbal jabs and slinging smart-ass bullshit that was about as subtle as a machete to the neck. The Boss moved quick. *Snick-click.* Switchblade. It spun in his hand. Blade up, then down, then slammed between the two bones that made up Jamarcus's forearm.

Kathunk.

Boss said that's how you do it. Never stick 'em in the hand. Those two bones, you can pin anybody anywhere. Boss said, "That's how they pinned Christ to the cross, you know."

The Boss is a tough nut. A hard lump of coal.

Candlefly is a piece of chocolate melting in a hot hand, a long lash of tall grass swaying in the slightest breeze. He's both a prick and a pussy.

Not impressed, Werth thinks.

So: kill him. That's what's got to happen. Except the Snakeface is here. But then: suddenly, he's not. He stays in the kitchen as Candlefly leads Werth along the downstairs hall. Candlefly walks, head tall. Werth hobbles. And all the while the man in the sharp tan suit is talking, saying, "I understand that you and Pearl have worked together a very long time–"

"Almost twenty years now."

"That kind of time forges bonds. So, I understand your reticence to give me the location your friend. Have you ever run a business before?"

"Eh. No."

They get to a door in the hallway. Werth knows where it goes: the wine cellar. Candlefly puts a hand on the knob, but doesn't turn it. "A business can live by men and their specialties, but it can also die that way. For instance, you have an employee who can do *one thing really well*. He's a gifted contract lawyer. Or he knows the ins and outs of your software. Perhaps he folds laundry with great elegance. While you have him, he improves business. But if you lose him? He takes that knowledge with him. This *hurts* business. You must *spread out the knowledge*. Create a little redundancy."

Werth clears his throat. Nods at the door. "We going downstairs?"

Thinks, Soon as he opens that door, I'm going to kick him down those goddamn steps.

But Candlefly ignores him. Keeps holding the door closed. "What we have here in the Organization is a business. But we have those with specialized knowledge. Effective while they're here, but..."

"You mean Mookie."

"I do mean Mr Pearl, yes, yes. He runs his own crews. He knows where the veins of Blue are. He knows and does *so much* in this business."

"He's just a soldier. I know everything he does."

"Do you? Really? Twenty years... I'm sure by now he does things his own way. Without your prompting. And when was the last time you went... *downstairs*?" He doesn't mean the basement. "Been a while, hasn't it."

"You don't know that."

"You let him handle things. That OK. It's a scary place."

"I'm not afraid of shit, pal."

But he is. He is afraid. Candlefly knows it somehow. Candlefly laughs.

"Oh, I'm afraid of it, too. It's perfectly normal to be frightened of the Great Below. You know, I have a theory. It's because of the Underworld that we – we as in mankind – are afraid of the dark. Because down there, the dark is real. Tangible. Isn't it? Horrible things, unknowable things, hiding down there in the shadows. Sometimes those things come up. Sometimes they eat. Sometimes they kill. Sometimes they..." A cruel twinkle in his eyes – he doesn't have to finish the sentence: *Sometimes they rape young women who end up having little goat babies just before dying.* "You come from that place. Part of you. And you hate it. And that's OK."

Werth is shaking now. He's trying not to but he is. He tells himself it's the Vicodin wearing off, that he needs a hit of Blue to calm him.

"I come from there, too, in a way. And I am not... able to return." Candlefly's entire body tenses as if he's experiencing a small moment of pain. "That's why I want to know what Mookie Pearl knows," Candlefly says plainly. "I want him to tell us what you and I do not know. I want to create a little redundancy. I don't want to kill him. I just want to talk."

"And *then* you'll kill him."

Another laugh. "No. Not necessarily. You say he's innocent."

"And you say he killed Casimir Zoladski. And in this town –
in this Organization – we deal with that kind of thing one way
and one way only."

"Maybe it's not true. Maybe I'm wrong."

"You really willing to find that out?"

"Of course. A good employer is a fair employer."

Werth watches Candlefly's eyes. Another difference between
him and the Boss. The Boss has sincere eyes. Hard like bullets.
Hot like cigar-tips. Candlefly's eyes are flashing lights. Shifting
left, right, shining bright.

Candlefly's got liar's eyes.

Werth nods. Lies right back. "Good. I trust you."

"Now," Candlefly says, "before we go into the cellar and I
show you something, I just want you to think about what you
want out of all this."

A radar ping in the back of Werth's mind. A selfish twisting
in his gut. "What?"

"Your reward. For being so loyal."

"Reward."

"Of course. Employees who go beyond the pale deserve
employee bonuses. You want a house here on the Upper West
Side? Done. A new crew? Easy. Something new to drive? That
can happen with a hand wave. Think about it, won't you?"

Then Candlefly opens the door.

Werth is left reeling. The gut punch of a sudden promise
– the potential for security, for *wealth*, is dizzying. He sees his
moment: Candlefly there at the top of the steps, looking back
at Werth with a smile on that handsome face.

"Coming?"

Werth swallows. Would be nicc to have a proper house in a
neighborhood like this one. All this time, people still treat him
like a freak...

"Sure. Yeah. Lead the way."

And the opportunity slips from his grip as Candlefly descends and Werth follows.

Werth's still got diamonds in his eyes as they reach the bottom of the basement stairs. Candlefly starts talking again, says, "You know the phrase, *carrot and the stick*? Some confusion over it. Some believe it's a carrot tied to the end of the stick – dangled at the front of the donkey's mouth so he moves the cart ever forward, the foolish ass thinking he's just one step away from a mouthful of delicious carrot. But that's not how I take it. I take it to mean that, in all things, we have two options: reward, and punishment. Honey or vinegar. Carrot and stick."

Werth's about to say something, but Candlefly turns on the light.

Revealed: the wine cellar. Oaken racks of dark bottles. In the back, a few cases of beer – good beer, not the cheap shit Werth likes to drink.

But none of that is as interesting as the man strapped to the chair in the middle of the floor. Werth knows him. How could he not? Mr Smiley's one of the biggest information brokers in the city.

He's a Snakeface. Doesn't look the part right now because Werth is standing here Blind. Now Smiley's just a man in a bright blue suit. Nice wing-tips. Manicured nails. And despite bring trussed up like a roast, he's grinning big and broad.

"Is all of this... truly necessary?" Smiley asks. The smile is strained. Lips trembling to hold their position. Werth can see that. The grin is big, but the eyes are dark. Suspicious. People tend to smile with their whole face, but this, this is just lips turning upward.

"You know him, yes?" Candlefly asks.

Werth nods. "Hey, Smiley. Surprised to see you here."

"Werth! My old *satyr* friend. Will you get me out of this chair?" Werth sees he's bound up with zip-ties. A lot of them.

Ankles and wrists, and then every two inches up the length. Too much for a man. Maybe not *enough* for a Snakeface. Especially one as slippery as Smiley. "It is *dreadfully* uncomfortable."

He's about to ask Candlefly what the deal is, but Candlefly's already talking.

"Smiley came to us. He had information we thought valuable. He's the one who told us that Mookie Pearl has a daughter, and that daughter is an enemy to our organization."

Smiley nods as much as the zip-tie around his throat and the belt around his forehead allow. "And your *hulking* associate made a dire mess of my teahouse. Not to mention cracking open the skull of my bodyguard."

Gorth? Mookie must have been pissed.

Smiley continues: "He didn't want that information about him and the girl let out. So I knew the first thing I had to do was come here and…" The smile broadens, tightens. "*Share.*"

"At what cost?" Werth asks.

"Oh, come now. I don't know what you mean!"

"You know just what the hell I mean. You didn't offer up this information out of the good of your heart." Werth looks to Candlefly. "He didn't, did he?"

A gentle shake of Candlefly's head. "No."

"What'd he want?"

"He had a laundry list of desires. A waive of protection fees for the next year, information on his enemies, a talk with the Lantern Jacks – who have been encroaching on his business in the last few months."

"Pumpkin-headed savages," Smiley says.

Candlefly lifts the back of his coat. From a back pocket, he pulls a small square box with a silver seal on it: a burning fly inside an old lantern.

He hands it to Werth.

"Fuck am I supposed to do with this?"

"Open it." Candlefly sighs.

He does. It's peacock powder. Smurf. Cerulean. It's untouched. A perfect little beach dune of blue dust. Does Candlefly not use? Does he *need* to use?

"I want you to *see*." Candlefly says.

"I know what Smiley is."

"Please. Just do me this concession." Candlefly, to make things clear, lifts his jacket, just to ensure that Werth sees the Walther hanging at his hip.

"Fine." Werth digs in a thumb. Takes too much – a callow and meaningless rebellion against this man – and smears it on each temple. The Blazes crackle and ripple. The pain of his body drifts out to sea. It's still there, but it's far off.

He turns. Sees the human façade fall away. The Snakeface is revealed. Squirming in his zip-tie bonds. Fangs clicking against fangs.

But then something else appears.

Something back among the bottles and barrels. A shimmer in the air, like a mist that dissipates when you look directly at it. A black shadow rises up through the floor as if the wood is insubstantial. Silver shining eyes. Fingers like scissors.

"Jesus. What… what is that?"

Candlefly smiles. Claps Werth on the shoulder. "I told you about the carrot. This is the stick."

Smiley cries out. Knows that something's wrong, that his time is coming. The Naga starts to thrash. The chair rocks back and forth. His mouth opens – a breathy hiss emits.

Smiley starts turning red. Body tensing.

His left arm starts to shift. Bulge like a hose with a kink in it, then squish down – it starts sliding through the zip-ties one by one. Swell up. Shrink back. Swell up. Shrink back. Then he starts freeing a leg – the shoe pops off, the whole foot tilts down at an impossible angle as Smiley starts to force it through each tight plastic loop.

The black shadow-thing moves fast.

Like a blanket it covers the top half of the Snakeface. Scissor-fingers plunge into the Snakeface's head and chest. Smiley spasms, body caught in the throes of a violent seizure. It isn't long before the spasms become a tremor and the tremors fade to a few myoclonic twitches. Those last shudders call to mind a piece of food being eaten. An apple. Or corn off a cob.

Candlefly squeezes Werth's bicep.

"Over here." As the shadow-thing... feeds, Candlefly brings over a leather bag. He opens it up. Inside: stacks of money. Twenties. Banded. "Here is the carrot. I want your help. I want you to tell me where your friend is."

"I... I can just call him. I'll have him come here."

"Yes. Do that. We need to know where he is."

"I already know where he is."

"Oh? Do tell, James. We can go pick him up."

Werth swallows a hard knot and gives the address to Candlefly.

Candlefly meets Sorago in the hall.

"Here's the address," Ernesto says, handing his old friend a written slip.

"I'll handle it."

"Let the Organization pick up the pieces on this one. Interface with Haversham, have them send a couple of their own to clean up the mess."

"And if they can't?"

"Then that's a win for us either way. The herd must be thinned. We must whittle this stick to a sharpened point." It was true. If the killers took care of Mookie and – bonus points – the daughter, so be it. If the Organization assassins ended up on the slab? Fine. At this point it was a numbers game.

"Pearl's a special case."

"Is he? He's the bull. We are the matadors."

"He's the one who saved the miner down in the tunnel."

"Was he?" That's news. "Perhaps he's a very lucky bull."

"Or smarter than we think."

"Hm. Fine, fine. Send some backup. Look to your friends in the caste."

Sorago nods.

"For the family," the Naga says.

Ernesto smiles. "May the Candlefly's light guide us through the dark."

13

The Underworld has many names because we have given it many names. The Great Below. The Deep Downstairs. Hell. Hades. Tartarus. Gimkodan. Naraka. It has many names and many places. This is not the only Underworld. There are many Hells beneath many parts of the world, all connecting at the bottom. The geography of our Hell is not fully mapped – it is a quantity that many have claimed impossible to know. But I feel differently. I feel it can be mapped. That its stories can and should be told. I will walk this sunless realm. I will start here, in the upper portions, in the place we call the Shallows. Then, into the labyrinth called the Fathomless Tangle. Then one day I shall find my way to the Ravenous Expanse. Where the eyeless gods of this place moan and gnash teeth the size of skyscrapers.

– from the Journals of John Atticus Oakes,
Cartographer of the Great Below

Nora fidgets. She chews an unpainted nail down to the quick. A bead of blood rises. She holds it up, sees the torchlight captured in the curve of the red.

"You sure that was a good idea, sugar?" Skelly asks her.

"It's part of the plan."

"A plan you just made up."

"We have to adjust. Things are… changing."

"You're bringing trouble to our doorstep."

"Part of the price." Nora shrugs. She tries not to act nervous, tries to act cool as an ice cube in a snowman's mouth, but all she can do is keep biting one fingernail after the next. "Nothing good is ever free."

Skelly paces. On one side of her face is the blue LED light from a camping lantern sitting atop an overturned oil drum. The other side, lit by firelight. A two-faced mask. Finally she turns, thrusts a finger up in Nora's face.

"You're playing with fire, kitten. You're telling them things just to rile 'em all up. I don't know if you have this all figured out as neat and nice as you want. There's gonna be blowback. I don't think you get that."

Everything's unstable, now. Things were supposed to go differently but they didn't and now here she is. Making up the story as it goes along.

"I get it!" Nora barks. "Jesus. What are you, my mother?" Calm down, you need these girls. "Listen. I know it's like I... threw a lit M-80 into a crowd. And maybe I did. But it'll clear a space. A space for me. For you. For the gang. I'll bring you guys with me. The Boss is sick. His grandson is..." Here she hesitates. Deep breath. "Dead."

Skelly walks up. Gets nose-to-nose with Nora.

Nora smells bubblegum and cigarettes.

"You better be right," Skelly says. "Because, baby girl, if you fuck us over or fuck us up, I'll crawl out of the corpse-pile dead or alive and skin you with *Santa Muerte* here–" The woman taps the hilt of the sheathed Bowie. "We square?"

"We're–"

Above their heads, above the floor, they hear a sound: *Whump whump whump*.

"Someone's here," Lulu says. Breathless with anticipation. Lulu seems to get off on this kind of thing. Fear. Danger. Like she's French-kissing Death in the broom closet.

Skelly shoots her a look. "Yeah, we got that, Lou." She turns to Nora. "They're here. Already. Let's hit the tunnels and–"

"No," Nora says. "If this was a hit squad they wouldn't be knocking. Listen to that sound." How loud it is. Him with those big stupid fists. Sometimes she thinks that's where the old man keeps his brains. "I know who it is. It's my father."

"See? Blowback's already started."

Another three knocks. *Whump whump whump*. Louder now. Skelly hisses, "What do we do?"

Nora jerks a thumb toward one of the posters. *Zardoz*. "I'm gonna hit the bricks. I've *got* to find some leverage. You stay behind. Talk to him. Throw him off my trail. Stay with him if you can. Last thing I need is that big dumb monkey messing up my plans."

"You really don't like him, do you?"

Nora doesn't answer. Instead she just walks over to the poster. Already two of the Get-Em-Girls are ahead of her – one in a pair of oil-stained denim overalls, the other in a black cardigan with a coffin stitched on the back, and in the front, cleavage so deep you could lose your car keys and money-clip down there. Maybe the whole purse.

The girls unpin the *Zardoz* poster at the bottom, then roll it up.

A tunnel is revealed.

Nora grabs one of the lanterns as Mookie knocks again.

Skelly and her share a look. Nora's not sure it's a friendly one.

She gives a flip little wave and a tight little smile even though her insides are a tumult of howling winds and breaking trees. Then she disappears down the tunnel and they re-roll the poster behind her.

Werth's not here and he's not answering his phone and Mookie's riding the razor's edge of this Blazes high – though by now it's not a razor's edge so much as it is the jagged teeth of a shattered mirror. By now the high is all coarse-grit sandpaper and hungry teeth.

So, hell with it. He stomps up to the door. Knocks three times. Figures he owes his daughter that much. Best not to come in hard.

Nothing.

Another three.

Goddamnit, Nora, answer the door.

He moves to the side. Peers in yellow-stained windows that are behind iron mesh like the door. Can't see squat. Goes back to the door. Rattles the chain and padlock. He wonders if they even come out through this door all that often. If they have a hole that takes them down into the Deep Downstairs…

That would let them move beneath the streets. Or even deeper. Hidden the whole time. Some gangs are smart and move that way. Not that the tunnels are safer than the streets – but that's the price you pay to stay outta sight. Plus, the dead-town of Daisypusher isn't even a half-day walk, sitting underneath both of the Marble Cemeteries on the East side. Go north and you'd get to Yonder, though the reasons for going there are few and far between. South you could work your way to the Oddments. Still, the tunnels in between are long and dark and full of who-knows-what. Gobbos. Monsters who are half-human but all-mad. Blue addicts. Cultists. Mole Men. Thugs who belong to Mookie and the Organization.

For now, he needs to refocus. He's up top. The sun'll be up soon. And he's got a door with a chain-and-padlock standing between him and his daughter.

He figures the heavy back-end of the cleaver will do the job.

But before he even gets to unsheathe it–

The door behind the cage opens.

He knows the woman. Skelly. Head of the Get-Em-Girls. She's an OK broad. Smart. Tough. Sassy. Doesn't take shit from anybody.

Pretty, too. He could stare into those eyes for hours. Not that she'd enjoy that. Having Mookie stare you down doesn't add up to a "romantic gesture" so much as it does the "piercing stare of a sociopath".

Still. Skelly's never done him wrong in the past. The gang makes a lot of noise about the Organization, but all the gangs do and he always figured it was part of their act: tough-talking authority-hating rockabilly roller girls, spitting in the eye of The Man, always wanting a bigger piece of the pie. They've never moved to do anything to back up all that boom and bluster.

But now Mookie's not so sure.

"Mookie Pearl," she says. "The biggest, baldest, most beautiful Daddy-o on the block."

He grunts. "Skelly."

"What's the tale, nightingale?"

"I'm bettin' you know why I'm here."

"I don't pretend to read minds. Though that's something I'd sure love to do. Can you imagine? Wouldn't you love to see what those dirty-birdies think about?" She tilts her head and the blue bangs hang like the tail-feathers of a drunken peacock. "Smart money says that everybody thinks about sex and death 24/7. I know I do. Sex more than death." She bats her eyelashes. "How about you?"

She's playing around, but Mookie can see it on her – the smile is forced. She's nervous.

"You have someone here."

"We have lots of someones here. But we don't run girls like that, Mookie. You want that sorta thing, you're gonna need to check with the Sinner Kids, maybe the Railroaders. I suspect they have a stable of beautiful honeys, oh, and boys too if you like that–"

"Stop. I'm looking for the girl calls herself Persephone."

"Ohhh. Don't you mean your daughter?"

A gut-punch. It staggers him. *That* information's getting out, then, too. Skelly eyes him. He doesn't say anything. He doesn't know how to answer that without getting himself in trouble. All Mookie can do is flare his nostrils, let out a short, sharp breath.

"We're all friends, here," she says. Gives him a wink.

Skelly pulls the chain around, unlocks the padlock.

She unlocks it, waves him inside.

And soon as he's through the door, a shotgun barrel jams into the side of his neck.

Figures.

They close the door behind him.

Soon as they do, Mookie grabs the shotgun by the barrel, yanks it out of the hand of the girl who's holding it. She yelps as he rips it from her grip. She breaks a nail in the trigger guard. He hears it snap. The girl turns away. He sees a fiery wrench tat on her bicep.

"You don't do guns in this gang," Mookie says. He points it at Skelly.

"We might've changed that policy. You don't know."

"I know now." He stares. "I don't have time to fuck around."

Skelly blinks. She's flanked by a couple other bad girls in thigh-highs. One's got a telescoping baton. The other a switchblade. They look confused, and give Skelly a quizzical look. She waves them off. Then she looks to the girl with the wrench tat."You OK, Lou?"

"Yeah." The girl cradles her paw. Mookie sees a little blood. Ripped the nail good.

He mutters a clumsy apology. Then a lightbulb flickers in the darkened refrigerator that is his brain. "Wait. Lou. You're Louisa?"

"Uh-huh. I go by Lulu."

"I know your girl, Karyn."

Lulu's face brightens. "Oh, hey. You know Karyn?"

"She's my butcher."

"She's beautiful."

"Yep."

"And her pussy tastes like angel sweat." Her lips suddenly wrinkle into an uncertain sneer. "Not that I've ever tasted angel sweat."

Mookie feels a bloom rise to his cheeks.

Skelly rubs her eyes. "Hey, dolls, this is sweet and all, but anyway to cut to the quick?"

"I want to see Nora," Mookie says.

"Don't think so."

"In case you missed the news, I've got a shotgun."

Skelly stands firm. "Ho ho ho."

"Jesus, Skelly, she's in trouble."

"She's just fine, Pops," says one of the stocking girls in the back. "You're the ones who are in trouble, Meat Man!"

Skelly shushes her. "Your babygirl's gone, you big gorilla."

"Gone. Like outta the gang gone?"

"Like, *not here at the moment* gone."

"So, she's coming back."

"She didn't say."

Mookie feels like a patch of skin got scraped off: rough, raw, abraded. "I don't got time for this."

"I'll tell you where she went," Skelly says.

"Will you, now? And what will it cost me?"

"You poppin' the clutch and getting' the hell out of here. Sound good, Pookie?"

"Pookie." He grunts. "Sounds fine. Where'd she go?"

"Jersey City."

"Jersey City. *Where* in Jersey City?"

"West side somewhere. I don't know. She knows a guy out there. Someone she's dating."

Mookie feels a hot steam blast inside: an acid reflux sear at the back of his throat. Jersey City is a shit-hole. And a maze, to boot. It will take him a while to get out there and put the word out that he's looking for her – he knows some folks in that direction, but not enough, not nearly enough, and soon as she sniffs the scent of him coming she'll be like a trapdoor spider back in her hole. And a boyfriend? A *boyfriend*? His daddy brain goes haywire, picturing her with some Jersey City shithead, him getting his greasy hands up under her shirt, the punk thinking he can do things to *Mookie Pearl's daughter*. And it's then and there that Mookie decides he's going to steal a fucking city bus and hit the Holland Tunnel and find this guy's house and drive the bus over his head.

Except–

Skelly's eyes. Her gaze flitting to him. Then the ground. Then to Lulu and they share a look, a look that doesn't take longer than a second sliced in half and it's then Mookie knows she's lying.

"Bullshit," he says, and he shoves past her. It is not a delicate shove, and Skelly almost loses her balance into the front desk.

Both of the garter belt girls step in front of him. One twirls the baton. The other flashes the switchblade in front of him – the swish of the blade cuts air in a sideways 8.

He holds them both off with the shotgun.

Mookie calls past the girls. "Nora? *Nora*, goddamnit."

"Back off, mister," says the Switchblade Sister.

"Yeah, get the fuck up outta here," says Baton Twirler.

Mookie ignores them. Stomps on the floor. Hears the boards reverberate. "She down there? I heard you got a hollow carved out for yourselves."

He goes to step past the two girls.

One swings the baton. The other comes at him with the blade.

Mistake. He blocks the baton with the shotgun, cracks her in the head with the stock of the gun. The other gets the shotgun's mouth smashed up against her nose. The knife falls out of her now-open hand, the blade stuck in the wood.

He stomps on the knife like a hammer pounding a nail. It's wedged in there good.

He calls again:

"Nora! *Nora.*"

He goes to take another step–

Skelly comes up alongside of him. He sees the glint of metal–

Then she sticks a giant Bowie knife up under his crotch.

"I'll spill your sugarplums, sugarplum. You know what happens to a testicle when it's pulled out of its sack? It unravels. Like a ball of yarn batted around by a mean old housecat."

"I just want to see my daughter."

"Rattle your cage all you like. That's not happening today, daddy-o."

He turns slowly. "You're making a mistake."

"Could be."

"You making a move at the Boss?"

"Could be that, too."

"Whole city does that, it'll be chaos. Already had the Lantern Jacks came at me. *They didn't make it.*" He sniffs. "This goes down, all the gangs are gonna want a piece of the island and what's beneath it. Bloodiest game of King of the Hill in history."

"Maybe we got an ace up our sleeve."

"You better hope."

Mookie's not real good at reading women, but he's damn good at reading criminals. And Skelly looks worried. All of them do. Skelly opens her mouth to say something and–

Gunfire.

Bullets pop and whine off the front of the building. Loud chatter. Fully auto. Punching holes in dirty glass. Mookie's about to yell for everyone to get down, and he reaches out with a massive arm to throw everybody to the ground–

But then he sees Lulu. Standing there stock still, the side of her neck open like a blooming rose. Blood starts to pump, a little at first, then a squirt. Her lips are red, too. A red far darker than her lipstick.

She starts to fall. Mookie reaches for her.

What he catches is a dead girl. Limp and lifeless. Eyes like the marbles in a mannequin's head.

Skelly's already crying out, running to the back. The other two girls follow with fleet feet–

Mookie hits the floor and army crawls to the door. He lifts up his cueball head, cracks the door and peers out. He has to know who's shooting at them. He wants to know who did this. So he can break a baseball bat off in their bowels. He thinks, it's gotta be a gang hit – they're all making moves now, all riled up and ready to dance–

His heart sinks when he sees.

The car is a black Cadillac Escalade. Two guys hanging out – a fat fuck out of the passenger side, a weaselface out the back window. Weaselface has a little Tec-9 submachine jobby, spitting fire and lead. The other has a long and mean AK-47.

He knows the both of them.

The Weaselface is Tommy Spall. The fat fuck is Karol Lutkevich.

Spall and Lutkevich. Two of the Boss's killers. Soldiers, technically, but specialized. Neither trucks much with the Blaze trade or the Underworld. They break legs, break heads, put bullets in hearts and brains.

Lutkevich changes the magazine. The Tec-9 in Spall's hands keeps on barking.

A couple bullets punch through the wood next to Mookie. For a moment he doesn't move. *Can't* move – pinned down. He's trying to parse this. What does this mean? The Organization's coming to hit the Get-Em-Girls? Are they here for Nora?

Or – and here, a chill runs over his hide like a tide of spiders – are they here for *him*?

He sees Lulu there. Bleeding out. Heels stutter-spasming against the floor.

He pulls the door, shoves the barrel out–

Takes a shot. *Choom*. The back window of the Escalade explodes in. The weasel – Spall – screams, his face suddenly a red mask of broken glass and buckshot.

It's enough. The fat fuck, Lutkevich, turns, sees that his partner's hit – he slides back over to the driver's seat.

People on the street are screaming. Running. Hiding.

Mookie's already up and out the door. Shotgun up. One blast, then another: both tires pop in a flip of black rubber ribbon. Spall, howling, leans out and fires a burst but the bullets go wild: he can't see anything through the blood.

Mookie shoots him in the head. A burping fountain of blood and brains.

Lutkevich: hand on the wheel, the AK up and pointed out the passenger side window. A chatter of bullets. Mookie ducks. Slides and slams his shoulder against the passenger side. Dents it. Soon as the bullets stop he throws open the door, slaps the rifle away with a meaty paw, drags Lutkevich part of the way out.

"You killed a girl in there," Mookie snarls.

"Suck my dick," Lutkevich says. Ballsy even still. "Time's over, Mook. New regime coming in. The Boss is sick. The prick kid is nowhere to be found. They want you dead."

Mookie closes the door on Lutkevich's head.

The man screams.

He keeps opening and closing the door until his head is shattered skull inside the meat-sack of ruined features. A broken vase in a bloody sock.

And then it's done. Both bodies, still.

Two of the Organization's own men. Dead by his hand.

That's a problem.

Somewhere in the distance: sirens. People hiding around corners, staring.

Cops. And soon: the Organization will come. They'll want answers.

They'll want his head.

Up here, he sticks out worse than a sore thumb. He sticks out like King Kong's dick. They'll find him soon enough if he hangs out here.

But...

Downstairs, they got nothing. He knows that place better than any of those assholes. Better than Werth, even.

He looks to the warehouse, and runs back inside to find the way down.

14

For as much as it is true that the Underworld is not a place of the spirit but rather a corporeal reality, that does little to negate the fact that the Great Below remains bound up with the energies of death. It has been seen from time to time that men who die upon the surface – men who die with purpose in their hearts, who die unexpectedly, who die in the hands of intense violence or grief-soaked tragedy – are given to leave their bodies as spirit and specter: a ghost of life, restless and insane. What is known is that these ghosts, when in proximity to a gateway into the Great Below, will eventually wind their way into that dark space. Wandering down, down, ever down. I've seen them here – the Cerulean gives me the sight. They move through the Shallows, toward the Tangle and through its catacombs. Though what happens if – or when – they reach the Expanse, I could not say.

– from the Journals of John Atticus Oakes,
Cartographer of the Great Below

Nora throws open the door to her apartment. Hurries inside, slams the door, chains it, turns all the locks, goes to the windows and closes the blinds and the curtains.

Then she sits. On the couch. Hands on her knees.

She starts shaking again.

Casimir is dead.

It hasn't caught up with her. Not yet. He's dead. And the blood is on her hands. Not literally, not anymore, but...

They were going to change things. *Together*.

And now...

Nora chokes back a sob. Kicks out with a foot, knocks over her coffee table. Everything feels like a rope slipping through her fingers, the frayed end almost in her hand and out of her grip.

All this time she thought she could go against her father, go against the Organization and control the Blue trade. What a joke. She had the money. She had no one or nothing holding her back. She played Mookie. Shot Werth. Bought some thugs. Got the Get-Em-Girls on her side. But she was David flinging stones at Goliath, and in *this* story, Goliath stomps David into a sticky puddle. The Organization came back on her like an ill-cracked whip. Her guys were bought back or killed. Her own Mole Men, executed down in the dark of the Underworld. Soon as those were gone, her territory was in the wind – the Organization soldiers took it right back. And then her Blue started to dry up.

She wants to bail. Get in a cab. On a train. Use the last bit of her money to hop a plane. Whatever, wherever. Just gone. *Run away*.

But then, another voice says: *you need to calm the hell down, bee-yotch. Focus up. You can fix this. You're already fixing this. The plan is the plan – you still need the gangs. You can still do this. Don't be a spaz.*

We do this right, we can still tear it all down and dance around in the rubble.

Then Daddy will listen. Then he'll really know who I am.

Nora feels under her couch. Pulls out the .38 she once used to pop a bullet into James Werth's hip when he caught her at her father's bar last year.

She knows what she needs. Time to make the gangs listen. Time to pay for their attention in the only currency that really matters right now:

Nora needs more Blue.

You're awesome, she thinks. You're a righteous mean-ass smart-ass little bitch.

Nora flips the cylinder. Sees the shiny ends of six .38 shells gleaming.

Then it's out the door to fix what's fucked.

The tunnel is lit with striations of pulsing light from squirming fungus tucked in the pockets of the open jaws and eye sockets of all the skulls lining the walls, one skull after the other, rows and stacks, not merely stuck to the rock but married to it as if they have always been a part of this place. The Blazes are like that: the blue stuff doesn't merely tear aside the façade to reveal the monsters, but when on it, the whole of the Underworld pulses with a different kind of energy. Like staring at the world under a blue light.

As Mookie charges forward, boots pounding on hard stone, splashing in murky puddles of water dripping down from the streets and sewer tunnels above his head – the Blazes crackle and hiss, the candles behind his eyes gone suddenly dark. It takes the wind right out of him. His legs buckle. He skids on limestone scree–

Mookie falls forward, catching himself on stinging palms.

Heavy breath. Labored. Wheezing. Too old for this. Too old by a country mile.

"You OK?" comes a voice from ahead of him. He's so disoriented that, for a moment, he doesn't know who it is. But then she says in that bourbon-and-smoke voice, "How's that classy chassis holding up, sailor?"

He hacks and coughs, suppresses a dry heave, and spits.

"Just fine. Drug picked a funny time to hit the bricks is all." He doesn't bother saying anything about that whole *I'm old and tired* business.

Skelly comes up, pats him on the shoulder. "Bluelight Special went dark, daddy-o?"

"Cut the slang shit." He stands – not easily, his legs still feeling like a couple Slinkies staple-gunned to his ass. She looks wounded. He mutters: "Sorry."

"You have blood on you."

He looks. He does. Hands. Shirt. It takes him a second–

"Lulu's dead," Skelly says. Is that fear in her voice? Anger? Both?

"I'm sorry."

He replays Lulu's final moments – open neck, blood up like from a water fountain, mouth agape, gone. And when she falls, he sees Karyn standing in her place.

Karyn. Shit.

Death is a fact of his life. He loses guys down here all the time. This isn't a forgiving place – it seems like the Grim Reaper has a house around every corner, in every pit, up every hollow shaft. Walls like these, lined with hundreds of human skulls, do little to shake the feeling. Whose skulls are these? He doesn't even know.

But it isn't about the dead. It's about those who get left behind. Survivors are like amputees: a part cut off them, a phantom feeling and false limb put in place as a piss-poor replacement. Hobbling around. Never quite whole again. He doesn't know how death is for the really truly dead, but for those left standing in its wake, it's the worst thing in the world. Like Karyn. Karyn, who thought maybe she was in love. Karyn, who had a partner in this life.

Karyn, who doesn't yet know that Lulu got a bullet to the neck.

A bullet maybe aimed for him.

Her blood is on him. In more ways than one.

The skulls around him no longer glow with swimmy, watery light – their open mouths and empty eyes have gone dark. The only light is from Skelly, who holds a torch – really, an old chair leg swaddled in gas-soaked rags and lit. The torch-flame pops and spits.

He wants to sit down in the silence and still cool air of this place.

He thinks, *just give up*. Let the gobbos come. Let them tear him apart, make charcuterie from his meat. Long pig pepperoni. Mookie salumi. Pearl prosciutto.

Or maybe one of the shadows would come for him. Sweep over him, silent as an owl, then down upon him–

But he's got work to do.

Mookie breaks the silence.

"Where'd the rest of your girls go?" he asks.

"Different tunnels. Split up just in case. All part of the plan."

"I need to know where my daughter is."

"I don't know where she is."

"It ain't Jersey City."

Skelly pauses. Eyes him up. "No. No it ain't."

Mookie pushes in against her. Chin out. Hands in fists. His shadow darkens her brow. "So then: where the fuck is she?"

That move – him standing there like a grizzly bear on its hind legs – usually gets most people to talk. Or at least flinch. Skelly stands firm.

"I *told you*, I don't know. That was part of the deal." She flips her Kool-Aid bangs back. "You really messed things up with her, you know. She's got it out for you."

"You don't get to tell me that."

"I'm just asking: were you a Bad Daddy, daddy-o?"

He shows his teeth. "You don't get to *ask* me that, either. I did the best I could."

"That so?"

No, he thinks. But all he says is, "Shut up and get out of my way."

"I'm coming with you."

He shoves past her. "No, you ain't."

She saunters after him, not as a trailing puppy but rather as someone confident in her inevitability to catch up. "Maybe I can help you."

"I don't need help. I do this alone."

"You need me."

"You're the enemy."

"Seems like maybe you're the one who's on the wrong side of this. Those thugs who shot at us – they were Organization men, weren't they?"

He doesn't say anything.

Finally, she asks, "You got a plan, then?"

He turns. Teeth grinding so hard they could mill wheat. "I'm gonna find out who killed Casimir Zoladski. Prove it wasn't Nora."

"Your daughter says she did the deed."

"What?" The air, sucked out of his lungs. "She tell you that?"

"She passed that message along. To your buddy. The goat-man."

Now: fire in his lungs. In his belly. Up his throat. "Werth came to you?"

"Mm-hmm. Was planning on killing her. Maybe killing all of us. She got the better of him. We roughed him up pretty good. She sent him home with a message: she killed Zoladski's grandson. Heir to the throne."

His head reels. He tries to imagine it: his daughter *murdering* someone. She said she was going to change things. But murder? He knew she'd gone mean, was maybe mean for a lot longer than he ever figured, but killing someone? That takes something he didn't know she had. You don't walk into their house and pulp their brains against the floor just because you can.

And *could* she have done that? Not by herself.

But then: a little tiny flare of hope, like a lit cigarette tossed up into the darkness. Skelly says, "I don't think she did it."

"Whaddya mean?"

"I know bad girls," Skelly says. "I'm a den mother to bad girls. Shoot, I'm a former bad girl myself. She's bad, all right.

Got a rattlesnake mind and bullwhip tongue. But I don't think she's *evil*. And that's what it takes to kill someone. You gotta have a little evil lodged up in there. Maybe a lot of it."

"What about you? You got evil in you?"

She hesitates. Steps closer. "Maybe a little."

"Me too." She presses herself against him. He smells her perfume. The lingering odor of an occasional cigarette behind it. He feels the heat coming off of her...

He shakes his head, pulls away from her. He says, "So I still need to find the killer. But I don't know how. I'm fuckin' lost over here."

"Too bad you can't just ask Casimir Zoladski himself."

It hits him like a fist.

"I can," he says.

"What?"

"I *can* ask him. I know someone." He waves her on. "C'mon. We need to head to Daisypusher. I gotta see a man about a ghost."

15

The gobbos are tribal. Possibly even hive-minded, as each individual gobbo seems confused, inept, like an ant who has wandered too far from the hill. But when together, they work together. They work as one. Tribal breakdowns do exist among them – some by belief, some by purpose, others by the way they look. Some gobbo groups are hunters, killers. Others are… well, I don't know that "religious" is the word, but they seem to congregate only at temples, gurgling and howling their dread songs to the Hungry Ones, the gods of this place. Some gobbos are fat and gray. Others pale, milky white, or with a rubbery, rusty skin. For a long time I thought that the Naga were the opposite: lone creatures, smarter by themselves than when together, generally distrustful of one another and operating on singular agendas. I no longer know if this is true.

– from the Journals of John Atticus Oakes
Cartographer of the Great Below

The two thug bodies fall like heavy rolls of carpet. They splash into the water of the sewer tunnel. Sorago quickly covers the manhole from underneath.

Two shadows emerge from the darkness of the tunnel.

Sirin and Sarnosh. Sirin of the golden eye. Sarnosh of the thick black scale. Both brothers in the assassin's caste. Two Naga loyal to Sorago. Loyal to the Candlefly clan.

Above, the sound of sirens. And humans, yelling. Such a
fearful, excitable lot. They're like ants whose hill was knocked
over by a child's boot.

Lucky to have rescued the bodies from the street before the
police arrived. The shootout with Mookie Pearl ended poorly
for the two human killers – for Sorago, that fact offers little
surprise. Those two were not assassins. They were dumb brutes.

But Sirin and Sarnosh...

At Sorago's nod, the two of them stoop by the two corpses.
Their teeth flick forward, glistening. They nip the necks of each
corpse. Fresh blood flows. Their tongues flicker out, catch a
copper smear on each, suck the blood back into their mouths.
Then they clamp their mouths on the wounds. Noisily gulping.

When finished, they stand.

Spall and Lutkevich's bodies are hollow, now: like tires,
deflated. Eyes bulge in shrunken faces. Fat tongues thrust out
of wine-dark lips.

Both of the Snakefaces shimmer. Their flesh rippling,
scales like an array of mirrors turning – and like that, they
are changed.

Spall and Lutkevich stand before Sorago. Over their own
dessicated corpses.

Dopplegangers. Fairly good ones, too – the eye color is
different (it always is); the skeleton beneath the skin isn't
quite right (it never is, and it's not even a skeleton so much
as it is a shifting cartilaginous mass meant to simulate a
skeleton).

But, otherwise, good enough.

Not-Spall and Not-Lutkevich step forward.

"Humans," Sorago says, making a face like he just ate a
week-dead rabbit. His fangs click together – the sound of a
thumb running across the tines of a plastic comb. "Inefficient
and weak. The only reason they have claimed the Infinite
Above is by dint of their number. But we start doing the good

work today, my brothers." And they really are his brothers. Both egg-mates from the same brood-whore. "You know the task at hand?"

They nod. Together Sirin and Sarnosh hiss: "May the Candlefly light the dark."

Sorago bends down. Grabs the cell phone off each thug corpse. Spies a flash of human pornography on the one screen: two women, each with her head between the other's legs. Like a crass facsimile of a Naga's breeding circle. He scowls, hands one phone to each of his egg-mates.

"I will call soon."

They nod.

"Destroy the remains."

Sorago turns and walks down the tunnel. As he does, he hears the sound of his brothers hissing and spitting on the three corpses -- the sizzle-pop of skin, soon the melting of bone. The smell in the air is one of vinegar and rot. Sorago smiles, and disappears into the dark.

Sorago stands in an alley between an open-air grocer and a small bakery. The human herd passes him by, bleating and bubbling. Unaware of who he is. To them he looks small, unassuming – a weak man unworthy of their gaze.

Camouflage, of course.

He dials Candlefly.

"My friend," Ernesto says.

Sorago explains what happened. Then adds: "Pearl is more of a problem than we anticipated."

He heard Candlefly *tut-tut-tut* on the other end.

"Surely, you don't think he can best you."

"Never." Sorago feels his pulse-beat quicken in his neck. The thought of some… lumpy, gone-to-seed human besting him? Is that even a meaningful question? Why would Candlefly ask him such a thing? A test. That's what it is. Always a test.

"He is but one problem of many. We have greater concerns."
On the other end, a liquid sound: Candlefly sipping a drink.
An espresso, most likely. "Sirin and Sarnosh are on the task?"

"Lieutenants. Then the gang-heads."

"Excellent. I want you to coordinate the next attack. If all is
to go as designed, we need the gateway opened."

"I shall lead the charge directly."

"No. We have the numbers. You won't be needed there. The
gob-folk will overwhelm those dead fools. You'll take one of
the Vollrath. Find the miner again. Morgan. Get what we need
from him. Don't let him escape without giving it up, this time."

"Yes, of course."

"And Sorago?"

"Master?"

"If you see Pearl or his daughter: end them yourself."

Sorago smiles. "I will deliver them into shadow."

"We didn't get the drop wrong?" Benny Scafidi asks, licking his
lips again and again – so often that the lips and the skin around
them are chapped. He just can't help it. He licks 'em to get 'em
wet, but then they get dry again and it's all: *lick slurp lick*.

The other Mole, Jenny Greenteeth, scowls at him and bares
her rotten chompers. "This is the place. I'm not a goddamn
idiot, Benny."

The two of them stand underneath the High Line Park
trestle. Benny's clutching a brown paper bag to his chest, a
narrow shoulder-width alley to his back.

"I'm just saying," he says. "Mookie would've been here by
now. Right?"

"Somethin' fuckin' goofy is going on," Jenny says, picking
at a pimple embedded in her eyebrow. "You know how I'm
stickin' it to that bag-boy from the Bronx? Raza?"

"Yeah, I know." A bag-boy: another drug runner like them.
Carry the drugs in a bag, pass it along to whatever dealer,

soldier or lieutenant it goes to. Benny nods and tries to repress a shudder thinking about crusty-ass Jenny getting all sloppy with some heroin mule in the Bronx. "But I think the one with the dick is the one that does the sticking?"

"Shut up. I stick who I wanna stick. Anyway, I called him." She waggles a filthy burner phone at him. "You know what he tells me? Says he was just on the phone with his crew chief, that ahhh, that lieutenant with the... the one with the glasses? And the mustache?"

"Ehhh. Bloom. Saul Bloom."

"Right, right. Says that he's on the phone with Bloom and suddenly Bloom is arguing with somebody and then there's a couple gunshots and Raza says he hears like, Bloom screaming bloody murder – then there's like, a, a, crunch? Like the sound of someone biting into a crispy fucking apple, that's how Raza put it. And then nothing."

"Then nothing?"

"Then *nothing*. It adds up to somethin' bad. The Boss is sick. Then somebody gets Bloom. And now Mookie's not here?" Her eyes pop and she clucks her tongue. "Something's up, Benny. Fuck fuck fuck."

Benny eyes the bag. His temples itch. His palms sweat. "So we could...?"

"Wait. Yeah." Her thin lips curl over puckered gums. "The Blue is ours."

It's like a trip to Disneyland. Benny feels elated. Like he's dancing with the angels. The Blue makes him feel impossible: like he can do anything. Like he can *see everything*. Fuck Mookie Pearl. Fuck Four-Top. Blue. *Blue!* He starts to unfurl the bag–

Just as a gun barrel presses against the stem of his neck.

"Oh, look," comes a girl's voice behind them. "Mole Men. How gross."

Jenny spits, but misses and the phlegm-blob lands on Benny's cheek.

He goes to wipe it away, but the gun presses harder into his head.

"Hand me the bag," says the voice.

Benny tries to turn around, but the girl says, "Don't even." Then to Jenny: "You. Take the bag, hand it to me over his shoulder."

Jenny scowls, but rips the back from Benny's reluctant grip.

"Hey," Jenny says, handing over the bag. "You're Persephone, eh?"

"Maybe I am."

"You used to run a crew of Moles downstairs. Femurcrack's crew. With Betty and that other guy. Magnum."

"*Man*gum," Persephone says. "They all ended up dead."

Benny feels his heart flip-flopping around like a stun-gunned rabbit. "Are... are we gonna end up dead?"

"Not today," Persephone says.

And then, like that, the gun barrel is gone from Benny's neck. He turns to see the girl darting down the alley, the brown bag of Blue in her hand. He weeps softly.

16

Some dead men become ghosts, yes – but it is also true that some ghosts refuse to leave the body. Those souls who are truly affixed to this world, who feel that they have work yet to complete, can linger behind in the body by sheer force of will. Though it is not a pleasant thing, being married to dead flesh. One corpse I spoke to from the town of Daisypusher said that it was a bit like being walled away in a tenement forever – everything falling apart, rats in the walls. Surrounded by eternal decrepitude. Things break down and no landlord comes to fix them. You dwell in the ruins of your own body. Ruins that will forever be crumbling.

– from the Journals of John Atticus Oakes,
Cartographer of the Great Below

A hundred feet beneath the old marble cemeteries on Manhattan's East Side sit the gates to the town of Daisypusher. Mookie and Skelly stand at these gates – a series of bones both animal and human wound to an old chainlink fence with coils of wire and swatches of black electrical tape – and stare through to the distant lights of the town past: a town that is carved out of the rock, itself a kind of tomb.

"Huh," Mookie says, the two of them standing bathed in the light of a couple dusty old lanterns lit with the glow of some phosphorescent fungus smeared on the inside of the glass. He taps one of the lanterns. "Nora and I used to chase

173

fireflies on the front lawn when she was little. I showed her that if you smushed their glowy butts it'd keep on glowing even after you smeared it on your cheeks. She cried for the little fireflies."

To this, Skelly says nothing. That sad look on his face. She wants to say, "Times have changed," because Nora's not the type anymore to cry over a little lightning bug. But she doesn't. She just kicks a stone with her heel.

Mookie then asks: "You ever been here before?"

Skelly gives it a look, shakes her head. "Heard of it. But no."

Above their heads, bats rustle wings, clinging to dark tree roots pushing through earth and stone.

"You don't have to be here."

She smirks. "And yet, here I am."

"Couple hours ago you were thinkin' on cutting me open from nuts to nose."

"Pssh. I wouldn't have done it."

"Maybe not. But you still don't want to be here."

She winds her fingers around a femur, stares through the gap. "No, I don't. Maybe you need someone to keep you safe."

"Maybe you need *me* to keep *you* safe."

At that, she smiles, and winks.

He continues: "Hell. Maybe this is a trap. Maybe you're just doing what Nora wants. You come at me…"

"Yeah, yeah, yeah." She waves him off. "Smart money says, if I come at you, you'll break me in half like a frozen candy bar. And if you come at me…"

He shrugs. "Lemme guess: you'll cut my nuts off."

Another wink. "You sure know the sweetest things to say. Gets my panties damp, big fella."

He grunts. Is that him blushing? Score one for Skelly. *That* gives her a thrill.

"How do we get in there?" she asks.

"Like this." Mookie kicks the fence. It rattles a mighty racket – bones against bones, bones against metal: an unholy cacophony like a symphony from the Devil's own orchestra.

Then they wait.

Doesn't take long before the gates shudder and start to drift open.

Inside the open gates stands an old woman – an old *very dead* woman, her desiccated flesh like dry, mouse-chewed leather against her bones, all of it ill-concealed behind a diaphanous gown that, once white, is now tobacco-brown.

Her eyes are like rotting grapes, rotating in their sockets until eventually they point their mushy pin-prick pupils toward the two of them.

Skelly suppresses a shiver. She's a tough cookie, or likes to think she is, but the Underworld... this place... all this *death*. Gets under her skin.

"Mookie Pearl," the old woman rasps. She coughs a few times. A clot of pillbugs tumble into her bird-claw hands. She tilts the hand, and the bugs fall to the ground. "You're a sight for sore eyes."

"Mother Cougar," he says, nodding.

"I mean that literally, by the way. My eyes are sore as stubbed toes. When I blink it's like I'm blinking past broken glass. Eyes're too dry, too dry. You got any Visine?"

"No. But I could get you some if you give me a day or two."

"Day or two? Heck, by then they might shrivel up and fall out of my fool head. I may just need you to lick 'em or something." Breath whistles through nostrils shriveled tight to her face. The undead – those whose bodies still contain the specters of the former inhabitants – don't need to do things like eat, breathe, or shit, but they often still do, if only out of habit. Or to make other people sick. "Whatchoo doing here, anyway? And who's the girlie with the hair?"

"This is my friend, Skelly. I'm here looking for someone."

"Who isn't? Well, come on in, then. We don't get many visitors of you *blood-pumper* types. You'll have to pay the toll, though."

Mookie nods. Comes up through the gates, waves Skelly on through.

As she steps up, Mookie opens his mouth. Stoops over. The old woman hobbles her gangly, poorly-held-together frame over. Leans in, sticks that rotten nose right up to his mouth. Skelly knows she's staring, but she can't help it.

"Go on," the old dead woman whispers. "Blow it on me."

He breathes. Slow and hot.

The old woman takes a long languid sniff.

"Meat," she says. "I always smell meat on your breath. I smell the spice. The fat. It's a beautiful thing, Mookie Pearl."

Mother Cougar pulls away. Then looks to Skelly. "You're next, sweetheart."

Skelly shoots Mookie a panicked look. If she could contain a single question inside her gaze it would be a loudly shrieked *"What the fuck?"*

He nods. Impatient like, "hurry up".

Skelly opens her mouth.

Mother gets all up in there. Another long sniff. "Oh, damn, what's that? Broccoli? Tofu? Jesus Christ, girl, you a vegetarian?"

"Vegan," Skelly says, but then she inhales through her nose and then a smell shoots up into her nostrils like a half-dead raccoon crawling up in there. Suddenly she staggers backward, blanching. Skelly turns away, bends sharp at the waist, and pukes.

Mother Cougar laughs, a gurgling guffaw. "Aw, shoot, girlie, that was your first time, wasn't it? My bad! I should've warned you not to breathe through your nose. Caught a whiff of my... *perfume*, it seems."

Skelly wipes her mouth. Looks to Mookie who gives her a shrug. He's smiling. A rare sight. "You think this is funny?" she asks.

"A little."

"Asshole."

"Yep."

"All right," Mother says. "Let's quit sniffin' each other's butts. See if we can't find you who you're lookin' for."

Now, at least, Skelly remembers why she became vegan in the first place.

The walk to Daisypusher from inside the gates isn't a long one. Five minutes and they start seeing the first ramshackle house: corrugated tin tilting atop crooked walls of mold-streaked plywood. A window cut out of the wood, a flickering fire-glow coming from within – a glimpse of a dead face, half-skin and half-skull, peering out.

It's a subterranean shantytown – the streets are paths cut between each hastily thrown-together junk-house. Mookie sees one house with a wall formed from the plow of a bulldozer; another with a roof made of the cellar doors stolen from some New York City sidewalk. One house across the way is lined with shattered broken subway tile – a sign for the Columbus Circle station hangs from wire outside a front door made from an old coffin lid. It's hard to count from here, but in the past Mookie figured there were fifty, sixty houses here. Now it looks like that number has grown.

There exists a kind of beauty here, too – all around, little flowers and birds cut from tin and wound with copper wire. Some of them are bedazzled with bits of colored glass while others are smeared with luminescent fungus. Other little tidbits of curious décor hang about: a rusted bird cage with an owl skeleton slumped inside, an old-school big blue mailbox spackled over with chewing gum; a series of hitching posts topped with human skulls that are each decorated in a unique way (glittery glass, teeth replaced with hematite, flowers painted on bleached bone, an American flag motif, ivy growing out of an open jaw).

In the distance, Mookie hears a subway train: *gung gung gung GUNG GUNG GUNG gung gung gung.* The ground shakes, the vibration crawling up his feet and legs. When it passes, a dog barks in the distance. Windchimes tinkle.

"So, who you need?" Mother asks. As she walks, her skin sounds like two rough roofing tiles scraping together.

"Man named Steve Lister."

She barks a laugh. "You know better than that. We don't go by our old names here."

"But you know him."

"I know him. Burnsy. That's what he goes by."

Burnsy. That figures.

As they walk, they hit the center of Daisypusher – a circle where the dead commune around a bubbler fountain made of misshapen gobbo skulls heaped in a clumsy pyramid. At its peak sits the cracked geode head of a Trogbody, dark and dirty water pouring out of the thing's open mouth, cascading down.

Dozens of dead folk eye Mookie and Skelly as they pass. The dead each bear the marks of their deaths. An armless girl in a pink dress smiles. A man in a rusty wheelchair – the spokes coiled with dead dry snakes – sits like a pile of moist garbage, flies buzzing all around him. A moldering hausfrau stands around in a pink bathrobe. A big no-eyed trucker type with a Peterbilt hat crosses his arms. A teen boy in a snazzy orange vest turns his head – the noose still hanging from his swollen, empurpled neck swings.

Mookie nods as they come closer. A few nod back. Others just stare.

The circle is ringed with trees – not real trees, but trees made of bundles of chain and fence and piled-high trashcans, the branches formed from twisting pipes, mannequin arms, and braided wire. Fake trees that cast long shadows.

Sitting in the makeshift tree branches are cats. Dozens of cats.

Each in various states of... unlife. Ribs showing through an old calico's side. A tomcat with half his face mashed in. Another cat that's just skeleton and skin hanging off the bones like old, wet curtains. Cat-bones click and shift in the branches. Mrowling and cooing and hissing.

Skelly stares up. Jaw slack.

Mother sees her. Laughs. "Girl, you gonna dress yourself up with skulls and death, you ought to know what it really looks like." The old woman snaps her fingers and lickety-split Mother Cougar is covered in cats – a whole coat of undead felines crawling up her arms and slinking around the hem of her gown, leaving it wet with a trail of moist decay. "Death ain't romantic, girlie. It ain't pretty. It ain't fashionable. Go on. Get a face-full. Gawk like a tourist!" Another laugh.

It's then that Skelly turns. Sees how all the other dead are staring. She stops walking as Mother pauses to play with her kitties. Mookie watches as Skelly stiffens. Her hand falls to her knife and rests on the silver skull of the Bowie's hilt.

"Relax," Mookie tells her.

"I don't like being made to feel like a heel," she whispers. "That old woman is cruisin' for a bruisin'."

"Cool it. You start shit here, you won't find me protecting you. You'll find me on the other side, hauling your ass out. These folks are dead."

"Yeah, I got that part, genius."

"I'm just saying, they got it hard enough as it is without you comin' in here like one day you won't be a body in a hole, too."

That shuts her up. Her hand drifts away from the knife.

Mother shakes herself free of all the cats but one: a lanky black cat that looks healthy until you see the roving stitch-scar that winds across the animal's body. Toward the belly, the scar is open, and a few bits of what look to be curls of dried potpourri come drifting out. Mookie catches a scent like death and cinnamon.

"These are my best friends," Mother says. "My *babies*. I find them up top sometimes – hit by cars or beaten to death by shitty blood-pumper kids or just dyin' because it's their time to die. They come to me without me asking. I bring 'em here and they keep the rat population down something fierce. This one got her back end crushed up by a taxi. Smelled pretty bad for a while, but she's good now. Ain't that right, Midnight?" She strokes the black cat behind the ears. "*Wooshy booshy kitty witty.*" The cat purrs like a guttering chainsaw – a sound too big for such a tiny beast. "Anyway. There's Burnsy's house."

Up ahead is an octagonal structure, the walls of which are wooden pallets woven together with heavy gauge chain and wire. The roof is slate – cracked, busted slate, but slate just the same. Mookie sees sudden movement atop the roof: a scuttling shape, a glistening light on a hardened carapace. A roach-rat. Half-roach, half-rat. Never in the same proportion. This one looks like it's got a bug's head and wings perched atop a fuzzy body with a long pink tail.

Then a black flash. The cat – Midnight – launches up off Mother's shoulder. Bounds over two roofs, *clang clang thud*, and hits the roach-rat like a fuzzy cannonball.

Mookie can't see what becomes of the roach-rat. But he hears its trill scream. Hears the sound as the cat feasts. *Crunch crunch crunch*.

"See?" Mother says. "Anyway. That house over there, that's Burnsy's place. Be nice. He's prickly. Probably on account of his skin and all."

Skelly gives Mookie a look. He averts his gaze and walks forward, guilt dogging his heels like a starving hound.

Mookie knocks. *Whonnnng, whonnnng.*

The walls may be wooden pallets, but the door isn't a door at all – it's an upside-down car hood. A racecar hood, number 57 painted in red letters. Freshly painted, too – though the fresh paint fails to conceal the bumps and pocks of rust beneath.

Inside, the sound of a chain rattling.

The door opens out. Mookie steps back, but he's too slow – it clips his chin. His teeth clack together over his tongue. He tastes blood.

He turns, spits a line of red on the stone.

And when he turns back, there's Steve Lister.

Burnsy.

Mookie's not a man given over to much guilt. In his line of work, guilt is a boat anchor around the ankle, a too-full colostomy bag hanging from the hip. It's a burden. A *does-nothing-for-you-but-slow-your-ass-down* burden. Guilt will make you hesitate. Shame makes you weak. And Mookie's tough. Tough like an anvil.

But this – the man's skin. His *body.*

He's like a giant walking third-degree burn. Blisters everywhere. Lobster flesh stretched taut. Burnsy's wearing a white I HEART NYC T-shirt soaked through with custardy stains.

The hair is a forest of charred stubs.

Big round unblinking eyes stare out.

The muscles around the mouth pull a pair of lips made of scar tissue into something resembling a scowl. A grim rictus of displeasure.

"You."

That's all Steve – Burnsy – says. *You.*

"Yeah." That's all Mookie can say in response.

"Die in a fire," Burnsy says. *"Blood-pumper."*

The hood slams shut with a clang.

Skelly says, "Hey, I guess you two know each other."

"You guess right."

"I'm also using my powers of perception to suss out that this crusty cat is *not* your biggest fan."

Mookie growls. "Well, shit. You must be psychic."

"What's the score?"

"I'm the one who killed him."

"... Oh."

He steps back. Pounds on the car hood. "Lemme in, Lister. I need to talk."

From inside: "Name's Burnsy now. Don't know any Lister."

"I got a favor to ask."

Now Burnsy's laughing. The kind of laugh where every time you try to stop, you just laugh harder. Like you're laughing in church and just can't quit. The funniest joke among the living *and* the dead.

"Do I wanna know how you killed him?" Skelly asks.

"In a fire."

She goggles. "You burned him *alive*?"

Mookie sighs. "Not on purpose. I didn't burn him alive. I was... listen, he stole from us. From the Organization. He was a stuntman on the side, but a driver for us–"

From inside: "A driver *on the side*, and a stuntman for *real*, you fat-necked thug."

"And he drove whatever needed driving. Dealers, people, pros, pimps, and above all else, packages. Turns out he'd been taking a cut. He got hooked on the Blue, but when he couldn't get his hands on *that* he started up with heroin and decided one day to run off with a package of Burmese Brown. They told me to stop him. I stopped him."

Skelly stares.

Burnsy yells, "Tell her *how* you stopped me."

"Goddamnit."

"Tell her."

"I hit him with a garbage truck."

Skelly's eyes go wide.

Suddenly, a chain rattles and the car hood door whips open. Burnsy stands there, a glistening red finger pointing, his eyes bulging. "So, I'm in my car, right? A '67 Mustang. Paint the color of mist just before sunrise. I'm hard-charging toward the Brooklyn Bridge around 3am, thinking that I was gonna be free, and who comes barreling up out of a side-street but this sack of lard driving a fucking *trash truck*. Truck plows into the Mustang. My heart breaks. My ride's over. But does he quit? Oh, no. No, no, no, no. He keeps driving. My car, my beautiful car, is smooshed on the end of the truck like a booger on a kid's finger and he pushes it forward into the front of a Duane Reade. Glass and metal crunch up. Car catches fire. And – spoiler alert – *I burn alive inside the damn thing*. I remember smelling my own hair on fire. Hearing the leather bubble and snap. The dashboard melted. So did my skin. And did he do anything to help? Put out the fire? Drag me out onto the sidewalk? Oh no. The bald prick, far as anyone can tell, hopped out of the truck and sauntered off like he was thinking of grabbing a late-night taco somewhere."

"I don't 'saunter'," Mookie says. Then, in a quieter voice, "I do like tacos."

"You fuck!" Burnsy shrieks. "*You insensitive fuck.*" Flailing his arms, he spins toward Skelly. "You know why I'm still stuck in this body? Because I got family to take care of. Because I got a wife and a daughter. Because they mean *everything* to me and this dumb hairless ape ripped my family apart–"

Anger blooms in Mookie's heart like fire in a stoked forge. Before he knows what's happening, he's got Lister by the throat and he's stomping forward into the dead man's house, thrashing him left and right, into shelves that contain strange cloudy jars and odd Byzantine brass boxes. Jars drop, pop, and shatter. Boxes clatter. A horseshoe clangs and rolls. A plastic box hits on its corner and vomits cat's eye marbles everywhere. Artifacts from Lister's old life – reels of film, a series of knob-toppers for a gear-shifter, a motorcycle helmet painted with lightning bolts – rattle but do not fall as Mookie jams the dead man hard against the wall of the house.

"*You* tore your family apart," Mookie yells. "You were the one who got hooked on that shit. Go on, tell us – that day you were taking a little spin, were you going home? Or were you going to sell the drugs? *Or* did you have a couple stuntman buddies in Red Hook where you were going to hole up and shoot poison into your arms until you could see God? Wasn't that your plan, asshole? You hadn't been home in months. *Months*. Trust me, I know. You want to know why you're still clinging to this world like a fucking flea on a dog's back? You wanna do right by your family, but only because you did *so wrong* by them for *so long*."

Burnsy's eyes glisten. He wheezes, "You got a... funny way of asking... for a favor."

Mookie roars, throws the dead man to the ground.

Skelly appears at his elbow. Pulls him aside. "Mook, he's right. If you need him, maybe you want to go easy. He's dead. You... did that to him." She pauses. "Like you said, they got it hard enough."

Mookie's chest rises, then falls. The breathing earth. A cooling mountain. A volcano finally falling quiet.

Mookie sighs and offers a massive hand to Lister. The words that come next don't come easy, like they're trying to grab Mookie's lips and crawl back down his throat before they fall out: "I'm... sorry about your family."

Burnsy grumbles, "And *I'm* sorry about yours."

Mookie retracts his hand. "What'd you say?"

"I'm sure you didn't have a mug that said FATHER OF THE YEAR either."

False alarm. Full eruption. Lava gushes. All Mookie can see – all he can *feel* – is ash and smoke and melting stone. With both hands he reaches for Burnsy, but the dead man is gone – scurrying through the archway formed by Mookie's legs, crawling on all fours like a whipped terrier.

When he turns, there's Burnsy. A tire iron in his hand.

He swings. Cracks Mookie in the elbow. Pain glows bright, radiating down to the wrist, all the way to the shoulder. And as Mookie is reeling back and waving his arm like he's trying to shake loose a bunch of ants, Burney takes another step back and pops the motorcycle helmet off the back shelf. Mookie bellows, an avalanche roar, then charges the dead man just as Burnsy drops the helmet over his own head.

The two of them go crashing through the wall and back out into the town of Daisypusher.

Skelly's not sure what to do.

The two men – one living, one dead, one a human bulldozer, the other a microwaved chimpanzee – kick king hell out of one another on the stone thoroughfare of Daisypusher.

Mookie's big, powerful, and slow. Burnsy doesn't have much power, but he's quick – and, being dead, he doesn't have much to lose. He fights like a rabid weasel.

The fight is a constant give-and-take, push-and-pull.

The big man's boot on the dead man's chest. The tire iron against the side of Mookie's skull. Burned face smashed into broken plywood. Dead man on Mookie's back like a rodeo man on the back of a Brahma bull, clinging to life for five, six, seven – *oh*, sorry, not eight seconds; dead man, meet big hand; dead man, meet hard stone.

They take the fight all around the octagon. Pummeling and spinning, hitting and kicking. Out back of the house is something bulky under a tarp, smaller than a car but bigger than a generator. Skelly doesn't have time to think about it because there they go again – stumbling and punching around the other side and back into what passes for the street.

She wonders if she should stop it. When her girls have a problem, she doesn't let them fight out in the open. For them, the battle is either on skates or doesn't happen at all.

Just the same, the fight sometimes needs to happen.

The girls. She hopes they're OK. Way they scattered after the attack on the warehouse – they know where to go. They know where to hide. She told them what was up: Boss is sick, a whole rain of shit could come down on everybody's heads, but it means opportunity, too. Back the right bitch – in this case, Persephone – and they might find their standing in this city to be *greatly improved* by the time the dust settles.

She's still not sure what to make of Mookie. First she thought, hell with this big palooka. King Kong's gonna fall and he's gonna fall hard along with the rest of his Organization. Staying with him was easy. He wasn't smart enough to see her as a threat. He trusted her. Which was insane. And stupid. If he was anybody else, she'd think it was part of some counter-plan to keep an eye on her, to keep her close so he can find Nora.

But no, the big dumb thug just plain trusts her.

And that's what gets her. Because here's this guy, supposed to be an enemy, and – what? He's just happy to have someone along for the ride. He's not *nice*. Not exactly. But he doesn't seem as bad as Nora led her to believe.

And he's a fine lookin' piece of meat. The bee's knees. The cat's paw. That doesn't mean he's a pretty man. He isn't. He's pit bull ugly. Got a face like a fist, a body like a bunch of tractor tires fitted around an oil drum.

But those hands. That jaw. He could crush her. Could *eat her right up*.

She shakes her head suddenly. No. *No.* Not going to do this. Not going to think this. She shakes the mental Etch-a-Sketch, clears her thoughts.

Right now, Burnsy's hugging the front of Mookie's (*big and powerful and handsome in the way you might admire the side of a mountain*) face, bringing the tire iron down between Mookie's shoulder blades – and Mookie's spinning like a drunken carousel, trying to grab hold of the blister-skinned corpse-walker.

Behind her, she sees they've drawn a crowd of dead folk. None of them hoping to intervene, by the look it. The hausfrau in the pink bathrobe seems to be really getting into it, a bloodthirsty grin on her zombie's face.

Fine. Time for somebody to do something.

Skelly walks up, draws her knife.

Then she bashes Burnsy on the back of the head with the hilt.

Bam.

She'd never hit somebody that hard unless she was planning on killing them, but – hey, this one's already stunt-jumped over the mortal coil.

Burnsy yelps and drops off onto his butt. To make sure he doesn't come back at Mookie, she kneels and puts the big blade up against his throat. And oh what a big blade it is – inches of steel reach beyond each side of the dead man's red, raw neck.

"You move I'll pop your head off like a Black-eyed Susan."

Burnsy sighs. Drops the tire iron. "Fine. Whatever." He pauses. "*I'm tired.*"

Mookie rubs his face. Wipes blood from his lip. Stretches.

"I'm tired too," he says.

"You boys ready to talk?"

"Long as he doesn't punch me anymore," Burnsy says. "Because, *ow.*"

Mookie shrugs, nods. "Deal."

And back into the octagon – now with one pallet wall knocked flat – they go.

As Skelly helps pick up the pieces of the broken home, Mookie stands still in the middle of it and lets the weariness wash over him. His body is pulsing with the after-effects of the fight. The pain a distant throb – all the more irritating because it's not front and center, not driving him like a knife in the ribs. Instead it's like a heavy bass booming on the other side of the wall when you're trying to sleep. He thinks about his daughter. About his ex-wife. About how his whole Organization is falling down around his ears with the Boss being sick and the gangs smelling the sour stink of an infected wound and how somebody – maybe Werth – sold him out. Then back to Nora, and how maybe a lot of this is her fault to begin with.

Where did I go wrong, he asks himself, but it's a question he already knows the answer to. And he knows it's not just one answer but a whole series of them, one after the other, the ants-go-marching one-by-one, hurrah, hurrah. Carrying his regrets and mistakes like little crumbs of poisoned bread. He reminds himself that when all this is said and done, if he's still alive, he's going to find Jess and tell her sorry.

Something he's never done.

Something he starts doing now.

"I'm sorry," he says. Lets those two words hang there for a while because he's not sure where he's going with them. Skelly gives him a look as she cleans up, and Burnsy – who sits on an overturned bucket – stops dabbing parts of his skin with a wet rag and stares. "I'm sorry about your family. Sorry about killing you. It wasn't my plan. I thought I'd smash your car, drag you out, give you a beatin', bring you back to the Boss. But then I saw the car was on fire..." He stares off at nothing, remembering the day. "I went to the trunk, popped it. Took the heroin. By then it was too late for you. I did the job. I got the drugs. I'm sorry you're dead and that death sucks."

Burnsy stands. Hissing in pain as he does. He looks Mookie up and down. "Fuck you, Pearl. Fuck you up, down, and sideways. Fuck you with a knife, a fist, a baseball bat, a fucking goddamn thermonuclear warhead shoved so far up your corn-hole your teeth glow. Fuck you to hell and back and deeper still. Fuck you from me, from my family, from the bottom of my fuckin' fuck-you heart, you fucking fuck-headed fuck-hearted animal."

Mookie nods. Says nothing.

Then: Burnsy offers a hand.

Mookie looks at it like it's a cankerpede.

"Still, thanks for being honest. And don't think I don't know. I know you killed me." He draws a deep breath, then lowers his voice. "... but I killed me, too. I hurt my family worse than you ever did."

Mookie knows that feeling all too well.

Burnsy continues: "I'm not forgiving you. That's not the kind of thing I can stopper up in a bottle and throw into a dark hole. Every day my skin feels like I'm being bitten by a thousand black widow spiders. Every day is a day I have to sneak up top to see my family – you know my wife got remarried? Some banker turd. My kid's smart, at least. Spelling bee champ. Good with numbers, too."

"That's something."

"But..." He fumbles around under some mess for a blue plastic spray bottle. He spritzes some all up and down his face. "What I'm saying is, you wanna ask me for a favor, I'll let you ask. At least."

"Really?"

"Really."

"I need to find a ghost."

"Find a ghost." Another water spritz.

"I heard you got into that. Tracking specters."

"Most of us Daisypusher types fall into that kind of work. We're good at it. Who you wanna find?"

"The Boss, his grandson–"

"Died, I know, I heard." Burnsy waves away Mookie's surprise. "Information has weight, and this place has gravity. News always trickles down. You want me to find the grandson's ghost? So you can solve the murder, I'm guessing."

"They say my daughter did it."

Burnsy whistles. "That I did *not* know. What do *you* say?"

Mookie doesn't answer. Can't answer. Won't.

"Right, OK. If he's down in the dark somewhere, I can find him. But this isn't a favor. This is a job. And I take this job, you gotta pony up."

"Whaddya want?"

"My family."

"I can't give you them back. Or you back to them."

"No, not that. I want them cared for."

"You said she's remarried, that the girl is… smart."

Burnsy stares hard, those bright white eyes like uncovered light bulbs. "And I want to be the one making their lives better, not worse for once in my… life. Unlife. Whatever. I want to take care of them. One last time."

"Name the price."

"Fifty thousand."

Mookie almost chokes.

"A *year*," Burnsy adds.

"Christ, Lister."

"That's the cost. Pay it or hit the schist."

Mookie's not good with math, but he knows what he makes a year and he knows that while the Boss is good for stuff like this, he has no idea how long the Boss is going to be hanging around what with the cancer and all.

A counteroffer, then. "Twenty-k a year for five years."

"Thirty for twenty."

"Twenty-five for ten."

The dead man stares. It's then Mookie realizes this is his *thinking-about-it* face. Most people's faces are expressive – the way the skin tugs at the cheeks, the way the eyelids narrow. But his flesh is stretched out. The eyes permanently exposed.

Finally, Burnsy nods. "Done."

They shake hands. Burnsy's hand is hot like beach-sand.

Skelly says, "I'm proud of you two crazy kids for making it work." In her hands is an old wooden box. Scalloped edges. Distressed brass trim.

"We're not exactly giving each other hand-jobs," Burnsy says.

Mookie nods at the box. "What's that?"

"That? Nothing." Mookie keeps staring, so Burnsy goes on: "I collect. Find all kinds of strange stuff above and below. Especially when I'm hunting up a spook for someone like you. I got soul cages. Monkeysblood crystals. Jumping vicar-seeds. Plus I got a wholly unholy host of funguses-amonguses. I've got crow-dimple, black-shelf, glow-worm, hob-tongue…"

But all the while, Burnsy's eyes are following Skelly as she moves to put that box back on the shelf. Mookie gently catches her hand. He looks to Burnsy. "What's in it?"

"Like I said, nothing."

"By nothing, you mean something."

Burnsy reaches for the box, but Mookie takes it, pulls it away.

He lifts the lid. Inside is a warped glass phial with a cork stopper. He picks it out of the box – Burnsy winces, mutters something about *being careful* – and, inside, a sap the color of milled wheat oozes sludgily back and forth.

"What is it?"

"I dunno."

"You're lying. You do know."

"It's a... a sap. Like amber. But more yellow."

"Where'd you get it?"

"Down in the..." Burnsy sighs. "Down in the Tangle. I was lost. I was following some of Oakes's old-ass maps and I fucked up somewhere. I came upon this gobbo campsite and they were there roasting cankerpedes and I knew they were all riled up because they were fighting and fucking and so I thought I better find a way around. Ahead was this little crevice – like a vent running through the wall and I thought, OK, I'm gonna crawl in there. I did and... fuck it if it didn't go anywhere but a dead-end, but *at* that dead-end I found these tubes. Like those wasps make. Mud-daubers? I broke it apart and..." He points to the phial with a blister-tipped finger. "That stuff came out. So I bottled it up."

As Mookie moves the glass toward the light, the dull yellow patina suddenly brightens as though flecks of glitter hang suspended in the sap. Gold like a burnished lamp.

"This is Ochre," Mookie says, his heart suddenly racing.

"No. What? I... y'know. Probably not. That stuff's a myth. Though, shit, careful with it, don't drop it for Chrissakes–"

Skelly steps up. "That the real deal, daddy-o?"

"I want to buy this," Mookie says. Could be fake. But what if it's not? What if it's really one of the Five Occulted Pigments? He's already got a little tin of what might be Vermilion – the Red Rage. To have a phial of Ochre? Golden Gate? Be a damn fine bargaining chip. He ever finds himself swinging on the end of someone's rope it wouldn't be the worst thing in the world to have these in his pocket to save his ass.

Or to save Nora.

"I can't do that," Burnsy says, a fast hand darting out and pulling the phial away. "You got what you came here for. I'll do the gig. You'll take care of my family."

"I can help you. I can..." Here Mookie's reaching, but it's worth a shot. "I can get you back on the payroll. With the Organization. Lister, c'mon."

"Mookie, go home, go get some sleep. You look like batter-dipped shit—"

Just then, outside, a hard bell clangs. Like an old iron dinner bell. Another bell joins in. And a third. A murmur of voices rise up amongst the alarm.

Burnsy bares his teeth. Grabs for the tire iron.

"What's going on?" Skelly asks.

"We're under attack."

17

Few can say what the gobbos actually want. Certainly by examination their wants and needs are crass, even evil: they enjoy the pain of others. They take great pleasure from the torment of human beings – they enjoy it the way a dog enjoys rolling around in roadkill, or the way a cat takes pleasure in torturing a rat. Gobbos hunt. They hurt. They eat. They breed. They steal. They kill. And yet that's just what we see of them: and until the Sandhogs broke into the Great Below years before, the gobbos had little exposure to mankind. So what did they do before they met us?
 – from the Journals of John Atticus Oakes,
 Cartographer of the Great Below

The bells are ringing.

Someone screams.

A sick, sinking feeling hits Skelly's stomach, like her guts have no bottom, like it's just a hole that pulls her into herself.

Some of the dead run toward the danger. They hold swords. Claw-hammers. Old-timey double-barrel shotguns, barrels rimmed with rust. Most run away. Faces frozen in mortified panic. Wretched limbs dragging them along.

A corpse in a moth-eaten tuxedo, a crumpled top hat held tight to his sunken chest, cries out as he hurries past. "Gobbos. *Gobbos.*"

Goblins.

She's seen them. At a distance. The Get-Em-Girls don't fuck with the Underworld much. Sure, they've carved out a few hollows here and there. They use the secret tunnels carved out beneath the city, winding in and out of forgotten subway stations and access passages. Once in a while a lone gobo creeps through the dark or the girls find a pack of them scurrying down some dark alley, but she teaches her girls to stay away. To call in the Organization. Let guys like Mookie handle it.

But she knows what they are. What they like. What they *do*.

Mookie draws his cleaver.

She bites the inside of her cheek. It hurts. It wakes her up.

Skelly draws her Bowie.

They begin to move. Through the fleeing corpses. The rotten stink coming and going in waves. Burnsy says, "The gobbos have always had a thing for this place. A few sneak around the edges, try to steal us away, God knows why. But they been gettin' ballsy recently. And coming in bigger and bigger groups."

Somewhere ahead a gunshot sounds. A shriek. A jabbered, inhuman cry.

Corpse-bodies jostle past.

Through the crowd, fire streaks in a wide arc.

A pop of glass.

A bloom of orange.

"Molotovs," Burnsy says. "They light the fence on fire. Keeps 'em back."

They push to the edge of the crowd. The dead gather ahead, some with lit bottles, others with weapons. She sees two clad in old-school Vietnam-era flak jackets. One's got a chestplate of armor made of soup and soda cans. Covering the arms are drainpipes and downspouts.

Past the houses, Skelly sees more bottles hit against the fence. Plumes of fire belch forth, sweep over the fence – the air warped around it, heat vapor shifting.

A few short, squat bodies clamber over the fence-top – on fire, burning, thrashing – and hit the ground and start running toward Daisypusher. Ten, twenty feet in, the bodies plop forward and stop moving. Still burning.

But then–

The fire starts going out. She hears the sizzle of flames. Something wet spattering.

From the edges in, the fire starts guttering. And failing.

Nearby, Skelly sees a dead woman swaddled in thick rags holding a rifle scope – just the scope, no rifle – to her eye. Mookie marches past and grabs it, takes a look down at the fenceline.

"Ah, shit."

"What?" Skelly asks.

He hands her the scope.

She peers through – at first she can't tell what she's looking at. But then she finds the fire, the last of it – and sees the gobbos on the other side, past the wire, past the bones. They're… doing something. She sees something dripping from the fence.

More climb on top. That's when she sees what they're doing. They're opening their mouths.

Something's pouring out. Geysers of spit or vomit, she doesn't know. Whatever it is, there's a lot of it. And it's putting out the fire.

Now gobbos are climbing up over the fence tops.

They hit the ground running. A dozen at first. Then another dozen. *More.* Jesus. She catches glimpses of open maws. Whipping tongues. And weapons: rusted knives and baseball bats swaddled in barbed wire. Is that a – some kind of antique? A blunderbuss?

Behind the goblins, a dark shadow rises. Like a black curtain blown loose of its rod. Floating behind, then over top the swarming gobbos.

Suddenly the scope is gone, snatched away by Mookie's massive hand.

She's about to protest, but he growls: "Here they come."

Mookie's tired. More than tired. *Empty*. Like he's a scarecrow that's been chewed out from the inside and all that's left is the burlap sack and felt hat. As the gobbos rush – thirty, maybe forty of the gibbering, howling gray-skinned, snot-slick mutants – there comes a tiny moment of doubt, a cigarette cherry in the darkness of his heart that burns hot and burns deep, and the doubt says: *You can't do this. You can't save this town. You can't fight anymore. You don't even want to. Sit down. Lie back. Give up.*

But then, that ember of hot ash is extinguished by a tide of anger.

He hates gobbos. *Hates them*. Sees what they've done. What they can do. They have nothing they believe in. A crazy loon like John Atticus Oakes thinks they have beliefs and even morals, twisted as they may be. He points to their temples, to some strange religious-seeming cave carvings, to their language that he supposedly helped to decipher. Says maybe they worship the Hungry Ones, the gods of the deepest dark. Mookie doesn't buy it. More important, he doesn't care.

They're awful creatures with no place in this world. Above or below.

And that drives him forward. He draws the cleaver. Nearby a pistol shot. He sees the top of one gobbo's head peel back, greasy brains bubbling over like a shaken beer.

The gobbos return fire. Mookie sees one gobbo skid to a halt, pointing a fat-mouthed blunderbuss. There's a ground-shaking *choom*, a pyrotechnic flash of light, a gout of sickly yellow smoke. One of the dead men next to Mookie, an older fellow with a big distended belly and a beard squirming with earthworms, falls back, body peppered with holes that don't bleed.

He screams and thrashes as cankerpedes come pouring out of those holes, squealing, squirming, *chewing* at him—

The gobbo starts to reload, stuffing a filthy wad of writhing, struggling rags into the mouth of the old-timey gun. The rest of the gobbos are only ten feet away.

Mookie bares his teeth. Twirls his cleaver.

And meets the tide of gobbos like a human seawall.

There comes a moment when Skelly thinks: it's all over. Mookie steps forward, spinning a cleaver that looks too heavy for her even to pick up, and then they slam into him like a collective fist. Then he's gone. Gone underneath a carpet of goblins. She catches a flash of bald scalp, a glimpse of a fist—

Her own Bowie knife at the ready, she resists every urge inside her body crying for her to *run, flee, hide, don't step over the edge, don't jump into the chasm*, and instead bolts toward the fray. A gobbo does a gymnastic tumble in front of her, springing up like a Jack-in-the-Box except *this* toy is armed with a chair-leg studded with fragments of chipped glass.

The gobbo screams. Leaps for her. She cries out, leans back, swipes—

Gobbo body hits ground. Gobbo head hits a half-second after, rolling away.

Mookie is already shaking off the gobbo tide the way a dog shakes water from his coat. One gobbo, cleaved in twain. Another kicked so hard his head crumples like a rotten pumpkin. He throws one to the ground, stomps on it. Tosses another in the air and cuts it in half at the waist. Dark blood spurts. Covers him.

Some of it's his, too. Red blood. Human blood. A gash over his ear. A bite on his hand.

She steps up. Without meaning to, they form a system. He throws them off, she sticks them in the belly, or hacks them across the back, or caps them like she's cutting the top off a pineapple. All this in a kind of slow motion, pockets of the battlefield revealed–

Mother Cougar pointing at the onrushing horde, her finger like a gun. Zombie-cats are her ammunition, screeching and leaping for the monsters, tearing with teeth, clawing at eyes.

Burnsy jumping like a maniac, up and over the heads of gobbos, bashing skulls with his tire iron. Cackling. And screaming.

Another burst of the blunderbuss: another corpse down. This time it's the one-eyed trucker, the fabric of his shirt and jeans rippling as a tide of venomous cankerpedes pours out. Bodies are dragged, kicking and thrashing, toward the gates. Abducted. For grim goblin purpose.

Skelly turns. Lops the arm off a fleeing gobbo. A corkscrew shiv clatters on the stone.

It's then she hears the screams coming from behind them. Back toward town.

The gobbos are there, too. Not possible, she thinks. They haven't broken the line. And the town is carved out of the stone – it butts up against hard rock.

It seems the monsters have found a way.

She yells to Mookie, tries to warn him–

But he's gone. Charging forward. Toward the blunderbuss gobbo.

She can handle this. She knows she can. She's a bad-ass chick. A deadly doll. She's a souped-up hot rod with a stacked rack. *She's one coo-coo crazy cooze, daddy-o.*

Skelly shakes the Bowie knife free of goblin blood, then runs back toward Daisypusher.

Choom.

Mookie sidesteps the shot – or thinks he does. Something tears into the meat of his bicep just as a pair of gobbos rush him. He bashes one in the face with the flat of the cleaver,

and swipes the blade left to slice the other's head in half at a
hard diagonal just as something pushes up out of the hole in
his arm–

He knows what it is. He feels it squirming.

As soon as the cankerpede pops its glistening black mandibles
out of the wound, Mookie grabs it and turns its head like a key
in a lock, twisting the head right off the body. He pulls the rest
of the foot-long worm from the wound – *spppplup* – trying not
to scream as each of the little razor-footed legs tears the edges
of the exit hole – and flings it against the stone.

Up ahead, the gobbo with the gun is frantically trying
to reload.

Mookie doesn't like that idea. He bellows and stomps
forward. The gobbo tries to backpedal and evade but he grabs
its hand, pulls the writhing rag-clot of cankerpede ammo from
the depths of the gun, and crams it forward, hard into the
gobbo's mouth.

Then he slams the gobbo's jaw shut, just to make sure.

It doesn't take long that the gobbo starts thrashing like he's
on fire – and his gray, greasy flesh starts undulating like a
blanket laid overtop a bunch of breeding snakes.

The cankerpedes are doing their work.

Mookie grabs the blunderbuss, breaks it over the gobbo's
head for good measure.

By now, the battlefield is looking thinned out. Good. A
gobbo flees toward the gates, a half-rotting cat clinging to his
rubbery head like a skullcap.

Mookie turns to find Skelly.

But he doesn't see her.

Then, somewhere, he hears her scream.

Back among the ramshackle houses of Daisypusher, Skelly
stalks the street with her big-ass blade pointed forward. Some
of the huddled dead point the way, back toward Burnsy's

house, back toward the craggy pocket end of this old corpse-town. "There!" a dead child in a dirty pair of footy pajamas cries. "Back there!"

For a moment she thinks she'll take a moment. Put the ol' roller skates on. The ground here is smoother, more sculpted – not too craggy, only a few lips of rock and stone. It'll allow her to move fast. Do her kick-ass roller-derby thing.

But then she thinks: *no time to lace up*. Just move, move, move.

So that's what she does. She moves.

Into Burnsy's place – a trio of gobs root around the place, throwing jars that pop, soul-cages that clang and roll. One of them holds up the wooden box with the phial of amber sap inside and it jabbers in triumph–

Just as Skelly cleaves its head open with *Santa Muerte*, her Bowie. It slumps backward, the box landing on its soft, oily belly.

The other two squeal in surprise–

Skelly uses that surprise. She smashes the butt of her knife into what passes for the one's nose, sticks the blade into the eye – and brain – of the second. As the nose-smashed gobbo reels, leathery lids blinking over bulbous eyes–

Slice.

She cuts its throat.

It tumbles into a puddle of its own black blood.

They came for the box, she thinks.

She picks it up. Wipes blood off it. Skelly steps back outside as a few of the Daisypusher dead gather around. The pink-robed hausfrau hurries up, points toward the rock wall – "I saw some of them go that way!"

Skelly thrusts the box into the dead lady's hands. "Here, Pinky. I need you to hold onto this. Give it to Lister– er, Burnsy, OK?"

A quick nod. "Sure thing, miss."

Skelly hands off the box and hurries away – she reaches the end of the carved out cavern in which Daisypusher sits, the rock wall that forms the *end of the line* for the far end of town. No gobbos–

But then she spies something at her feet – a pile of earthen dust sitting there like pencil shavings.

It's funny how the brain sometimes misses a beat. Or takes too long to connect ideas. It's only a half-second when Skelly walks up, sees the pile, and then answers her own mystery. They must've bored a hole in the rock above our heads.

Except that last thought suddenly becomes: the rock above *my* head.

She looks up. Another wrong move. She should have sidestepped, backed away, any movement but standing there and craning her head heavenward.

A ring of goblin faces greet her from within the rock.

A ratty noose drops down–

It catches around her neck. She screams.

Suddenly it's pulled taut. She can't breathe.

They begin to haul her up.

Head pulsing. Legs kicking.

Her knife clatters to the ground.

She tries to scream again, but now it's just a squeaky hoarse whisper.

They pull her up through the hole. Body scoured by scabrous rock.

They laugh as they drag her through the darkness.

18

The greatest trick the monsters have is that they can look like us. Maybe soon they'll learn to act like us. Maybe one day they will even become us. Am I mad?

– from the Journals of John Atticus Oakes,
Cartographer of the Great Below

It's been a long fucking day down there.

Davey Morgan takes the train back out to Staten Island. Battered and bruised. Put through the wringer. Same way he feels every day on the job.

He loves it anyway. It's who he is.

Even now, as he returns home, he knows there's no night of R&R awaiting. His daughter Cassie is off at NYU, but he could call her, could have her come over. They'd eat some ice cream from the corner store, maybe watch a movie. Maybe *Die Hard*. It's his favorite movie – how could it not be? She pretends it's hers, too. Maybe it really is, but that doesn't matter. What matters is that she does it to make him happy. Even says all the lines along with him. Such a good girl.

But tonight's not about the R&R, it's about more work. They're coming up on the blasting radius for the nexus of the three tunnels. He's got to sit and work on the blasting pattern. It'll come to him. How to open up Water Tunnel #3 without bringing the other ones crashing down on their heads – drowning his crew and drying up the city.

He steps into the house. Peels off his boots. Roots through the fridge for a beer.

"Daddy."

He turns. "Cassie!" There stands his daughter. His baby girl. His heart swells.

"Look at you, girl. Surprising an old man like that." He winks and points the beer at her. "You should be more careful. Could give a fella a heart attack."

She smiles. "Can I have a hug, Daddy?"

A hug? That's not like her. She's not the *huggy* type. Not after their mother passed. Still. NYU's been hard on her. He sets the beer down, steps forward–

Her eyes.

Oh, god, her eyes.

Those aren't her eyes.

Move you old bastard.

He turns, throws the beer bottle–

Already "Cassie" is ducking it – brown bottle pops, foam everywhere – and she moves fast. He grabs for a French knife out of the block next to the toaster, but it's too late – Cassie spins him around, wrenches his head back. He feels his vertebrae pop. He sees her mouth open: foul teeth descend. Snakeface, he thinks. Which means Cassie is dead. Or bled out somewhere.

He brings the blade up into Not-Cassie's gut.

Then teeth tear into his neck.

The world lifts upward as though pulled on strings.

Darkness launches forth to replace it.

Sorago stands over the miner's body as the Vollrath slithers forward and plunges its blade-fingers into the corpse's head and heart.

Then it begins to noisily drink from the body. Not blood. But information. Knowledge. *Memories.*

The Naga presses his tentacle-hand against the wound in his gut. It comes away sticky with smoldering blood. The human wounded him. Disappointing. It'll heal because he'll make it heal. The medicine lies there on the floor before him, after all.

"Do we have what we need?"

A LIFE OF PAIN AND LITTLE PLEASURE.

"That is not what I mean." Then he adds: "Dread Chevalier." An unpleasant honorific, but the Vollrath seem to prefer it.

I SEE IT ALL. THE DEATH OF HIS WIFE. THE GRIEFSTRUCK WORKMAN. ARTHRITIS. PROSTATE CANCER OF WHICH HE WAS UNAWARE.

"Do you have the blasting plan?"

I HAVE ALL THE BLASTING PLANS. I HAVE HIS KNOWLEDGE.

"Good."

HE KNOWS THE ONE KNOWN AS PEARL. I SENSE RESPECT. AND FEAR. AND A MEASURE OF AWE.

"We're not worried about Pearl." Sorago pauses. Candlefly isn't concerned. Mookie Pearl is a thug. Just like Spall or Lutkevich. He's a pawn in a game he doesn't even understand. Unless... "*Should* we be worried about him?"

On this, the Vollrath is silent. It pulls away from the corpse of Davey Morgan and hovers there behind, rippling in a non-existent wind.

WE HAVE WHAT WE REQUIRE.

Sorago hesitates. "Good. Then if you'll excuse me."

He kneels down by the body, plunges his fangs into the dead man's neck, and begins to drink in great coppery gulps. As the blood slides down the back of his leathery throat, he already feels the warmth of his stomach wound begin to tingle and itch.

And ultimately, heal.

••••

Candlefly paces.

He opens and closes the blade of a cigar cutter again and again, each time imagining Mookie Pearl's nose, thumb, or balls getting snipped.

But once in a while Ernesto's mind wanders and he imagines his own flesh inside the cigar cutter's razor mouth – this is his fault, isn't it? He thought to dismiss Pearl. *Just some thug.* Twice now he's disrupted their plans – a child kicking over a sandcastle. He stopped them from taking the knowledge from Davey Morgan's brain. And now? He thwarted the attack on Daisypusher.

Which means they don't have the Ochre.

Which means...

He cannot abide that thought.

Renata will be gravely disappointed in him. She will tell the children. Oscar won't understand. But Adelina, she is a cruel girl, in her way. Like Mookie's own.

His wife is not a Candlefly, not by birth, and the others will laugh at him. They will mock his ambitions. Ambitions they expect him to serve alone.

A spike of anger at that: the families want him to fail. They expect him to do this alone. They don't understand what's at stake. They believe him *incapable*.

He'll show them.

He receives a text from Sorago:

It is done.

There. One part of the puzzle down.

He does not do this "texting" thing – so instead he just dials Sorago.

"The attack on Daisypusher failed," Sorago says.

"Yes, I'm well-aware. The Vollrath here know all."

"We should have sent them. I should've gone. Let me go still–"

"No. I'll need you here soon. Take Sirin and Sarnosh. Find the girl. I have a new idea."

"The girl."

"Nora Pearl. *Find Nora Pearl.*"

On the run. Hungry. Tired.

But excited, too. Things are twisting out of her grip, but Nora knows that if she can just regain her hold – even one finger's worth – then as it all falls apart she'll be there to make something of the pieces.

The plan is still in play.

She's already gone to the Sinner Kids – those white faux church-boys from the Upper West Side. Already secured the promises of the Haitians and Jamaicans of the Black Sleeves in Harlem (and just now she wishes she'd grabbed a cup of goat curry to go since they do their business out of a little restaurant called Oxtail Billy's). It wasn't easy to get the gangs to follow her: but offering them some low-cost Peacock Powder was a good start – and puts some money in her pocket.

Plus, claiming to have killed Casimir Zoladski gets her mad respect. You have to listen to me now, she thinks. What she tries not to think about is just what that respect has cost her. Look forward, not backward. What's behind you is just a big stupid wall of pain. Ahead is the promised land.

Now: time to meet the Majestic Immortals in Washington Heights.

They're a mean-ass crew. Strange mix, too: Dominicans, Puerto Ricans, couple Jewish kids. They wear hoodies with a crown and halo on the backs and fronts. Nora was just a kid when it happened, but she's heard that, ten years back, they pushed out another gang trying to step on their corners, the Electric Mongols. Chaos-sowing lunatics, anarchy-with-the-circled-A types. Wore 3D glasses. Dropped a lot of acid. The Immortals ran them out, but not before stringing up the bodies from streetlights. Hands and feet chopped off. The crown and halo carved into their foreheads.

She hears the Mongols have resurfaced recently – sometimes they pop up in the Bronx, sometimes in Queens. But they're not her problem. Not today.

Today is about the Immortals.

Nora wants them on board. *Needs* them on board. After the Mongols came through and the Immortals handled it, the Organization punished them for taking action on their own. Cut their supply. "Rezoned" their territory.

They've got an axe. She wants to help them grind it.

The Immortals operate out of the top floor of a new-law tenement house in one of the old Irish blocks of the city. Nora expects to have to plead right at the front door. Usually they've got a guy watching the stairs – walk in, and there he sits. Now it's just an empty stool. They're usually more careful than that.

Into the stairwell.

The lights are dim. Flickering and snapping. The stairway is painted in a swimming pool blue. Nora heads up the steps, feet echoing. Ten flights. It will be a hard walk but not an impossible one. Washington Heights is already on a steep-ass hill. And you don't live in New York without learning to walk some stairs. When she first moved here, she was used to life in the burbs – walking three floors sucked the life right out of her. Left her wheezing. Made her look like a real rube, total amateur hour, lost her some cred right out of the gate. Thank god she had a lot of cred to lose. Getting her father to clear out that entrenched gobbo nest at the restaurant earned her big ups around the city. People knew what she could do, then.

But she blew it. She didn't have the people. She remembers reading about the Iraq War and how when America kicked the stuffing out of Baghdad how the biggest issue in getting everything back to normal was *infrastructure, infrastructure, infrastructure*. Not just putting streets and water and sewage back in order, but also putting *people* in place.

She didn't have people. Didn't have a *coalition*.

That's what this is about. She has an opportunity. An opportunity that's different today than it was a week ago but ever since...

Well.

Let's just say it's time to evolve. Like a good animal she survives through adaptation.

Four flights. Now five. Heart and feet pounding in alternating rhythms.

She could use some Blue. That would keep her moving. But she's only got a few more hits and doesn't want to waste them here. That's OK, she tells herself. Soon as this all shakes loose she'll be in control of her own supply. Hell, her own *re*supply. Maybe after all is said and done her father will finally see what she is. What she's capable of. He won't ignore her anymore. The reality of the situation will hit him full in that confused gorilla face of his, and then *he'll* come work for *her*.

That's the prize. The one that makes her feel like a kid on Christmas morning. Waiting to open the present you've always wanted.

Her Christmas mornings were never like that. She got presents. Mookie gave Mom money, Mom bought stuff. But Mookie – *Dad*, ugh – was never there. Maybe he was when she was really little, but by the time she was seven or eight, he hardly ever left the city. When he did, he and Mom fought like a mongoose and a cobra. Few times a year she saw him, he was itchy, edgy, sleep-deprived. Beaten to hell, too. Mom would patch him up. She even got good at stitches. That was the one time the two of them didn't fight. He'd sit on the toilet, wincing and bleeding. And Mom would hover at his side, behind him, in front – Bactine, Band-Aids, gauze, peroxide, swabs, needle, thread, a fistful of Tylenol. Bloody rags in a trashcan. Stain-stick for the shirts.

That's what she really wanted for Christmas in those days: just to have Daddy come home and be with her.

But that turned sour by the time she was a teenager.

No amount of money he'd send would matter.

And now all that money is hers, anyway.

Sometimes she thinks: I can still take the inheritance. I can still blow town. I can go anywhere I want.

She thinks that, but she keeps going up, up, up.

Six floors. Seven.

It's on the seventh floor that she sees the first fly.

A fat one, too. Fat like he's been feasting on a Thanksgiving turkey.

Buzz, buzz.

Eighth floor.

That's when she sees the gun.

It's just lying there. Little .38 snubnose. Blued pitted steel.

Three steps up above that is an empty .38 shell.

She smells it, then, the stink of gunpowder. Hanging there. Not too strong.

But there just the same.

Alarm bells go off. *Run run run.*

No. Hold your ground, she tells herself. This is New York Fucking City. Stand tall. Hang tough. Nobody abides a coward in this town. You want to go up against the Organization, you can't shake like a leaf anytime there's a stiff breeze.

Ninth floor.

Blood. Just a speckling – a few flecks of it. Still a little wet. Not dried yet.

Turn and go, nobody will know you were here. This isn't good–

She has to see. Has to know. Information is power. If she comes and goes without finding out what happened, what's the value? There has to be value. She has to own this, *earn* this, learn *something* she can use.

At the top of the tenth floor steps, she sees a dark-skinned hand draped between the bars of the stairway railing.

She's shaking now. Trying not to, but shaking.

A leaf in a wind.

Shut up. Stupid girl. Don't be weak.

Keep walking.

Walking.

To the top.

Bodies. Five here. Hoodies. Crowns. Halos. Blood.

One shot in the head, his brains caught by the hood of his sweatshirt. Another with bullets stitched across his chest.

But the third and fourth…

Their necks are ripped out. A Hispanic kid, his throat torn from the front. A black girl, Dominican maybe, the side of hers chewed open.

Ahead is the door into their safehouse.

It is no longer safe. It hangs open. She sees the hallway and a handful of doors, and in that hallway and between those doors are more bodies. Another five, easy.

Then a door down that hallway squeaks open.

A bulldog of a man in a cheap gray suit steps out. Grinning at her. She knows his face. One of the Organization lieutenants. A hands-on hitter. Spall. Or Lutkevich. They come in a pair and she's not sure which one is which, but he's damn sure one of them.

He waves at her. Little waggling fingers. Playful-like. *Toodle-oo.*

They're ahead of her. They knew. Somehow, they knew. The Sinner Boys gave her up. Or the Black Sleeves. She told them where she was going. Damnit. *Damnit.*

The bulldog's got a gun. A shotgun. Pump action with the sling hanging loose.

But then he does a strange thing: he drops it. Holds up his hands as he walks toward the door, toward her. "Hey," he says. "Wait there. Let's be friends."

Big smile.

A trick. It's a goddamn trick. He knows the shotgun has a spray pattern. Won't get a good hit on her from here. Pellets. Just pellets.

He's going to get close. Stick her with a knife.

Fuck this. She knows enough. Time to run.

She pivots. Down the steps. Feet running a rumbling drum roll – fast, too fast, almost tripping, toe of one foot almost catching the heel of the other–

She catches herself on the railing. Down, down, down. *Go, go, go*–

Ninth floor.

She's watching her feet now.

Mistake. Nora almost runs into him.

The other one. *Of course* the other one. Spall and Lutkevich. Those names, you always say them together. Partners in knee-capping.

(Partners in… throat-ripping?)

The skinny one has that same smile. Waves the same way. Wiggle, waggle.

She's caught. Trapped like a rat between two cats.

Except this rat has a trick.

Her hand darts into her pocket. Finds the scales there – scales from a dead Snakeface, scales purchased from an old blobby half-and-half at the Oddments bazaar. Magic trick time. She pops one scale under her tongue. The taste is like licking a bloody battery.

The trick is she disappears. She can't feel it, but she can see it. Disconcerting as all hell to have your hands fade from view, to lose sight of your own peripheral eye sockets – you never think about those until they're gone.

The killer before her looks shocked – one minute she's there, the next, *poof*.

Good. She leaps the railing – hits the stairs going down. Body slams against the wall. Feet still echoing. The scale hides her from sight, but she's still on all the other senses. They can hear her. *Smell* her. Nora wishes suddenly she didn't wear that perfume all the time – the one that smells like gardenias, the one her father bought her a few years ago for Christmas.

No time to worry about that now.

Eighth floor. Through the door. Another stairway on the far side. It won't connect up to the tenth floor but connects to all the others. In the hall, a small black kid peers out his door, holding a raggedy Elmo doll. As she darts past, she gives him a gentle shove backward, whispers, "Hide!" Then she closes the door.

Nora keeps running.

She tries to soften her steps. Bolts across to the far side of the hall. Opens the door. It squeaks. It *bangs*.

Still, she's on the other side. The lights are brighter here. Doesn't matter, they won't be able to see her. And nobody's here.

Time, then, to wait. To hide in plain sight.

Nora eases up against the corner. Presses herself tight against it. Willing herself small. *Calm your breath.* Her teeth start to chatter. She tenses her whole body till it stops.

Nothing. No movement. Nobody here.

Just the buzz of fluorescents. The distant sound of someone yelling.

She's not sure how long she stands there. Two minutes? Twenty?

But she's lost them. She has to have. She creeps out from the corner. With each step she brings her foot gingerly down, soft heel to easy toe. Tip-toe gently toward the steps –

Bam. Something hits her in the solar plexus. The air goes out of her. She staggers back, looks forward. Nobody's there and–

The air shimmers.

The other fat one appears. Smiling.

"We have magic, too," is all he says.

Then someone grabs her from behind. Long arms wrap all

the way around her. It's impossible, even as tall as the other killer is. These arms *feel* like they wind around–

Like snakes.

Oh, no.

The thin one laughs as his fangs sink into her neck.

And he keeps laughing. She can hear that laugh, echoing into her heart and her head. Dull and throbbing around her fading pulse-beat. She tries to cry.

She can't.

19

This is what I have discerned from looking upon their cave drawings and reading their crass hieroglyphics found at their temples: I think the gobbos are slaves. We think them as animals, as monsters, but I believe they are a race of people – subterranean hominids long separated from the genetic line that created us, or created the Neanderthals. I further suspect they found their way into the dark to survive some cataclysm of the above world. The Deluge? An Ice Age? Some… volcanic pyroclasm? Their myths are unclear. They came down here thinking they were alone, but they were not. Entities waited here at the bottom of the labyrinth: Those Who Eat. Chthonic gods, entrenched at the center of the maze like worms in a dog's heart. And I believe those gods enslaved the gob-folk, whether out of fear or appeasement, or out of love or even some other heretic magic, I cannot say. I believe if we can break the goblins free of those gods, they can be tamed. Even made to live among us as people. Wouldn't that be grand?

– from the Journals of John Atticus Oakes,
Cartographer of the Great Below

"Skelly's gone," Mookie says. His voice is more a croaking bleat than the booming growl he's used to. He drops her Bowie knife on the ground. "I found this. Nobody's seen her. Which means they took her. Which means I *lost* her."

Burnsy paces in front of Mookie just outside his house.

Around, the dead of Daisypusher hover. Some clean up goblin bodies. Some weep. Some console.

"Was she someone to you?"

"No. Yeah. I dunno. A friend of my daughter's, I guess." Just one more way I failed you, Nora.

"She seemed all right," Burnsy says. A tepid sentence, but spoken with the weight one criminal affords another. She's a stand-up guy. Like you could trust her.

Could he? Mookie doesn't know. Was she planning to stab him in the back when he wasn't looking? At this point, it doesn't matter.

The cleaver hangs at his side. Wet with clotting gobbo blood. And matted with hair.

"I gotta go after her," Mookie says.

"Do you?"

"This is on me. Maybe if I figure out where they're going, I can catch up–"

"Where *are* they going? They could go south. Could go north. Could find a shaft down into the Tangle. Will she be a breeder? A sacrifice? A test for their weapons? Food? A free fuck? You don't know what they're gonna do with her, which means you don't know where they're taking her. The Underworld's a big place, in case you hadn't heard."

"Yeah, I *heard*." Then, quieter, "I still have to try."

Just then – a raspy throat-clear at the door. It's the woman in the pink robe.

"Burnsy," she says, holding out the scalloped box.

"What the–?" Burnsy steps up, takes the box. "Florence, what the hell is this?"

"The girl gave it to me. Said to protect it. I think those gobs were lookin' for it."

"It *is* Ochre," Mookie says. The Golden Gate.

Burnsy takes the box, then mists himself with the blue spritz bottle: a nervous gesture if not a necessary one. "Yeah. It is."

"Why would they want it?"

"No idea. I don't even know what it does. I just know it opens a gate."

"To what?"

On this, the dead man says nothing. Does he have an answer? Or doesn't he want to say? Whatever the case, Burnsy hands the box to Mookie. "Here. Take it. If I'm gonna be looking into this murder thing for you, then someone's going to need to protect the box. I figure a human cement mixer like you ought to do the trick."

Mookie takes it. "You sure?" The dead man nods, but then says:

"That means you don't go after Skelly. I can't have you carrying this stuff straight to the gobbos. If they were looking for this, then you need to take it up top." Burnsy lowers his voice: "Mook. Go find your daughter. Quit fuckin' around down here. If they think she did it, then they're gonna go after her. And you need to be there."

"You're right." Mookie slides the box of what-may-be-Ochre into his satchel. Next to the container of Vermillion. *Golden Gate and Red Rage*. Both myths until now. Could that mean that the Death's Head is real? Maybe, Mookie tells himself, he can still find it. Can still bring it to the Boss and cure him. Especially now that Casimir is dead. He suddenly thinks to ask Burnsy, "What do you know about sacrificial offerings? We found marigolds, mezcal, chocolate on the kid's body."

"Day of the Dead-style *ofrendas*? Sounds like someone's trying to appease someone. Or something."

"Found two broken chain links in the pockets, too. Iron."

Burnsy's crispy brow furrows. "Sounds like a summoning and binding."

"What?"

"Someone called up something from the Underworld and then... locked it the fuck down. Bound it. Maybe to the body."

"That's bad, right?"

"It's rarely good."

"Thanks for your help, Burnsy."

"We're not fuckin' fuck-buddies. But I'll go do the job. I'll find the ghost of the grandson. And I'll keep my barely-there ear to the ground for your girl, Skelly."

"I can't leave that task to you."

"You gotta. Because you have other shit on your plate. But you owe me, Mookie Pearl. You owe me and my family like you wouldn't believe."

From Daisypusher to a long unused subway station. Then to a subway tunnel. Then to the 2nd Avenue station. Then up the stairs. To the street.

Into the light. Again.

Everything hurts.

Afternoon coming into evening. Mookie hasn't slept. He's barely eaten. He had the hell kicked out of him by not one but two goblin hordes. And the mistakes he's made seem like ghosts walking with him as he staggers up out of the subway tunnel.

Skelly: dragged away. Lulu and Karyn: one dead, the other forced to be alone. Werth: maybe betrayed him.

And his own daughter? Hates him. Hates him enough to go after his entire Organization. To maybe murder a young man. To bring it all down on Mookie's head.

His ex-wife. Jess. *Jessamyn*. When was the last time he even *called* her? To check in? To do more than send her an envelope full of money?

Jesus. What an asshole he is.

No wonder they all hate him. No wonder everybody betrayed him.

Grampop's voice in his head: You're dumber than a truck full of broken toilets...

As his phone finds the signal, his cell dings. A text message coming in.

Mookie comes up to the corner, people moving in streams past him, and he checks the phone, shielding it from the glare of the sun.

One message from Werth. All caps.

CALL ME.

Mookie thinks about ditching the phone. But he doesn't *know* that Werth sold him out. And he doesn't know that Werth knows he suspects, either.

He dials the old goat.

Werth answers.

"Werth, what the f–"

"Mookie, shut up and listen. We have your daughter. You hear me? *We have your girl.*"

"You sonofabitch."

"I want you to come in, Mook. It's time to talk this out. Things have changed, you understand? You need to get right with this. There's still room for you here."

"Still room? Room for what? The fuck are you talking about?"

"The Boss is... listen, things have changed. Candlefly's got the wheel."

"Candlefly? And you're on board?" Goddamnit. "You sniveling fuck."

"I'm texting you a couple pics so you know we're serious."

We're serious. Werth and Candlefly?

"I'm glad Nora shot you," Mookie growls. "But I won't be so gentle."

"Shut up and look at your phone."

The phone dings.

Deep breath. He looks.

"Nora," he says. Voice a pained whisper. It's her. Sitting on a chair in a wine cellar. Hands bound behind her. Feet bound to the chair. They beat her. Her face is bruised and bloodied.

Head slumped forward. Mookie imagines that Werth did that. To get even.

Back on the phone.

"See?" Werth says. Sounding strained. Tired. Like all this was inevitable. "You can still do right by us. Come in. Play nice. We can all get on the same page. You can make out good. They wanna do right by us if we do right by them."

"I'm going to break you in half. I'm going to beat you to death with your own horns. I'm gonna shove your hooves up your–"

"You don't have room for that kind of bullshit here. The house, Mookie. Be here in the hour or else."

"I don't know she's alive. Nora. It was just a pic. She might be–" He can't even say the last word. It catches in his throat, a frog in a net. "I don't know she's alive."

"Here." A fumble of the phone. Skin or fabric rasping against the receiver.

Then: "Mookie."

Nora. It's her.

"It's me, honey. It's Daddy."

All she says is, "You reap what you sow."

Then Nora's gone and Werth is back on the line.

"Satisfied?"

"Go to hell."

"The house. One hour. Or she eats a bullet."

Click.

PART THREE
MEAT & MONSTERS

20

I seek to push deeper into the Great Below. Deeper than any human has pushed. I want to see the Ravenous Expanse. All I have are stories carved into walls or overheard from a roving pack of gobbos. I want to see the deepest gods, Those Who Eat. I want to stand at the edge of the Maw-Womb. I think I hear them, those gods. It's just a tickle at the back of my mind, like a little earwig burrowing into my ear. It's like tuning a radio past the static and listening for the snippets of voices in the chaos, and what I hear, what I've put together, is that if I go deeper, if I go to the heart of the Underworld, I will find the secrets of this place. I will learn why the goblins exist. I will learn what the worm-gods want. I will know where to find the Occulted Pigments and what they do. By forging downward I will learn the fate and future of the world above and how our two worlds need one another, because I believe that they do. When I go down into the Expanse, I will have the truth of this place hewn into my heart.

– from the Journals of John Atticus Oakes,
Cartographer of the Great Below

Gasp. Twitch. Thrash.

Skelly lurches awake on a pile of bones.

Animal bones, by the look of them. The delicate skeletons of mice and rats, of squirrels and pigeons. Larger bones, too: cat bones, a dog skull, the antlers of a deer, the horns and half-a-skull of a big bull. A mound. Tall as Mookie. Big as a Jersey sand dune. And this one is not the only one – the room is a wide-open cavern, heaped with piles of bones and bodies.

All of it bathed in the eerie green fire-glow from trash barrels, oil drums, and torches stuck atop crooked poles. Light and smoke like waltzing wraiths.

Shapes move in the half-light. Gobbo-shapes. Some squat and plump, others with sagging chests, scurrying about on bony arms and knobby legs. The smoke climbs up sheer walls, walls unexpectedly straight for this place – the Great Below, a land of craggy caverns and twisting tunnels, of slanted walls and jagged teeth.

This is one of their temples, she thinks.

On the walls, gobbo faces are carved into and out of the rock: broken teeth and howling mouths, crumbling noses and cratered cheeks. The eyes, though, the eyes are always cast downward. Looking to something far below.

To the carvings on the floor, maybe. The floor is marked with long, dark, lean shapes, winding around the piles of the bones and bodies. Like snakes encircling wrists, like ropes around necks.

A moan. Behind her. Skelly almost cries out, almost weeps in shock–

A man's voice: "Shhh. *Shhhh*. If they see you're awake, they'll come."

She turns. Sees someone else here atop the pile of bones. Sprawled out, half-covered by dead animals. It's an old man in an MTA uniform. Half his face frozen in a palsy, the eye sagging in its socket, the mouth drooping like a melting clock in a Dali painting.

"Who... who..."

"I'm Walt Meyers... I... I work for–"

"The MTA."

"Right. The uniform." A wet, humorless chuckle. "I did maintenance. On the tracks. I... I've been here a couple weeks." His breath is a damp wheeze. "I don't feel great. Think I'm on the way out. You don't want them up here. They... they did things."

He lifts his arm. A couple bones rattle. The uniform is torn under the armpit and–

Eggs. She knows what they are. She's heard the stories but never seen them up close and now she wants to cry out, maybe throw up. They're like frog eggs she used to see as a kid when she'd stay on her uncle's farm in Jersey. They had a creek, and there in the creek she'd see these globby, translucent eggs that almost looked like frog eyes. Dozens of them clustered together in the water, the tadpoles inside visible and twitching.

These are like that. But bigger. The things inside aren't tadpoles. They look like fat grubs pulled out of a tree or up from a sickened lawn. Bulbous and without limbs.

Grubs. Baby gobbos.

"I got 'em here and got one behind the ear–" He turns his head and there, on the palsy side of his face, a single egg covers his whole ear. When he moves it quivers like a Jell-O mold. "And a half-dozen between my legs, too. They... they broke my knees. Snapped 'em when I tried to get up and run. You can't run. You can't hide."

Tears weep from his one good eye.

"We have to get out of here," she tells him.

"There's no escaping this place. People have tried. We're not alone here. Soon as your eyes adjust you'll see them. Some are dead. Some close to it. Occasionally one wakes up on the pile, crawls down the heap. Or makes a run for it. Like me. They catch you. They're everywhere. And when they have you that's when they come up. Lay their eggs. Some don't lay eggs at all. I watched two of them attack a heavy-set fellow two piles over and…" His voice drifts off and he licks his lips. "Here." A dry whisper."You wanna see something?"

He gestures with his head.

Skelly follows his gaze up.

The floor is all dark shapes, and at first she thinks the ceiling is, too.

But soon as she realizes the reality, Walt confirms it. "It's a map," he says. "Took me a while to figure it out. Lot of it is just nonsense, what I guess must be tunnels or passages folding in on each other. But in the middle of it is something I know all too well – the subway map. Just Manhattan, not the boroughs, but you can see their curves, how some are together and then breakaway. Can almost make the shape of the island. Like Manhattan's circulatory system. It's almost… *arterial*."

Skelly tries to parse it. A map. Of the underground of the city. Or at least, what's just beneath it – what in the Underworld they'd call the "Shallows". She can see the pocket where the town of Daisypusher sits. A lot of the tunnels are thin and small, noodles and tapeworms tied into one another. But along the far eastern side of the map runs a big fat line, like a pipe. And another thick line is carved at the top of the island and runs into it, and a third one comes in toward the bottom but doesn't seem finished. Where this tunnel ends is a symbol like Skelly's never seen before: a triangle with what looks to be a mouth in its center.

She points the thick lines out. Asks what they are.

"I was trying to figure out the same thing, but then I realized–"

A scream cuts the air like a hatchet. A woman's scream. Walt reaches up, pulls her low to the pile, hisses, "Look."

A young woman stands atop a pile of corpses. She's far enough away Skelly can't make out much about her face, but she sees the woman turn and shake and begin to flail, head cast back so far the scream rises out of her like smoke from the burn barrels.

The gobbos come fast. But not fast enough to catch what suddenly erupts out of her. Her body twitches like it's being shot. Skelly hears the wet *pops* and sees the silhouettes of things wrenching free from her body. The scream is cut to a gagging sound. The shadows of grubs fall from her armpits. From between her legs. From up and out of her mouth. *Plop, plop, plop*.

A splashing sound. Then a chorus of high-pitched squealing, like someone trying to drown a litter of piglets in a washtub.

The gobbos come. Take away the grubs. It calls to mind ants carrying larvae.

As for the woman's body? It collapses onto the pile. Utterly still.

Just one more for the mix.

Skelly bites her hand. Stifles her own cry. Can't stop shaking.

"That happens," Walt says. Then, sadder, more distant, "That's what's gonna happen to me."

Not me, Skelly thinks.

"Don't think about it. Here, look. Those pipes there on that map," Walt says. "Those are water tunnels. The city's water comes from upstate. Reservoirs. Two tunnels are done, but the third's being dug. You can see the third ends at the funny-looking symbol there. Don't know what that is."

Her first thought: I need to tell Mookie.

Her second thought: And then he needs to come down here and burn this place to the ground.

But that means she has to leave. Has to find a way out – through the bones and bodies, through the dozens of goblins crawling all over this place.

She feels at her side. Her knife is gone. She feels a tiny stab of remorse at that – the knife was a custom job. Cost her a pretty penny. Though now she's not so sure the skull fetish is one she wants to keep.

On her other hip is a surprise.

Her skates. They're still there. Laced to her belt loop.

"I'm going to get out of here," she says, untying her skates. As she does, the heel of one skate knocks loose the jawbone of what might be a deer skull. The bone bounces down the heap, rattling against every other bone as it falls.

Oh, no.

Gobbos – some just shadows, some lit against the flickering green fire – stop. And turn. They start jabbering, grunting. Picking up weapons.

Then they start moving toward the bone heap.

Candlefly tries to remain calm. But he knows his rankled irritation is showing. Even as he speaks he hears it bleed through.

"What was *that*, exactly? You reap what you sow?" He takes a few steps closer to the thug's troublesome daughter. "Some kind of code phrase, perhaps? I have a great deal riding on this–"

Nora frowns. "Please. We don't have code phrases. We're not close."

"Then what was it? Please. *Do tell.*"

"You wanted him to come," she says. "If I got on the phone and sounded all weepy and needy and nerdy, he might not have bought it. But play it tough and he knows this is the real deal. Hello, I'm not very nice to him, if you haven't noticed?" She squirms. "You going to untie me or what?"

Candlefly hesitates. Then he nods toward Sorago.

The Snakeface glides silently toward her, begins undoing her bonds.

"You didn't need to keep me tied up in that chair," she says.

"Yes. Well. I wanted to make sure you kept your end of our bargain."

As she stands out of the chair, she stretches. "I did. He's on his way."

"A nice touch with the–" He points to her bruised face. "The makeup."

"Good enough for a cameraphone."

"You really don't care for him at all, do you? Your father."

The girl hesitates. As though she's thinking about it, earnestly considering it. "No. I don't know. He wasn't a good dad."

Candlefly chuckles. "Trust me from experience. Few fathers are good fathers. You should respect yours a little more."

"Oh? You have kids?"

"Two. Adelina and Oscar. Twins."

"You trying to convince me to grant my father clemency?"

"Clemency. Oh my. Such a big word for a little girl."

She stiffens. "Not so little. And I like books. You got a problem with that?"

"Of course not."

She looks at the floor. "Hey. I gave him chances. Chances when I was a kid. Chances when everything fell apart. Chances even now. Just a few days ago I offered to have him work for me. But *once again*, he refused." She rolls her eyes.

"A missed opportunity."

"I guess so." She looks up now at him. She's got fascinating eyes – pointed and gray, like the tip of a sharpened pencil. And it's like they're pleading with him. "You won't kill him?"

"No," he lies. "We won't kill him."

Another pause. Finally, she nods. "Good."

"Let me ask you something else."

"If you must."

"It must have surprised you. To find Casimir like that on the floor. Having met a truly brutal death."

Her gaze meets his. "I already told you, I killed him."

"Did you?"

"I did."

"Ah. Well! You're lucky then that I consider his death no more than a speed bump in our relationship. Besides–" He can't help but smile at this. "It's nice to be working with someone so robust. So *vigorous*. What you did to the young man was…" He shudders, as though feigning excitement at the girl's deception. "What a partnership this will be, Miss Pearl. A brand new day is here."

She struggles to unlace the skates. Get them on her feet. The gobbos are coming. Clambering up the heap. Bones clatter. Goblins hiss.

One skate on.

And now they're here.

A gobbo with sallow cheeks and bulbous blood-red eyes comes at her, jaw creaking open and a tubule tongue searching the air – a glistening egg already gleaming at its tip, pushing out like a cancerous tumor through bubble-gum-pink lips.

Skelly cries out. Swings with her one free skate. The wheels are Zombie wheels with hard, anodized aluminum centers. She clocks the gobbo in the side of the head, makes a mushy dent. The tongue recoils, and the creature rolls down the bone-heap with a rattle.

She kicks out. Sends another one tumbling.

A third comes up on her left. No tongue, and it takes her a second to realize what's in the thing's hand. It's a Christmas stocking – grimy, greasy, and it swings like it's got something heavy in the foot. Then she hears the jingle of change–

The gobbo swings the Christmas stocking right at her head.

She's too slow. She feels it. She brings the skate up and *knows* it'll land too late–

The gobbo is suddenly bowled backward.

With Walt on top of it.

Skelly backpedals, the osseous heap shifting beneath her. It's hard to get purchase, hard to find stability–

The gobbos come at her.

But Walt is there again. He launches himself in front of her. Waves his arms–

"I'm all egged up!" he cries, a yawp of throaty rage. "You come at her, you might hurt your precious *babies*. That what you want?"

They hiss. Test him by swinging weapons – knives, broken bottles, boards with nails in them – at the air in front of his head. He whimpers with every swing.

It buys her time. She tries not to hurry, tries to focus and do it right. Skate on. Pulled tight. Laces taut.

The gobbos fan out. Walt's just one man. They are legion.

He swipes at them. Throws bones that rebound off goblin heads.

But it doesn't matter.

Because here they come.

Skelly doesn't want to look. She closes her eyes and lurches forward. The skates work against her with the shifting pile beneath her, but it's all she has.

She's just lucky goblins aren't tall.

Hands on hot, rubbery skin. A shriek beneath her. Her elbow connects with something–

When she opens her eyes, she sees no more goblins ahead of her.

All she sees is the downward slope of the heap.

She hits it with her head, and topples down the hill, head over feet, feet over head, end over end again and again – bones cracking her in the head, cutting her skin–

Something slashes her cheek–

Then a sting in her palm–

Green glow a swirl around her, everything a dizzying blur–

Until she lands at the bottom. Shoulder first, hard on stone. There's a starburst of pain, but no time to think about that now. She scrabbles on hands and knees, more pain in her left hand–

The shattered ribcage of a small mammal has become embedded in her palm. Blood flows around dirty little bones.

It's an absurd thought at a time like this but she thinks: I'm going to need some high-octane antibiotics to handle that.

She shakes her hand. The ribcage falls free, clatters on stone.

Ahead of her, goblins emerge from the shadows around the burn pile and into the light of a flickering green torch. It's then she realizes many have faces reminiscent of human babies: fat cheeks and wet mouths, big eyes, wispy hair. But there the comparison ends. These are human infants by way of a demonic coupling, ashen skin and colored eyes, rotten teeth and egg-laying tongues. As they come closer, she gets her bearings, takes a deep breath...

Skelly screams.

And then she skates.

Werth sits upstairs in the foyer while Candlefly remains downstairs with the girl. The old goat drums his fingers on his lap. They're really making friends with Nora Pearl, now? How will Mookie react to that? Werth isn't sure how *he* feels about that. He'd just gotten used to thinking, OK, regime change, it's sink or swim, fuck or walk, play or die. And now Candlefly is making eyes at the enemy? The little shit who killed Casimir Zoladski? How does that make a single fucking *mote* of sense?

"Don't worry," Candlefly had said. "I don't trust her. One move and she's done."

"And Mookie?" Werth asked. "He gets to stay? We'll give him a chance? Because I need him. He's good people." He neglected to add: and you don't want him on your bad side, cause he'll hit you like a goddamn cannonball.

"If Mookie wants in, he can have in," Candlefly said. "Now make the call." Then he handed Werth the phone and...

Now he's upstairs. Waiting. Mookie will show. He has to.

Haversham paces nearby. "They're going to give Pearl a chance?"

"That's what Candlefly said. He's gonna let him try to make nice. See if we can't... all be a big family again."

"We'll never be a family again. We're just a business." Haversham stops. Stands and stares off at nothing. "Maybe that's how it should've been all along."

"Go to hell, Haversham. The Boss treated you like he was one of his own."

"Yes, of course, I..."

"And..." Here Werth stands, hobbles over, keeps his voice low. "And Candlefly? He's gonna treat us like resources. Like *employees*. And hey, speaking of the other 'employees', where are the other lieutenants in all of this? You try any of them?"

"I tried calling."

"And?"

"I'm... not getting any answers."

"Jesus. Not a one?"

"Not a one."

"That isn't good, Haversham."

"I suspect..." Haversham's voice trails.

"You suspect they've been put six feet under."

"Liquidated is the word I was going to use."

Werth rolls his eyes. "Of course it is. What about us? Are we going to be liquidated? Is that their plan for us? Jesus Christ, look what they did to Spall and Lutkevich. They're not even... them anymore. Just Snakeface fuckfaces in disguise."

"I don't think so. It doesn't make sense. We're still here."

"We are, at that."

"Maybe we're the new regime."

Werth's gut tightens. His body hurts. His *mind* hurts, too. "I hope so, Haversham. I really fucking hope so."

Every part of her is electric with fear and aversion. Skelly's brain has to work overtime to convince her body to cooperate, to barrel forward on a pair of roller skates through what may very well be the bowels of hell. This is the act of racing toward a cliff, of walking into a punch, of springing headlong into certain doom.

But she has no choice. Skate forward or die standing.

Only problem: she hasn't skated in years. Skelly used to do derby. A lot of her girls still do. It's part of their look. But that's the thing. For her, these days it's *just* aesthetic. The skates are hers, sure, but she's been running a gang, not rollin' around a flat track.

She's out of practice.

And this ain't no flat track. She doesn't have her girl-pack with her. No jammers, no blockers, no pivot. She's fresh *meat* here.

Soon as she starts to skate forward – toward the onrushing gobbos – the wheels bounce over a lip, a lip she realizes too late is part of the floor carvings, the massive stone etchings of monstrous worms and snakes winding around each mound of death. It jars her; she almost falls forward, but she twists her hips and leans into it, getting her skates beneath her–

And that's when she realizes, those carvings are just what she needs. They're a smooth track.

Yes. *Yes*. As the goblins rush toward her, she reaches out her hand–

And catches the flickering green torch.

Soon as she meets the rushing goblins, she skates by them in an arc, swiping the torch across their faces and into their field of vision. They squeal and shriek. One launches himself at her with a rattling bike chain in hand but she ducks, feels the skate wheels hop the lip and land in the track of the carved floor–

Another twist and she stays in the track.

She rides the shape of the monster, winding around one heap and then another, the serpent tracks forming massive coils and knots around each–

There. *There*. The way out. An archway. Fire-lit. The

arch a carving of eyeless worms whose flesh is marked with strange symbols.

Ahead, through the arch, the darkness shifts–

She thinks it's just her eyes. *Skate, goddamnit, just skate.*

But then something emerges. A black shape, a reaper's cloak without the reaper in it. It rushes toward her. She sees shiny eyes, like nickels catching light, hears the sound of blades scraping together–

In the derby, when you're a blocker, you have to keep your center of gravity low so you don't fall – and that gives you speed, too.

Skelly shrinks herself small, hunkering low as she blasts forward.

The reaper's cloak flutters over her head.

Then through the archway.

Where the stone is no longer smooth.

The wheel hits rough-hewn stone. Clips on a crag. Skate-nose caught.

She pitches forward, her head cracking against a toothy outcrop. She sees flashbulbs go off – the tunnel ahead slopes downward. And once again her body is a rag doll thrown down a hill.

21

I have a dead man to lead the way. The undead of Daisypusher know this place better than most, almost like it's intuition, or second nature – a nature born as they die. It suggests again to me that while the Underworld is a physical place, it resonates with the energies of death, creating a profound sympathetic bond between what we experience in our afterlife and the corporeal channels of this realm. Regardless, my guide is a dead man who has chosen the post-life name of Cerberus, not because he has three heads but rather, ironically, because he was killed by three dogs while trying to protect his daughter from their attack. She was mauled, sadly – lost fingers, needed some reconstruction of her jaw. But she lives while he dies. That is his mission, he said: to help after death to pay for the surgeries she yet needs and to make her life better even as his own is forfeit. We should all be so lucky to have so strong a mission in life or beyond it.

– from the Journals of John Atticus Oakes,
Cartographer of the Great Below

He knows they see him. Mookie stands at the door. Knows now that there's a camera pointed at him. This is it. This is his last moment to do differently. He tells himself, I could turn and run. Fuck the Organization. Fuck Werth. Hell with my daughter. She's done me wrong too many times now, and I don't owe her anything but the sight of my turned back.

But that's not Mookie. What would he do on his own? Die on the vine like the last grape hanging, that's what. His is a life defined by others. Whether it's helping them, hurting them, or just plain doing what he's told. He's not the man running the machine. He's just a rubber belt fed through hungry gears.

Before he does anything, he takes out his tin of Blue, presses a pad of cakey peacock powder between his fingers, and massages it into his temples. The horse-kick hits. A few chills after. Then it's all melted butter and smooth jazz.

He opens the door and goes inside.

Mookie's at the door. Barbarian at the gates. Werth watches as Haversham ushers Mookie inside. Like a man leading a dire wolf in on a leash.

Mookie. With a heavy cleaver hanging at his hip in a sheath. And his beat-to-shit leather satchel dangling over his beefy shoulder.

Candlefly approaches from around the corner. Smiling. Hand extended.

Mookie sees him. But then looks past him.

Right at Werth.

The lip curl. The narrowed gaze. The popping knuckles. Hate waits hot in that gaze. He thinks I betrayed him, Werth thinks. Shit, maybe I did.

"Mr Pearl," Candlefly says, his voice more *unctuous* than usual. He doesn't wait for Mookie to return the handshake – Ernesto reaches right in, pushes his hand into Mookie's gargantuan grip.

His eyes suddenly go wide.

Werth hears the grinding of knucklebones.

"You've got an impressive…" Candlefly's head cranes on his neck. The pain in his wince is obvious. "Handshake."

"Boss said it was how you got someone's measure," Mookie growls. "I wanted you to have my measure."

"Consider it so."

"My daughter."

"–is downstairs."

"You hurt her."

"She *attacked* us." A lie. Werth knows they sent people after her.

Candlefly tries to retrieve his hand. But Mookie doesn't relinquish the man.

"Where's the Boss?"

"Upstairs. Resting. *Recovering*." Werth hears that and thinks: yeah, right.

"I want to see Nora."

"Of course," Candlefly says. "This way, please? Though, first you'll have to… let go of my hand?"

Mookie says nothing, instead makes the sound in his chest of a tomb being opened. He finally lets go of Candle-fly's hand.

"Shall we?"

Candlefly heads toward the cellar steps.

Mookie walks after, once more giving Werth a look. In that look, Werth can practically see himself being torn limb-from-limb in the dark behind Mookie's eye.

Werth gives him a nod. As if to say, "It's OK".

All Mookie does is bear his teeth like a rabid dog.

He follows the two of them downstairs, walking with Haversham.

Down into the wine cellar. Racks of wine necks and bottle bottoms. Barrels in the back. Warm lighting. Everything smells of wood and must and the faint sour tang of spilled wine. And there, in the middle, in a chair:

Nora.

Mookie pushes past Candlefly. He runs to her, drops to his knees. Cups her head in his hands. "You're all right?"

She wrenches her head away, then gently pushes his hands

away from her face.

"I'm fine," she says.

He goggles at her. "You're... not hurt. Or tied up."

"Duh."

"I don't get it." He turns. Gives a desperate look to the others, then back to Nora. "They hurt you."

"Just a little." She smiles, then tilts her neck to show off an already-healing wound. *A Snakeface bite*. "You got played, Daddy. It was the only way to get you here. Make you think I was in danger. You'd do anything for me, I said."

"Nora–"

"There's a new business arrangement. You're at the bottom of it."

"The hell?" Mookie doesn't understand. All he knows is one sentence is tumbling through his head again and again: You got played, Daddy.

"I'm going to be your–"

Then: a sound. Off to Mookie's left. A heel-scuff.

Nora's gaze flits in that direction. Her eyes go wide. Then she looks right.

She mouths the word before she says it: "No. No!"

Suddenly her gaze locks with his and all she says is:

"Run!"

She hates him. That's what she tells herself as he comes into that wine cellar like a beast led to slaughter. He was married to the mob. They were his family. Not her. Not Mom. And now...

And now here he stands, the poor dope about to have his manhood rubber-banded and sliced off by the very Organization to which he pledged his fealty–

That hate inside her rises hot and feels just. It tastes of sweet comeuppance. *You deserve this, you dick.* She's old enough now to recognize that this is a teenage hate, the petulant hate of children for their parents, but it's so deep-seated, so *integral* to who Nora is, she can't help but take pleasure at it.

She thought everything had gone sideways. Casimir, dead. An attack on the Get-Em-Girls. The death of the Majestic Immortals. Then: she gets taken by a pair of Snakefaces to what she assumed was *the grave*. But Candlefly – the face of the *new* Organization, or so he said – offered her a new deal, instead.

Bring in your father and you can be his boss.

Then he clarified: His Keeper. His *Master*.

Some girls for Christmas want Barbie Dream Cars or ponies. Other girls want makeup, or a new cell phone, or hell, when she was 12 she wanted a pellet rifle (which she did not get). But now, all she wants is a collar around Mookie's neck. And she wants to be the one holding the leash.

And that's what she's about to tell him.

She's about to say, I'm going to be your boss. You're going to be my little bitch. You'll do everything I want. You'll furnish me in Blue. You'll kill anybody who gets in my way. You'll get me a puppy for my birthday. You asshole.

Before she can say any of that, she sees the darkness move between wine racks.

A Snakeface assassin emerges – one of the killers who attacked her and brought her here. It's the thin one, but the fat one is only a step behind.

And then off to the right is the third.

The one Candlefly calls "old friend".

All of them, fangs out. Tentacles searching the air silently.

It's then she realizes: they're going to kill my father.

That's when it all melts away. The anger. The hate. Like ice in the Devil's mouth.

She doesn't expect the word to come out of her, but there it is, screamed aloud, betraying everything she wanted, everything that she believes herself to be:

"Run!"

••••

He didn't see that coming.

The first thought that pops into Werth's head as chaos takes hold is an oddly calm and quiet one: The little sociopathic bitch has a heart after all. Buried somewhere under that glacier she calls a soul.

Then the thought is gone as it all goes to epic shit.

Nora screams for her father to run.

But Mookie does no such thing. He lurches to his feet. Puts his daughter at his back in a protective stance and stands tall as the first two Snakefaces close in.

The one that looks like Spall leaps – and meets Mookie's thundercrack fist, head snapping back and shattering a bottle. Red wine spills like blood.

The other – Not-Lutkevich – tries to tackle Mookie from the side, but it's like a dog hitting the side of a school bus: he thuds dully into the slab of meat that is Mookie Pearl, and Mookie picks him up and slams him down on his knee. Like a child breaking a twig over his leg. Lutkevich rolls to the ground, doubled over.

But Sorago–

Sorago's *fast*.

He twists out of the way of a backhanded hammer-fist, comes up around and behind Mookie as if the laws of physics are no longer in service – fangs thrust forward, glistening.

They plunge into the back of Mookie's neck.

Werth thinks, This is it, goddamn, Mookie's down for the count, and he looks to Haversham, but Haversham is just staring, a bug-eyed fly-catcher who's never been in the shit, who's never been in the fray with bullets knocking splinters out of the doorframe inches from his head, who lives a life of spreadsheets and appointment books.

But Mookie isn't done for. Not by a long shot.

The big sonofabitch spins. Sorago barely holds on with squirming tentacle-fingers, fangs still embedded in Mookie's neck. The other two – Sirin and Sarnosh, Werth thinks their names are – lurch up, hissing, arcs of spat venom just missing Mookie's face.

Mookie drives his hulking body backward. A rack topples. Glass shatters. Sorago drops, flailing.

Candlefly sees an opening.

Werth watches, horror-struck.

The man reaches into his suit.

Draws a small pistol. A Walther. Points it not at Mookie–

But at Nora. She rushes to meet him, a sudden glimpse of the father within the daughter, a feral tiger sprung free from its cage–

Candlefly clips her across the face with the gun. She hits the floor and rolls into a ball, clutching her cheek. He points the gun at her.

Then–

Mookie, now free of Sorago, slams into Candlefly. He drives him forward into another rack: bottles fall, thud, roll free. Candlefly tries to bring up the gun but Mookie knees him in the groin, grabs the man's wrist and *twists*–

Snap. Bright white bone spears – like sharp teeth, Werth thinks – poke free from Candlefly's wrist as the man cries out.

Mookie hefts Candlefly up by the throat, drives a cannonball fist into the man's face – *boom* – just as Not-Spall's fangs sink into the meaty back of Mookie's neck.

Another hit. Candlefly's face rocks back. Blood squirts from his nostrils.

Not-Lutkevich coils around Mookie's leg–

Fangs sink into Mookie's calf.

A third punch. Candlefly's face looks like a package of ground chuck. A red, half-collapsed mess.

Now Sorago steps in.

The assassin doesn't move swiftly. He stands up from the wreckage of a wine rack, dusts himself off. Werth watches the Snakeface stalk across the floor with confidence.

The Naga comes up behind Mookie like a shadow.

Werth thinks: Help him!

But help who? Which one?

Instead, he does nothing.

Sorago's fangs again sink into the side of Mookie's neck.

Mookie's hand darts to his side. Grabs the cleaver there. Unhooks it from his belt, raises it up–

It hangs over Candlefly's head. The Sword of Damocles. Swaying gently.

His arm drops to his side.

The cleaver drops to the floor. The corner of the blade *ka-chunks* into the wood and sticks there.

Candlefly's breath comes as a ragged whistle through a ruined nose. Blood bubbles up from lips split and torn by his own now-loose teeth. He wipes his face across the sleeve of his suit, leaving a crimson streak on soft beige.

With his unbroken hand, Ernesto pushes gently on Mookie's chest.

The big thug falls. The floor shakes. A lamp rattles.

Werth stands. Stock still, like any movement might be construed as a treachery against... someone, anyone. He doesn't know what to do. Every part of him is paralyzed by indecision and uncertainty. His loyalty is flapping loose in the wind.

Blood on his fists. Rage in his heart. One of Candlefly's teeth stuck in the meat around his knuckle. The poison runs through him, turning his blood to slush. Squeezing his muscles so hard they lock up tight and lose all sense of tension. He stands. Still awake. Still aware. But he can't do anything. His mind is unmoored from the rest of him. His body adrift, a boat on an ocean without a sail or a rudder – him the captive captain, unable to command his ship. And then one more bite and no more punches and Candlefly wipes his messy face on his nice suit and puts one finger on Mookie's chest and pushes. It doesn't even feel like he's falling. It feels like the world is lurching upward. Like the train next to you is drifting backward when really you're the one moving forward.

The ground hurries up to meet him.

There, flat on his back. He sees Nora. Now up and crawling. The man, Candlefly, is yelling at his Snakeface friend – something about being slow, no hurry, while he was getting pummeled to a pulp. Then Haversham, that weak-kneed weasel, points to Nora and sounds a cry of alarm–

She's getting up now, getting her legs under her–

Run, baby, run.

But Candlefly stalks toward her. Gun out. As she tries to stand he bashes her in the back of the head. Mookie tries to scream, tries to tell Candlefly he's going to rip his spine out his mouth and reinstall it through his asshole, but all he can do is whimper and mewl as Nora rolls over–

Candlefly straddles her–

She holds up her hands like that matters–

Then Candlefly puts a bullet into her gut. *Bang.*

Mookie bites through his own tongue.

Tastes blood. Smells gunpowder. Sees darkness.

Lights out.

22

We are lost in the Tangle. Its labyrinthine passages confound. Passages up, holes down, tunnels east, caverns west – endlessly looping upon themselves. Direction has no meaning. Nor does time. It's like outer space – or, perhaps, its opposite. I've seen many places – rooms, if you will – that are distinct. Rooms of stalagmites and stalactites that look like bloodied teeth, grottos with rock outcroppings that look like faces, old goblin nests filled with the remnants of stolen humanity: a child's tricycle, a stop light, a fireman's mask. Dangers abound, too: pools of stinking sulfur, drips of snotty acid from stone above, pockets of gas – some that choke, some that conjure sleep, some that will strip the skin from your bones. Cerberus, who I've since learned is really named Danny, is still leading us forward, but though he claims to know the way, his roving gaze tells me we're lost. To my mind, we have only one important direction to reach the Expanse: down, down, always down.

– from the Journals of John Atticus Oakes,
Cartographer of the Great Below

A goblin hand touches her face. Skelly gasps, cries out – consciousness slamming back into her like the action on a pistol. Her hand feels on the ground, finds a rock–

Bam. Clocks it into the side of the monster.

"Ow, fuck!"

She staggers to her feet.

A long tunnel. Subway tile merged with porous stone. The only light comes from flecks of glowing blue stuck in the pores of the tunnel walls. Like fireflies crushed into the rock.

Burnsy is on the ground. Clutching his head.

"Oh, shit," Skelly says, hurrying over. Helping him up.

"You brained me with a rock."

"Sorry, daddy-o."

"Daddy-o. Who does that? Who still uses that word?"

She shrugs. "Kind of our thing. The Get-Em-Girls." *Whatever's left of us, anyway.* "It's a habit. I don't... I don't know."

"Yeah. Well. A guy rescues you from a pack of goblins and nurses your cuts and he gets a rock to the dome to pay for it. That should teach me."

A wave of guilt washes over her. "I thought you were... one of them."

"I'm ugly, but I'm not *that* ugly. Anyway, if you're up, it's time to move. I haven't heard any of those fuckers for a while, but that doesn't mean they're not still out there, searching. They'll give up eventually – they have the patience of a twitchy cricket – but I still don't want to take my chances." As Burnsy talks, he starts packing up gear into an old 80s-era Jansport backpack.

Her wounds suddenly flare with fresh pain – a slow sting that transitions to a hot throb. She lifts her hand to her face, where the bones cut her, and feels her palm is sticky. And it smells like a dead animal.

Burnsy must see her face because he says, "It's gopher grease."

"Do I wanna know?"

"Not really."

She blanches. Sniffs it again. "I think I wanna know."

"There's an animal down here. It's like a gopher, but it's all white, has eight legs, and is blind as my mother–"

"So, nothing like a gopher."

"We call 'em gophers, all right? You know, just for being a smartass I'm gonna tell you the whole thing. That grease on your hand is from their anal glands."

"Oh, god!" She gags, turns, tries to wipe her hand on the wall.

"Whoa, whoa, don't do that. That stuff is at a premium. It heals cuts like you wouldn't believe. Keep that goop on you, goddamnit."

She winces. Lets her hand hang so she doesn't have to smell it.

Backpack slung over his blistered shoulder, he waves her on. "Let's go, let's go. We gotta move. I got a lead on the dead Zoladski kid."

"Change of subject," she says, hurrying after him. "How'd you find me?"

"Luck, mostly."

"You just… stumbled upon me."

"Nah. Not *that* lucky. I was looking, trust me – I told Mookie I would. The luck part is that I found a ghost that had seen you. The poor demised fucker didn't know what he'd seen, of course – mostly he was just reliving his last moments in his head again and again – but he'd seen the gobbos dragging you and some of the other folks from Daisypusher. I knew the location of the temple. Went to scout it and there you were. Half-conscious. A pack of gobbos on your tail. They took you one direction, the Daisypusher dead in another."

They round a curve in the tunnel and she can feel a gentle slope downward.

"And how'd we get away from them? The goblins."

He doesn't have to answer her. All he has to do is point.

Up ahead is a souped-up Yamaha four-wheeler. With big-ass wheels swaddled in spiked, studded chains. Like chains for driving on winter roads but juiced up on steroids. On the front of the quad is a goblin skull with plastic googly eyes. The rest of the thing is painted red, white, and blue.

"Go America," she says, somewhat breathless. "This is what you had under that tarp out back of your house, wasn't it?"

"You got it. She's an all right ride. Better than walking on foot. Doesn't get into the nooks and crannies, but she'll take me most places in the Shallows, even carry me through some of the Tangle if I need her to." He winces, straddles the seat. "Chafes the shit out of my thighs to drive, but such is the not-quite-life of a reanimated burn victim. Hop on."

He pats the seat.

She eases behind him.

He pops on a pair of goggles. Gives her a pair, too. They're shop goggles made of clear – if dirty – plastic all the way around.

Then–

Key in the ignition. The engine gutters, then grumbles to life – a fat, slovenly dragon awakening from slumber after eating all the villagers.

"Let's go find ourselves a ghost," he says.

Then he guns it.

Time oozes. It twists. It crawls, centipede-like, away from Nora's grip. She does not know how long she's been here. How long since they killed her father, since they shot her in the stomach. How long since she thought she had the world in her hand and Mookie Pearl by the leash. How long since it all went to shit.

How long since Candlefly – whose face was now a mincemeat pie baked in a bloody crust – dropped her here in this bedroom to bleed out and die. How long since he whispered in her ear, "You betrayed me, and so now you suffer a death that creeps up on you, the anticipation slow as your misery mounts."

She lies on the bed. Breath coming in little shallow rabbit gasps.

I'm dying.

Bullet in her middle. Tore up – what? Her stomach? Liver? A kidney?

A little voice reminds: It was always going to come down to this. You knew that, didn't you? You kept coming at the beast. One day the beast would return the favor.

Then, a defiant voice: Not. Dead. Yet.

She slides a trembling hand into her pocket. Finds her tin of blue. Pops it: not much left but enough for now. She almost fumbles it, drops it on the bed but manages to cup her fingers into a little shovel and scoop out some Cerulean.

Nora presses powder to each temple. Blue flecks flaking onto the white pillow and bedsheets.

It washes over her, a tide of fire, hot like a habanero, then warm like whiskey.

Soon her breathing grows deeper. Fuller. The Blue won't mend her – it's strong enough for superficial wounds but not a gut-shot.

But it'll keep her alive for a little while longer.

She stays like that for a while. Stilling her breath. Willing the wound to go numb. Trying to imagine how she's going to escape. Trying *not* to think about her father. That last one: an impossibility. Her mind wanders to him. Is he dead? He must be. This moment, she thought it'd bring her happiness. To see the man who poisoned her life himself poisoned? But was that what she wanted? For her father to *die*?

It isn't. She just wanted him to finally pay attention. That was all. All of this was to force him to see her. To see who she was, and who she'd become because of him.

And now he's dead.

And she'll be dead soon too if she can't figure out what to do next.

••••

I'm gonna die.

Again.

Skelly escaped the gobbo temple and thought that was the end of it. Now here she is, reminded of her own mortality once more. Death doesn't stare her in the face so much as *whip past her* at what feels like a hundred miles-per-hour.

The quad barrels through downward-sloping Underworld tunnels. The quad bounds and growls. Tires bounce over hard rock, giving the whole vehicle a bounce and a lift where Skelly's stomach feels like it leaves her body and gets left behind. Burnsy's loving it. Hooting. Letting go of the handlebars and holding two blister-red fists up in the air. It's then she remembers:

He was a stuntman.

I'm driving though hell on a four-wheeler with a formerly-living stuntman.

Once again her brain reiterates what she now feels is absolutely true:

I'm gonna die.

It's not liberating, this feeling. Her life does not flash before her eyes. She is, in fact, married to the moment. Married to every scraggy rock that passes within inches of her skull, bound to every rough-rimmed pothole the quad drops into, fixed permanently with the air in her face and the bite of the goggles around her eyes and the skitter of roach-rats and cankerpedes as they flee before the coming four-wheeler.

Once upon a time, she fancied herself a tough bitch. Now she's not so sure.

At least she isn't pissing her pants. Small favors and all that.

The tunnel twists. It pulls hard right; tires grind on loose stone, spraying gravel against the wall like buckshot. Then a serpentine left – before curving right again.

Suddenly – *whoosh* – they're out of a tunnel and into a wide-open cavern, a massive sepulchrous chamber with twisting salt columns that look like piles of melting soft serve peppered with ice crystals. The ceiling looks melty, too – colors like paint melting. But that's not what truly draws her eye and lends this cavern a graveyard vibe.

The room is home to what must be hundreds of statues.

No. Not statues. *Skeletons*. Put back together. Rearticulated. Made to stand up. Hollow-eyed skulls tilted on bowed spines so they are forever staring down.

At first she thinks they're children, but as soon as they pass one and she sees the deformation of the bones, the bulbous off-shape of the skull, she realizes:

These are goblin skeletons.

As if she were not afraid enough.

Burnsy must sense her fear – maybe in the way she grabs him tighter. He shouts back at her, "Goblin graveyard! Don't worry! They fear their own dead – won't come near the place!" The quad winds through the bone garden. Then he yells, "Hold on!"

They hit a skeleton. It bursts. Bones rattle around them. Something that might be a knucklebone pops off the front of her goggle.

She's about to scream at Burnsy, but then he points–

"There! *There*!"

A flickering shape at the edge of the bone garden. Pale. Human. Walking forward, toward a tunnel. The shape blinks in and out of existence. Erratic and intermittent, a light switch flipped on, off, on, off by a mischievous child.

A ghost.

She's never seen one. She knows they're down here, but unless you're looking for them, they tend to be invisible. Just foggy shapes at the periphery of one's eye.

But they're looking for this one, and so there he is.

Burnsy revs the engine, and the four-wheeler lurches ahead of the flickering specter. Then he cuts the brakes and spins the quad around as it stops. Skelly's stomach, trailing behind, suddenly comes plunging back into her body. A wave of nausea mitigated by a spike in adrenalin damn near knocks her flat.

Burnsy kills the engine. All is silence. The ghost makes no sound as it moves toward them in a herky-jerky shuffle. It stares at nothing – the eyes are barely eyes at all, more like holes in an old tablecloth. The toothless mouth stretches open impossibly, the throat a black cave that keens with a faint moan that calls to mind a distant wind. The body is naked. The flesh pale, smooth like porcelain, the manhood a shriveled, crooked thing.

Burnsy hops off the quad. Skelly follows, her legs almost giving out.

He lifts the seat. From underneath he removes a flat metal shape – brass, ornate. He pulls up, and it pops into the shape of a hollow cube. Each piece looks delicate as a bird bone, all the little Byzantine brass bits tied together at junctions by fraying red thread. The corners of the box are little decorative skulls – human – with brass tacks for eyes.

"Soul cage," Burnsy says, striding toward the ghost. He stops ten feet in front of it and waits, holding the cube up in his blood-blister hands.

Skelly moves to his side as the ghost continues inevitably toward them. She cannot repress a chill. Visions of death wash over her. She sees herself, dead by a hundred ways – hanging, burning, gunshot, drowning, plane crash even though she's never been in a plane. She sees Lulu, her neck ripped open. Her own mother, dying in a hospital bed from emphysema – the gurgled whisper of a woman drowning in her own body.

Burnsy elbows her. The death visions break apart like old bread. "Getting near a ghost and staring it down does that to you," he says, like he knows.

"Don't know what you mean, jellybean," she says, but even she hears the quaver in her voice.

"The soul is in the heart, in case you were wondering. That's the core of us. Not what's in our heads, but what's felt in our hearts." He holds the soul cage at chest level, and step-by-erratic-step, the ghost comes toward them. Burnsy doesn't shove the cage at the specter but rather lets the specter walk up to the cage–

It disappears through the wraith's chest.

The ghost freezes perfectly still – as if someone hit the *pause* button.

There's an electric snap – the hard smell of ozone followed by a whiff of the grave.

The ghost's mouth opens even wider. The eye sockets stretch and distort. Limbs stiffen and begin to elongate and then droop like wilting flower stems–

A scream rises from its mouth. This is the scream of a victim, a man about to be murdered, a woman watching her own child die, the sound not just of death but of great suffering and sorrow wedded together in one horrible howl.

Another electric snap.

And then the ghost is gone.

And the vision hits them like lightning.

Here, then, is Casimir Zoladski. He's entering the Boss's house. Keys on a hook. Jacket on a hanger. Upstairs. Calls, "Dziadzia? You here? Granddad? Haversham?" Shoes echoing in the hallway. Someone behind him: the Boss. His grandfather. The old man is without a scrap of clothing. His white shriveled body sags. Wisps of hair on his chest, arms, thighs. Pubic bush like a wire brush.

The old man coughs. Can't help it. It's the cancer.

Casimir spins. He has something *he* can't help, either: he laughs.

The Boss's cough subsides.

He stares at the boy with some commingling of hate and pity.

"You're not ready for this, are you?" the Boss asks.

"Dziadzia. You..." Casimir fails to speak the obvious: "You're naked." Instead he shifts his tone to one of caution and uncertainty: "You're supposed to be at a meeting with Haversham. Are you OK?"

"I'm OK."

"I'll call Haversham–"

"No, you won't."

Casimir looks at his watch. His thoughts, broadcast: I'm supposed to meet her. Images in his mind: a girl. Tartan skirt. Blue cardigan. Mean eyes and a wicked smile resolving into a softer, happier countenance. A name: Nora Pearl. He's waiting for her. He loves her. Or thinks he does. Could be little hearts around his head like pink birds.

"Answer the question," the kid's grandfather says, sneering.

"What... what question?"

"You're not ready for this. To take over."

"N...no. I'm not."

"That's disappointing."

"I know. It's just–"

"You're weak. I knew it all along. Your father was weak, too, but in a different way. He was weak in the mind. You're weak in the heart. You don't have the stones for this."

"I don't."

"Then I'm sorry."

"Sorry for–"

The Boss roars, leaps. Hands around the kid's throat. Casimir backpedals. The Boss begins uttering something, some strange chant or prayer. It sounds like *"Ugatha thra iss ashana ugatha vithra mell tanta"*, and it gets louder and louder as he wrings the boy's neck–

Casimir tries to turn, but falls–

The Boss is on him. Grabs his grandson's head with preternatural strength. Smashes it forward. Just once. Once is enough to pulp the kid's face like an orange shoved into the bell of a juicer. The young man's body shakes violently. The Boss rides it out like a rodeo cowboy.

And then the body is still.

Blood pools.

The old man walks away. Returns with a brown paper bag.

The objects of ritual. A marigold in each hand. Broken iron chains in the pockets. A smear of chocolate on each fingertip. And then a splash from a bottle of mezcal poured on the blood pooling beneath his smashed-in face.

All the while, that chant—

ugatha thra iss ashana ugatha vithra mell tanta
ugatha thra iss ashana ugatha vithra mell tanta
ugatha thra iss ashana ugatha vithra mell tanta

Then the Boss's body tightens up as though in a seizure of his own. Fingers stiffening and splaying outward. Jaw creaking as it extends wide, wider, widest. Eyes rolling back.

The floor shudders. Dust falls from a light fixture.

A black shape rises from below. Swirls around him, a tornado of ink and shadow – tentacles, worms, fingers, whirling around and around–

Then entering his wide-open mouth. Squirming like snakes. His cheeks bulging. His abdomen distending like a starving child's belly.

Thirty seconds of this. Then a minute. Then five.

The last of the shadows – a flicking tail – gulp down and are gone.

The Boss eyes go all black: an oil spill. Then clear again.

Brown irises are now crystalline blue.

The Boss makes a sound like: *Guhhhhh*.

Then: another whipcord of lightning. The world lights up. Goes dark.

Burnsy falls on his ass. Yelps as he does. Skelly's already on the ground. Curled up in a ball. Holding her throat.

The soul cage glows. Faint light. Slow pulse. It makes a sound, too, a sound you can't *hear* so much as *feel*. Like a television left on in the other room with the volume down, just a faint white-noise whine.

The ghost of Casimir Zoladski is gone. Trapped inside the cage.

"It's... done," he says. Then he shivers. He babbles, he can't help it: "I do this all the time but – never gets easier. The death. How they die. They're trapped in there. Replaying that moment. As they... march on. Restlessly shambling through the Shallows, through the Tangle, all the way toward... well, toward the end, I guess. Toward whatever waits in the Expanse."

Skelly sits up. Stares at the soul cage vibrating.

"He killed his own grandson."

"Yeah. Fuck."

"Wh... why? What happened?"

"Some kind of summoning. I told Mookie that's what it might be. But it ain't in the kid. It's in him. In the Boss. Bound in his... skin. Or maybe it's wearing him like a fucking jumpsuit. I don't know. But it's something from the deep. From in the Tangle. Or maybe from all the way down."

Now she's really shivering. "You ever been... all the way down?"

"Into the Expanse? No way. I don't know anybody from Daisypusher that has. I mean, I've heard the stories. I've even heard of maps you can buy that'll take you there, but I figure they're a load of unhappy horseshit. Not exactly a short trip, either. The Tangle is hundreds of miles long in every direction. Probably more. And frankly, I dunno why'd you wanna go. If this place really is home to a host of starving and insane subterranean gods, I can't see the value in walking up to their front door and paying them a visit." He waves it off, pulls out that blue mister bottle and spritzes himself with water. "Fuck it. We gotta go. Get this soul cage back to Mookie. Give him the ghost. Show him what we saw. You ready to ride?"

Skelly's about to say something about, uh, *hell no*, she is not ready *at all* to hop atop the Vomit Comet again and would he please be so kind as to drive just a little more slowly so she doesn't become a ghost herself, OK, thanks, daddy-o?

She doesn't get those words out.

There's movement at the far end of the room. And sound: a horrible, discordant sing-songy chant. Like a choir of oinking pigs and snarling wolves.

Gobbos. A dozen of them.

Carrying a pair of corpses.

The goblins don't see them. Not yet. Too many salt pillars and skeletons are in the way, and they're a hundred yards distant.

She ducks and hisses, "I thought you said they never come down here!"

"They don't! But they still bring bodies from time to time. You kill any back at that temple?"

"I dunno. I think maybe."

"That's probably them. Nice work." She's not sure if he's being sarcastic or sincere.

"We have to find another way. Go deeper to find another way."

"Uh-huh, uh-huh." But he doesn't move. He's staring ahead. "See over there?" She follows his pointing finger, and sees two salt columns that have collapsed.

"Yeah, so?"

"Let's roll."

She gets on, thinking he's going to turn this thing around, head the same direction the ghost of Casimir Zoladski was heading.

That's not what he does.

Burnsy starts the engine.

"Oh, no," she says.

"Oh, yes," he answers. Revving the engine. *Grrrrrooom. Vrrrggrrrgrrroom.*

"Oh, no no no no no hell no."

"Oh, yes yes yes yes *fuck* yes."

The quad leaps forward like a starving puma. Tires breaking goblin bones. The gobbos ahead see them. They begin to gibber and wail in alarm. Corpses drop. Weapons up. Rusty machetes and glinting shivs. One's got a slingshot, with something squirming in the slingshot's pocket. And still Burnsy heads right toward them.

Accelerating.

She figures out what he's doing two seconds before he does it.

It's too late–

He cuts the quad left, then right again–

Tires bounce up onto those collapsed salt columns.

Columns that, fallen, form a ramp.

Skelly screams.

The quad races up – and is suddenly airborne.

Gobbos watch from beneath. The slingshot lets loose, but whatever creature serves as ammunition rebounds off the four-wheeler's undercarriage with a metal *plunk*.

The quad in flight, Skelly experiences an odd moment of bliss – an absurd sensation that all her life has led to this strange and singular moment. Ramping a jacked-up hell-quad over a dirge-singing pack of goblins with a burned-to-death stuntman at the wheel.

I'm flying, she thinks, half-giddy.

The tires hit ground. The flight is over. Her pelvis almost shoots up through her ribcage.

Burnsy whoops and cackles as the quad races out of the bone garden and back into the twisted tunnels of the Fathomless Tangle.

23

I asked Danny – Cerberus – how he does it, exactly. How does one navigate the Tangle as a living dead man? What is his secret? He explained it to me thusly: he can feel all the ghosts of the Great Below. Always. Together they form a sensation that exists at his margins, a psychic awareness that is hazy, non-specific, and ever-present. He can, with some concentration, explore this formless mass of spirit psyches like a man reaching into a murky pond to feel around in the mud for a snail, or a coin, or a lost key. He can see who they are, can even see through their eyes, and in this way can begin to put together a picture of the spectral movements through the Shallows and into the Tangle – and so, a map, an imperfect map, is formed. Of course, that ends once the ghosts reach the nadir of this place. Once they approach the Ravenous Expanse, he says, they disappear – like a candle flame snuffed beneath an overturned cup.

– from the Journals of John Atticus Oakes
Cartographer of the Great Below

Mookie lies caught in the grip of a terrible dream, the kind that keeps shifting, worsening – a dream shot through with betrayals from him and against him, a nightmare thick with the feeling of being lost in the dark and without a friend. All the world and what's beneath it is his foe. Werth cutting his throat. The Boss laughing. Davey, dead in the water tunnels beneath the city, goblins planting eggs in the sockets of his torn-out eyes, his mouth still forming the breathless words necessary to condemn Mookie for his inaction. Grampop, cursing Mookie from the dark, calling him names. Skelly, belly swollen with some half-and-half baby about to be born. Faces of death. A mounting tide of ghostly faces, bulging and spilling on the beach that is Mookie's mind.

Now he stands at a pig farm. Black-bristled, white-bellied Mangalitsa hogs sniff, snort, and grouse in the green-gray mud. Above his head, a steel sky threatens rain. He smells wild animal musk. Pig piss. Hog shit. Footsteps slapping mud behind him.

Jess. His ex-wife.

"You made a mess of things," she says.

"I know."

"You coulda done anything with your life. Coulda stayed a Sandhog."

"That job wasn't for me."

She rolls her eyes. One of her signature moves. Jess always had a little attitude. A little fire at the end of her tongue, a sparked flint in her eyes. That's why he liked her. She was tough. She needed to be to deal with him. Nora's got that spark. *Maybe too much of it.*

"You were just afraid of becoming like your Dad."

"Who isn't?"

"You didn't have to be a Hog. You had choices, Mikey."

"Mook. Mookie." A hard wind kicks up. "*Not* Mikey."

"You were Mikey to me then, you're Mikey to me now, and nothing can change that. What's done is done." She laughs softly. "You had the chance to be lots of things. I almost got you that garbage man job."

"I don't want to be a garbage man."

"You already *are* a garbage man, just without the uniform. But fine, OK, whatever. You didn't want to be the trash-man. What about that job Bobby Pallotta offered you? Bouncer at the – what was that strip club?"

"The Lady Lair. Didn't pay enough."

Above, the sky shifts – sudden clouds move swiftly overhead. Faces appear in the clouds, faces he can't make out. But all of them are in pain.

"Could've been a skip tracer. Deshawn Washington was a–"

"He wasn't the skip tracer. Deshawn was a repo guy. You're thinkin' of his brother, Demarcus, from Queens."

"To-*may*-to to-*mah*-to, Mookie. Either of those damn jobs would've been–"

"Still not enough money!" he roars. "We had a mortgage! You had to have that... that goddamn Chevy Malibu. We sent Nora to that girl's school. *We needed real cash*, not fucking... Monopoly play money."

"I told you, I would've gotten a job."

"No! No wife of mine gets a job."

"Big man with big balls doesn't want his little wifey to work? You're *smarter* than that, Mikey. Everyone says you're dumb, but I see it in your eyes – you're smarter than that." Jess walks up, thrusts her finger in his chest. Over her shoulder, he sees a glimpse of something, someone: a tall man in a beige suit. Candlefly. Then he's gone. Jess keeps talking. "You think because your wife works, what, you're not a tough guy anymore? Wife brings home some coin your dick will shrink a couple sizes? C'mon, Mikey. I could've helped. You never let me help. And then when you left..."

"I kept sending money. You never had to work. I took care of that. All you had to do was handle Nora–"

"She was a good kid. She didn't need handling. She needed her father."

"Jess, I know I made mistakes–"

There. Over her shoulder again – Candlefly. Closer this time. Near the red barn with the peeling paint. He starts to push past Jess, but she catches his hand.

"Where do you think you're going?"

Candlefly's gone. Mookie growls. "There's... something. I gotta go do something." *I gotta go kill someone.* He feels for his cleaver but it's gone. Right. Damn. Stuck in the floor. But wait – is this a dream? Maybe it's not. Shit. *Shit.*

"You leaving us again."

"Jess, I gotta–"

"Doesn't matter. She's dead. Look."

Mookie follows Jess's stare.

There's Nora. Face up in the mud. Blood pumping from her gut, pooling in divots of greasy mud. The pigs start sniffing at her. Mookie turns, sees Candlefly smoking a cigar in the distance, smiling. The pigs start to bite at Nora's feet. One pulls her boot off. Starts eating it. Another starts in on her heel.

Candlefly is laughing now. He's far away, but that deep laugh carries.

Mookie launches himself over the fence. Into the mud. Boots stuck. He can't pull them out. The mud is sucking at his feet, drawing him down, down to his knees as the pigs move in and begin to eat Nora, chewing off her fingers, moving to the face and eating her nose and ears and working on her chin. One stoops and laps at the blood like a dog–

A whisper in his ear. Candlefly. "How did it feel to watch your daughter die?"

"How did it feel to watch your daughter die?"

Candlefly slaps the canned ham that is Mookie Pearl's head. *Pat, pat, pat.* Harder: *whack.* The man's eyelids flutter. His face, shot through with dark striations. Bruise-colored arterial fractals. A side effect of the Snakeface's poison. Sorago's in particular.

Three doses. Enough to drop an elephant.

And still Mookie Pearl almost cleaved his skull like a cantaloupe.

Impressive. And a shame. If there was a chance to still bring Pearl into the fold, to make him part of the plan...

An option, no longer. This road only ends at one place. Alas.

"I thought you were going to kill me, I really did." Here in the wine cellar with Mookie Pearl bound to a chair with honest-to-god heavy gauge chain, Candlefly puffs on a cigar: a Honduran, not a Cuban. A far better smoke. A mouth-feel like velvet. The taste and smell of chocolate, cherry, and, if he may wax poetic, old books. Candlefly is not himself a fan of old books, but his cousin, Grigor – well. Grigor is a book-sniffer of the highest order. "You certainly tried. You've made quite a mess of things for us, did you know that? You stopped our first attack on the miner, Morgan. Then you thwarted the attack on Daisypusher. But you're a speedbump, not a wall. Where is the Ochre? You have it. You must. Our... spies no longer detect its presence in the Underworld."

Mookie's eyes finally open all the way.

They see Candlefly and go wide.

The thug tries to say something, but it comes out as frustrated gibberish.

"Ah!" Candlefly says. "You're upset. Probably because my face looks so pretty again." He showcases his own visage like a game show hostess framing a prize with elegant hands. "It's been almost twenty-four hours since you pummeled my face into *pâté* and I look good as new, don't I? I cannot share how or why. Old family secret."

"You're..." Mookie starts, his lips drooping, but the words slowly forming. "Not human." A string of drool oozes from his mouth, pools beneath his chin.

"Do you want a prize for figuring that out? I assumed it obvious by now. Perhaps I overestimated your intelligence."

"Fuck... off."

"With such startling wit, how could I ever think you stupid?" A cruel twinkle in the man's eye. "You are right, Mr Pearl. I am not human. Not entirely. My entire family is... of mixed heritage, you might say. The Candlefly roots go very, very deep, indeed – roots that drink from the oldest bloodlines."

"You're a... half-and-half."

"So crass. Hardly. Do I look like an aberration? Some mutation with dolphin flippers and a monkey's tail? A cock like a lizard's tongue? A tongue like a goblin's cock? *Please*. We are not the stock of some common shadow, not born of some randy gob-folk or from a Naga with his septic seed. Ours is a far more refined heritage. A proud tree. Strong and tall and with many branches."

"Fucking... monster... either way."

"Yes. Perhaps. But don't act like you're any better. We're all monsters here, Mr Pearl. Varying only by degree. Now: I come to ask you a question and I ask it again: *where is the Ochre?*"

"Up... your mother's... *ass*."

"My mother, Catalina, were she alive still, would slap that vulgarity out of your mouth, Mr Pearl. Such... profanity only makes you seem more foolish. Vulgarity is the crutch of weaker men. Now, you don't want to tell me where the Ochre is? Fine. I'll have the Vollrath suck it out of your head and your heart. What you know, we'll know. I should've done that to begin with, but I wanted you to see my pretty face one more time. Just to let you know that you failed."

"If the... Boss were alive... he'd skin you like a deer."

"You mean, Konrad Zoladski?" Candlefly steps back, points to the wall behind him where the Boss sits perfectly still, hands folded in his lap like a ventriloquist's dummy. Then the Boss hops off the chair like an eager child and walks over to the table. It takes a second to register on Pearl's face. The look of shock is truly precious to Candlefly.

"B... boss." That word comes out of Mookie's mouth, and it is the sound of horror.

"Mookie," the Boss says. "You disappoint me. I thought you were loyal."

"I... I am. I didn't–"

Candlefly nods. The Boss hits Mookie.

The old man hits hard. Harder than any old man has a right to hit, especially when punching some thug whose head is harder than a bowling ball. But Pearl's head rocks back. His nose mashes flat. Blood pours.

Of course, the old man isn't really the old man. Not entirely. Not anymore. Candlefly wonders if Mookie realizes that his old master is no longer human.

And never will be again.

Times like this, he wishes he were psychic. Cousin Hiram would come in handy in that instance, but Ernesto is not on speaking terms with most – all? – of the Bellbooks.

Mookie blubbers through blood. Hardly words. Just guttural utterances.

"We're going to go now," Candlefly says. "Soon as you have your wits about you – and what copious wits they are, as we've learned – we'll be sending someone else downstairs to have a little chat with you. And then it'll all be over."

He pats Mookie atop his big bald head.

The Boss chuckles.

Mookie weeps.

Werth waits for Candlefly at the top of the cellar steps. Pacing. At the far end of the hall, Sorago watches him with those dead serpent eyes. Werth gives the Snakeface a nervous smile, then turns away.

The door clicks. Candlefly steps out.

Werth starts in: "You said Mookie was on the up-and-up. That he would have a chance. That, that, fuck – that we would all get on the same damn page. Candlefly, are you listening to–"

Werth's breath lodges in his chest.

Candlefly steps aside and another figure emerges from the cellar.

The Boss.

The Boss.

White T-shirt, suspenders, suit pants. In his hand is a black plastic comb, which he runs through his white hair.

Werth tries to say something. All that comes out is a squeak of surprise.

The old man looks... healthy.

No. Not just that – he looks like the Konrad Zoladski from ten years ago. Tighter stomach. A little taller. Broader chest. The wrinkles are not so deep. The eyes are bright and young.

"Werth," he says, giving a clipped nod and a toothy smile. "Good to see you."

"B... Boss. You... the cancer..."

The old man winks. "Feeling like a new man. I think I'm gonna beat this thing."

"How?"

"My friends from the Candlefly family here have some old world medicine. Some real *rarified* stuff, if that's the word. Knocked me flat. Felt like I was going to die, but now..." He slaps his chest hard, too hard. "I feel like I just rolled off the Detroit assembly line with all new parts."

"It's goddamn good to see you again." Werth looks to Candlefly who stands there in the hallway looking oddly amused. The man in the suit speaks:

"Did you need something, Mr Werth?"

"I just... I wanted to talk about Mookie."

"Regrettable," the Boss says. "But we deemed him disloyal. For killing my grandson and all. Him and that demon daughter of his. Shame. A real shame."

The old man stares him down.

It's then that it hits Werth: Zoladski's eyes don't look right. They're clear, bright, sure. But they're also the wrong color.

His eyes are normally dark. A brown so dark they might as well be black.

These eyes are crystal blue. Blue like Hawaii water.

The Boss pats Werth on the shoulder.

"I'm going to go have a sandwich now."

Werth nods. "Sure, yeah, of course."

Candlefly says, "We'll talk later."

Then the two of them are gone. Werth feels alone until he remembers Sorago – he looks to the Naga, and sees the Snakeface staring at him. Wicked smile plastered on the serpent's face.

Nora rests for a little while. Regaining strength.

But then, above her – the air shifts. She feels a presence. Like someone is standing in the room with her.

She lifts her head. Pain gathering in her gut like water collecting in low places.

A black shape, black as night, stands by her bed.

Dead dark eyes that flash like quarters watch over her.

She thinks, It's a nightmare, a hallucination, but it's not. She sees it. The Blue *allows* her to see it.

"Wh... what are you?"

A voice in her mind:

WE ARE VOLLRATH.

"What... do you want?"

WE WANT TO SEE YOUR MIND.

Then the thing leaps upon her.

Ghost-scalpels cut into her. Invisible fingers probe.

Visions emerge like pages from a book flipping past, faster and faster until they tear out of the book: a school play, a skinned knee, her parents fighting, shattered plates, a broken microwave, her father storming out the door, a funeral, her graduation with no one there to congratulate her, the check from the lawyer, her first hit of Blue, her first gun, a gut-shot old goat, her father's face of fear and disappointment and rage.

She tries to push back, tries to find a psychic handhold in the storm of images – it's like fighting through wind and rain, through cutting ice and hammering hail. But the Blue lends her fortitude, and she pushes on – her own mind pushing back against the trespasser, and then it's like she pokes a hole in a dark sheet–

A whisper through static, snippets of voice through a screeching frequency –

It's like the door falling off an airplane in flight: a sucking vacuum. New visions pull her forward then draw her down. Like hands out of grave-earth grabbing. The horror of a dead city, *this* city, New York: a gutted carcass. Hollow buildings, windows like frightened eyes. Creatures moving among the streets. Survivors screaming. A car on fire. An infant's wail cut suddenly short. Shadow things stalking alleys. Goblins running in packs, faces smeared with blood. Snake-men coiled around lampposts. And just below the surface, the worms crawl. Worms bigger than city buses. Big as buildings. Worms that pass underneath and tent the street, sending manhole covers blown skyward.

Werth paces the second floor hallway. Haversham stands nearby, idly fingering a button on his cuff. Werth keeps his voice low. "This is fucked up, Haversham."

"Yes. I know."

"Some weird shit is going on."

"I… know."

"The Boss ain't the Boss."

"We don't know that."

Werth stops pacing. "We *do* know that," he hisses through his teeth. "We do. You didn't see his eyes."

"I didn't see him at all."

"Well, he's here. Downstairs. Go have a look."

Haversham doesn't budge. All he says is, "Maybe it's good the Boss is back."

"Good? *It's not him*. And did you see what they did to Mookie? Shit, Haversham, we're on the hook here. This is on us. We're the last ones to have any chance to do anything." He hears his own words, knows he's barely making any sense. "The girl. The little... Mookie's daughter. She dead?"

Haversham shakes his head. "No. She's alive. For now. The Vollrath wanted time with her."

"What the fuck are those things?"

"I don't know."

"This isn't how we do things."

"Maybe this is the new order."

"It isn't. Can't be. Won't be." He stops."You have a gun, Haversham?"

The question hangs between them like dangling spider.

Finally, Haversham nods. "Yes."

"Good, because you might need it when the shit hits the–"

From the study, a phone rings. A simple old-school rotary ring. Werth recognizes it: it's the ring of Mookie's cell phone. That's where they threw Mookie's stuff. Stuff Werth's supposed to have already gone through, but he hasn't because... it feels like the final nail in the coffin of his bond with the big lug. He goes into the study, picks up the phone from under the leather satchel Mookie had slung over his shoulder, next to the cleaver–

He answers it. "Who is this?"

On the other end, a female voice: "Who is *this*?"

She sounds familiar. Her voice tickles some part of his brain–

"*You*," he says, suddenly realizing. Skelly. The queen bee of the Get-Em-Girls. The one who ran him through the wringer.

"I want to talk to Mookie."

"Mookie's not available."

"I have something for him."

Werth stops. Breathes into the phone. Then finally he hurries to the door and shuts it gently. "What kind of something?"

"I'm not telling you that, *Werth*." So she knows who he is, too.

"You're pretending what, I'm the asshole here? I trust you about as far as I can drop-kick you. And since these days I'm basically an old gimp, that ain't very fucking far."

"*You* sent guys to my place to kill us. One of my girls is dead."

"Guys sent to your place? I didn't do that."

"Quit lightin' up the tilt sign. Your pants are on fire, liar."

"I'm not–"Again he hears his voice. It's agitated. Ladled with anger. He tries to calm down but keep the urgency in his voice. "You want the truth? OK. Mookie got busted. He's here at the Boss's place chained to a chair and a table because he's on the hook for Casimir Zoladski's murder. He probably doesn't have long before they…" He pictures one of those reaper-cloak shadow-things going to town on him. "He doesn't have long. So what do you have?"

Silence on the other line. Once upon a time, you'd hear a dial tone, but now – now he's got to talk into the void. "Hello? Hey. Did you fuckin' hang up on–"

"I'm here. I know who killed the grandson."

"Lemme guess. Some handsome prick in a beige suit."

A pause. "No."

"Then who is it? And how the hell do you know?"

"We have the ghost of Casimir Zoladski."

Jesus.

"Who killed him?"

"You can see it for yourself."

"I can't… I can't get out of here. They've got me trapped. Just tell me who did it."

It's then she tells him the story. Of what she saw. Of what she still sees when she closes her eyes. She tells him the whole story: the naked old man. The surprised grandson. The attack. The chanting.

"The Boss?" That question, blurted out far louder than Werth hoped. He says again, quieter this time: "The… Boss did this? Don't fuck with me."

"He's not the Boss anymore. Not entirely, at least. It was a ritual. He summoned something. Maybe into him."

The eyes. Those new baby blues.

It fits. Werth can't help but admit it: it totally fits.

All this time and the Boss killed his own grandson.

Skelly keeps talking, asking him what she can do, how she can help to free Mookie, asking him about Nora, asking him all kinds of things.

But as he stands there, he sees something.

He moves aside the cleaver – Christ, the thing's as heavy as Viking battleaxe – and lifts the flap of the satchel. Two things catch his eye: first, a box, and second, a little jeweled metal ball with a latch.

He opens the latch.

Red dust lies in a little dune. He sniffs at it. Even just the smell sends a surge of adrenalin through him: neck tendons tighten like the rope around the neck of a pissed-off dog. His heart goes a mile a minute. Jesus.

It's the Red Rage. Vermillion. Has to be.

It's myth. A legend. All bad news.

Or is it?

He swoons with the possibilities.

He mutters into the phone: "I'll handle it."

Skelly protests: "Wait, wait–"

He ends the call.

Then closes the little container of Red and pockets it.

Deep breaths. In, out. In, out. He wills his heart to calm itself.

When he's cooled down, he roots around the satchel. Beef jerky. A flashlight. A pair of brass knuckles. Then he finds Mookie's little tin of Cerulean. Werth takes a hit. It's time to scrape the barnacles from his third-eye and start seeing the world as it really is again. The Blue washes over him. Almost sweeps his legs out like the ocean coming up over the side of a boat.

He shakes it off, then keeps digging.

He opens the scalloped box. Inside lurks a phial. A cloudy yellow sap oozes within the glass. Crystalline glitter shimmering in the goop.

Werth isn't a student of the Pigments, but goddamn if that doesn't look like Ochre. Could it be that Mookie's walking around with an old-timey test tube full of what Oakes called "Golden Gate"? That means Mookie's got *three* of the Five Occulted Pigments in his bag. Two of which were thought to be relegated to the stuff of legend.

He shoves them back into the satchel. Nobody's looking right now; it's safe here.

With the Red in his pocket, Werth hobbles back out into the hallway. Haversham's still out there. Fidgeting.

"I'm a man on a mission," Werth says.

"What?"

"I'm going to go free Mookie Pearl." He forms his fingers into a gun."Be ready."

24

My guide can... go no further. We were crossing a chamber – a bridge of bones and ratty rope swayed across a small underground river of rusty, blood-colored water. I crossed first, and I could hear the rope creaking, could even hear threads snapping. The bone bridge rattled and dipped, making me dizzy and nauseated. (How long has it been since I've eaten? Does it matter? Am I even hungry?) I made it to the other side, but the both of us did not cross at the same time lest we discover too late that the bridge would not support us. As Danny crossed over, I heard the sound – a loud crack like a gunshot – just before a piece of rock from above broke free and smashed through the bridge three feet in front of Danny. The bridge floor was gone – but the bridge itself held together. For a moment, all seemed fine. Danny even laughed, and then I laughed, and he took one step... then the entire bridge fell to pieces. It tumbled into the water and with it, Danny. He hit the river and began screaming. I saw shapes: lean shadows, long fins, silver teeth. First two, then ten, then three times that. Swarming Danny as the waters swept him away and under a shelf of granite. He was gone. Now I move forward without Danny. The cruelest thing I can tell you is that I think I'm glad it happened. Because once he could no longer follow, I began hearing the voices. Whispers crawling in my mind. Urging me forward...

– from the Journals of John Atticus Oakes,
Cartographer of the Great Below

Nora's mind is a cacophony of whispers.

Hillview, Fifth and 78, blood in the streets, Vithra, Morquin, Hyor-Ka, soldier Vollrath, knights to queens, riser shafts, valve tunnel, Candlefly, Woodwine, Bellbook, a man a mile.

She sees a pattern of dots. An explosion. Water. Stone dust. Bone dust.

A voice booming in her mind, shoving past the whispers: YOU ARE STRONG. Go to hell, she thinks.

WE ARE HELL. WE ARE THE TOLLING OF ITS BELLS. WE ARE THE WHISPERS OF THE WORMS. WE ARE THE FIRST. WE ARE VOLLRATH.

Again the dots. The blast. A gush of dark water. Blood oozing on marble floors. Casimir's face smashed – *Caz, no, gods, no*; she came in the house, found his body upstairs, the blood still wet, *run, run, they found him out, run–*

A city empty, howling monsters, massive worms coiled around skyscrapers.

Please get out of my mind.

BUT IT IS SO DELICIOUS.

Nora screams.

Werth grunts as he hobbles down the steps. He limps, gimp-like, around the corner. But the pain isn't enough to stop him. He can feel the tides turning – he knows what to do now. Knows where his loyalty belongs.

"Going somewhere?"

Sorago. Spine bowed. Hands flat at his sides. He steps forward, blocks the door to the wine cellar.

"I want to talk to him," Werth says. "Before he... before whatever it is you're gonna do to him."

"That is not an option."

Shit shit shit. He can't take this guy. He has no chance in the world. The assassin would dismantle him like a baby calf under a carpet of army ants.

"Listen. I lied. I don't want to talk to him. I want to–" And here he gives bunny-ear air quotes. "'Talk' to him. Know what I mean?"

Sorago stares.

"I want to beat his monkey ass for doing this to me. To us. To the *Boss*."

Sorago still says nothing.

The Snakeface's eyes flit to behind Werth, and it's an unlikely voice that saves him.

"Let him do it," Candlefly says. Then, to Werth, "I'm glad you're coming around. Besides, if it will make you feel like a valuable asset to punish treachery with a little violence, who am I to stand in the way?" Werth feels embers of victory swirl and bloom with triumphant fire until Candlefly adds, "In fact, I'll not only *not* stand in your way, I'd like to come downstairs and watch."

That smile. Like oil on a puddle.

Fuck.

"Yeah," Werth says, no longer sure how he's going to make this work. The plan was always simple and stupid: go downstairs, unchain Mookie, fight their way out of this place and make a break for it. Use the Red stuff if they had to. That's now a dead-end non-option. He could try to overpower Candlefly, but he's not sure that's a winner of an idea, either. Mookie beat the man's face into ambrosia salad, and one day later the guy looks like he's even handsomer than before.

Candlefly opens the door, gestures for Werth to go first.

No other choice now.

Time to improvise.

For a moment Mookie thinks he's being wrapped up and choked out by one of the Snakeface assassins: serpent arms snaked all the way around him, squeezing him like an antelope in an anaconda grip. But then he gasps awake and realizes it's just the chains.

He tastes blood. Old blood. *His* blood. A mouthful of iron and salt.

From somewhere, a scream. A woman's scream. A girl, maybe. A little flare of hope in the darkness: It's Nora. She's alive, my daughter... but like all flares the light streaks and fades and then it's back to the eternal night of dead hope. Because she's dead. She has to be. Candlefly *told* him she was dead to taunt him.

But taunt him with truth, or a lie?

How much of this has been a lie? Was her captivity even real?

A freeing thought blooms in his mind: *Davey could be alive, too, and Lulu and Nora and maybe this is all a dream like with the pig farm or maybe this is my Hell – maybe I'm lost in the deep downstairs and this is what I see as I starve and die while wandering the Tangle.*

His head swims.

Footsteps. The door ahead of him opens.

His heart hammers. His cheeks flush with a murderous hunger.

Werth.

To make matters worse, Candlefly steps in behind. His hands are in his pockets. He takes a slow heel-to-toe step. He is the very picture of nonchalance.

Werth paces in front of the table.

Mookie says nothing, just a rheumy, rumbling growl.

"He's not going anywhere," Candlefly says. "Take your shot."

"I'm psyching myself up," Werth says.

Mookie blubbers, "Hey, goat. Your master is tugging your leash."

"Shut up, Mook." Werth's eyes flash.

"Don't be a pussy, Werth. You wanna hit me, here's your chance." He thrusts out his chin far as his bonds allow. "I got a big melon. Easy target. You little gimp. Little weak-kneed limp-dick. Glad my daughter dug a bullet into your hip. How'd it feel to get owned by an eighteen-year-old girl in her school uniform, you fucking–"

Werth comes up on him – a fast hobble, one hand out, grabbing Mookie by the chin. Raspy calluses against Mookie's stubbled jaw.

"There we go," Mookie says through clenched teeth. "Cranky old goat."

"How's it feel to know your daughter's upstairs, dying on a bed?"

The flare reignites.

Dying. As in, not dead. As in–

Alive.

Nora.

He almost faints.

But Werth shakes his head back and forth.

"Pay attention, you thick-necked piece of shit. People always said you were stupid but I always figured you were smart. How smart are you, Mook?"

It's then that Werth raises a quivering fist.

Mookie looks up. Sees the old goat open the fist a little. Inside, something glints. Light shining off jewels. A ball. Davey Morgan's teaball. Werth's thumb pops the latch.

A glimpse of bright red powder.

Vermilion. The Red Rage.

Werth turns his thumb, tilts the teaball. Red powder coats his palm. As he works his hands, it greases the knuckles.

Then he hits Mookie hard in the side of the head.

And again in the face.

The jabs aren't hard, but Mookie knows to make it look good. How smart are you, Mook? He rocks his head back, pretending the take the hit hard. Will the powder mingle with his blood? Will it look like part of the damage done?

With each strike, the thought clear and bright in his mind: *Nora is alive*.

Candlefly's hand catches Werth's arm.

It's then he realizes, it's over. He's busted.

The man says, "Good enough. Has to be something left of him for the Vollrath to eat."

Werth mumbles something in the affirmative, steps away from Mookie while pocketing the teaball. Mookie's head lolls on his shoulders, the red powder mingling imperceptibly with the blood already on his face. But nothing happens. Not that Werth knows *what* should happen, exactly, but the Red Rage is legendary for the anger and strength is places upon those it affects. And yet, Mookie still sits docile as a trussed lamb.

A shadow passes. Werth jumps, startled.

One of the reaper-cloaks is here. Appearing out of nowhere. A flutter of black and—

It moves toward Mookie.

No, no, no.

"Come," Candlefly says.

"But..."

"Let the Vollrath have its meal."

Werth realizes he's not sure how you gain the effects of the Red Rage. Cerulean, *that* goes on your temples but who's to say the Red Rage shouldn't be eaten? Or cooked and injected like heroin, or smoked like a couple sugar cubes of crack? These are esoteric occult drugs, maybe you burn it in a pyre with three dead rats and inhale the fumes – could be anything. Could even be that the drug is fake. Why wouldn't someone sell Mookie a measure of fake Vermilion? Good money. *Easy* money.

It's over. Done. His one chance, lost.

Candlefly gives Werth a nudge up the steps.

The shadow rises behind Mookie. Shiny eyes gleaming.

Its fingers drive into the man's bald scalp as if his skull is as insubstantial as fog.

Werth heads upstairs, tasting defeat and pondering the future.

He sees nothing but the strange refraction of light and the watery shimmer in the air. Then Werth and Candlefly head toward the steps as something cold drives down deep through his head – no, his *mind*. Then another set drives into his heart, into his *soul*, and every synapse lights up, a switchboard of sadness and sorrow and death. Images flit by like fast hands flipping photos: Mookie bouncing Nora on his knee, Jess throwing a plate at Mookie's head and Mookie breaking a chair on the kitchen counter, Mookie hiding in the back at one of his daughter's school plays and leaving just before it ends, *flip, flip, flit, flit*. And then it all burns up: an image like spilled blood, a sheen of oil, a strike of a match and a *cracklewhoosh* of flame–

Red bleeds in at the edges. Blood and rust and magma.

His heart kicks into high gear. From zero to tachycardia with the flip of a switch.

A buzz and a howl in the hollow of his head–

The knives exit heart and brain, soul and mind–

An empty vacuum. Fire fills it. Anger blooms like a plume of acrid smoke.

A sound: *bink, tink, tunk* – chain links bending, bowing, snapping. His body swells. Everything cramps. Pain, sweet pain, delicious misery. He feels sharp like a broken tooth, raw like a scalded tongue. He stands. Chain links drop to the floor. The shadow-thing thrashes on the ground behind him like a bug under a magnifying glass. Screech, wail, spasm. Its pain is his pain. Mookie's breath comes in shallow gasps. Fingernails in palm-flesh. Teeth gritting. He stoops by the thing, and tears off its eyes. It thrashes.

Everything hurts. The hurt is pleasure.

Saliva pools in his mouth. His dick is hard as rebar.

He begins to climb the wine racks.

Upstairs, Werth thinks, it's time to go. Just make a break for it. There's the door. *Run, you asshole, run.* He almost laughs. Like he can run! Best he could do is limp-stagger-stumble toward the door and the moment he tried Sorago would be on him like a fast cat on a sick rabbit.

He feels Candlefly watching him.

"That was curious," Candlefly says.

"Was it?" Werth tries to play cool.

From upstairs, Haversham wanders down.

"You seem to have a lot of anger toward your old friend."

"Guess I do."

"It doesn't make sense."

Werth freezes. Sorago tilts a head toward him. *Eyeing up the kill.* Candlefly steps closer. Werth's mouth goes dry.

Candlefly says, "I'm beginning to think our trust in you is misplaced."

Sorago smiles. Hisses. Squirms closer.

That's when a fist punches up through the marble floor.

It grabs Sorago by the ankle.

It drags him back through the hole, the Snakeface's writhing body collapsing as it's sucked down into the cellar.

An eerie silence follows.

Candlefly gapes.

Werth almost laughs. Because he knows that fist – fat knuckles, pink scars, each finger thick like a goddamn bratwurst. And the look on Candlefly's face, one registering genuine *holy-shit* surprise, is a prize without value.

Mookie. The Red Rage took. The transformation is a thing of fear and horror, but also victory.

Candlefly gives Werth a look. "You."

Werth gives him the finger.

The floor suddenly shudders. The marble begins to crack. Another tremor, this one rougher than the last. The ground quakes, then–

Mookie crashes up through the floor. Bloody. Beaten. Covered in marble fragments like shards of eggshell.

He's huge.

Bigger than normal. Neck thick as a tree trunk. Biceps rippling as though snakes swarmed beneath the skin. His eyes are black dots in red seas. His wrecking ball skull pivots, leers toward Candlefly.

"You."

Candlefly doesn't hesitate. He pulls his pistol. Empties the magazine into Mookie's chest. Werth's ears ring. Gunpowder haze fills the air.

Mookie's shirt is torn.

On the skin are stuck flattened mushrooms of lead.

Which drop to the floor, one by one. *Plink, plunk, thunk.*

Mookie roars, stomping toward Candlefly.

From upstairs comes another scream. Nora.

Like that, Mookie turns, bounds up the stairs, his feet cratering each step. And as Candlefly turns his attention to the fleeing monster-man, Werth ducks down the hallway and hides.

Mookie is hell on two feet, the Beast that slouches toward Bethlehem. He is Behemoth and Leviathan. He is the end of the world surfing on a tide of blood and lava.

He hears his daughter scream. He moves fast. Skin tight. Muscles bulging. Bones heavy as oaken crossbeams. At the top of the steps is a Snakeface masquerading as the killer Lutkevich. Killed you once. Kill you again. The black-scaled Naga lunges, fangs out. Mookie punches through its face. Pulls the back of its head through its mouth. Then throws the lifeless blood-pumping body back down the stairs.

The other one–

Spall. Not-Spall. Golden eyes. Lithe. Climbing up the walls. Lunging at him from the ceiling. Mookie bats it to the ground like a badminton birdie.

Then he stomps on the monster's head. Once. Twice. Three times, it's red paste and porcelain bone. Plump brains ooze.

Mookie throws open the door.

He cries out for Nora – but her name is hardly a name, and in the hollow of his head he hears the echo of his ragged roar.

The shadow thing is lifted off Nora's body. She feels the pressure gone. Feels breath fill her lungs and the noise flee her mind. The thing screams.

And then, just as her eyes open, she sees it torn in half. Its eyes drop to the floor like loose buttons before the entire creature disappears as if it never even existed.

Her father stands by the bed.

Except, it's not her father. It can't be him.

He's bigger. Far bigger. *Inhumanly* bigger. It's like what was fat is now all muscle, inches of sinew and tension – brawn in its purest form – layered onto his already prodigious form. His eyes are blood red. His lips peeled back, white teeth bared – a picket fence of crooked slats.

He growls something. It might be her name.

Then his hands close around her neck and begin to squeeze. Throttling her. His eyes are sad but his mouth twisted up in rage. She tries to cry out, tries to beg and plead, but as he shakes her she feels something in her gut give way – fresh blood flows. She thinks he asks her: *Who are you?* Like he no longer recognizes her. Who is she? Who she is, suddenly pouring out of her. Like an overturned glass, a broken teacup. She catches a glimpse of herself in a gilded floor-to-ceiling mirror standing in the corner. Nora now understands what someone means when they say a person looks "ashen". Her color is indeed the pile of ash in an ashtray: the color of rain puddles and clay, the color of cemetery slabs. Monster-Mookie chokes the color – and the life – right out of her.

25

I've found a body. A golem – a Trogbody. I missed the corpse the first time, dismissing the strange shape as just another part of the insane topography of this place, but I doubled back (without meaning to), this time with a glow-stick in my hand. (That's what I call it when I find a way to break apart some of the glowing fungi and smear them on a branch or stick – it affords me reasonable light down here in the dark.) The golem lay collapsed against the wall, his geode head smashed open, the rose crystals glittering within. His body like lava rock: black and shot through with holes, for his flesh was once bubbles in cooling lava. He had a book, if you can call it that: a stone book, the pages slate and looped together with a binding of dry twine. Some kind of religious book, all symbols. But I remind myself that our alphabet is just symbols, too. I see eight pages with large glyphs carved upon them. I see a dead tree with a some kind of bottle in its hollow; a fat-bellied bell hanging from a bound scroll; a candle with a fly atop its wick instead of a flame; a gravestone with a horse-head at its crest; a monstrous pig with sharp teeth; a tower made of crystal; a musical note with a worm or snake wrapped around it; and finally, a lamb with a key held in its mouth and another around its neck. As I beheld the book, the voices in my mind returned with renewed vigor.

– from the Journals of John Atticus Oakes
Cartographer of the Great Below

Everything is fire. Everything is alive and angry and vibrating at a frequency Mookie's never felt before. His fist pulses like a heartbeat. It's covered in blood and flecked with bits of marble and splinters of wood. Pulling Sorago through the floor felt like the best meal of his life. Punching a hole through the one Snakeface and stomping the other's head into a treacly mush and tearing that reaper-cloak fucker in half felt like that moment just after an orgasm: toes curling, then a deep and enduring *satisfaction*.

But now: hands around his daughter's throat. Crushing her trachea. Her gray face going blue. Eyes popping out of her head. He's killing her. He knows he is. And it feels great. Which in turn feels awful. Like he's watching someone else do it from inside their mind. The Rage has him. It begs him to do it. To pop her head off her neck and throw it through the door.

He tries to quiet the fire. But this isn't fire. This is napalm. This is lava. It sticks to the walls of him and won't let go.

Her face looks suddenly unfamiliar to him. You don't know her, a horrible voice inside bleats. She is a stranger. She is an enemy.

She hates you.

She betrayed you.

Kill her.

He tries to say her name. Tries to ask her who she is. The words don't sound like words. All she manages is to squeak out a single word:

"Daddy?"

And that does it. The water that quiets the fire. The wind that cools the magma. It's still there. Inside him. Inside his *belly*. But for now the cast iron door is shut. The fire is contained inside the furnace that is Mookie Pearl.

He lets his daughter go. She gasps. Blood flows fresh from her wound.

Then: a voice from behind him.

"Mookie Pearl. Loyal until it all starts falling apart."

He spins.

Standing there in the door: the Boss. A small man made smaller by Mookie's size.

That accusation: *disloyal*. All the years that Mookie has given to the Organization – to the *man* standing before him – come rushing back. A cruel accusation, disloyalty. Mookie's been nothing but loyal. The furnace door inside him pops open again. The fires of anger belch out. Napalm spills.

He stomps forward, cracking the wooden floor. He reaches for Zoladski–

But suddenly the man leaps in the air, fast as a jungle cat. He clings to the ceiling. Wisps of white hair waving. Mookie sees his blue eyes glittering.

Through the roar of blood in his ears, Mookie thinks:

The Boss doesn't have blue eyes.

Something roils beneath the Boss's flesh. Something that no longer aims to be contained. Mookie swipes at the Boss, but the man drops from the ceiling, and skitters backwards into the hall – and as the old man moves, his body rises as his arms lengthen and his legs distend. As he stands to full height, what was once a small man is now as tall as Mookie.

The creature's fingers stretch and splay. Something begins to grow from their tips. Black spears glistening. Slicing at the air. Similar nails poke through the man's shoes.

His jaw shifts, cracks. At first Mookie thinks it's opening wider and wider like the mouth of a Snakeface, but then the lower jaw breaks in half and peels away, all the way back to the man's ears. What it reveals is not a human mouth at all but some kind of leech maw: rings layered upon one another, a threshing contorting sphincter of shark's teeth.

All sense of loyalty to the man is gone then. Because the man himself is gone.

Mookie looks forward to killing this thing.

He storms forward. An inelegant approach – the single-path march of a locomotive looking to explode a cow upon its tracks. But he can't help it.

The Red Rage cares little for finesse.

The Boss drops to all fours and scuttles forward, nails clicking.

Mookie clasps both fists together: a knuckled hammer. He leaps forward, bending at the hip, dropping the hammer of his flesh–

The Boss is gone. Mookie's coupled fists hit the floor.

The scuttling sound comes from behind him.

The thought strikes him: He's fast. A stupid, obvious thought; one proven true as the Boss soundlessly leaps upon his back.

Claws like iron nails drive deep into Mookie's side. His flesh is hard, unyielding, able to stop bullets, and here Zoladski has no difficulty. The wounds are cold in the heat of his rage. He stands, screaming, flailing. The thing's mouth clamps down on the flesh just below his neck. Razor teeth spin and bore. Something wet and cold like a tongue slithers into the wound and begins to coil around his spine. His body lights up with a fireworks display of pain.

Nora staggers out of the room. Numb. Bewildered. At first she thinks, I've peed myself, but it's not piss, it's blood, her blood. Her throat throbs. Her head pulses. Images of a dead city parade before her. Like now there's an open door inside her mind and anything can come through it. She sees visions of goblins cooking humans over barrel fires. Of snake-men slithering through the darkness of an alley.

She sees a pattern of dots.

She says it aloud: "Pattern of dots. Blast. Bone dry."

Again: "Pattern of dots. *Blast*. Bone dry."

And a third time. The words don't make any sense to her. But there they are.

In the hallway, Mookie the Monster fights...

It's him. It's Konrad Zoladski. Except he's not human anymore, either.

Nobody's human anymore. We're all monsters now.

The two smash into walls. Bannisters. Wainscoting. Pictures tumble off walls. A vase shatters. Blood sprays.

Then the Boss-Thing crawls onto the back of the Mookie-Monster. It bites down. Back of Mookie's neck. Crunch. Tongue splashing in blood. Her father drops to his knees. Wails in pain.

A body. Nearby. One of the Snakefaces. With the golden eye. A gun at its hip.

Suddenly it's in her hand. She barely remembers picking it up. Barrel wavers. Sights dip and swerve.

Bang.

A wall sconce goes spinning on the wall like a prize wheel.

She pulls the trigger again. This time, the bullet finds its target. It clips the Boss-Thing in the head – it wrenches its neck backward and howls in pain, letting go of Mookie's neck in the process. Nora gasps. Sobs. Steps through a doorway into a study and collapses on the floor, all the strength leaving her body as warm blood splashes.

The Boss is back up. A flap of skin has peeled back from his forehead – like a bundled tear in the felt of a pool table made by a stuttering cue – and beneath is something that looks less like flesh and more like a bottomless hole.

Mookie turns. Sees Nora stagger into a nearby room.

A small voice beneath the hurricane of rage: She's safe.

That moment of distraction is all it takes. The Boss leaps, the suit and shirt tearing as his midsection extends, stretching like taffy–

Mookie catches the old man by the throat.

There. The steps. Sorago stalks up them toward the scene. Looking like he's been run over by a city bus – dust and splinters and smoking motor oil blood.

He's flanked by a pair of walking shadows: black sheets with knife fingers and eyes like shining coins. They float up the steps like foul wraiths.

Zoladski's body begins to bend and coil around Mookie's arm—

Snap.

Mookie's arm breaks, bending the wrong way at the elbow.

Werth hides. In a coat closet, of all places. He pulls out his phone. Texts Haversham: **HAVE THAT GUN READY.** Upstairs, the ground shudders. Banging. Crashing. Gunfire. The walls of the house actually shake.

Werth thinks, I have to go. Now's the time. Run away. Get out of the city.

But Mookie. Mookie saved his ass. And he didn't do shit for him.

Loyalty, Werth thinks. Do I even know what the fuck that is anymore?

He decides, suddenly: yeah, yeah he does.

The old goat man creeps out of the coat closet. Another gunshot upstairs. Something – not some*one* – screams. Werth darts back into the foyer, then to the bottom of the staircase: there, at the bottom, is the body that rolled there. The Snakeface that was pretending to be Lutkevich and now is just a dead Snakeface, skin like gunmetal scales hanging on black leather. At his feet is a gun. Werth picks it up–

Just as Candlefly comes in from the kitchen. A phone pressed against his ear. Ernesto is looking up toward the ceiling as the house shakes. Werth catches snippets of him yelling over the din: "–still don't have the Ochre, and now this–"

But then he sees Werth.

And Werth has the gun pointed.

Werth makes a gesture: *Put the phone down.*

Candlefly scowls, rolls his eyes, and sets the phone on the floor.

"You're making a big mistake," Candlefly says, then adds: "Etc., and so on."

"You're a bad man."

"Who said I was a man?"

"Then what are you?"

Candlefly's smile spreads – like jam on toast. "A daemon."

Werth pulls the trigger. The bang is loud: too loud, impossibly loud, and the kickback on the pistol is worse than he figured, so bad that he can feel it vibrating in his arm, *in his chest*, like a fist punching him in the heart–

He suddenly can't get a good breath.

Candlefly looks behind him at the bullet hole in the wall.

Then says, "Thank you, Haversham."

Haversham? Werth turns. Sees the company man behind him. With a small Walther. Little smoke signals drifting from the barrel, carrying one message: *I've made my choice.*

"Haversham," Werth blast. "You shit."

Haversham pulls the trigger again, and it's lights out for James Werth, the old goat.

It's not pain so much as pressure. The arm goes the wrong direction, and Mookie can feel the unnatural way it bends. The Boss-thing wraps its elongated body around it, tightening and twisting, making the break worse.

And now Sorago, the Snakeface he dragged through the floor and left for dead, is coming up the steps.

With two of the black shadows.

Panic. Anger. Two warring feelings. Part of him wants to stay here, stand his ground. Keep fighting. Fight till they whittle him down. Fight till he dies on his feet. He could do it. Burn up like an asteroid tossed into the sun. Go nuclear. Take someone with him.

But Nora's face floats before him, again pushing the wall of fire back. The panic tells him it's time to go. Panic is a rat on fire; a bear hounded in bees. It wants to run. It wants to escape the pain. Most of all, it wants to live.

Mookie, though, doesn't give a shit about living.

He cares a hell of a lot about Nora living, however.

Which means it's time to figure out a way out of here. The window, he thinks. Maybe the window. Nora's in the study. There's a window in there.

Panic wins. But not before anger takes one last bite. With his good arm Mookie grabs Zoladski by the head, rips him off his broken arm – an act that only makes the break worse, compounding the fracture as bone bites through skin – and pulls the Boss-thing's undulating body upward, its leech-mouth gnashing–

Then he smashes his head forward as he pulls his hand toward him.

His big bald dome crashes into the creature's mouth. Teeth shatter against his skull. Embed in the meat of his forehead. The thing screams.

It's distracted.

He wings it toward Sorago – who now stalks the hall toward him.

Snakefaces are fast, lithe, a bundle of snakes in humanoid form – but right now Sorago's slow, probably from getting dragged down through marble and wood and metal pipes.

It knocks him down. The shadows duck it by disappearing through the floor.

It affords Mookie an opening. A short one.

He seizes the moment. Runs like a Mack truck toward the study door.

Mookie dives through it. Slams it shut behind him. His panic is a gleaming beacon, a lighthouse beam swooping over his very few options. They'll be through the door in two seconds. *Move, move, move.* He reaches out with a big arm, grabs one of the bookshelves, yanks it out of its mooring. It brings hunks of plaster wall with it as it tears out anchors.

He smashes it up against the door. Then grabs another bookshelf, rips it off the wall, and adds it to the pile. Then he presses his back against it just as something hits the door like a shark smashing its nose into a diver's cage.

"Nora?" he says. Barely managing to find a human voice.

But Nora is face down on the floor in a puddle of blood.

Ernesto Candlefly had stayed out of the way, called home to the family. Spoke first to his wife, then to his Uncle Borja. Explained what was happening. Or tried to. Then came along James Werth with the gun, and Haversham – *of all the people* – to save the day.

Konrad Zoladski's transformation, on the other hand, was a beautiful thing. And only just beginning, by the look of it. The monster that Mookie Pearl became should have been easy pickings: strong, yes, but slow. No match for a god. But this god had yet to realize his full form.

And so, this charade is now prolonged. As Candlefly ascends the cratered steps, he sees that Mookie is pinned behind the door of the study. Zoladski – or, perhaps it is time for Candlefly to begin thinking of him by his proper name, *Vithra* – slams against the door again and again with the rage of a starving devil.

Sorago hurries up to Candlefly as Candlefly emerges.

"I failed you," the assassin says, bowing his head.

"Shut up, old friend. This will be over soon enough. Vithra will handle it."

"But–"

"Look. He's almost torn the door apart." He has – already it is splintering against the onslaught of his metal claws. But oh, what's this? Is that a glint of envy in Sorago's serpentine eye? Good. Punishment for his failure. Let him fear that he's fallen in Ernesto's estimation. That is something Candlefly can use.

●●●●

The door is splintering. Rocking against the bookshelf.

Nora. *Nora*. She's dead. She's really–

Her back. Still lifting gently. Rise and fall. Breath. Life.

On a nearby table is his bag. And his cleaver. That's where Werth got the Red Rage. Did he also take…

"Nora," he roars. Nothing. No movement.

He needs to get to the satchel.

Wham. The Boss-thing is through the door. Books rattle. His claws are tearing the mahogany back off the bookshelf now.

Mookie storms across the room. Grabs his bag, opens it. His giant hands can barely handle this task – they tear the bag in twain. At first he doesn't see it and he thinks: they have it, or Werth took it, or it's gone, we're dead, she's dead; and again panic scrabbles against his mental walls like tarantulas on fire.

But then–

There. The box. The Ochre. Werth didn't take it.

The Golden Gate.

Gate. That's what they need.

Some way out. To anywhere.

The glutinous golden sap crawls in the glass.

A dread thought hits him: I have no idea what to do with this.

Drink it? Rub it on his temples like Cerulean? On his gums like blow?

Shit! He should have asked Burnsy.

Stupid, stupid, stupid. They're all right. You are dumb as a, as a…

He can't even think of a good metaphor. He's that dumb.

Burnsy would laugh at him right now. Marvel at his pain.

Wait. Burnsy. What was it Burnsy said? Not to drop it. *Don't drop it, for Chrissakes*. That's what he said. Why? What happens if one were to drop it?

Mookie clutches the phial to his chest.

The shelves against the door rattle. Books tumble. Splinters fly.

The Boss is almost through.

Mookie bellows, then pitches the glass against the floor. The phial shatters with a *pop*. The golden fluid spreads quickly, almost as if alive – oozing, shimmering, pseudopods of fluid crawling outward. He hears a sizzle. Smoke rises from the hardwood.

A flash of bright bronze light–

Where the puddle of Ochre was, now there's nothing: just a hole, a pit, a yawning abyss rimmed with the oozing remnants of the glittering sap.

Fear stares up through that hole. And yet, what choice do they have?

Mookie knows he has to move fast. Panic is unspooling in the chambers of his heart like a clot of cankerpedes. He pulls away from the bookshelf. Launches himself across the gap to Nora. Swoops her up in his good arm. The bookshelf shatters inward – books and splinters everywhere. The Boss-thing stands in the gap, broken leech mouth clicking and chittering–

The cleaver is at his feet. Mookie kicks it to the hole – it tumbles in.

The Boss springs toward him.

Mookie feints right, moves left–

He leaps into the hole as Zoladski sails past.

Darkness.

A shimmer above.

A *pop*.

Mookie and Nora fall.

26

The gobbos came out of nowhere. A hunting party. Jars of still-living milk-spiders (for they can only be eaten alive), a few rimstone cankerpedes on skewers – and something else, a wolf-like beast with hooves instead of paws and barbed quills instead of fur. They had it hanging on a spit, carried between a quartet of goblins – I saw its head hanging limp, pale tongue lolling. It had no eyes. A long, prodigious snout – but no eyes. I thought to hide as they passed, pressing myself into a crevice. They passed by, but then the final gobbo in the ranks – a young one by the looks of it – was playing with his milk-spider in the jar. Rattling the glass, tapping it. The bulbous white spider running around in circles. The gobbo fumbled the jar. It broke. The spider saw its opportunity and ran – right onto my foot. The young gobbo followed, wailing and gnashing its broken teeth. That's when it found me. Shrieked in alarm. The others came. I pressed myself deeper and deeper into the fissure – I was by then quite thin and able to slide through the stone. Then one of the goblins thrust into the crevice a jagged spear. The lance struck me in my side. I screamed and pushed through the crevice, losing skin and hair in order to manage it. The spear-wound is already infected. I'm bleeding very badly. I fear this wound is a mortal one.

– from the Journals of John Atticus Oakes,
Cartographer of the Great Below

"Is he dead?" Candlefly asks.

Sorago lifts and shakes the corpse with one of his tentacle-feet. The goat-man's body is limp, his life having leapt the fence and left the paddock empty. "He's dead. What should I do with him?"

"Take him into the Below. Let the roach-rats feast. Let the goblins have his flesh in whatever salacious way they choose." Candlefly sparks a cigar. *Puff, puff, puff.* Victory, it turns out, tastes so much sweeter than failure.

They do not have the Ochre.

Because it was here all along! And then Mookie went and used it, opening the gate that they needed open. Yes, *fine*, Candlefly didn't precisely intend to open the gate *here*: he thought it'd be a bit more dramatic to do at the Empire State Building observation deck, but the door was open. An unexpected triumph.

Mookie did not thwart their plans. He in fact guaranteed their success.

What a fool.

Puff, puff, puff.

Still. In his way, he was a capable soldier, wasn't he? More capable than his own. It's then Candlefly feels a tiny sting of remorse: did he back the wrong horse? The inhabitance rite would have been better spent on Pearl. Certainly Pearl could have been manipulated into killing his own daughter just as the Boss was nudged into murdering his own grandson? Blood from one's line must be spilled – and Mookie and Nora were already at each other's throats.

Well. Too late now. He can't put this monster back in the cage.

Or, rather, can't take the monster *out* of the cage.

And though the Boss technically failed to put Mookie down, it all worked out in the end, didn't it?

"Anything else?" Sorago asks.

"Yes, my old friend. Tomorrow is the big day, and I'd like to take out as many birds as possible with the stone we throw. Now that Nora Pearl isn't out there stirring the pot, let's bring the gangs together. At a single location near the dig – it will be more convenient that way. Down by the docks. Makes the most sense." He blows a plume of smoke. Before Sorago can confirm, Ernesto holds up a finger. "Never mind. Zoladski should call. They fear him. They'll listen."

"They will fear me, too."

"Don't be dramatic, old friend. Dispose of the body."

Sorago hesitates, and nods. The tension is palpable. Relegated to a common corpse-dumper? Ah. The envy. Good.

He calls up the steps: "Konrad. Come down here, please."

Nothing.

Hm.

"Konrad! Your presence is... requested."

There. The Boss appears from within the study. He has returned to his human guise. Jawbone fused back together. Body shrunken into the little old man. He begins to descend the steps, scowling.

"You don't command me," Zoladski says. "You are not my master. *I* am the master here. Until my brothers and sisters come to this world and claim it for themselves, I am the only god of this place. You don't command me. *I* command *you.*"

Candlefly shrugs one shoulder. "Not so much, no. When you wanted to leap into the gate and follow after Pearl and his daughter, what happened, exactly?"

"I chose not to leap."

"Yes, see, I remember it a bit differently? I remember yelling for you to stop a hair's breadth of a moment before you leapt into the hole. And what did you do?"

"I chose–"

"You chose *nothing*," Candlefly barks. "You did as I commanded."

The little man bristles. His jaw twists – the skin and bone separate for a moment, revealing a glimpse of the leech-mouth within. "You dare speak to me this way?"

"I do dare. Because you can't hurt me. And I *can* hurt you. I saved you, Mr Zoladski. And I summoned you, Vithra. Both of you listen up, because it's time to have a little talk, mm? You like to see yourself as the first of your kind to rise up out of the Maw-Womb and infiltrate this world. An *advance guard*, if you will. A lovely delusion, but a delusion just the same. I brought you here and *bound* you. Maybe it wasn't me doing the ritual, but it is the ritual of my family – the *ofrendas*, those offerings, the blood of your kin spilled. And now you – a very powerful old god – are trapped inside an old man's body. What do you think happens if I decide to terminate that body? Do you think you will wriggle free, a butterfly from its vulgar cocoon? Or do you think that perhaps you will die along with it? Let me answer for you: it is the latter. The body dies. The *god* dies."

Zoladski quivers in rage.

His hands move fast–

Black spikes spring from fingertips–

He swipes at Candlefly with enough strength to take Ernesto's head off.

It scares the hell out of Candlefly. But he doesn't flinch. And he is rewarded for his apparent fearlessness. The claws stop an inch shy of his face.

Zoladski – Vithra – tries desperately to push further. To get one claw-tip to *touch* Candlefly's dusky cheek.

"Can't do it, can you?"

"I... can kill everything else. Everything around you. Everything you love."

"You can. And then I can end you. With but a thought. That is my power. To simply *wish* you dead, and you die. You are not my master. You are my prisoner. All of your brothers and sisters writhing in the Maw-Womb will be. Did you really think my family was summoning old subterranean gods in order to bow and scrape and kneel? Please. Far better to make a god serve you, don't you think?"

Ernesto laughs. He feels good, suddenly. The loss of Mookie Pearl stings but...

Things still look pretty good from where he's standing.

The black nails retract into Vithra's fingers.

"You'll pay for this," the god says.

"Yes, likely. One always pays a cost. But I think it will be worth it. For now, I have a task for you." It is then that he tells Zoladski-Vithra what to do, and the very act of commanding a god feels oh-so-good. The god listens. Simmers with hate. And at the end of it: *nods*.

Triumph.

He smiles, stretches, then says: "I'm going to go lay my head down. Big day tomorrow, after all."

Ernesto wants to be well rested when this city falls to him.

27

The voices are loud now. My side throbs. The skin around it is black and puffy – tendrils of infection, some red, some the color of wine, spread out beneath the flesh. My breathing has gone shallow but the voices promise me I'm close, so close to what I seek. Here the ground slopes at a hard forty-five degree angle. I can barely stay upright as I walk downward, my calves burning, my hands raw from bracing against the rock wall. The voices now are deafening in my ear. They're showing me something: tubes in the wall made of a fine crust, and within those tubes, a slow crawl of golden sap creeping. Is this Ochre? I believe it must be. They tell me what to do. I break one of the tubes off gently. I hold it in my hand the way a prophet holds a scroll containing the Word of God. And I break it against the ground and marvel in the howling pit that is created.

– from the Journals of John Atticus Oakes,
Cartographer of the Great Below

It's like falling through a hole in a layer cake. Speckled schist, black stone, pale sand, white pebbles like loose teeth, blue slate – they all hurtle past, down to up, no ground beneath, for what seems like an eternity. Tree roots, glimpses of skulls embedded in rock, glowing fungus in crooked striations. The flash of a milk-spider scuttling. A face in the rock. A vein of electric blue Cerulean. All whipping past.

Mookie has not lost his daughter. He holds her close with his one good arm. He hears her pulse in her neck, in her chest. He feels it in her wrist. But he is wet with her blood. And he feels her eyelids fluttering against him. Hears her soft moans of pain.

But he knows they're going to die. This fall cannot end well. He doesn't know much about science, but he knows enough about terminal velocity to suggest that whatever they hit – rock, water, a big room full of pillows and stuffed animals – they will die.

He hears a keening windy wail followed by a vacuum *pop*–

Then there's a blinding golden flash.

The world rushes up to meet him.

But it's not like falling and hitting ground. It's like he has been in the same place all along, cradling his daughter, and now he and the world are... syncing up. Brought together and made whole again.

He scrambles to stand–

His legs care little for that plan. They're weak, wobbly like those of a newborn fawn, and he falls. The Red Rage has left him: the fires have gone out. He tries to say something, but his throat is dry and feels like he's gargling cut glass. All the fight goes out of him. He doesn't know where they are – he sees a dim orange glow not far away like the way a sunset comes up through a line of trees, but everywhere else is dark, dark but for a few pinpricks of purple like a wall of stars, and way up there is the gate from whence they came, a burnished bronze disc cut from the darkness, an upside-down *pit*–

–and it's then Mookie gives up. He crawls to Nora and curls up next to her – she moans, mutters something, "Pattern of dots, blast, bone dry." The words mean nothing; he's not even sure she said them. Maybe he's hallucinating. All he can do is hold his daughter close as he lapses into something that resembles death more than it does sleep.

Words slither into his ear, wind around his mind, words that make no sense–

Morquin
Hyor-Ka
Vithra
Uthuthma
Mathokor
Pelsinade
Lith-lyru

His eyes shut tighter. A wind whips over the contours of his scalp – it's cold in one instant, hot in another. He pulls his daughter to him. Keeps her close. Keeps her warm.

Then he hears Nora's voice: Pattern of dots. Blast. Bone dry.

Then voice: Hi, Daddy.

Candlefly: Roots that drink from the oldest bloodlines.

More words-like-worms, these sung as a swift song:

Candlefly Woodwine Glasstower Bellbook Gravehorse Hogstooth Lambskey Wormsong

Pattern of dots.

Blast.

Bone dry.

A scuff of sound nearby.

Mookie startles awake.

A gobbo stands only ten feet away. Paunchy belly hanging over a maggoty white penis. It watches Mookie with bulging eyes as it scurries up to what looks to be a flat stone carved with symbols. It lays upon them a spool of thread, a handful of coins, and a bundle of dead, dry marigolds. It hisses at Mookie before hurrying away.

It doesn't attack.

Thread. Coins. *Marigolds*.

Like those left behind on the corpse of Casimir Zoladski.

What was it Burnsy said? *Ofrendas*. Offerings.

Mookie checks on Nora. Her brow is feverish. Her breathing, shallow.

He needs to know where they are. The way out has to be near.

Mookie stands. He sees that they're on a blasted stone shelf. It goes on and on, as far as he can see – except for the side that drops off into a faint fiery glow. Above is just empty space. Mookie has become accustomed, down in the Great Below, to having a roof of rock over his head, often so close that he had to stoop or even crawl. But here he can see no ceiling at all. Just endless dark. And little pinpricks of purple up the walls like violet eyes watching him.

He walks toward the edge of the shelf. Space seems to distort here. The edge seems close, but before long he realizes he's been walking for several minutes. He turns. He can barely see the dim shape of Nora there. All around him are altars like the one the gobbo used. Many are home to unusual items: a scattering of coffee beans, an old Hershey bar, bits of broken colored glass, a six-pack of beer, a disemboweled rabbit, a chopped-up cankerpede.

And near the altars are small stone circles – campfires, Mookie realizes. Dead. Ash piled in the centers.

Nearby is his cleaver. Lying there, sheathed. Fallen through the hole.

He leaves it. What good will it do him now?

To the edge, then–

As he gets closer to the precipice, the shelf tilts downward and Mookie has to be careful not to lose his footing. He still feels weak and his broken arm dangles uselessly at his side. The pain isn't a dagger stab so much as a tumultuous wave pounding against toothy rocks. If he falls, that arm won't do much good to stop his descent.

And a descent here means sliding over the edge into… where?

It's soon that he sees.

An abyss. Dark, but for the distant magma glow.

It's enough light to see the shapes moving.

Massive shapes. Like giant worms turning, coiling together and then apart. Whispers rise up: *Morquin, Hyor-Ka, Vithra–*

He pulls away. The whispers grow quiet.

That way is not the way out. It's an escape, perhaps – but a permanent one, too terrifying to conceive.

As he backs away from the cusp, a dread thought strikes him:

This is it.

This is the Ravenous Expanse.

His heart grows cold.

They're at the bottom of the Great Below.

He cannot calculate how far down this is. Hundreds of miles. If "miles" mean anything here. They fell through a gate that may not have been a corporeal one.

They're impossibly far from everything. From the city. From the light.

From medical attention.

Nora is going to die down here. In the dark. With a father she hates and ancient gods squirming in the light beneath them.

Mookie wants to weep. And fling himself into the abyss.

No. *No.*

He's got to fight. He made it this far.

She's not dead yet.

Neither is he.

"Nora. Sweetheart."

She stirs. Moans. Her face a rictus of pain – like fingers pull at its edges, the skin tight against her skull. Here she looks small and weak. Once she would have played up that fragility to dupe him into helping her. But now it's no ruse.

"Honey, please, god, Jesus, wake up."

Her eyes flutter open. She sees him. Terror-struck. She swipes at him, tries weakly to push him away: "You monster, you're a monster, get off me–"

"Honey, *honey*, we're alive, but–"

"I hate you. *I hate you.*"

"You don't mean that."

Her eyes roll unmoored in her eye sockets. Then they refocus. A small voice: "Daddy."

"Nora. Sweetheart. I'm here." He wipes hair from her brow. Feels the heat coming off her. "I'm going to go see if I can find a way out. I'm going to climb—"

"I didn't do it." Tears run down her cheeks.

"What? Sweetheart, just relax."

"I didn't kill Casimir. I loved him." She blinks away tears, presses her face into his forearm. Damp and warm. "He and I were going to run away together and get married. And then work against his grandfather because, because he knew a lot about the Organization and he said, he said Konrad didn't trust him or even like him and I loved him and…"

Her words dissolve under the onslaught of sadness. She sobs. "I'm sorry," she says. "Sorry about all of it."

All this has the whiff of the confessional. Mookie doesn't like it.

"No," he says. "No apologies. Not now. I have my own. Doesn't matter. We're gonna fix this, Nora. I'm gonna fix it. Stay here. Rest. I'm… I'll be back."

He kisses her on the brow. She's burning up.

"Daddy, you never went to see Mom—" She starts babbling. "Werth is dead and Skelly is dead and I see Mom standing there next to you—"

It's hell to turn away from her.

But he has to.

He walks, and then he climbs.

The walls are deeply pitted and pocked with chambers, almost like the eaves and pockets of a burial chamber – fortunately, that means he has plenty of handholds.

*Un*fortunately, one of his arms is broken and worthless.

–more useless than a pair of tits on a lawnmower–

Still, Mookie has to climb. There has to be a way out up here. A tunnel. A way up and through. Then maybe he can find a vein of Cerulean. The Blazes can't cure Nora but they can forestall what's coming. Buy them time.

A cruel voice asks, Time for what?

He can't answer that. So he shoves the voice down in a dark hole.

He climbs.

One hand palms a rough rock. Heavy boots find a toe-hold. Then he pulls his prodigious body up with that arm, leaning into the rock so he doesn't fall. He feels his hand one inch at a time up and up and up – sliding across sharp rock cutting into his palms, but he can't just let go because he doesn't have his other hand to anchor him.

It's miserably slow going. He almost loses hold more than once. Hugging the wall helps, but as he climbs – ten feet, then twenty, now thirty – he becomes painfully aware that one of these times he's going to fall and crack his head open like an ostrich egg.

And then Nora really will die down here.

It's an unsolvable problem. He can't go up. But he can't go down. What was it Jess used to say anytime they had a fight? "It's the Lady and the Tiger, Mikey. Can't win for losing with you." He suddenly misses her. It's a physical pain, this longing – it lives in the space between his heart and his guts. God, how he fucked everything up.

Above him in the wall is a pocket carved out of the rock – big enough to fit him. He pulls his way up to it, draws himself into it with a long, guttural grunt.

Here he's bathed in twinkling violet light.

On the wall of this little chamber are tiny mushroom caps. The caps glow purple. Not all of them, but the part that glows forms a small icon.

An icon shaped like a smeary, melting skull.

He plucks one. Smells it – earthy, moldy, but something else, too. A vinegar tang. His eyes lose focus. He feels dreamy, tired, unhinged and disconnected.

Mookie pulls it away from his face.

His fingers are stained with purple.

Caput Mortuum.

Death's Head.

Not a pigment in the rock like Cerulean. Not a sap like Ochre. It's fungus. One of the Five Occulted Pigments – the most sought-after one – is a goddamn mushroom. He knows the legends. It's life wrapped in the guise of death. Rumors say it'll extend one's life, cure diseases, maybe even make a person immortal.

He laughs. To be dropped down to the very bottom of the Deep Downstairs – to the nadir of the Underworld – is suddenly not a punishment, but a blessing.

He thinks suddenly: *I could eat one.* It would fix him up. But no. He doesn't know what it'll do. What if it put him to sleep while it mends him? Nora comes first.

Mookie pockets all the mushrooms he can pluck off the wall – almost a dozen – and begins climbing down, trying desperately not to fall.

"I'm coming, baby," he breathes against the rock. "I'm coming to make it all better."

Someone is standing over her. A shape. Gauzy and flickering. Mookie yells, screams, "Get away from her!" He runs toward Nora, boots cracking on crumbling rock. With each footfall new pain jolts through his shattered arm but he doesn't care because whoever is standing over his daughter is going to pay.

The shape begins to move away from her. Walking slowly toward the shelf's edge, toward the abyss, toward what Mookie assumes must be the Maw-Womb.

No.

No, no, *no*.

It's then he sees. Sees that the person walking away from Nora is–

Nora.

Flesh shifting, shimmering. Opaque. Fading in and out.

Her ghost.

His daughter's ghost.

Mookie wails. He refuses to believe it – she can't be dead. Not now. Not after all this. Not after the fortune placed in his pocket: *Caput Mortuum*. Life-saving Death's Head. He barrels toward the body. Collapses on it. Feels her neck.

No pulse.

Lifts his hands to her mouth. No breath.

He stands, almost falls, but gets his feet under him.

He hurries over to the ghost walking ineluctably toward the edge.

Nora's eyes are empty caves. Her mouth a pitch black tunnel – soundless and without breath. Hitching step by hitching step she shambles forth.

He waves his hands in front of her. Tries to grab her, but his hands pass through her.

He weeps. Blubbers. Tries to hug her, hold her, shove her–

She moves past him. *Through* him.

She'll walk to the edge. He knows that now. That's where all the ghosts go, isn't it? To the cusp and over. Into the abyss. Toward the writhing worm-gods beneath.

It's then he decides: If she goes, I go.

Food for worms.

Gnashed by the teeth and heat and acid of the Maw-Womb.

He staggers back to the body. Weeping. Pulling her limp, rag-doll body close against him. He kisses her brow – a brow already gone cold. He wipes hair out of her lifeless eyes–

And leaves a purple streak across her forehead.

A message. An opportunity. *One last chance*.

He fishes in his pocket. Pulls out one of the mushrooms – still glowing in his palm, though the glow has softened. He pries open her dead mouth–

Mookie looks over his shoulder, sees her ghost is close to the edge now, moving faster than he anticipated. The ghost skips ahead five feet, then ten, disappearing and reappearing as she closes in–

He shoves the Caput Mortuum death-cap into her mouth.

Forces her jaw to chew. But it's rubbery – a dead jaw is not meant to chew.

So he takes two fingers and shoves it down her throat. Far as it will go.

The ghost is almost at the edge. Arms out. Head up. An angel about to be received into hell.

He massages Nora's cold throat.

Feels the clot work downward.

The ghost disappears over the edge. Mookie feels his heart fall with the specter – the sound that comes out of him is a strangled, grief-struck bleat.

But then:

Nora's body shudders. Gasps. A great heaving intake of breath. A seizure overtakes her. She judders like a truck on rough road. A scream bubbles up and flies free–

Her eyes focus on Mookie.

"What have you done?" she shrieks.

And then she falls limp once more.

At her neck is a pulse. At her mouth, breath.

She's alive. He holds her close. Kisses her temple.

She's alive.

28

This is the Ravenous Expanse. This is the Maw-Womb. A great abyss carved out of the rotten heart of the world. A deep nothing burning with distant fire. Toward the heart of the flame: the Deep Shadows, the Hungry Ones, Those Who Eat. I feel their hatred toward me even as they call me closer. They hate all us for what we have. It bleeds off of them, that jealousy. They have no fealty toward us or this place or to anything. Their loyalty is only toward themselves and their own cruelty. This is the knowledge I take with me to my death. I hobble to the edge, but I refuse to fall. I crawl back from the brink and nestle up against the wall, the infection in my side now like tree roots wrapped around pipes and breaking sidewalk. I slumber into death now – surrounded by the tiny violet eyes watching me from the outcroppings of rock above me and around me.

– from the Journals of John Atticus Oakes,
Cartographer of the Great Below

Morning. Impossible to tell but for the brightening of dark to gray.

Skelly checks the address. It's an old grocery store warehouse down by the harbor docks. They had a fire here years ago. Everything's still closed up, scorched with the tongue-kiss of an old flame. She shows up in a black slicker and a Yankees baseball cap, her rockabilly persona drowned like a rabbit in a mud-hole – but she's not here to show her colors.

Even though that's what she's supposed to do.

After leaving Werth with whatever it was he had to do, she and Burnsy parted ways. He gave her a pager number, to which she said, "People still use pagers?" His answer: it's a dead technology. Then she checked on her girls. After scattering to the four corners of the city they'd meet back at another safehouse in the Meatpacking District.

And then yesterday night she got the call.

She let it go to voicemail.

Glad she did. It was him. *The Boss*. Calling a convocation of all the gangs in the city still loyal to him. Said he has "big plans". Offered "new opportunities for leadership". Didn't mention the death of his grandson, which by now half the city had to have heard about.

A tantalizing call to those in the dark.

Tantalizing for those who want to play ball. And tantalizing for those who see an opportunity to make a move against the king and knock that daddy-o off the board.

But they don't know what he is. Skelly knows. And so last night she made calls. Calls to every contact she had: Bull Mosley of the Black Aces, Denton Lansdale of the Bruisers, Carly Espinoza of the Railroaders. She couldn't get anybody from the Immortals, the Sinner Kids, the Black Sleeves. The Lantern Jacks told her to go fuck herself. So did the Bloody Nomads, the Killarney Boys, and the Devil Bitches. She didn't tell them the truth. Not all of it. All she said was that she had intel that this was a trap.

By the look of the cars here, the only one who really listened was Bull Mosley. Maybe he believed her. Maybe he just didn't give enough of a damn to show up.

It's two hours after the meeting was supposed to begin.

She steps inside the warehouse, ducking out of the gray day into deeper darkness.

A minute later she staggers back outside, and pukes in a puddle.

••••

A tremor shakes the ground. A furnace blast of heat scorches the air. Mookie jostles awake. Nora still lies asleep in his lap. Mumbling. Moaning. As though caught in the throes of a never-ending nightmare. He feels her stomach, lifts her shirt – the fabric peels away from the flesh with a Velcro rip, the dried blood sticking them together. Underneath it, no gunshot wound. Just a star-shaped pucker.

She's healed.

Again the ground shudders.

He looks down at the pile of *Caput Mortuum* mushrooms. They no longer glow. The light, gone from them. Are they inert? Powerless now? He thinks, eat one anyway. You need to heal. But... Skelly. Werth. Others might need them. Mookie pockets the rest of the spongy skull-shrooms, then stands up.

He shuffles slowly toward the edge, arm dangling. Passes the cold campfires and strange goblin altars. Sees his cleaver again there, decides this time to pick it up.

The rocky shelf cracks. Splits.

A brand new problem.

He steps close to the edge, careful not to go sliding into oblivion–

His foot slips.

His ass hits the shelf. He starts to slide–

Cleaver. He uses the cleaver and drives it into the rock–

It buries. Catches. He holds tight. It stops his fall.

Mookie pulls his body back over the ledge. Climbs to his feet. Now he's able to see. The orange glow burns brighter. The worm-gods are closer to the surface. A breeding ball of hell-snakes. Rising slowly to the mouth of the abyss. They're coming up out of the Maw-Womb. To be born. To be vomited up.

He hurries back. Wakes Nora. She sucks a breath through trembling lips.

"Something's different," she says.

"I was just gonna say that same thing."

"Something's different with me."

He blinks. "You're alive."

"I'm alive." Like she doesn't believe it. "How?"

"These." He pulls out a handful of the mushrooms. By now the purple glow has dimmed to a violet miasma.

"Death's Head," she says.

"Yeah. A lucky find."

"Lucky." But the way she says it, it sounds like she's not so sure.

An explosion sounds from somewhere beneath them. It reminds Mookie of the dynamite blasts down in the Sandhog tunnels. Davey Morgan, even back then, was the Master of the Blast. He'd say, "Every explosion is a snowflake, you see? Every type of rock, every shape of the wall, needs a charge designed for it. Gotta find the right touch to bring it down proper-like. You don't caress it just so..." He'd clap his hands together. Cloud of dust from slapped palms. "Boom." Then he'd go about designing the borehole pattern that would open the tunnel but not bring the whole thing falling down on their heads, a cascading pattern of holes fitted for the dynamite–

Pattern of holes.

Pattern of dots.

Blast.

Bone dry.

"That's it," he says. A shiver runs through him.

"What?" Nora asks, weakly.

"That's what you were mumbling about. A pattern of dots. Blast. Bone dry." He closes his eyes. Rubs his face with his one good hand. "They're going to kill New York City. The whole. Damn. City."

Skelly stands outside for a while, drawing breath.

But then, inside, she hears something: a cough.

Someone is still alive in there.

Impossible. Through all that…

There, again: the cough.

She has to go back inside. Just to see. Just to make sure.

She creeps back inside.

Don't look, don't look, don't look. Eyes shut. They're all dead. Nothing worth lookin' at, sugar-pop. Don't breathe through your nose.

She almost steps on an eyeball.

Then almost throws up again.

From behind her, the cough. Sharp. Wet. It almost scares her out of her own skin.

In the corner, both legs broken in multiple places, is Carly Espinoza. The head – and only female member – of the Railroaders. Blood wets her chin.

"I know you," she bubbles. And coughs again.

"Carly, I'm so sorry…"

"Ain't right. Ain't… human. What he did. What he was. One minute he was the Boss and some of us was gearin' up to maybe bring his ass down – and next minute he's something else. Big and fast. Like an animal. Like the Devil." Her eyes lose focus.

Skelly kneels down. Holds Carly's hands.

"Guess he thought I was… dead. I ain't dead, motherfucker," Carly says. "I'm gonna kill him, girl. Gonna… kill him ten different ways."

"I know." Skelly doesn't know what to say. She wants to run, go back outside and throw up again, forget all this ever happened. And yet, she remains. Stay hard. You're tough. You gotta be. "What happened?"

"He… took a phone call. Then he left."

"What did he say? On the call."

"I… I dunno. Not much. Something about meeting people somewhere. The hole. That's what he said. And something about the Lincoln Tunnel."

"He said that? The Lincoln Tunnel?"

"N...nah, he just said, 'the tunnel', but what else could he have–" Her words are lost beneath a wet, rattling cough. She drools a pink froth: spit and blood.

Skelly stands. Blinking back tears.

Carly lifts a limp hand. "Help... help me up."

"I... can't. Your legs..."

"I'm OK. I'm gonna be–"

Her eyes roll back in her head. Her body seizes.

Skelly stifles her own cry as she runs outside. The morning air feels good. She breathes deep. Tries not to think about it. Gets out her phone. Calls the police.

Then she sends a text to Burnsy's pager.

WE NEED TO MEET ASAP 911.

Because she knows what's happening and where.

Mookie tries explaining it. Tells Nora that when you blow a hole in a wall, you drill these holes. Different pattern for different jobs. On paper, that pattern looks like a series of connect-the-dots – meaningless to anybody who doesn't know how to imagine the blast pattern of a series of dynamite sticks. He explains that right now – maybe today – the Sandhogs will be working on digging Water Tunnel #3 like they always do.

Except there's a point where the tunnel passes near Tunnels #1 and #2.

New York City gets its water – *all* its water – from outside sources.

Cut off both tunnels, and with the third tunnel not expected to be finished until 2015, you destroy the city's water source. That will render the city uninhabitable. People will be evacuated. It will be a no man's land until they manage to pipe fresh water back into the city. Can't bring in water by truck – the city at a conservative estimate uses over a *billion* gallons per day.

"That," he says, "is how you kill New York City. You cut off its water, it's like cutting off its head." And the way you do that, he explains, is by fucking up the detonation of Water Tunnel #3 just as it's near the other two tunnels. The wrong blast pattern – an ill-designed "pattern of dots" – will cause all three tunnels to blow. The water will cascade into the Great Below, but never reach the city.

That's what they're planning.

They have to be.

He doesn't know why. But that has to be it.

Another boom below them. A sharp crack of stone like a glacier breaking. The tremor this time is sustained. He can hear them now, their wet flesh sliding against one another. The worm-gods as they rise to the vent of the Maw-Womb.

"While we wait here, the city's going to die," he says. A morose thought. He suddenly doesn't hate the city so bad. He can't imagine its streets dark. Some will stay behind, won't they? Criminals. Lunatics. Mole Men. And the monsters will rise. Maybe that's what it is. Maybe they want a playground. A place for gobbos and snake-men, for rock-bodied golems. For all the monsters and the starving worm-gods that birthed them.

As though on cue, one of the gods launches up out of the rift – the size of the ancient worm dwarfs anything Mookie's ever seen on land or at sea. It's a giant worm of black segmented flesh, with one mouth containing a hundred smaller mouths, a thousand dead eyes at the fore of its shunted head.

When it rises, a deafening whisper fills Mookie's mind:

HYOR-KA.

Nora makes a small, afraid sound.

The world shakes.

Another worm-god rises, this one lacking the segmented body and featuring a ragged line of rock-like spikes along its dorsal ridge.

Another screamed psychic whisper:

UTHUTHMA.

The first worm-god ascends, squirming in mid-air like a mosquito larva in pondwater. It slides toward the crackling golden gate left in the air high above, and it's fits perfectly – like the worm-god and the impossible hole were made for one another. A vacuum hiss, a booming echo. The beast wriggles into it and is gone.

The next worm-god heads for the same hole.

Mookie stands up. Helps Nora stand, too.

"Come on," he says. "I know how we get home."

29

Their voices awaken me. Lith-lyru. The Bleak Hymn. The Song of Despair. It sings me to awake. One last moment of consciousness before I die, or so I thought. There greeting me in the dark: a tiny skull-shape clinging to a rock. The face of a small button-cap mushroom. It's then I realize: I have found it. The prize at the bottom of the Cracker Jack box – Caput Mortuum. The Death's Head pigment. Rumored to cure all ills but rumored also to confer... other effects, permanent ones, upon its eater. I do not care what they are. The song is loud now, its watery echo and discordant notes vibrating in my heart, urging me to eat, eat, eat. So I do. I eat the mushroom. I feel it. I feel the change. It is time now to join the gods.

– from the Journals of John Atticus Oakes,
Cartographer of the Great Below

His belly is full. Bursting, practically. Any moment now Candlefly expects the buttons of his shirt beneath his suit to pop off and ricochet around the limousine like wild bullets. Since being here in the city he's eaten fairly light: a salad here, a little fish, a cup of oatmeal, and of course the requisite amount of human blood (warmed up – he, unlike some of his fellow daemons, prefers it that way as cold blood tends to unsettle his stomach). But this morning! Ah. Time to let loose a little. So close to the end now, his body was all but *begging*

319

for a hearty breakfast! Three eggs, two pancakes, real maple syrup, blood sausages.

Powerfully delicious. And now he feels like his furnace is full of coal. Ready to burn.

Haversham sits next to him – a damp dishrag on all the good feelings. Sweaty palms on trembling knees. Finger continually pushing his glasses up his nose.

"You seem tense," Candlefly says. He grabs Haversham's knee and squeezes hard.

Haversham almost yelps. "I…" Then he swallows whatever he was about to say.

"Is it about the old goat? You did well, Haversham. What's your name again? Your first name. Milton."

"Milton, yes." Haversham clears his throat, coughs into his hand. "It's not about that."

"By the gods, Milton, we'll be at the dig site in–" He checks his watch. "Less than ten minutes. Don't make me chase this down like it's a stray dog. You can tell me."

"I just don't understand what we're doing."

"What do you mean?"

"What… all this is about. I thought it was about…" His eyes shift left and right as though he's worried someone could be listening. "The *Organization*. Our *business*."

"The business of a criminal enterprise, you mean? Illicit goods and prostitutes and protection rackets and the like?"

"Well. Yes."

"It… *is* about all that. Or will be again. But first we have to… soften the city up a little. Are you a cook?"

"What?" A flash of confusion mixed with irritation. "No."

"You get a tough cut of meat like a… chuck roast or a pork butt and you can't just apply heat and eat. You have to roast it. Low and slow. Maybe a little smoke. Let the tough connective bits break down. Let the fat and juices warm up and seep into the meat. Then you can just… pull it apart with your fingers.

This city is like that. It's a tough hunk of meat and I need it yield to my fingers. Do you understand?"

"Y... no. Frankly not."

"This city is going to fall. Today. We're going to knock the giant to the ground and when he falls, his body will be ours. The city is the giant. A metaphor."

"I understand the metaphor."

"Good. Could we have done this without the Organization? Of course. But when the city is evacuated–"

"Evacuated?"

"–most of the people will leave, but you know who won't leave? The criminals. They will remain. The Organization and its lieutenants and the gangs beneath them would have all remained here in the city. And they have a hold on the Underworld. I can't have that. That hold must be mine. The *city* must be mine. For if I am to command gods–"

"Gods, what gods?" By now Haversham is really shaking quite violently, his eyes glistening with tears that have yet to fall. It's all done quite a number on him. Candlefly wonders, is this what post-traumatic stress disorder looks like?

He figures, why not blow the cork right out of the bottle? If Haversham handles it, fine. If not... then perhaps he catches a bullet in the temple and that's that. Candlefly certainly *likes* Haversham, especially with his most recent display of loyalty. He's got a keen business mind. Candlefly needs that. So: stress test time.

"I am not human," Candlefly says. "I am a daemon. With an *ae*, not just an *e* – we were the first offspring of the Great Below, you see? Our eight families were the first children of the Hungry Ones, the first progeny of both man and god. We betrayed the gods long ago and locked them down in the dark and they cursed us in turn: they ensured that those of the daemon families could not enter the Great Below, not without great pain and madness brought upon them. The gods have long sought an opportunity to return to the Above just as we have hoped for a way to once more go Below. Katabasis for us. Anabasis for them. And so with all the signs and portents, it seems the time is now. The Underworld beneath Manhattan – one of many Underworlds, if you must know – has been discovered and opened and now we intend to bring the worm-gods home. Ah, but the Hungry Ones despise humanity and hate the light. They will be weak when they arrive and so as they wait in the seven sacred goblin-folk temples, we will prepare the city as a ritual space. The house must be abandoned. Cleared of its prior residents before the *new owners* move in. Except, ah yes, one final trick: the gods shall not own this city. The Candlefly family will. And we will own the worm-gods, too. All part of an ancient bargain helping to ensure our own version of hell on Earth."

He chuckles, then claps Haversham on the back. The priggish man runs his fingers through his hair with splayed fingers. He's sobbing, now. Great hitching, heaving sobs.

"It's all right, Haversham. It's quite a lot to digest, but you've done well for us. I'll give you some time to... process. But I suggest you make peace with it soon. Yes?"

Haversham barely manages a nod.

"Most excellent, my new friend. To the dig site, then."

Mookie and Nora stand at the lip. The ground trembles. He holds her hand.

"You're gonna need to hold on to me," he says.

"I know."

"Tight. Tighter than ever."

"I know."

"That means you're gonna have to trust me."

"I do."

"You do?"

"I swear."

Beneath them, the worm-gods roil.

Another one pulls away from the others and begins to rise to the surface. Mookie shields his eyes, sees a flash of three mouths and not a hundred eyes, but rather one: a cyclopean orb the color of the sun at sunset.

"This is us," he says.

Nora lets go of his hand. She gets on his back. Wraps her arms around him.

Mookie pops the top of the sheath, withdraws the cleaver.

The beast begins to rise.

Everything tells Mookie not to do this. Every inch of his gristly frame screams at him, a chorus of horror.

He jumps. Roaring as he falls. Nora screaming.

They arrive in the middle of the dance.

That's how Candlefly thinks of it: *a dance*. Because it's beautiful, really. Graceful as anything you'd see on a stage. And so much more *real*.

They step past the bodies in hard hats and yellow slickers. Necks twisted like wrung-out hand-towels. Limbs separated from bodies. Sandhog corpses strewn about.

It's still going on. By the trailer. Even more of Vithra has emerged beyond the container of Zoladski's flesh, a glorious evolution of form: the neck three feet long, the limbs long and lean like whip-cord saplings, all claws and teeth and ripping skin and eviscerated bodies. The men of the Sandhog union give back in violence. These are tough men, men of the earth, men of salt and stone, but they are still just *men*, and Zoladski has become so much more.

On the other side, by the elevator leading into the rather epic hole, Sorago continues his work. His really is a dance – as Sandhogs rush him he pirouettes, sidesteps, bites one as he shoots another and beheads a third with a curved blade. Another set rush him. One is flung into the pit, another finds his head cleaved, yet another finds himself embroiled in the deadliest kiss as Sorago's jaw unhinges and swallows the man's face whole.

Haversham looks the color of a green potato.

"Looks like they're almost done," Candlefly says. "Enjoying the show?"

"Of... of course."

He isn't, but oh well. One day perhaps he'll learn to appreciate true beauty.

The cleaver buries into god-meat.

Thwack.

It takes everything Mookie has to hold on. As the god-worm rose to meet them they met the god-worm in turn, and the hit was violent. And now Mookie's hand strains to grip the cleaver's handle. He tries to bring his shattered arm forward to grab something, *anything*–

As the beast rises above the surface of the rim, a booming whisper:

PELSINADE

So that, then, is the name of their ride.

A ride that won't be their ride long. Because Mookie's grip is slipping. Nora's not a big girl, but the weight on his back is too much – and Mookie's himself far too large and with a busted arm, to boot. He has no stability. The heat here draws out sweat and his hand on the prodigious handle of the cleaver starts... to... slip...

The worm-god's skin is not smooth like the others – bundles of squirming cilia like the fingers of sea anemones rise up in clusters – and Mookie sees one of Nora's hands reach out and grab a bundle while the other stays wrapped around his neck.

Stability. Just a little. Maybe enough.

They cling to the side of the creature like ticks on the belly of a bird.

••••

Nora is dead.

She knows it as sure as she knows anything. And yet, she can feel her heartbeat. Can feel the sound of blood in her ears. This isn't dead like the dead of Daisypusher. This is a different kind of dead. Worse and better in equal measure. It's not that she's dead inside but that something inside of her *is* dead. She just can't put her finger on what.

Thinking about this helps distract her from the fact that they're riding some kind of hell-born worm deity to the surface – or to wherever the shimmering gate above their heads is going to take them.

Even as the wind rushes past them, even as she fails to control the fearful whine in the back of her throat, even as she holds one arm around the neck of the man who for so long she hated and wanted dead in that teenage-fantasy way, she thinks about it.

That little skull mushroom gave something back.

But it took something, too.

She just doesn't know what.

Eventually the police will come.

But for now the dig site is loud and remote and protected by two rings of very robust fencing. Nobody will know anything unless they pass overhead and see all the cock-eyed bodies and bright puddles of red.

They take the elevator – just a cage dangling from a crane – down into the massive quarry-like hole. Sorago and Vithra already wait at the bottom among a new batch of corpses. Some Sandhogs. A few EPA inspectors. A geologist.

Vithra's limbs twist and crack as they slowly return to human form. Zoladki's clothes are now in ribbons. Once he returns to the shape of the little old man, he looks like a homeless person, perhaps one cast out of his capitalist tribe when the markets took that nose-dive a few years back.

Sorago and Vithra stalk up to meet Candlefly as he exits the cage.

"The plan may continue," he says. "Sorago, your... friends are waiting, I assume."

"Yes. Near the juncture of the three tunnels. They're blasting in two hours."

"Good. It is a journey of many miles, so go. And take a walkie-talkie. We'll need it to speak."

Vithra cocks Zoladski's fuzzy caterpillar eyebrows. "I want to kill more. I'll go too."

"You won't. You'll stay up here in case we encounter any problems."

The old man's face tightens. "But I want to go."

"And I say you'll stay."

"My brothers and sisters will be waiting in the nesting temples before night falls—"

"Do not defy me, Vithra."

"You *could* come down with us." A flash of cruel irony in Zoladski's eyes. "Oh, but you can't, can you? What happens if you go down into the dark, Candlefly?"

Ernesto doesn't lose his smile. It's painful to keep it plastered to his face like that, but he feels it's necessary. "You're about to make me lose my good mood, old man. Stand back and let us work to free your brothers and sisters. Unless you care to see that mission complicated?"

Silence.

"Good," he says. "As I thought. Now, let's find the detonator. I want to be the one to hit the plunger when the time comes."

Layers of earth – the mantle of this planet in its many colors and textures, the stratum of the Great Below laid bare – whip past as Mookie holds onto the cleaver embedded in the worm-god's back. The air is heavy, the smell of soil and minerals bright.

Then there is a static crackle, the sound of stone shearing–

A fresh thunderous *boom*–

The beast known as Pelsinade launches forth into a massive open chamber like an eel dumped from a bucket. Its belly hits. The ground trembles. Limestone stalactites from above drop like swords into the earth, some sticking into the stone, others shattering.

All around them is a temple. A massive goblin temple. Mookie sees piles of bones. And corpses.

And hundreds of gobbos.

Mookie and Nora hang from the side of the worm-god.

He thinks: I'm going to have to kill all of these things if we're going to escape–

But then he sees. They are all dropping to their knees. They're ululating, tongues fluttering in their mouths. The sound is haunting, an infernal trilling fast dissolving into a warbling chant.

Mookie tries to pry the cleaver free, but he has no leverage. To Nora he says, "We're just going to have to drop."

"It's almost three stories."

"Just hold tight. I'm tougher than you think."

He feels her arms around his neck. Even in this place of death, it gives him comfort. It's the closest thing to a hug he's had from her in years.

"Ready?"

She makes a nervous, uncertain sound.

He drops.

They slide part of the way along the rounded curve of the worm-god's body. After that the drop is only fifteen, twenty feet – but with her weight on his back and his own bulk, his legs hit and pain jars up into his legs and a thought pops in his head like a muzzle flash (this is how Werth must have felt all the time) and then he tucks and rolls and Nora is flung from his back and he lands on his goddamn arm and–

He grits his teeth, bites his tongue. Don't cry out, don't wail, don't make a noise you big dumb shithead.

He lifts his head.

He's face to face with a gobbo.

Its eyes are closed, hidden beneath leathery, callused lids.

Its uneven mouth is open. Tongue flapping.

It's breath smells like roadkill.

Mookie stands – so much pain, a fire stoked anew, now in his legs and his arms, but he has to *go*, has to *move* – and he sees Nora nearby. She holds up her hands; she's OK. He waves her on, then points past the worm-god's tail which lays coiled around a pile of animal corpses. Beyond it is an archway – an exit.

She nods.

They hurry forward past the chorus of keening goblins.

He's panicked. And in pain. Nora can sense that. He's like a zoo animal testing the limits of his cage: up and down one tunnel, then back out and up another tunnel. He grabs some nearby glowing fungus, has nothing to use as a torch and smears it all over his knuckles and holds his hand aloft. They're bathed in a nauseating green glow.

She tries to ask him where they are, but he just shushes her – and a not insignificant part of her wants to bite back, wants to shush *him*, wants to let loose with a fusillade of cruel barbs. But she has to choke it down. Stop. Grow up. He saved you.

Another voice within asks, Did he really?

She feels her skin. Cold. Corpse-cold.

The walls are warm but she can see her breath.

She can't see Mookie's breath.

She feels a nervous, acid edge in her stomach. Who are you? What are you?

Finally, Mookie points. "Look." He seems excited. Or agitated. Both.

It's a vein. A blue artery in the dark wall. Brighter than a human vein, this is the color of electric lemonade, of blue raspberry, a color you don't find in nature except on tropical birds.

Cerulean. Peacock Powder. *The Blue Blazes*.

Some of this vein has been tapped already. The lower portion broken apart, the blue long-gone. But not all of it. At Mookie's head height, the vein is still strong.

He grabs a rock with his glowing fist. Brings it hard against the Blue.

Once, twice, three more times.

Chips of blue fall. A cloud of shimmering powder fills the air.

He grabs a few chips. Pops them between his finger. They break apart, cakey and light. He gives her some. Then rubs some on his own temples. She sees the drug take hold in him. His head tilts. His vertebrae crack from butt-bone to base-of-skull like one long string of knuckles. He sucks in a pleasurable breath.

She rubs it on her temples, too.

And nothing happens. No sinking into a warm pool. No kick in her tail.

Nothing.

She decides not to say anything. Not now. Not here.

"I know this vein," he says. "My Moles were working it. We're near the Canal Street station. Come on. This way. We can get into the Sandhog tunnels using one of the old boltholes that Davey and I carved years ago."

Nora hurries after. The Blue still hasn't kicked in.

That worries her.

It's not a plunger, Candlefly discovers. It's a big red button in a box ringed with ruggedized rubber. He's disappointed, honestly. He'd like a plunger. Like in the movies: stand before it, hands on the plunger – press it down and *boom*.

A small fleck of dirt in the eye of a truly lovely day.

Near him, Vithra suddenly shudders.

"Cold?" he asks.

"Something has changed," he says.

"Oh?"

Vithra falls silent. Candlefly shrugs. Always such drama from the gods.

As they wind through the tunnels, Mookie grins at his daughter. He knows that in the eerie glow of his makeshift light source, he may look manic and mad, but he can't help it.

"I like this," he says.

"What?" Nora asks.

"You. Me. Working together. Father and daughter."

"Yeah, it's... great."

"I just mean–"

"This isn't how I imagined it," she says.

"How'd you figure it?"

She says nothing.

He fills the silence, says, "I never imagined it at all."

"I know." She gives him a look. It isn't a nice one. "That's the problem. Isn't it? You never imagined us as much of anything. You had your work. Then you had those... *people* out in Staten Island. Some brat named Nora. Some nag named Jess."

"It wasn't like that."

"It was and you know it."

He stares at the ground. "I always thought about you guys. I always tried to be there. I just..." Mookie's not good with words. Especially not now: all the pain, the fatigue, everything, it's drawn him out, hammered him thin. "I never wanted my life to get near yours. My life is all..." He sighs, gestures around him. "It's this. It's the ugly dark. It's goblins and addicts, dead men and snake venom. It's just... trash and horror and blood. I never wanted that for you."

"Well, it found me."

"I know. And I'm sorry."

She stops. He continues for a few steps, looks back.

"When this is all over," she says, pointing her finger at him, "I want you to go visit Mom."

"I'll call her–"

"I said, *go visit her*. Promise me."

"She may not want to hear from–"

"Promise me!"

"I… OK, yeah, I promise."

She stands still. Staring at him with a look he cannot parse.

"Can we go?" he asks.

"Thanks for saying you're sorry."

"I am. I am sorry."

She swallows hard, then nods. "We can go now."

He finds the bolthole carved by Davey a long time ago. Covered up with a false limestone pillar carved with an X etched into the rock.

Mookie shoulders into the stone, pushes it aside.

A small passage is revealed. A musty breeze breathes upon them.

"C'mon."

The men in the tunnel are Sandhogs, yes. But Sorago knows that they're more than that. They're men of the 147½ – a cabal within the union that know of the monsters, that are familiar with the ways of the Underworld, that protect the city's most vulnerable projects from intrusion by malefic forces.

A malefic force such as Sorago.

He runs through the tunnel, feet echoing on the round concrete beneath him – a tireless journey. He is at present alone, and alone they may defeat him. It takes a lot to admit that, for he is a woefully efficient killer – but they will be many and they will be prepared.

That is why he cannot go in alone.

Ahead he sees the first sign of them.

Gobbos.

Not just a pack. An army. Fifty of them. Or more. Among them, black shapes – the reaper-cloak Vollrath, the advance knights of the Hungry Ones.

Sorago is not a zealot of the worm-gods. Few Snakefaces are. This is a strange role for him, to help bring them to the light of the above world. But it is all for a good measure. Candlefly says that it is his will and the will of the whole family that they will not serve the gods but rather be served *by* them. And that is a mission Sorago can get behind.

Not that the gobbos need to know that.

The Vollrath know but don't seem to care – what that means, Sorago cannot say.

All that matters is that they gather like this under a single purpose.

Normally getting gobbos to work together in this number is an impossible effort: a Sisyphean task that will inevitably roll back upon you. But now they are bound by the whims of their worm-gods.

Which means Sorago now has an army to bring with him to the end of this tunnel.

They hear the screams.

Echoing through the concrete tube that is Water Tunnel #3.

Mookie lifts the concrete piece back in place. Then grabs a handful of nearby dust and blows it back over the seams, making them disappear.

"It's already started," he says. "You stay here."

"What?"

"I can't risk you getting hurt. Not again." The thought alone almost kills him.

"I'll help. I'm not some weak-kneed little brat. I just need a weapon."

"We don't have any weapons."

"We have you."

Pride blooms in his cheeks. It tightens his fists to sledgehammers.

But still–

"I can't. Nora, I can't. I don't want to lose you again."

She sneers suddenly. "You'll lose me if you don't let me come. You let me out of your sights, Mookie, and I'll walk. I'll walk out of this tunnel, and you'll never see me again. *Stop* keeping me at arm's length. *Stop* treating me like a little girl. You want me back in your life? Then we do this together. You want me gone? Then do it alone."

A glimpse of the old Nora. No. Not the old Nora, but a recent one – the cruelty of a teenager, the acid response to what she must perceive as betrayal.

But strong, too. He sees Jess in there.

And maybe he sees himself, too.

From down the tunnel comes yelling. Hollering. The bellows of hearty men. Sandhogs. Must be. Seconds later, the sound of drilling vibrates the concrete.

She looks around, reaches down, picks up a rock. "Look. I have a weapon."

He sighs.

Then he nods.

"You can come," he says. The decision is a small knife in his heart. The only comfort is that the knife could have been so much larger.

30

[gibberish written on bound swatches of human skin, inked in blood and coal dust]

– from the Journals of John Atticus Oakes,
Cartographer of the Great Below

The slaughter comes quickly but not without cost. As expected, the men of the 147½ are prepared for an assault at any time. They plan for this, they run drills, they come armed. The gobbos sweep over them like a tide. The men draw guns – a shotgun from a gearbox, a pistol from a hidden holster under a slicker – or they grab those tools around them that serve as weapons: pick-axes, hammers, wrenches. The goblins are armed, too, their best weapons brought to bear against the flesh of men: A mace made from a baby goblin at the end of a stick, its wormy mouth and sharp teeth ready to bite; a whirring sharpened blade made from the end of an old box fan, the fan running off a tank of gasoline on the gobbo's back; a slingshot firing oblong marbles of hematite into the exposed eyes of goggle-less Sandhogs.

It starts to go pear-shaped. A bark from a shotgun blows the gas tank on the gobbo's back. Liquid flame sweeps over five, six of the creatures, thrashing and crackling like logs in a fire as they burn. A newly one-eyed Sandhog runs at the gobbos one by one, poor depth perception not preventing him from bringing a sledge against their heads, *wham, wham, wham*. Pistol fire. A swung axe.

But then Sorago and the Vollrath step into the fray.

Sorago doesn't bother with the dance. He walks – nay, *strolls* – among the fracas, as casual as an old man in Central Park. Any who come at him are dispatched with teeth, pistol, or blade. Legs cut out from under men. Holes punched through hardhats by a four-barrel derringer, splashing brains down the backs of necks. Venom spat in open mouths.

The Vollrath do their jobs. They move to the end of the tunnel, to the massive wall ahead of them that, were it laid on its side, would look like a mountain range but is instead the barrier of schist and granite that prevents this tunnel from moving forward. The tunnel is peppered with holes in a specific pattern – a pattern designed by Davey Morgan to create the most efficient blast. In each hole sits a stick of dynamite like a nesting bird, and from each stick is a braid of det-cord, and each cord winds together into one. The Vollrath know their targets. They pick the explosive experts. They pick the drillers. They leap upon them as a blanket, covering them, ethereal fingers like ice picks caring little for the corporeal barriers of hard hats, skin, or bone. They take control of them, riding them like men ride horses, marshaling them forward as puppets.

They begin to work with great efficiency.

The remaining goblins – two dozen left chanting and screaming their crass gobbo vulgarities – gather to watch the men work. The men wheel over long bore-drills, press the spinning bits (each as thick as a child's wrist) into the stone. A spray of bits. The men would normally wear face protection but that would cause a delay. Here the flung scree chews into their faces, stone shrapnel biting skin. Their faces are soon a mask of red. It doesn't matter. They don't need to see. Only their minds are necessary. And their hands.

As they drill one hole, they move to the next.

And the other two men gingerly take dynamite out of existing holes, and slide them into the freshly bored pockets. One by one, a new pattern of dots emerges. A new blast pattern. One plucked from the wealth of knowledge stolen from Davey Morgan's head.

It is an unstable pattern that will end it all. It will drown the tunnels. It will dry up the city.

A new era will begin, with the daemon families ascendant. The Underworld will be brought fully to bear upon an unsuspecting world. The city above them will be the first settlement of the Great Below.

The drill is loud. A deafening rock-chewing buzz.

Smoke rises from the drills and from the rock as it burns. The smell stings the nose. It isn't long before the entire chamber is lost to the haze. The chamber is home to two massive fans – meant to blow smoke out of the chamber so that workers can see – and Sorago thinks to plug them in, get them going.

He doesn't have the chance.

It's only when a gobbo runs by him screaming silently – a rock still sticking out of the creature's misshapen head – that Sorago realizes something has gone terribly, terribly wrong.

He turns.

Mookie Pearl walks among them.

It is so impossible that Sorago can almost not conceive of it. The man went to the deepest pits of the Great Below – broken and beaten – and now emerges here?

Sorago hisses and stands ready.

The thug barrels through the ranks of the goblins, one arm swinging useless at his side – his other hand smacks, punches, throws, twists gobbo heads like they're bottle caps. A girl steps into the fray next to him, a rock in her hand. Bashing. The thick treacle of gobbo blood speckling her face like flecks of black pudding.

It's her. It's the man's daughter.

The gutshot girl.

Doubly impossible. For a moment Sorago doubts everything: the plan, his own eyes, the very gods he cares little for. But then it all snaps forward; he has no time for doubt.

He has only time for killing.

The plan must be saved. The dynamite is in place.

Mookie Pearl and his daughter must die.

Don't think about the dead men. That's the thought running through Mookie's head. Sandhogs of the 147½ lie scattered about, broken, destroyed – tough men, men far better than Mookie has ever been, men who deserve better than what they got down here in the dirt. A man a mile? This mile has been the bloodiest of them all.

He can't think about them.

He can only think about what happens if he fails.

About his daughter. About what happens after.

Gobbos fall beneath his one fist, beneath his stomping boots, beneath his smashing head. Ahead, he sees a sledgehammer. Meant for breaking rock after a blast. He curls his foot under it, lifts it up in the air–

The hammer spins. He narrowly catches it in a meaty paw.

Then he sweeps the legs out from under three, four, five gobbos at a time. As they drop, squealing, trying to stand, he pops their heads like blisters.

Movement. Ahead. Then gone.

To his right–

Fast through the smoke.

Sorago, the Naga assassin.

A four-barreled pistol in one hand. A curved blade in the other.

Mookie lifts the sledgehammer, not a moment too soon. The Naga's gun barks one round, then two. One bullet *pings* off the metal head, the other pops into the handle, sending a cough of splinters into Mookie's cheek. He backpedals; Sorago leaps.

The Snakeface crashes into Mookie. His legs still hurt; his one arm doesn't work. He teeters and falls.

Teeth sink into the meat of his shoulder.

The cold saline rush of venom travels down his arm. Already the muscles start to deaden. Already he can feel the sudden gallop of his heart followed by an immediate slowdown. His head cranes back.

He sees Nora.

She cries out for him.

The gobbos have her.

The rock wasn't enough.

She knows that now. Somehow she thought – what? She thought her pride mattered. That this moment of standing with her father, of him choosing her, was all she needed. In a way, that's still true. She holds onto that choice he made like a piece of broken boat in the open ocean; it's the only thing that keeps her from sinking into a watery grave of abject hopelessness. Her back presses tight against the wall, jagged rock in her flesh.

The gobbos have her surrounded. They've swarmed.

She holds up her arms as one slashes a knife made of jagged glass. It opens a wound across her forearm. Fresh blood splashes. Another lunges at her feet; she kicks it away, but all it does is bowl over and cackle madly. Another snaps its teeth at her. She tries to bash it with the rock, but the rock slips away, cracks into another monster and is lost in the smoke. Her only weapon is gone.

They move in.

She can't go any farther.

Her father hits the ground, the Naga atop him. His teeth in her old man's shoulder.

The drills growl through stone.

She hears something else, too – a higher whine, a chugging engine.

Through the smoke, a black shape charges. Like an ancient beast born from fire. Except this beast doesn't have four legs: it has four wheels. A jacked-up quad with chained tires blasts into the chamber and comes right for her–

It mows through the gobbos. Greasy gray creatures are flung forward, screeching.

A dead man with boiled skin sits up front, leaning forward on the four-wheeler. A goblin runs up the front of his vehicle, and he bashes it with a tire iron.

On the back is a familiar form.

"Kelly," Nora gasps, the time for nicknames gone. The leader of the Get-Em-Girls hops off the back with a Louisville slugger and bashes a gobbo's leg crooked, then caps the head. The two girls crash together in a hard hug. "How–"

"Long story. Here, you need this."

She hands Nora a switchblade. The blade springs free with a click of the button.

Nora smiles.

His arm is dead weight, a slab of salami hanging off his body.

But the rest of his body still works. Even as his heart pulses like an old frog's neck – *lubdub, lubdub, lub...dub* – he knows that what Nora said is true.

He's the weapon here.

And what his Grampop said so many years ago is true, too: "You got a hard head, Mikey."

Hard as diamond, but nowhere near as pretty.

He rolls his body over, using his dead arm like a bludgeon. Sorago doesn't expect it and is bowled over. Mookie rolls with him. Pins him. Lies on him like a beached whale. The gun comes up, presses into his forehead–

Mookie jerks his head aside as the gun goes off. *Bang!*

Ears ringing. High-pitched whine. This is a test of the emergency broadcast signal...

He brings his hard head down against Sorago's.

Once. Then twice.

A third time. Fourth, fifth, sixth.

He rears back one last time–

Sorago's mouth fills with fresh venom to spit–

A switchblade buries into his forehead.

Nora presses it further. Then twists.

Crunch.

Sorago's legs kick once. Then are still.

"You saved me," Nora says. "I save you."

The Vollrath work, unaware. Drill buzzing. Dynamite in tubes.

Suddenly, the first drill cuts out. Then the second. Engines gutter. Drills slow, then stick in the rocky holes they were drilling. Smoke curls upward in lazy circles.

The heads of the puppet-men turn and look.

Behind the drill stands a corpse-walker with a beet-red blister-face. He holds the power cords that connect the massive drills to the generator.

The generator still grumbles – a quiet chug compared to the growl of the drills – but the dead man has unplugged the machines from it.

And on the other side, a girl with a bleeding arm bends down and uses a small knife to cut the det-cord leading to the bundle of dynamite.

The Vollrath let go of the bodies. The men drop. Still alive. Barely.

SOMETHING HAS CHANGED.

The thought goes out, a frequency shared by all Vollrath.

THIS WILL NO LONGER BE OUR TIME.

Then:

WE RECEDE UNTIL

And the Vollrath sink through the floor, escaping the Shallows. Returning to the Tangle from whence they came.

Nobody is answering on the other end of the walkie-talkie.

"The Vollrath are leaving," Vithra growls.

"Shut your mouth," Candlefly snaps. Suddenly this nice day is as gray as the sky above. He tries to raise Sorago. "What's going on down there? Over." Just an empty radio hiss.

"Something's changed."

"I said, *shut up*."

He grabs the button, hits it with the flat of his palm.

There's a buzz and a crackle.

The det-cord, so he understands, is fast. Many times the speed of a bullet. Miles away but traveling ten thousand feet per second…

There should be a boom right about–

Now.

Nothing.

No distant *whump*.

No earth shake.

How irritating.

"You," he says, pointing to Vithra. "Go."

"What if I say no?"

"Then your monster-god brethren get to stay down in the dark and I turn you off like a light-switch. You said it. *Something's changed*. It's gone wrong, and I need *you* to fix it. Now *go*."

The old man's face stretches into an inhuman sneer. "As you *wish*."

He heads toward one of the tunnels branching off of the quarry.

They fade through the rock. The reaper-cloaks abandon their men and are gone. Leaving Sandhogs behind, bloody but breathing.

Mookie stands. Arms useless. Heart barely thudding. He feels like a heavy stack of bricks on the back of a donkey – swaying left, swaying right. But still he stands. Thanks to the Blue Blazes shooting through him like a hot jet of magma.

"Thanks," is the only word he can manage. He says it to everyone.

"We shoulda let you die," Burnsy says.

Skelly punches him in the arm. Mookie gives her a rare smile. He knows it's an ugly thing, his smile: all lop-sided, his underbite forcing his teeth to poke out over his upper lip. But she smiles back. And winks at him. A small moment, but one that makes him happy.

Nora links her arm in his. "We better get you–"

The radio at Sorago's hip crackles.

"Sorago. Answer me. Over."

They share a look. The radio hisses. "What's going on down there? Over."

"They're up there," Nora says. "Waiting."

"Motherfucker was probably gonna be the one pushing the plunger on this dynamite," Burnsy says. He walks over and yanks on the sheared det-cord, pulling a dozen sticks of dynamite from their hole.

"Not a plunger," Mookie rasps. "Button."

Burnsy grabs his crotch. "I got your button right here."

"Would you guys be quiet?" Skelly says. "You hear that?"

"Hear what?" Burnsy asks, but she shushes him, taps her ear.

Somewhere far off is an infernal roar.

"What is that?" Nora asks, voice low.

"Him," Mookie says. "The Boss."

"Oh, shit," Nora says.

Skelly pales. "I saw... I saw what he can do."

"We have to go," Nora says. "We have to leave."

"But where? How?" Skelly asks. "This is a dead-end. And the way out is a one-way street straight toward–"

The wail and roar again. Closer this time.

"We can't fight him," Skelly says.

"I'm gonna have to," Mookie says. Everything hurts. He can barely lift a fist to swing it. If only he had the Red Rage. Maybe he could grab some dynamite and... "Hold up. I got an idea."

His voice is sluggish. Mush-mouthed. But he tells them in a string of broken words.

Burnsy's blistery lips twist into a dramatic frown. "I fucking hate you, did I ever tell you that?"

"Sorry." Mookie shrugs. "Better hurry. Gotta get these fans set up."

Vithra runs on all fours, loping forth like the spawn of the Devil and the meanest wolf in the woods. His long limbs spring him forward, leech mouth squirming and gnashing. Claws clicking on concrete.

He's going to kill them. Whoever is here, he's going to rip them into so many ribbons. Then decorate himself and the walls. The idea thrills him. To make something pretty out of so much blood.

He hates humans. Disgusting things. The hairless apes crawled out of the trees and claimed dominance over the land and sea and sky. And he and his brothers and sisters were forced to stay down in the dark with the earthworms and voles and eyeless crickets. It was the daemons – daemons like Candlefly – who forced the Hungry Ones into the deepest pits and would do so again given half a chance. And it was the humans who kept them there. Millennium after millennium.

But with the city gone, they will have a kingdom once more to call their own.

He'll find a way to dispatch Candlefly. The man is arrogant. He oversteps his bounds. He will leave an opening, and Vithra will crawl through it.

But first, the end of this tunnel. The blast didn't work. It won't matter. He won't need dynamite. He'll use his claws. His teeth. The whole of his body. He'll launch himself into the rock and tear through it like he's tearing through some poor fool's belly to get to his guts.

The tunnels will break and the water will flow and he will swim in it as the city above goes thirsty. As the men are moved out. As the monsters move in.

Ahead is a haze of smoke. Whirling like a sideways cyclone. He hears the thrum of distant fans.

He cares little for the machinations of man. He continues forward.

Hungry. Always hungry.

It's then he sees something ahead—

Something smaller than him. Racing forward with equal speed.

A beast of the Great Below, he thinks.

But then he sees. It is no beast.

It is a machine. On four wheels.

Vithra howls at it in rage.

Nora presses the walkie-talkie button, holds it to Mookie's face. He clears his throat. Tries to get his growl on, sound as much like Sorago as he can manage.

"Detonate," he says. "Over."

Candlefly hears it and laughs.

He punches the button.

Vithra leaps over the quad. It passes underneath as he hits the ground again.

Trailing behind are a dozen sticks of dynamite. Connected to the braid of det-cord.

There's a sizzle. The cord burns.

The man that was once Konrad Zoladski is caught in a wave of fire. Hot white heat hits him like a tractor trailer. But there's something else, too – an intricate cage the color of bronze. It breaks apart, spears of metal tearing through him–

And with it, a howling specter. A face, familiar. Casimir. His grandson. (Is he even Konrad Zoladski anymore?) The specter is a torn ribbon, a rain of knives, a howling mouth and a thousand eyes. Wraith-hands, *hands of wrath*, plunge into his mutated flesh and rend it asunder and fire fills the gaps.

Then the wave of white is gone, buried in darkness as the lights go out and the tunnel crashes down around him.

A fresh wave of smoke blows in, but the giant fans, running on generators, push it back. Burnsy sighs. "She was a good girl, that ride. God bless America." He holds his hand over his chest and stands stiff.

"Guess we timed it right," Nora says.

Burnsy drove the quad forward, the accelerators held down with electrical tape – he bailed off the back soon as he got it going in a straight line.

Skelly leans against the wall, exhales a heavy breath. "Are we done?"

They listen. No more bestial sounds from the dark.

"Think so," Mookie says. It feels like his voice is coming back. The venom is still in him, but his heart is picking up the pace. Returning to the normal drum-beat he hears in the hollow of his head.

The radio crackles.

"What happened? *Who is this?* Over."

Candlefly's voice. They share a look. Mookie grabs the walkie with a numb hand, uses the meat of his palm to press the button.

"You're damn right it's over," Mookie says. "All your buddies are dead, Candlefly. Tunnels One and Two are intact.

You should run. Because I'm going to come for you soon as I see daylight. And when I find you, I'm going to tear you into hunks like a piece of fresh bread, and I'm going to dip those parts of you into your own blood."

Then Mookie drops the walkie and stomps on it.

"Did you really need to stomp on the radio?" Burnsy asks.

Mookie shrugs. "Felt good."

"Let's find our way out of here," Skelly says.

Water Tunnel #3 is collapsed. No way to get past it. And no Boss-thing corpse in sight. Down here it's dark, and they're thankful Burnsy brought a pair of headlamps.

Mookie directs them toward another bolthole. It will take them back out, he says, toward the Canal Street station. They walk for a while in the underground. They don't talk. Occasionally they hear the wail and gibber of a goblin in the distance.

A sound, it seems, of the madness born of mourning.

As they walk, Nora starts to feel it. She almost forgot, almost felt normal.

But then–

It's just an itch, at first. A twinge in her belly. Then a tickle over her flesh like the tiny legs of a thousand ants dancing. Anxiety begins to crawl up inside of her. Soon it's more than that; it's full-bore panic, scrabbling and slamming itself against the walls of her mind. Sweat pours out of her. Her mouth is dry as a desert wind. Her hands curl into claws; the muscles in her legs start to clench and cramp.

They get to an old rusty door with a cracked wire-frame window. A subway train blasts past on the other side. Lights strobing. Mookie goes to open the door.

She cries out.

He stops. Turns. The headlamp light shines bright in her eyes. She can't see his face, but he can see hers and she wonders how she looks. If it's half as bad as she feels–

"What's wrong?" he asks, pulling her close.

"I can't... go."

"What?"

"I can't go with you. Out... up. Back."

"You're not making any sense."

She stifles an unexpected sob. "I'm... different. I belong here."

"Nobody belongs here," Skelly says. She pulls Nora close, but Nora draws away – her touch feels like burning. "Nora, whoa–"

"Oh, God," Nora says. "It was the mushrooms. Wasn't it?"

"You're on mushrooms?" Skelly asks.

Burnsy steps past. "Whoa, whoa, whoa. What mushrooms?"

"We found the Death's Head," Mookie says. "It's a mushroom. She was... dying. Dead. I gave it to her..." He pulls them out of his pocket: the glow is gone. They're shriveled and dry like little dessicated organs.

"Aw, shit," Burnsy says. "Mookie. Nora. I'm so fuckin' sorry."

"What?" Nora asks. "What is it?"

"You're right. You can't leave. You're... part of this place."

"No, no, no," Mookie says. "That's bullshit. I can pick her up right now, and we can get the hell out of here." He reaches for Nora, but she pulls away. She pulls away from all of them. Begins backing down the tunnel. Even receding ten feet calms her pulse-beat, lessens the itching.

"I'm fine," she says. Suddenly puffing out her chest. Holding up her chin and blinking back tears. "I can handle it."

Stay tough, she thinks. Take this like you've taken everything else. Suck it up, you stupid girl. Even still, her hands dart out, brace herself against the walls of the passage so she doesn't collapse. Don't let him see you like this. Don't let him see you weak.

Mookie reaches for her, but she pushes him away.

Burnsy leads Mookie off and she hears the dead man telling him, "Mook. Listen. The stories about the purple skull – I didn't know it was a mushroom, but people talk just the same. Always figured the old tales were bullshit but...It's like the myths, right? Inanna or Orpheus or–"

"I don't know shit about that!" Mookie roars, and he picks up Burnsy and slams him against the wall. "Don't you fuck with me, Lister."

Burnsy talks fast. "I'm just saying I've done some reading since I been down here and the old stories say that when you eat of the Underworld, you can't always leave. Now, that ain't universally true – shit, the Blue stuff alone makes that clear – but I've *heard* that the Death's Head is different. That it's like a trap. It keeps you alive but it also...*keeps* you, you know what I mean?"

Nora can't help it. She turns around. Faces away. Arms crossed. The stance of the petulant teen, she thinks, but it helps her. Calms her not to look at them. Her eyes forward, staring down the passage, she can't help but think: Is this really my home now? This horrible place? She still feels a hard pit in the middle of her. Like a hard stone in the space between her heart and her stomach.

Skelly holds her hand. For a while they just stand. Like people at a funeral, the awkwardness of their grief laid bare. Mookie presses his head against the stone wall of the passage. Burnsy looks down.

Finally, Nora says, "I said I'll be OK, so I'll be OK."

"You can come to Daisypusher," Burnsy says. "We'll get you a place."

"Living among the dead," Nora says. She just barely manages to stifle a sob. "Awesome. Love it. Let's do it." She hears the sarcasm in her voice and feels a stab of shame.

"Better than dying."

"What happens if I go out there?" she asks. "What happens if I *leave*?"

Burnsy shrugs. "Not sure we want to find out. Not today."

"OK. OK." She sniffles. "Let's do this. Let's go."

She starts to storm forward, back down into depths. Mookie catches her shoulder, but she pulls away. He turns toward the others, asks, "Can you guys give us a minute?"

Skelly kisses her on the brow. Then she goes through the door. Burnsy nods, gives her an awkward clap on the shoulder. He follows after Skelly.

"This can't be true," Mookie says. "I'm gonna try to get you out."

"Good for you. I don't need your help." She knows she sounds like a little bitch, but the words keep coming. "Go home, Mookie."

"Don't." He pivots her, looks in her eyes. "Don't do this. Not now. Don't pull away. I'm your dad. You're my baby girl. For a long time I couldn't take care of you and I'm not gonna lose you now. Not to this place. I'll fix this."

She sucks in a deep breath. Hesitates. But then: "OK."

"OK?"

"I said OK."

"I love you," he says. "And I'm so sorry."

"I'm sorry, too." Those words, a stone thrown that shatters the whole dam. Waters flood. Drown her. Tears fall. Her cheeks feel warm and wet as her nose starts to plug up. "I love you, too."

He pulls her close. Wraps his one arm around her. It's strong enough for three, four arms. "I can stay a while if you want."

"It's OK. I'll go with... Burnsy, is his name?"

"Yeah. He's all right." Mookie pauses. "I killed him. A while back."

"Oh."

"I know. But he'll get you squared away. I'll bring blankets. And food. Anything you need. You still like those little – shit, what are they called? The little chocolate buttons with the tiny white dots–"

"Non-pareils."

"Yeah. Those. I'll bring you a big bag of those."

She kisses his cheek. "Bye, Daddy."

He can't seem to say goodbye. Looks like he tries, but his mouth can't form the words. Instead he nods, musses her hair like he used to do when she was little.

Then he's gone.

31

I'm between. I mean that. Like, I don't belong anywhere? I'm alive but bound to the land of the dead, which means I'm not all that alive, am I? I'm just a prettier zombie than the rest of these people here in Daisypusher. I feel between in a lot of ways, actually. I'm not a good girl, but maybe I'm not such a bad one. I love my father, but there's a still part of me that hates him, too, because of Mom. I don't know what I want to do. I don't even know who I am. Burnsy tells me that's called "being human" and, worse, "being a teenager", but I think maybe he's just trying to be nice. I'm just... between. I'm nowhere. I'm nobody. Maybe that's OK. Maybe I can do something with it. For now, this place is my home. Not Daisypusher. I don't belong here either. I mean, all of it is home. The Underworld. I press my hands to its walls, and I can feel it there. Almost like it's aware of me — as much as I am of it. One day soon I'm going to explore my new home. All of it.

– from the Journals of Eleanor Jessamyne Pearl,
Living Dead Girl

It's an accounting of the dead.

First: Werth's apartment. Mookie cleans it out. It's a – well, a rat-trap isn't the word because of all the cats. Turns out, Werth really liked cats. Or hated them and had them anyway. Maybe that makes it a really good rat-trap? Mookie doesn't know, doesn't care. He gives away everything that has value.

Takes the cats to a shelter. All of it is hard to do with his one arm in a sling and the rest of his body feeling like it's been put through a meat slicer. When he's all done he stands at the door of the apartment and closes it and says goodbye to Werth inside his head. He's still not sure how to feel about him. He liked Werth. But Werth treated him like shit for years. And at the end...

Well.

That poor old goat.

A day later: Karyn's. At first he can't tell her. He pretends that he's here about losing the cleaver. But she's distracted. She tries to push some charcuterie on him – good stuff, too, cantimpalo chorizo, salchichon, Jamon Serrano ham. But he can't do it. Can't take from her again and again, and finally he just spills it. Tells her all about Lulu. How he was there. How she died. He doesn't spare a detail. What's the point? He was never a good liar anyway. She breaks down. He sees it: the love was real. Not just a thing born of intensity. A lot of love isn't love, it's just a strong feeling that over time fades, but this, what Karyn feels, is true blue. And it kills her. And she kicks him out because he was there and, even if he didn't kill Lulu, he can be her scapegoat. He wants to be. *Deserves* to be. She can pile all her grief and blame upon his ox-like shoulders and boot him out the door. Which she does.

On the third day: Davey Morgan's funeral.

The cops found Cassie Morgan, Davey's daughter, unconscious in her NYU dorm room. Half-dead, saved by a wandering RA. She's at the funeral. Looking bleak. Barely keeping it together. Her emotional state blown apart like rock by dynamite. Mookie doesn't bother trying to talk to her. She wouldn't remember him, anyway. That was another lifetime. Besides: what would he even say?

The funeral – there's a line out the door of people waiting to pay their respects. Sandhogs from the 147 and the 147½. EPA guys. Bunch of cops and firemen. They loved Davey. He ran dozens of crews over the years. He is beloved.

Few of them recognize Mookie. The ones that do give him looks.

You ain't welcome here, Mikey.

He isn't. But he stays just the same.

On the way back from the funeral, he puts some money into an account. For Lister's kids. For Lister's wife. He doesn't know how long that money will last now that the Organization has gone to hell, but he does what he can.

Later, he talks to Skelly. She said she's been down to see Nora already and asks him, has he gone yet? He tells her he hasn't – he's sent her a care package, meats and cheeses and those non-pareil things, but he says he's got one more thing to do before he sees her.

"I gotta go see my ex-wife," he says. "I made a promise."

He knows something's wrong when the plane turns over the ocean. Candlefly can feel it bank hard to the right – and then they're flying in a new direction. Traveling south along the Spanish coast, not across the country. Which means he is not going home.

Home is Mallorca.

They're heading toward…

The Canaries. That has to be it.

This is not good news.

As soon as everything went to hell – in some ways, quite literally – at the dig site, Candlefly knew it was done. Something had happened. No – *Mookie Pearl* had happened. A rogue element he again underestimated. His mistake. A big mistake. A final one.

He told Haversham to run.

Haversham didn't hesitate. He turned tail and bolted.

As he ran, Candlefly shot him in the back of the head.

Then for him it was time to book a private plane and get out of here – already they were calling what happened a terrorist attack. If that got attached to him in any way, that would blow back on his family. They'd stayed hidden and out of sight for a long time. How crass and hollow it would be to suffer now not from some supernatural danger but from the mortal bureaucracy of American Homeland Security.

And now this. A turn of the plane.

A half hour later they land. The pilot doesn't show his face. The door opens, and the steps descend. Outside, to one side is the snow-tipped peak of Mount Teide. On the other, the steel-blue ocean. And ahead: men with guns.

Ah. That's how this is, then.

They walk him down a trail. To an old church with a dead tree outside that looks like a skeleton's hand reaching toward – and forever failing to reach – heaven.

At the steps he sees her:

Renata.

His wife. Beautiful – those dark eyes, those broad hips, the way the wind feathers her shoulder-length hair. She looks like an eagle, cutting a dark, strong, noble shape.

The men with guns step aside and he thinks: I am pardoned. At least in part. This, then, a sign he is not welcome home, but at least a sign that he is still allowed to be with his family. He runs to embrace her at the top of the steps. He holds her close.

"Where are the children?" he whispers in her ear after kissing it. He calls for them: "Oscar! Adelina!"

She pulls away from him. Icily, she says, "They did not come."

The men with guns step in behind him.

"Renata–"

"The family is displeased." A pause. "All the families are."

"My love–"

"Our bond is broken," she says. "I am no longer your wife. I am once again a Glasstower. I am not a Candlefly." His heart breaks. He almost collapses. "And neither are you. Goodbye, Ernesto."

She cups his face with both hands, and then pushes past him. He reaches for her, tries to go with her – but the men with guns push him back. He tries to strike one.

A butt of an AK-47 crashes into his face. He feels an explosion behind his eyes.

They drag him into the church. And it's then he sees what is to be his fate.

An old gate. To one of the many hells. The Underworld beneath New York is just one of many – one of nine major hells, to be exact. All of them dead-ending in the Expanse. Where the Hungry Ones still dwell.

This gate is just a hole ringed with stone. The rest of the church innards never existed. It's just a façade, a false temple meant to fool crusaders so many years before.

Above it is a rope on an old pulley. At the end of that rope hangs a noose.

He screams. Tries to fight. Another hit to the nose. The nose breaks. He can't see through the tears now. He tastes blood along with the salt air.

They wind the rope, not around his neck, but around his ankles.

Then they push him down, down, down–

He cries, "I cannot go! It is forbidden! Wait! *Wait*–" But his words are drowned out as the pain seizes him. The pain is like being robed in fire and ice, like being drowned in lava and frozen in a glacier. It feels as though his skin is being stripped away. As though hot iron rods are thrust up into the marrow of his bones. It hurts in his teeth. His balls. His soul.

It hurts eternally.

For he is immortal. And now, so is his pain.

••••

Jess lives in a small house on Staten Island. It was their house once. But Mookie took his name off it a long time ago. Same as he took himself out of their lives. A fact he regrets now. He's old and has nothing. Almost nothing. He can see Nora. He'll see her every day if she'll let him. It's better than nothing, yeah. But it's so much less than what he could have had.

He needs to tell her what happened. He can't tell Jess the truth. How could he? He doesn't want to poison her with that nonsense. Mookie never let her see any of that before and doesn't want to start now.

So he can't say, "Our daughter is alive but down in the dark."

Or could he? Could he tell her everything? Could he show her?

He's not sure. He holds the idea. Lets it swish around his head.

First, the hard part: knocking on the door.

Things have changed around here. Not a surprise. A new look out back: white picket, a classic fence, instead of the chain-link he put up. He hears a dog barking out back, too. A little yap. Like a terrier or something. *So she has a dog.* Potted plants line the steps. Mums. She wasn't much of a green thumb, always killed plants, but as far as he knows, mums are pretty hardy flowers.

He stands on the stoop. One arm in a sling.

He's faced gobbos and inhuman crime lords and ancient worm-gods and yet here he's more scared than he's been in a long time. Mookie wants to run. Like a gun-shy puppy.

But then he's doing it even before he realizes it.

Knock knock knock.

Footsteps. Fast approaching.

The door opens and a young girl, maybe twelve years old, stares out. Red hair in pigtails. She squints. "Who are you?"

"Who are *you*?"

"I'm…" She catches herself. "*Not telling* you that. Mom!"

She runs back inside the house, slamming the door.

A minute later, a woman comes to the door. A short, squat woman. Hand inside a dishtowel, which is itself inside a glass as she cleans it. "Help you?" she asks.

"You're not Jess."

"No. I'm Marie."

"I want Jess."

"Jess Stevens?"

"No. Who the hell is Jess Stevens?"

"Lives down the block."

It strikes him like a fist to the gut. *She got remarried.*

"Mid-forties?" he asks. "Hair the color of a penny?"

"No. Early thirties. Blonde. Bartender at Coyle's." The woman suddenly narrows her eyes. "Wait, are you talking about the woman who used to live here?"

"Yeah. Jess Pearl."

"Who are you?"

"Her husband." He sighs. "Ex. Ex-husband."

The woman's face falls.

"I'm sorry, but…." She looks suddenly uncomfortable. "She's… she's dead."

"What?" He almost laughs. "She's not dead."

"She died… not quite two years ago. Bad hit-and-run accident. Some drunk plowed into her. Accident, I guess. We bought the house out of auction from her – your, ah, her? – daughter. She'd just turned eighteen or something and we put in a bid…" She stops talking. "I'm so sorry."

Impossible. His thoughts spin around inside his head like a tornado. One second he wants to cry out, push past this woman, find out where they're hiding Jess. The next second he wants to punch her in the mouth, knock her head clean off her shoulders for lying to him like that. Then he wants to collapse here on the stoop, curl up in a big broken ball of grief and gristle, and weep till the sun goes down and the moon pops up.

All he does is mutter, "Thank you" in a voice he's not sure is his own. Then he shuffles away from the front door and takes ten steps.

He stands there. This was their house. That was his wife.

Hit-and-run accident.

She died.

She's dead.

We bought the house out of auction from your daughter.

That wouldn't have been long before Nora came to him the last time. When she lied to him. And got him to wipe out that nest of gobbos. And shot Werth. Jesus. He always wondered where she got the capital to set up shop so early. From this. From the house sale. And from insurance and whatever money Mookie'd been sending to Jess.

He'd been inadvertently funding his own daughter's attacks against him.

He didn't even know his own ex-wife – the mother of his child – was dead.

No wonder Nora hated him.

He does all he can do. He goes home, to the bar, and drinks himself to sleep.

He wakes up at the bar. A plate of chicken fingers in front of him, mostly cold. He knows he didn't put it there. Nor did he put the bottled water there.

He lifts his brow. Bleary-eyed, he sees Nora sitting next to him.

"Hey, Daddy-o."

The voice. Rich, dark. Bourbon and cigarettes and chocolate. No. It's not Nora. It's Skelly. Or Kelly. That's what she said: "Call me Kelly from now on." So he does.

"Hey," he says.

"Hey back."

She runs her hand across his scalp like his head's a bowling ball and her fingers are seeking the holes. He holds up the water. "This you?"

"No, it's a water bottle."

"Funny."

"I thought so."

"Thanks for the water. And the chicken."

She pats the top of his head. "My pleasure, big fella."

"You want some meat?" he asks.

"That a come on?"

"I got meat in the fridge."

"Nope, still not sure if this is a come on or not."

He musters a chuckle, then goes and fixes her a plate. "I'm a vegan."

"Ah, shit. Sorry?"

She sighs, then says, "I used to love a good hamburger. Still miss it from time to time."

Then she picks a piece of prosciutto and pops it in her mouth.

He grins. "That's the sexist thing I've ever seen."

"What now?" she asks.

"For the first time in a long time, I dunno. I always came back here, but then the call would come. I'd be on the job." He stares at the racks of liquor he'll never drink. "Always on the job. But now there's no job."

"Maybe that means it's time to move forward."

"I wish I knew what that even meant."

"It means you pick a path and walk down it."

"Yeah?"

"Yeah."

"Where do I start?"

She holds out her hand and starts to lead him away from the bar toward the steps and up them. "It starts here. It starts tonight."

ACKNOWLEDGMENTS

Every book is the product of more than just one person, even though the author is the one who wears the laurels on his crown.

Thanks to my wife and child for putting up with the weird bearded hobo who lives with them and writes these fanciful stories.

Thanks to dangerous deviant Dave Turner who, despite his city-dwelling pretensions, is a most excellent reader and editor of books.

Thanks to Robin Laws, who gave me reason to conjure the character of Mookie Pearl for the anthology, *The New Hero*.

Thanks to Lee Harris and all the Grumpy Cyborgs who helped make this book into what it is.

Thanks to Stacia Decker, agent extraordinaire, who knows her way around a hard-ass novel edit and who kicks ten kinds of ass. No, eleven. *Twelve*.

Thanks to author friends like Stephen Blackmoore, Adam Christopher, Gwenda Bond, Kim Curran, Mur Lafferty, Lauren Beukes, Myke Cole, Saladin Ahmed, Delilah Dawson, Karina Cooper, Matt Forbeck, Matt Funk, Jimmy Callaway, Dave White, Joelle Charbonneau, and Dangerous Dan O'Shea who repeatedly inspire me (and frequently conspire *with* me).

And thanks to all you people for picking up and reading his book. You are why I'm here after all, allowed to do this crazy author voodoo.

ABOUT THE AUTHOR

Chuck Wendig is a novelist, screenwriter, and game designer.

He is a fellow of the Sundance Screenwriting Lab. His short film (written with co-author and director Lance Weiler) *Pandemic* showed at the Sundance Film Festival in 2011. That same year, *Collapsus* – a digital transmedia drama, also co-authored with Weiler – was nominated for an International Digital Emmy and a Games 4 Change award. He has contributed over two million words to the game industry, and was developer of the popular *Hunter: The Vigil* game line.

He currently lives in Pennsyltucky with his beautiful wife Michelle, their taco terrier Tai-Shen, their red dog Loa, and their son (known as "B-Dub").

You can find him at his website, terribleminds.com, where he remains busy dispensing dubious writing wisdom. Said dubious wisdom is collected in eBook form, such as in the popular *500 Ways to Be a Better Writer*. His next book for Angry Robot is the third Miriam Black novel, *The Cormorant*.

terribleminds.com

MEET MIRIAM BLACK.

"Trailer-park tension, horrified hilarity, and sheer terror mixed with deft characterization and razor plotting. I literally could not put it down."
LILITH SAINTCROW

BLACKBIRDS

CHUCK WENDIG

MOCKINGBIRD

CHUCK WENDIG

SHE KNOWS WHEN YOU WILL DIE.

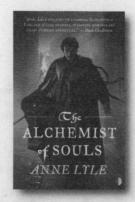

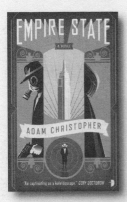